MEET THE MENAGERIE . . .

MR. DOYLE . . . Sorcerer and alchemist. A man of unparalleled intellect. When evil threatens to consume the world, he gathers those who will fight.

CERIDWEN . . . Princess of the Fey. Solitary and beautiful, she holds the elemental forces of nature at her command.

DR. LEONARD GRAVES . . . Scientist, adventurer, ghost. He exists in both life—and afterlife.

DANNY FERRICK . . . A sixteen-year-old demon changeling who is just discovering his untapped—and unholy—powers.

CLAY . . . An immortal shapeshifter, he has existed since The Beginning. His origin is an enigma—even to himself.

EVE . . . The mother of all vampires. After a millennium of madness, she seeks to repent for her sins and destroy those she created.

SQUIRE . . . Short, surly, a hobgoblin who walks in shadows.

continued . . .

00647690

THE NIMBLE MAN

A NOVEL OF THE MENAGERIE

CHRISTOPHER GOLDEN
AND
THOMAS E. SNIEGOSKI

ACE BOOKS, NEW YORK

THE BERKLEY PUBLISHING GROUP
Published by the Penguin Group
Penguin Group (USA) Inc.
375 Hudson Street, New York, New York 10014, USA
Penguin Group (Canada), 10 Alcorn Avenue, Toronto,
Ontario M4V 3B2, Canada (a division of Pearson Penguin Canada Inc.)
Penguin Books Ltd., 80 Strand, London WC2R 0RL, England
Penguin Ireland, 25 St. Stephen's Green, Dublin 2,
Ireland (a division of Penguin Books Ltd.)
Penguin Group (Australia), 250 Camberwell Road, Camberwell, Victoria 3124, Australia (a
division of Pearson Australia Group Pty Ltd.)
Penguin Books India Pvt. Ltd., 11 Community Centre, Panchsheel Park,
New Delhi - 110 017, India
Penguin Group (NZ), Cnr Airborne and Rosedale Roads, Albany,
Auckland 1310, New Zealand (a division of Pearson New Zealand Ltd.)
Penguin Books (South Africa) (Pty.) Ltd., 24 Sturdee Avenue,
Rosebank, Johannesburg 2196, South Africa

Penguin Books Ltd., Registered Offices: 80 Strand, London WC2R 0RL, England

This is a work of fiction. Names, characters, places, and incidents either are the product of the
authors' imaginations or are used fictitiously, and any resemblance to actual persons, living or
dead, business establishments, events, or locales is entirely coincidental.

THE NIMBLE MAN: A NOVEL OF THE MENAGERIE

An Ace Book / published by arrangement with the authors

PRINTING HISTORY
Ace mass market edition / October 2004

Copyright © 2004 by Christopher Golden and Thomas E. Sniegoski.
Cover art by Christian McGrath.
Cover design by Judith Lagerman.
Interior text design by Kristin del Rosario.

ISBN: 0-441-01215-9

ACE
Ace Books are published by The Berkley Publishing Group,
a division of Penguin Group (USA) Inc.,
375 Hudson Street, New York, New York 10014.
ACE and the "A" design
are trademarks belonging to Penguin Group (USA) Inc.

PRINTED IN THE UNITED STATES OF AMERICA

10   9   8   7   6   5   4   3   2   1

For Pete Donaldson,
who understands that imagination is its own reward.
—C.G.

For Joseph Sniegoski, my Dad,
who never saw anything wrong with loving monsters.
—T.S.

ACKNOWLEDGMENTS

I thank Connie and my kids so often they might be sick of it by now. But thanks to them again, even so. Boys, when you're a little older, this one will make you smile. And, of course, thanks to Tom, who always believed we'd make something of this world, even way back at the beginning.

Many thanks and deep, respectful bows to Ginjer Buchanan, who *got* it completely. Thanks are also due to my whole clan, with love, as well as to Jose Nieto, Rick Hautala, Amber Benson, Bob Tomko, Pete Donaldson, Lisa Clancy, Allie Costa, and Ashleigh Bergh, for keeping me sane.

—C.G.

As always, my loving thanks to LeeAnne and Mulder, you guys keep me on my toes, and to Chris Golden, who challenges me to be better.

And thanks tied up in a big red bow must be given to my mother, Ginjer Buchanan, Dave "Boombah" Kraus, Mike Mignola, Eric Powell, Don Kramer, Greg Skopis, Kenneth Curtis, Jean Eddy, Lisa Clancy, Dr. Kris, David Carroll, Jon and Flo, Pat and Bob, Pete Donaldson, and Tim Cole and his disciples of doom. All part of my menagerie, each and every one.

—T.S.

1

WITHIN the silent halls of the Boston Antiquities Museum, the shadows were in motion. Red alarm sensors shone brightly but recorded nothing out of the ordinary. Only the nearly somnambulant passing of security guards disturbed the dust that eddied up on currents of air. Hidden cameras revealed only exhibits and artifacts in otherwise empty rooms.

Yet there was one room that was not empty.

The exhibit was Egyptian, devoted almost wholly to the Twelfth Dynasty. Though its collection of stone fragments, papyrus, masks, and sarcophagi might impress school-children, to those educated in the area of antiquities the ex-hibit would have been wholly unremarkable. Or nearly so. Those who noticed anything at all out of place would likely have attributed it to simple human error, to a curator who had made an honest mistake.

In one corner of the room Mr. Doyle thoughtfully stroked his thick mustache and admired a small sphinx. The piece had been unearthed at Katna millennia before and bore the name of a daughter of Ammenemes II, but the curators of the museum had badly mislabeled it. He shook his head and his heavy gray brows knitted with disapproval. If he had them there, he would have given them a tongue-lashing for being so careless. Of course, on this night their carelessness had worked in his favor.

The moment he tore his attention away from the priceless sphinx, Doyle caught sight of the object that had drawn him here. With a grunt of satisfaction he crossed the room to a marble pedestal and peered through the thick glass enclosure atop it at the artifact inside. It was a crystal spider set inside a gold frame, perhaps five inches in length and four at the widest leg span. A small placard rested atop the enclosure.

> Crystal Spider, circa 1995 B.C., discovered at Lisht, believed to have been a gift to the illegitimate pharaoh Nebtawyre Menthotope III during the "seven kingless years" preceding the Twelfth Dynasty.

"Well, well. Hello, my little friend," Mr. Doyle rasped, standing a bit straighter and smoothing his greatcoat as though he was in the presence of respectable company. Which was not at all the case.

"So?" came a voice from a shadowy corner of the exhibit. "How did I do?"

He glanced in the direction of that voice. There was a large, ornate sarcophagus on display, and beside it several lighted glass enclosures that contained burial jars apparently associated with whomever had been put to rest within the sarcophagus. Eve stepped from amidst this tableau of death with grace and nonchalance, the same way she would walk into a bar or step onto a subway train. She wore tight new blue jeans and a formfitting green turtleneck beneath a stylishly long brown suede coat. With her silken black hair and exotic features, she was beautiful in a way only cruel things are. A tragedy, to be sure, for though Eve could be cruel, she had so many other facets, so many better qualities.

They were old friends, these two, but it had been quite some time since they had seen one another. Doyle understood. He was just as guilty as Eve of letting their acquaintance grow fallow. With lives as busy—and as long—as they both led, the years could go by with the deceptive speed of clouds in the sky. When each one was so much like the last, it was easy to lose count.

As always, they were becoming reacquainted in a time of crisis. It was the nature of their friendship. He had contacted Eve for assistance and her efforts had produced results in less than a day. He had located her on the island of Mykonos. Fourteen hours later she had knocked on the door of his sprawling townhouse on Beacon Hill with the news that led them here.

Doyle smiled indulgently at her, as he would have at a daughter of whom he was particularly proud. "How did you do? Remarkably well, Eve. I've inquired all over the world in search of a Lemurian Spider." He turned his focus back upon his prize. "Bangladesh, Cyprus, Istanbul, Minsk. I confess to feeling more than a little foolish that you located one right here beneath my nose. And so quickly. How did you manage it?"

Eve strode across the room to join him, leather heels scuffing the floor. "We all have our specialties, Doyle. For instance, how did you get us in here without setting off any alarms? Without the guards noticing?"

A rare tremor of amusement passed through him. There had been so little humor or camaraderie in his life of late. Too many times in the past he had been betrayed by colleagues and friends, so he had come to count on his enemies as far more reliable. Eve was one exception. There were others, but he had not seen most of them for a very, very long time.

With a mischievous smile he touched the enclosure around the spider and whispered a minor incantation. The glass turned to damp mist that fogged the air around their heads and warped the thin beam of red light that should have triggered an alarm the moment the enclosure had been removed. It did not. When the mist had dissipated, Mr. Doyle picked up the crystal spider and examined it more closely.

"As you say," he mused, "we all have our specialties."

Eve allowed herself an appreciative nod and then began to stride impatiently around the exhibit hall. It was typical of her.

"Relax, Eve. We're not leaving just yet." He shot her an admonishing glance. "If the whispers Dr. Graves has been hearing are correct, we don't have time for certain niceties. I'm not going to be able to take my new toy home to play with it."

He began to pry the crystal spider out of its golden frame.

"Hold on," Eve protested, hurrying to his side with a rasp of suede and denim. "Do you have to do that? You know how much I love the sparkly things. The spider would look nice on my mantel next to that Buddha with the clock in his belly."

He ignored her. It had grown warm in the museum in spite of the cool air blowing out of the vents, but Mr. Doyle had been a magician long enough to know the heat had nothing to do with the actual temperature. His face felt flush and the gold softened in his fingers, peeling away like hot wax.

"Fine," Eve sighed. "This thing wasn't easy to find. Just doesn't seem right to ruin it. How many bits and pieces of flea market junk do you think survived from Lemuria?"

Doyle sniffed in contempt. "More than you realize. I doubt there's a major museum in the world that doesn't have at least one Lemurian piece misclassified as Egyptian or Greek or Etruscan, even Japanese. It's one of the great failings of the human mind. One of our primary irrationalities. We see the improbable and call it impossible, and would rather accept convenient untruths than seek out unpopular solutions."

"Do you have to be such an elitist asshole about everything?"

The man flinched and, crystal spider in his hands, turned to glare at her. They were allies and sometimes friends and he was fond of Eve, but there were times when her behavior puzzled him. Other times it reminded him that though he had put a great deal of distance between himself and the odd primness of the era of his birth, he had not entirely escaped it.

"No," he replied at last, "just about some things. And most certainly about history and archaeology. I would think you of all people would understand."

Her eyes narrowed and a hint of fury glimmered in them a moment, and then passed. She sighed. "You are the most aggravating man."

Mr. Doyle cleared his throat, back rigid, and nodded once. "Yes. I believe I am." Then he bent to his task once more. The job was nearly done, and it took him only another minute or so before he had removed the gold entirely from the elegantly designed crystal spider. It was a marvel from an age far more distant than anyone would have guessed.

"So are you going to tell me how this is going to help us find your dead sorcerer friend?"

The edges of Doyle's mouth tugged upward, his mustache twitching in the smallest of smiles. He stared at the

Lemurian Spider in his hand, felt its edges sharp against the callused flesh of his palm.

"Our quarry is not precisely dead, lovely Eve. And this? With the proper incantations, it will weave us an answer."

Eve arched an eyebrow. "What the hell does that mean?"

He felt the words rising from deep within his chest, as though they had been born not of his mind but of his heart. When he spoke them, his voice was higher and lilting, the way he had sung the melodies his mother had taught him as a boy in Edinburgh.

"Atti mannu kashshaptu sha tuyub ta enni."

Mr. Doyle turned from her, raised the spider, and hurled it with all his might at the wall. Eve shouted and lunged to stop him, but for all her uncanny speed she was too late. Her eyes were wide and her gaze ticked toward the wall. It was clear she expected the spider to shatter.

Instead, it stuck to the wall.

For several long moments nothing happened. The only sounds in the room were the hum of electricity in the walls, the shush of the air filtration system, and Doyle's own breathing. The illumination cast by the display lighting in the otherwise darkened room only contributed to the gathering and shifting of shadows in every corner, and they seemed to darken, to cluster more closely, as Doyle and Eve stared at the crystal spider.

"All right," Eve said, *"what* is—"

She never finished the sentence.

With a grating, clicking sound, the spider began to move. Its legs scratched at the wall as it crept upward, and Mr. Doyle narrowed his gaze, peering more closely until he could make out the thin strand of crystalline webbing it was leaving behind.

Eve slid her hands into her pockets and gave her hair an insouciant toss. "You know, with all I've seen—which is pretty much everything—you'd think I couldn't be surprised anymore. What is it doing?"

"Watch," he chided her.

And so they stood in silence in the midst of the Egyptian exhibit and watched as the spider spun its crystal web, clicking up the wall and then to the left, moving back down to diagonally cross its original line. Soon enough a pattern began to take form.

"It's a map," Eve said. She stepped closer and looked up, head tilted back as she studied the circumference of the web pattern and the shape it had taken, the grid that was forming along the length of it and the large open rectangle in the center.

Brows knitted, Eve turned to stare at Doyle. "It's a map of Manhattan."

The spider paused for several long seconds at a spot upon its web that corresponded to where Greenwich Village would have been on the map. When it at last moved on, it had left something behind. Amidst that crystalline web, at one particular junction of gleaming thread, a tiny crystal stood out from the pattern of the map.

A chill passed through Mr. Doyle like ice sliding down his back, and he stared at the map. Slowly he nodded. He had wondered for so long what had happened to the Mage, what had become of Lorenzo Sanguedolce, that it seemed unreal to him, looking at that crystal and knowing that it symbolized an end to his search.

He nodded gruffly and glanced at Eve. "All right, then. To New York."

SHORTLY before dawn, with heavy storm clouds aiding the night in its quest to keep morning at bay, the limousine swept through midtown Manhattan. Its tires sloshed through pools of rainwater, and the windshield wipers hissed as they beat their hypnotic rhythm upon the glass. New York had its reputation as the city that never slept, but on that Sunday morning it seemed, at least, to be dozing. The limousine was not the only vehicle about— they passed several taxis and police cars and a handful of automobiles whose drivers were likely about on business of questionable intent—but the streets were lonely never-theless. With the storm hanging so low over the city and the rain driving down upon the limousine, New York seemed very inhospitable indeed.

In the back of the limo, Eve rested her head against the tinted window and gazed up at the cityscape that unfolded with each block. Twenty-four-hour neon storefronts, digi-tal billboards, and the glass and steel faces of thousands of corporations. In her life she had seen the rise and fall of cities more glorious than this one, and yet there was some-thing about New York—with its old-fashioned personality and its vast ambition for the future—that she admired.

Her long legs were stretched out, and she had slid down in the seat. From time to time her mind drifted so that she was in a sort of trance state in which ghosts of the past haunted her memory, but she did not sleep. Eve never slept during the night.

In the driver's seat, Squire yawned, revealing teeth as jagged and numerous as a shark's. The gnarled, ugly little man glanced into the rearview mirror and saw her watch-ing him. His grin was hideous.

"Hey, babe. Good morning. You were zoning out back there so I didn't want to interrupt."

Eve stretched languidly against the leather upholstery, aware of the goblin's hungry eyes but unconcerned. She twisted her neck, muscles popping. Across from her, be-hind the driver's seat, Doyle slept in a sitting position with his hands clasped, corpselike, over his chest. He snored lightly, head bobbing from time to time.

She glanced at the driver again. "Usually you can't keep your mouth shut, Squire. I appreciate it."

"My pleasure," he said.

The goblin returned his attention to the road. They had passed through Times Square and were now rolling south on Seventh Avenue. Squire was a cautious driver. Doyle had paid to have the limo customized so that Squire could see through the windshield and still reach the accelerator and brake, mainly because the goblin liked to drive. Of all the services the creature performed for his employer, chauffeuring was the one at which he had the least amount of skill. Eve would not deny that Squire had his uses, but there were times when they were outweighed by his more annoying attributes.

"So, what's this about, babe?" the goblin asked, casting a quick glance over his shoulder, his gnarled features silhouetted by the greenish light from the limo's dashboard. "I mean, I need my beauty sleep and the boss rousted me without telling me much. What's the hurry?"

Eve closed her eyes and sighed. "If I explain it to you, will you stop calling me 'babe'?"

"I can try."

She nodded, opening her eyes and sitting up straighter in her seat. Her black hair fell in a tumble across her face and she swept it back again. "That's good. Doyle would be unhappy if I ripped your throat out."

The rain pelted the limousine's roof and sluiced down the windows. The engine purred and Squire kept both hands on the wheel as they slid through another intersection. Once again he caught her eye in the rearview mirror.

"Don't be that way, darlin'. I don't mean anything by it. And I'd have to be blind not to notice what a looker you are."

Eve's upper lip curled back in a hiss that revealed her fangs. "That could be arranged."

"Okay, okay," Squire protested, shrugging. "Just making conversation. You don't wanna talk, we won't talk."

Eve turned her gaze out the window again as they passed closed shops and newsstands with their metal rolling doors locked down tight. A tall, thin man in a hooded rain slicker hunched over as he walked his dog, the little beast leading him along by its leash, creating confusion as to which of them was the pet. Given the hour, Eve was tempted to believe the dog was in charge.

"I know very little," she began, still peering out into the rain.

"That's more than I know," Squire noted. He fished around the front seat and then held up a pack of cigarettes in triumph. The limo slowed as he tapped one out and used his lips to draw it from the pack.

"I've forgotten more than you'll ever know," Eve said, and her voice sounded hollow even to her, tinged with a melancholy she rarely allowed in herself. It was the rain. The damned rain. For some reason it always put her in mind of a simpler time, long ago.

Squire either missed her tone or ignored it entirely. "All right, you know so much, then spill it." The goblin pushed in the dashboard lighter, the unlit cigarette rolling like a toothpick between his lips.

"You're not going to smoke in here," she said.

His wiry eyebrows went up, and he glanced at her in the mirror. "I'm not? No, I guess I'm not."

Eve glanced over at Doyle. He grumbled in his sleep now, brow knitted in consternation. She was not surprised. He was not the sort of man she would ever expect to have sweet dreams.

"It's pretty simple, actually. You know the story of Lorenzo Sanguedolce?"

"Sure. Sweetblood. That's what all the arcane books call him. Sweetblood the Mage."

Eve nodded once. She had expected Squire to know the story. Anyone even tangentially involved with the magical community would have. Tales of Sanguedolce could be traced back as early as the eleventh century, and though he seemed to have changed his name several times, the stories about him cropped up in journals from a dozen countries over the course of hundreds of years. He was called Sweetblood, but it was unclear whether this was a literal translation of his Italian surname, or if the surname was simply another variation on that descriptive appellation.

By all accounts Sanguedolce had been the most powerful sorcerer who had ever lived. Yet early in the twentieth century, he had simply disappeared. None of the dark powers in the world had laid claim to having destroyed him, and though there were rumors and whispers, no mage was ever proven to have knowledge of his whereabouts, or his possible demise.

"You know your boss has been looking for the mage for a very long time?" Eve asked.

Squire chuckled without humor. "That's an understatement. Never thought it was a great idea, myself. You know what they say about searching for Sweetblood."

"We may have found him."

The goblin jerked the steering wheel so hard to the right as he spun to stare at Eve that he nearly plowed the limousine into a squat blue mailbox on the sidewalk. In a panic, Squire hit the brakes and got the limo's nose headed in the right direction again.

Eve watched him in the mirror. Several times the annoying little creature opened his mouth and closed it again, as though for the first time in his life he had no clever or boorish remark to make. She knew it would pass, though. With Squire, it always did.

"Hell," the goblin said, the word coming out in a harsh

grunt. "All the stories say . . . ah, hell, Eve, *all* the stories say that would be a bad idea."

Squire kept his hands on the wheel and his eyes on the road. A taxi cut in front of the limousine despite the fact that there were only a handful of cars on Seventh Avenue. Ahead a light turned red and the goblin began to slow the limo.

"True."

The word came from Doyle. Eve glanced over at him and saw that his eyes were red and his face somewhat flush. He had not slept nearly enough, but that was not unusual. Magic had suspended the aging process in him, had even partially reversed it, but there was no escaping that the man was still human. An alchemist and magician, a brilliant writer and scholar, a believer in both the goodness of the world and the darkness that tainted it, Mr. Doyle was among the most powerful magicians on Earth, but he was also just a man. Human.

Eve envied him that. She could not even remember what it meant to be human.

"Boss, you're awake," Squire said, turning to glance back at Doyle now that he was stopped at the red light.

Tiredly, Mr. Doyle smoothed his jacket and ran his fingers through his silver hair to straighten it. "And you, my small friend, have a gift for stating the obvious."

"What can I say?" Squire muttered happily. "I'm blessed."

The light turned green, but Squire was careful to look in both directions before the limousine picked up speed again. Behind him, his employer tugged out a pocket watch and clicked it open. He checked the time and then slid the watch back into his vest pocket.

Doyle cleared his throat and glanced at Eve, then turned his attention to Squire again.

"The warnings about what would happen to anyone

who searched for Sweetblood are dire," the magician absently admitted as he began searching the inner pockets of his jacket for something. "But I suspect they were spread by Lorenzo himself in an effort to dissuade the curious."

Eve stared at him. "And if you're wrong?"

Doyle raised an eyebrow and stared at her, his eyes as silver as his hair. "If I'm wrong, then we handle it."

"That's your plan?" Squire asked. "That's not much of a plan."

"There isn't time for subtlety," Doyle replied. "My search has always been a casual one, rarely the focus of my efforts. But Dr. Graves has word that someone—someone with malevolent intentions—has indeed located Sweetblood."

"And we need to get to him first," Squire said, nodding to himself as he turned the limousine down a side street, the rear tire bumping up over the curb.

"Precisely."

The goblin turned south again at the next corner, and soon enough the city was changing around them. The skyscrapers had given way to brownstones and rowhouses, and there were trees growing up out of the sidewalk. They passed a park that seemed remarkably free of litter and graffiti.

"All right," Squire said. "I get it. But I was still half asleep when you got me out of bed to drive you, so there's still one thing I'm not understanding."

"Only one?" Eve taunted.

Doyle frowned at her. "What's that, Squire?"

"Where do the glass spiders come in? You said something about glass spiders, didn't you? Or was that in my dream?"

Before the dapper magician could answer, Eve spied their destination, the address plainly exhibited on the front door of the brownstone. The sky had begun to lighten, but the drenching rain and the heavy cloud cover would shield her from the sun.

"Stop here. This is it."

The goblin pulled the limo to the curb. Doyle leaned across the back seat to peer through Eve's rain-streaked window, eyebrows raised. Then he popped his own door open and slipped out. Eve stripped off her suede coat, folded it, and left it on the seat, then followed suit. The rain began to dampen her hair immediately, streaming like tears upon her cheeks. Thunder rolled across the sky, echoing off the faces of the buildings. Lightning blinked and flickered up inside the clouds as though behind that veil the gods were at war.

Doyle slammed his door without another word to Squire. His gaze was locked upon the brownstone, and he stared up at its darkened windows as he strode around the limousine to join Eve on the sidewalk.

Her nostrils flared and she sniffed at the air. "Does this seem too easy to you?"

"I'm not certain that's a word I would choose," Doyle replied, wiping rain from his eyes.

Eve pushed her hair back from her face and rapped on the limo's passenger window. When Squire rolled it down, she bent to peer in at him. The goblin's eyes went to her chest, where the tight cotton of her turtleneck stretched across her breasts.

"Up here, you little shit."

A dreamy smile spread across his features. "Sorry. What can I do for you?"

"Open the trunk."

He reached for the release, there was a small pop, and then the trunk lid rose. The sound of the rain pelting the metal altered at this new angle. Eve went to the rear of the limo and reached into the trunk to retrieve a parcel wrapped in soft leather. She unfolded the leather and

folded her fingers around the stock of the sawed-off shotgun, and she smiled as she dropped the leather wrap into
the trunk and slammed it shut.

Turning to Doyle, she cocked the shotgun. "Too easy."

"Perhaps," he replied. Then he nodded toward the brick
steps in front of the brownstone. "Would you like to get the
door?"

Eve strode purposefully up the short walkway, not even
bothering to check the windows of the surrounding homes
for prying eyes. That sort of thing was Doyle's problem,
and he dealt with it often enough. She went up the four
steps and paused on the landing, then shot a kick at the
front door. The blow cracked it in half and tore it from its
hinges. The bottom part of the door flew across the building's foyer and shattered the legs of a small table; the top
half swung like a guillotine from the security chain that
still connected it to the door frame.

With preternatural swiftness she darted inside the
brownstone, swinging the gaping double barrels of the
shotgun around as she scanned the parlor on her left and
then the formal living room on her right. Nothing moved.
Nothing breathed.

Doyle stepped in behind her. Eve glanced at him and
saw the corona of pale blue light that encircled his eyes,
the aura of that same glow surrounding his fingers. The illusion of the kindly, aging gentleman had disappeared.
This was the magician. This was who Doyle was.

"Anything?" he asked.

Eve's eyelids fluttered as she inhaled. She glanced at
the stairs that led up into darkness. "Nothing that way."
Then she narrowed her eyes as she stared into the shad-
owed corridor that led toward the back of the brownstone.
"But that way . . ."

"Magic. Yes. I feel it."

Doyle went past her, heedless of any danger. The blue

light around his fingers and leaking from his eyes grew
brighter, and he was a beacon in the darkened corridor. Eve
tried to make sense of the layout of the place in her head.
Living room and parlor in front. Probably a back staircase
somewhere, a pantry, big kitchen, and the sort of sprawling dining room that had been popular in the first half of
the twentieth century.

There were framed photographs on the walls that had
obviously hung there for decades and wallpaper that had
gone out of style before John F. Kennedy was President.
Yet there was no dust. No cobwebs. No sign that time had
continued to pass within that home while it went by on the
outside.

The corridor ended at a door that was likely either a
closet or bathroom, but there were rooms to either side, elegant woodwork framing their entrances. Doyle did not
even glance to his left, but turned into the room on the
right. Eve was right behind him and nearly jammed the
shotgun into his spine when he came to a sudden stop.

She moved up beside him, staring into the dining room.

Six figures sat in a circle around the elegant dining-
room table, all of them clasping hands as if joining in
prayer—or a séance. There were candlesticks on the table
and several on a sideboard; Doyle waved his hand and
each of the wicks flickered to life, those tiny flames illuminating the room. Perhaps the old magician needed the
light to see by, but Eve did not. She saw better in the dark.

Of the six, five were very clearly dead, and had been so
for a very long time. Though their skeletal fingers were
still clasped, they were withered, eyes sunken to dark
sockets, only wisps of hair left upon their heads. In many
places all that remained of their flesh was tattered bits
clinging to bone, like parchment paper. Eve peered more
closely. She had not smelled death in this place, so she
wondered if it was some sort of illusion. But no. There was

an earthy, rot odor that lingered in the air. It was simply that, like dust and other sediment of time, the stink of putrefying flesh seemed to have been suspended somehow.

The five withered corpses were of indeterminate age and race, but at least one of them had been female. And then there was the sixth member of this chain, a woman in a blue dress, her brown hair up in a tight bun, with small framed glasses resting on the bridge of her nose. Her eyes were closed and her face peaceful, as though she might well have been in the midst of a natural slumber rather than eternal repose.

"Yvette Darnall," Doyle observed.

Eve glanced at him, saw the puzzlement on his face, and knew that it matched her own. "You know her?"

"A mystic and psychic. She disappeared in 1943."

"Or maybe she didn't," Eve said, her gaze once more surveying the hideous gathering, the sunken faces waxy and yellow in the candlelight. "Maybe it was just that nobody knew where to look."

Doyle frowned thoughtfully and stepped further into the room. Eve followed but her nostrils flared and the hair rose on the back of her neck. Her fingers hooked into talons. She sensed something in the room, and she knew that Doyle had felt it, too.

Yvette Darnall opened her eyes.

Eve and Doyle froze. For just a moment there was a kind of terrible awareness in the psychic woman's gaze, and then her eyes rolled upward so that they seemed completely white. Her head lolled back and her jaw went slack, mouth falling open.

One by one, the five cadavers did the same. Some of their jawbones cracked. When the most dessicated among them lay his head back, it simply tore off above the jaw with a sound like snapping kindling. Upon hitting the hardwood floor, his skull shattered into dust and bone fragments.

Yvette Darnall began to moan, and so did the chorus of the dead.

She choked as a stream of milky, opalescent mist issued from her throat, and a moment later thinner tendrils of the same substance flowed from the gaping mouths of the dead. Eve recognized the material. *Ectoplasm.* Malleable spirit flesh. But she did not think it was the ghosts of these dead summoners or even of the medium herself who was manipulating the ectoplasm here.

It coalesced in the midst of the table, and as it did, Eve saw that Yvette Darnall had begun to decay. Whatever this power was, it was drawing on whatever essence remained in her; it had kept her here for more than sixty years as a spiritual battery, and now it was using her up.

The ectoplasm churned like thick, heavy storm clouds and began to take shape. In a moment Eve could see human features forming, a man with a long, hawk nose and thin lips, with wild unkempt hair and a shaggy beard.

The face in the pooling ectoplasm narrowed its eyes as though it had seen them, and it sneered imperiously, gaze rife with disapproval. When it spoke, its lips moved without sound, yet its voice issued from the wide, gaping mouth of Yvette Darnall.

"Doyle," the voice rasped scornfully. *"You damned fool."*

2

THE ectoplasmic head of Sweetblood the Mage drifted in the air above the circular table. Tendrils of supernatural matter extended from the manifestation to anchor itself to the ceiling, the walls, and the table below it. The ghost flesh moved, its lips forming words, but the voice of the world's most powerful sorcerer growled at Doyle not from the ectoplasm but from the grotesquely open maw of the withering spiritualist, Yvette Darnall.

"And to think I once called you 'apprentice.'"

"I always respected you, Lorenzo," Doyle said, attempting to conceal the exhilaration he felt at moving so much closer to actually locating the archmage. "But I never understood your decision to retreat, to hide yourself away. The world has need of you."

Doyle recalled his first meeting with Lorenzo Sanguedolce, in Prague, during the spring of 1891, and their immediate dislike for one another. Even after the relationship shifted to that of teacher and student, their animosity stood firm. There wasn't anyone, on this plane of existence anyway, that Doyle disliked as much, but the ways of the weird did not take into account one's personal feelings. Sweetblood was needed; it was as simple as that.

"Do you have any idea the risk you have taken in searching for me?" the undulating spiritual mass asked, the power of its voice causing the psychic's body to visibly quake. *"Do you think I have stayed away from the world all this time on a whim?"*

Eve stood beside Doyle, tensed for a fight. He could feel the aggression emanating from her lithe form, millennia of experience having taught her always to expect a fight. "I could be wrong," she said, "but I'm going to guess he isn't all that pleased to see you."

Doyle shot her a hard look. "Your enhanced senses are absolutely uncanny," he said dryly. Then he turned his focus to Sweetblood again.

"You must listen, Lorenzo. Damn me if you will, but others are on your scent as well. One way or another, you've been found. But the others who track you have grave intentions."

"And you, fool that you are, you think I need your help?" Sweetblood rasped. *"You may have done their work for them, Arthur."*

The disembodied head gazed down upon the grotesque gathering at the table beneath him, at the rapidly degenerating form of Yvette Darnall and the circle of desiccated corpses clutching hands, with a look of utter disdain forming upon his spectral features.

"You're no better than this damnable woman and her band of psychics. They too attempted to locate me. Their curiosity cost them their lives," the spectral head went on, showing not the slightest hint of compassion. *"Fortunately, I was able to use their folly for my own ends."*

Eve sniffed. "Nice guy."

Doyle ignored her, focusing on Sweetblood, trying to gauge by the rate of Darnall's deterioration how much longer their connection would remain active. "Obviously," he said, gesturing toward the circle of cadavers. "You used them as an alarm to warn you when someone, or possibly something, was coming too close. The psychic residue of their search led us here, drawing us away from your true location."

The acrid aroma of burning flesh permeated the room, and Doyle frowned and glanced away from the ectoplasmic face to find that the body of Yvette Darnall had begun to smolder, the tight bun of her hair emitting a gray, oily smoke.

"Indeed. And in this pocket of frozen time, I might work my power through these decaying idiots and destroy the interloper, the next fool. I never expected the next fool to be you."

Doyle could not help but smile. "You have always underestimated me, Lorenzo."

The entity appeared to seethe. Flames burst from the bodies of the other mystics, as if by the very fire of its anger, their clothes and parchment-dry flesh were consumed. *"You're a careless fool, Arthur, and this latest misstep only proves it."*

Eve stifled a laugh with a perfectly manicured hand, refusing to make eye contact with him. It was at moments like this when Doyle remembered why it was that he so often chose to work alone.

"Cast all the aspersions you like, but they will not alter the truth. Dark powers descend upon you," Doyle declared, fingertips crackling with leaking magickal energy. "Better that *I* should find you than some malevolent—"

"Imbecile!" Sweetblood bellowed, enraged, his voice erupting from the gaping lips of the medium who had become his conduit. The ectoplasmic features that loomed above the fire-engulfed cadaver contorted, and the ghostly tendrils that connected it to the dead woman writhed and

pulled away to flail whiplike above them. *"Persist, and you may doom the world."*

The burning corpse of Yvette Darnall stood up abruptly, knocking over the flaming chair in which it had sat for the last sixty-one years. Like some fiery marionette, embers of flesh falling from her form, the dead woman leaned across the table to point an accusatory finger at them.

"Go home, apprentice," said Lorenzo Sanguedolce, through the charred and smoking remains of the medium. *"You meddle in matters beyond your comprehension."*

And with those final words, the instrument of the mage's admonition exploded, spewing fiery chunks of flesh and bone. Doyle and Eve watched as the room was consumed by fire, the ectoplasmic manifestation of the archmage evaporating with a sizzling hiss. The spell that had kept the room in a timeless stasis had collapsed, age rushing forward, drying the wood, speeding the fire. Time and flame sapped the moisture from the dark mahogany, reducing it to kindling. The heat seared his face, yet Doyle stared into the flames until he felt Eve's powerful grip close upon his arm.

"I wouldn't count on the last word," she snarled over the roar of the fire as she began to pull him toward the exit.

Doyle roughly removed her hand and ventured further into the room.

"Have you lost your mind?" she shouted after him.

"Go," he told her. "There's still a chance I can salvage what we came for."

It was becoming ever more difficult to see, as well as breathe, and Doyle quickly scanned the floor for the precious item he sought. Silently he prayed to the Ancient Kings that it had remained intact.

"Arthur, let's go!" Eve called from the doorway, as his tearing eyes fell upon his prize: Darnall's blackened, jawless skull lying upon the smoking wood floor.

Removing a handkerchief from his pocket, Doyle folded the white silk and used it as a buffer to protect the soft flesh of his hand from the searing heat emanating from the charred skull. There was only the slimmest chance that what he was about to attempt would work, but there was far too much at stake not to at least try. He inserted his index and middle fingers into the hollow eye sockets of the medium's skull, searching for the soft gray matter of the brain beyond the missing eyes. The tips of his fingers sank into the gelatinous muscle of thought. He let slip an exultant sigh; the flames had not yet melted the woman's brain. There were still things to be learned from her.

The beams and walls of the burning room moaned and creaked. It would not be long before the ceiling caved in, the upper floors of the brownstone coming down as the entire building was consumed by the supernatural conflagration. Beneath his breath, Doyle uttered an incantation of retrieval, letting the ancient magick travel through his body, coursing down the length of his arm, through his fingers, and into what remained of the dead psychic's brain. Images of Yvette's past—of heartbreak and ecstasy and quiet contentment—flooded his mind, making themselves at home, as if eager not to be forgotten with the passing of their host. The deluge of memories was overwhelming, and he nearly stumbled into the fire as he magickally ransacked the recollections of a lifetime.

Behind the remembrance of a torrid lesbian affair with a beautiful dark-haired girl nearly half her age, and beyond an exceptionally awful production of *La Boheme*, Doyle found the elusive bit of information that he had been searching for and claimed it as his own.

He plucked his fingers from the skull, tossed the now empty shell back into the flames, and wiped the viscous, hideously warm gray matter from his fingers upon his scorched handkerchief. The fire raged all around him, attempting to block his path and consume him, but the mage knew the language of fire, speaking to the conflagration politely and with respect, and it allowed him to pass unharmed through the doorway and into the smoke-filled hall.

In the corridor, where smoke billowed and flames had already begun to lick across the ceiling and ripple up the walls, Eve waited. Her face was covered in dark patches of soot that resembled war paint. Her eyes darted about like those of a desperate animal. Her kind did not do well with fire.

"I can't believe you're not burned to a crisp."

Doyle moved past her silently on his way toward the exit.

"At least tell me that you got whatever it was you risked being burned alive for," she said, following close on his heels.

"I did indeed," he said as they hurried across the entryway and out into the damp pre-dawn air. "Time is short, now. We must act swiftly. He's far closer than I would have guessed."

Squire awaited them on the sidewalk in front of the burning brownstone. The goblin held an open umbrella, rain sluicing over the edges, and he wore a nervous expression upon his grotesque features.

"A real gentleman's gentleman," Eve muttered as she reached him.

Sirens wailed in the distance, but they would be far too late to save this building. As they moved toward the car, Eve cursed loudly. Doyle turned to face her, only to flinch as something wet and heavy struck his shoulder, slippery on his neck. Suddenly the predawn was alive with the staccato thunder of one damp impact after another. In the midst of the rain, something else was falling from the sky.

"What the hell?" Eve snapped, shielding her head as the

toads continued to fall, bouncing off the brick steps, the streets, and the cars below them. Multiple car alarms wailed, partially drowning the rather offensive sound of soft flesh striking hard pavement.

Doyle stared about in alarm. *Things are worse than I thought.* Squire scrambled up the steps to shield them both from the pummeling rain with the large, black umbrella.

"This can't be good," Eve snarled, pushing bloody, ruptured amphibian corpses out of her way with the tip of her designer boot.

"Be thankful it ain't cats and dogs," Squire said, as the rain of toads continued to fall all around them.

Far worse, Doyle thought.

JULIA Ferrick turned off the engine of her Volvo wagon in the underground parking garage on Boston's Boylston Street and wondered, as she so often did, what had happened to her *real* son.

"I was listening to that," the imposter growled from the passenger seat. He had insisted on listening to one of his homemade music mixes on the drive to their family appointment, and when she had turned off the engine, it cut off a headache-inducing grind in midverse.

"And you'll hear the rest of it on the way home," she said with exasperation, placing her keys and the parking garage receipt into her handbag. His name went unsaid. More and more, of late, she had trouble calling him Daniel, or even Dan. She didn't know him anymore. Jesus, she craved a cigarette.

"I wanted to hear it now," he said curtly, refusing to make eye contact with her.

Julia looked at him, avoiding her gaze as if he would turn to stone if their eyes met, and wondered when exactly the aliens or the goblins or maybe even the Gypsies had come and taken away her real son and replaced him with this grim doppelganger. She ran her thumb over the tips of her fingers, where the nails were short and ragged. It was a nervous habit born out of quitting smoking. Anytime she looked at her nails, she thought maybe lung cancer was preferable to the complaints she got when she tried to get her manicurist to fix them.

"C'mon," she told him, opening her door. "We're going to be late."

She slammed the driver-side door closed, but the six-teen-year-old did not move. Dan just sat there, sweatshirt hood pulled up over his head, arms folded across his chest. His skateboard was on the floor in the back, and her eyes flickered to it. The skate punk thing was just the latest identity he'd tried on, and she wondered how long it would be before he shed this one. Every time she saw him in those baggy pants, she shivered. To her eyes, he looked like a criminal. That was a terrible thought, but there was no escaping it. It was difficult for her to conceive that these kids looked at themselves—or at each other—and thought that they looked good.

The one thing that never changed was the music. Whether it was Taking Back Sunday or Rancid—and wasn't that band name apropos?—it was much the same as the clothes he wore. Julia simply could not understand the attraction. She wasn't a fool. She didn't expect him to listen to things she liked, old Peter Gabriel and David Bowie, or Genesis. Music was a personal thing. It spoke to your heart, or it didn't. But with a couple of exceptions, the sort of thing Danny listened to was just . . . it was awful. Ugly. How could he not see that?

Julia knew that he'd had a rough year—his father walking out on them, the condition that gave his skin a weathered, leathery texture—and she wished she could make it all go away, give him the perfect life she'd hoped for since he was a baby. But life threw you curves. No way could she have predicted his medical problem. Trying to balance her sympathy for him with her frustration at his behavior was enough to drive her to drink . . . or at least to run back to her cigarette habit and beg a pack of Winston Lights to forgive her.

Things were bound to get better. That's what she told herself while she was biting her nails. Things *had* to get better. She was determined to help Dan in any way she could and had begun homeschooling him with the finest tutors and making appointments with the best dermatologists and psychologists. Julia still remembered the loving little boy he had been. He had filled her with so much happiness. She wanted that boy back.

No matter what it cost.

"Daniel Ferrick, get out of that car right now," she yelled, her voice reverberating against the low concrete ceiling of the garage. There was a quaver in it, but she promised herself she would not break down.

Slowly, he turned to look at her through the glass and scowled. His skin was getting worse right along with his attitude. They had first diagnosed it as a unique form of eczema, but she soon came to realize that none of them really had the first clue what it was. They kept going for tests and various special medications, and pills were prescribed, but nothing seemed to help. When the two pronounced bumps appeared just above his temples last week, he had nearly had a breakdown. And in private, in her bathroom with the shower running, Julia had wept for him. She'd snuck a cigarette and blown the smoke out her bedroom window, hoping he wouldn't smell it. Whatever else might be done for him, Julia knew they both needed to see the family psychologist.

"Doctor Sundin is going to be really ticked if we're late

again," she said, tapping the glass with the knuckle of her hand. "Let's go."

She couldn't even remember the last time she'd heard him laugh or seen him smile. It tore her up inside, but at the same time, it was becoming increasingly difficult to live with.

The passenger door popped open and Dan slunk from the vehicle. The hood of his sweatshirt was pulled so far down over his head that it completely hid his face in shadows. Over the last week or so he had begun wearing gloves in public to conceal his skin condition, and the way his fingernails had started to grow tough and jagged. The way other kids dressed these days, nobody had seemed to notice.

Julia reached out to her son and rubbed his head through the heavy cotton hood. She remembered her teenage bout with acne but could not even begin to imagine what it must be like for the boy. He roughly jerked away from her affections.

"Don't do that," he spat at her. "It hurts me."

The boy's mother bit her tongue and walked toward the garage's Boylston Street exit. She glanced at her watch. If they hurried, they would only be a few minutes late. Julia hoped Daniel would speak to Doctor Sundin about his self-image problems, and how they affected his relationship with her and his father. She planned to avoid any mention of his clothes or his music. Those things got under her skin, but they were superficial. The real problems were so much deeper.

As she glanced back to confirm that Daniel was indeed following, she wondered how much of his personality change could be attributed to Roger walking out on them. Irreconcilable differences, he'd told his lawyer. *The son of a bitch took the coward's exit,* she thought, remembering all the sleepless nights as her son yowled in his bed, the skin condition so irritating that he scratched himself bloody. Then there were the violent mood swings, and the complete change in the boy's personality. *Yeah,* she thought. *Roger got off easy.* There was a small part of her that envied him. *The bastard.*

Julia Ferrick pushed the disturbing thoughts from her mind and turned to wait for her son to catch up. She was standing in front of a high, wrought-iron fence, and beyond it she could see children at play in the yard of the day care facility headquartered there. The kids squealed and laughed as they ran about under the supervision of their minders. It was a nice sound, one that she hadn't heard in a very long time.

"I'm coming," Dan mumbled, head down, gloved hands shoved deep into his sweatshirt pockets.

"I know," she told him, trying her best to keep her temper in check. "I just thought I'd wait for you."

Dan kicked at a piece of gum, crushed flat upon the sidewalk. "Don't do me any favors," he mumbled as he scuffed at the pink refuse with the toe of his sneaker.

Julia Ferrick was about to say something she was sure to regret when she noticed that a little girl, no older than five, now stood on the other side of the metal gate, watching them. The child sniffled, her hand slowly rising to her face to rub at her eyes. The little girl began to cry.

"What's the matter, sweetie?" Julia asked.

"Don't feel good," the small child whined, beginning to cry all the harder. Julia moved closer to the gate, wanting to get the attention of one of the day care workers, when the child in front of her began to retch. Thick streams of milky white vomit poured from her mouth to splash upon the sidewalk, spattering her shiny, black patent leather shoes.

Julia was about to comfort the little girl through the thick bars of the metal gate when motion at the periphery of her vision caught her attention. She glanced down upon the puddle of vomit at the child's feet.

It was moving.

Now matter how badly she wanted to, Julia Ferrick could not pull her eyes away from the horrific sight. The child had regurgitated maggots—not just one or five or even twenty, but hundreds of them.

"I trew up bugs," the child whined over and over again in a dazed chorus. "I trew up bugs. I trew up bugs. I trew up bugs."

Julia felt that she might be sick as well and finally tore her gaze away to look upon the playground for help.

"Could somebody—anybody—help here please!" she cried out, on the verge of panic. Then she saw that the staff was in a panic of activity, the other children sick as well, all of them throwing up as the little girl at the fence had done.

One of the staff members fainted, hitting the ground dangerously close to an undulating pile of maggot-infested sick.

"Got to call 911," she mumbled, reaching into her bag for her cell phone. "This isn't right. It isn't right at all."

Julia hit the emergency button that would immediately dial for help and brought the phone up to her ear, gazing into the playground at the children all in the grip of sickness. They were all crying, some curled into convulsing balls on the ground. Even the little girl at the fence now lay at the base of the gate, trembling as if freezing.

This is a nightmare, she thought as the voice on the other end of the phone asked her to state her emergency.

The words were about to leave her mouth when she noticed that her son now gripped the black iron bars of the gate in his gloved hands. His hood had fallen away to reveal his closely cropped hair and the condition that had changed his face and the skin of his entire body. The bumps upon his forehead seemed more pronounced, red and angry as though ready to burst.

As he stared intensely through the bars at the children overcome with illness, Daniel Ferrick made a sound the likes of which his mother had not heard for a number of years. In any other circumstance, she would have paid a great deal of money for a chance to hear it again.

Her son was laughing.

EVE could smell the prominent stink of fear upon the commuters milling around the main terminal of New York's Grand Central Station. The city was freaked, but given the circumstances, could she blame them?

The toad rain ended around thirty minutes after it had begun, followed by random incidents of bizarreness that they had heard about on the radio in the limousine on their way to the station: spontaneous human combustion, stigmata, spectral rape, and myriad other claims that were coming in seemingly by the minute. And if what Doyle was hinting about was even remotely true, this was just the tip of a really nasty iceberg.

Now, perhaps ninety minutes after sunup, she followed the mage as they wound their way through the early morning commuters that seemed paralyzed by the turn of events. Eve was careful to avoid any patches of daylight coming in through Grand Central's high, ornate windows. Fortunately, though the rain of toads had stopped, the more conventional showers continued, and the clouds outside meant she didn't have to work on it that hard. She had slipped her suede jacket back on, but had been careful not to let it get wet.

Announcements were made over the station's PA system, departures and arrivals, but nobody seemed to be going anywhere. The crowd teemed with people unsure of what they ought to be doing. Should they go on with their day-to-day lives? Go to work and ignore the fact that toads had rained down from the sky? Exposure to the preternatural had that effect on some people. When they had gone to bed the night before, their perceptions of the world had been solid and clear, but now all that had changed. They had been shown just a hint of the truth that she, Doyle, and certain other unsavory types in the paranormal circles had known for most of their lives.

The world was anything but "normal."

Some tried to laugh it off. She could hear them among the crowds that milled about. But beneath their levity she could sense the tension, smell the fear as it took root and prepared to blossom.

Eve sympathized. They were in Manhattan, and thanks to all the nasty shit going down, she just knew she was not going to be able to stop at Barney's for a little shopping expedition. It pissed her off. A visit to New York always meant a Barney's trip for her. The last time she had picked up a spectacular silk top and Prada boots that were totally out of fashion now. Doyle dressed well, for a man, but this was because he was a product of his era and not because he had any real appreciation for clothes.

It was a weakness for Eve. She might even have gone so far as to call it an obsession. There was no sin in wanting to dress well, she always said. So few people caught the irony. After all, without her own sins, clothes might never have been invented.

Doyle stopped at the top of the marble staircase that would take them underground, into the subway system.

"We're going down?" she asked, still fascinated by the weird vibe she was picking up from most people within the station.

"Yes," he said, taking hold of the brass railing and beginning to descend. She followed. "Despite Sweetblood's best intentions, a link had been established between the medium, her psychics, and the mage."

Doyle went around a random commuter who stood frozen on the stairs, clutching the handrail as if for dear life. He had been very brief in the car, giving to Squire only their destination, as if he had needed time to process the information that he had obtained at the brownstone. Eve found it particularly nasty that Doyle had to stick his fingers into somebody's brain to find what he was looking for. Better him than her.

Not that she hadn't rooted through her share of viscera in her time. It was only that brains were so grotesquely unpleasant to the touch.

"So you got Sweetblood's location out of the medium's brain?" Eve asked.

"With some minor difficulty, yes," Doyle confirmed.

"Don't you think that was kind of sloppy on your old pal Lorenzo's part?" she asked him curiously. "Leaving that kind of information lying around in somebody's head when he's supposedly all hot and bothered about not being found?"

They reached the bottom of the stairs and proceeded through a pair of double doors into the underground system.

"That is where Sanguedolce's arrogance worked against him," Doyle said.

Eve thought he sounded more than a little arrogant himself. She didn't know what it was with mages, all of them so full of themselves that she was surprised they could fit their swollen heads through their front doors.

"He never believed that another mage would demonstrate the skill necessary to actually track him," Doyle said, grim satisfaction etched upon his face. "And, Heaven forbid that they did, he left a warning that should have successfully ended the trail."

She looked about the platform. There were people waiting, but not half as many as there should have been at this time of the morning. "But Sweetblood wasn't counting on you being the one doing the looking, was he?" she asked, playing with the man's cockiness.

Doyle's smile was fleeting. "He never recognized my talents," the sorcerer said, walking to the end of the platform. A homeless man surrounded with shopping bags full of empty cans snoozed against a wall, and Doyle was careful not to wake him as he peered down the tunnel into the inky darkness beyond. "He thought me incapable of mastering the weirdling ways."

"I guess you showed him," Eve muttered, standing by his side. She noticed that some of the commuters had begun to watch them with interest. "If you're thinking of continuing this little expedition down into the tunnel, you might want to use some of that mojo you're so good at so nobody calls the transit police in to arrest our asses."

Doyle looked away from the tunnel and toward the small crowd waiting for the next train. "Ah, yes, prying eyes," he said, his own eyes sparking with mystical blue energies. "Perhaps I'll make them see us as workers from one of the utility companies," he said, a strange, lilting spell upon his lips as he raised a hand, barely visible wisps of supernatural manipulation streaming from his fingertips to work their magic upon nosey commuters.

Eve heard the rustling of plastic bags and turned to see that the homeless man had awakened from his slumber and was staring at them.

"You don't want to go down there," the man said, his voice gravelly and rough, as if not used to speaking. He hooked a dirty thumb toward the tunnel entrance behind where he sat. "Some nasty shit goin' on down there." The poor soul was covered in grime and was dressed in multiple layers of clothing, the shoes upon his feet held together with wrappings of electrical tape. A foul odor of misery wafted up from him, an aroma he seemed perfectly content to wallow in.

Doyle had turned from the subway crowd. "A friend of yours, Eve?"

"Just a concerned citizen," she told the mage.

The man brought his legs up to his chest. "Stuff not meant to be seen by the likes of us," he said, beginning to rock from side to side. "Somethin' bad's comin', I know," he said, his pale green eyes glazing over as he rocked. "And it ain't ridin' the train, oh no. It's comin' in real style. That's it. Real style."

Doyle stared at the rambling man, then reached into the pocket of his coat and drew out a small billfold. Eve wasn't exactly sure how much money it was, but Doyle didn't even glance down to count it as he leaned forward to present it to the homeless man. "Thank you so much for your assessment," he said. "We'll keep it in mind."

The homeless man took the money from Doyle and looked at it briefly before stashing it amongst the layers of his clothing.

"Coming, Eve?" Doyle asked as he stepped down off the platform into space. There was a good seven feet to the tracks below, but that didn't seem to hinder the mage's progress. It was as if the air beneath him had thickened, and he drifted unharmed to the tunnel floor.

"Don't spend that all in one place," she told the man as she followed the mage off the platform. Eve leaped down into the darkness and landed in a graceful crouch, careful to avoid the electrical bite of the third rail. Electrocution wouldn't kill her, but she doubted it would be a very pleasant experience.

Able to see as well in the darkness as in the light, she spotted Doyle waiting against the tunnel wall. He gestured for her to follow.

"Quickly now," he urged.

The subway tunnel was filthy and she made a conscious effort to keep from making any contact with the walls. "Damn. This is not a place for suede. I should have left my jacket back in the car." She had purchased the coat only recently in Milan and did not want it ruined.

"Your clothing should be the least of your worries, my dear," Doyle said as he held his hand out before him, a sphere of light glowing from a space just above his palm, lighting his way.

"Are you trying to scare me?" she asked, watching the rats scurrying about in the shadows, bothered by their presence. "Me?"

He stopped before an ancient metal door, its surface caked with ages of dust, dirt, and corrosion. It was also padlocked. "You mean after all you've seen thus far, you're not scared already?" He placed one of his hands against its rusted surface.

A subway train squealed somewhere close by, and she wondered if it was coming their way. "I've faced the wrath of God," she said, watching him at the door. "I've had more terrifying *dates* than this."

A tiny smile played at the edges of Doyle's mouth. "Ah, yes. Sometimes I forget." Doyle took his hand away from the door. "We'll need to get through here," he said, pointing to the rusted padlock. "Do the honors?"

Eve reached over and tore the lock free with a single tug, rust smearing her palm and fingers.

"I don't suppose you have anything that I could use to wipe my hand?" she asked the mage as he went through the door. With a sigh, she resigned herself to the fact that her wardrobe was going to be ruined.

Eve wiped her hand upon her denim-clad leg and joined Doyle in the tiny entryway. There was a metal staircase leading down into further darkness, which her companion had already begun to descend, his eerily glowing hand lighting the way. That staircase ended at another door, which led to a cramped hallway that took them to another even older-looking door that had been sealed shut with planks of wood nailed to the frame.

"Let me guess," Eve said as she grabbed hold of the first piece of wood and ripped it from its moorings. "You want these removed as well."

Doyle stepped back, giving her room to work. "Astute as well as beautiful," he observed. "Traits not commonly found together these days, I'm sorry to say."

Eve smiled. "When He made me, He broke the mold."

The last board came away from the frame with a metallic shriek as the old nails were torn from the wood, and the door stood revealed.

"Allow me," Doyle said, sliding back a corroded deadbolt on the door with some minor difficulty. The rusted joints squealed as he yanked the door open, a damp, ancient smell wafting out to greet them.

"Smells old," Eve observed, following the mage through the doorway and out onto what appeared to be another, far more antiquated version of a subway platform. "Even by my standards."

"It should," he replied, raising his arm to shed further light upon the forgotten chamber. "It's been sealed up tight since 1899 when the major construction was begun on the subway tunnels above us. This was part of the old Grand Central Depot."

There is definitely something to this place, Eve thought. Something in the air that hinted of a power as old as Creation. *Whatever is going on here, there is more to it than rains of toads or some antisocial sorcerer hiding out.* She walked the platform, her footfalls leaving prints in the inch-thick dust that had settled there since the close of the nineteenth century.

"Very good, Lorenzo," she heard Doyle say to himself, his voice a sibilant whisper in the lost station. "But not good enough."

She sensed movement close by, the stale air rushing around her, and turned to see a shape shambling out of the darkness of the tunnel they had just journeyed through. Eve tensed for a fight, but it was the homeless man who had tried to warn them off before. She frowned. Doyle had cast a spell before to blind people back on the platform to their presence. But this filthy creature had seen them.

He leaped up from the tracks to the platform, where he landed without making a sound.

"It appears there is more to our poor soul than meets the eye," Doyle said. "I'd thought madness responsible for his resistance to magick. Now it seems not."

The man strode toward them, his duct-taped shoes making a strange scuffing sound upon the concrete-and-dust-covered surface of the platform.

"What gave him away?" Eve asked, watching the figure with a predator's gaze. "It was the seven-foot jump that clinched it for me."

"I'll leave you to deal with this complication," Doyle said, his voice reaching her from somewhere on the platform behind her, "while I endeavor to bring our search to an end."

Eve didn't respond to Doyle, choosing instead to keep her eyes upon her would-be attacker. "Don't want any trouble," she told the man.

The homeless man stopped his advance, glaring at her with eyes that now seemed to glow with an eerie inner power. "The mage must not be disturbed," he roared, in a new and terrible voice.

She wondered if he was possessed.

But then the man began to grow and his clothes tore as his musculature was altered, bones twisting grotesquely along with his flesh. As she watched the transformation, she doubted that this thing had ever really been human at all. Spiny protrusions erupted from the new flesh beneath the old. The creature reared back, stretching to its full height, and she saw that it had more than doubled in size, torn skin hanging from its body in tatters.

"For nigh upon a century have I guarded this place," its voice rumbled through a mouth filled with jagged, razor-sharp teeth. "I shall not fail in my duty now."

It came at her then with speed belying its size. She dodged from its path, leaping onto the wall and clinging there, insectlike.

The demon fixed her in its gaze, head cocked, yellow eyes glinting with surprise. It tilted its head back and sniffed the air as she hissed. Eve sprang at it from her purchase upon the wall.

"Vampire," it growled in disgust, slapping her viciously away, the sharp protrusions that adorned its body shredding the soft suede of her Italian coat as well as the delicate pale flesh beneath.

Eve rolled across the filthy floor and came up quickly, coiled upon her haunches. She felt the bestial side of her nature awaken, the canines elongating within her mouth, fingernails curling to talons.

"Did I forget to mention how much I hate that fucking word," she spat, and she lunged at her foe, a thirst for the blood of her enemy taking her to the brink of madness.

It was a place she had been so many times before.

3

A stray cat with fur the color of copper and one white ear trotted along Rue Dauphine, darting out of the paths of tourists strolling the New Orleans streets and sniffing at air redolent with the aromas of the city's famous cuisine. Most people did not even notice the stray. Despite the glitter of its later development, it was still an old city at heart, home to countless rats, and stray cats were not only inevitable in such an environment, but welcome. An old Cajun man sat on the stoop in front of a barbershop whose window frames were badly in need of a new coat of paint. He called out to the cat as it passed, almost as though the two were old friends. Otherwise the stray went on without interruption.

If anyone had taken enough interest, they might have observed that the cat seemed far more single-minded than most of its species. Rather than wandering, lured by tempting smells or idle curiosity, it seemed to have purpose.

Most of the traffic in the French Quarter was on foot. Quickly, though, the stray was moving away from the core of the Quarter, and there were more cars rumbling by and fewer people on the sidewalks. There were children searching for summertime diversions, but none of the street performers who normally livened up the cobble-stones of the Quarter.

Soon the stray left Rue Dauphine and began a winding journey that took it past buildings that had been beautiful once, their balconies and facades elegant and proud. Now they were falling apart, paint faded and cracked, and where there might once have been flowerpots upon the balconies or outside of windows, there were now cases of empty beer bottles and washing hung out to dry.

On a corner, the cat paused and perched on its haunches, staring first into the air above it at something visible only to its eyes, then across the street at a barroom called Charmaigne's. Only the first half of its neon sign was glowing, and even that was dim in the sunlight. A pair of police cars were parked askew in front of the place, and across the street was a third car, this one with no police markings but with a blue light spinning behind the rear windshield.

No spectators had gathered on the sidewalk outside the barroom. It wasn't that kind of neighborhood.

The cat stared for a long minute at the grimy plate glass windows of Charmaigne's. The barroom door was propped open with a cinder block, but with the sunshine so bright, it was only darkness inside. At length the stray set off across the street. It paused beside one of the New Orleans P.D. squad cars, then slipped beneath the vehicle. The cars had been there long enough that the engine was not even warm above the stray.

With a practiced, feline nonchalance, the cat went up onto the sidewalk and slipped into the steamy, fan-swirled gloom inside Charmaigne's. Two uniformed police offi-cers stood just inside the door on either side, as though they were concerned someone might try to escape the stale-beer and bad-cigar stink of the place. A third officer stood in the center of the barroom with a man in a white shirt with rolled-up cuffs and a loosened black tie. His hair had been cut with a military severity, and he wore a gun on one hip, a badge clipped to the other.

At their feet was the corpse of a boy, perhaps fifteen years of age, who lay on his belly in a pool of his own blood. His face was sideways, one cheek on the floor in the coagulating crimson, the other turned upward, the diffuse sunlight in the darkened barroom creating an otherworldly sheen upon his ebony skin. He was not the only corpse in Charmaigne's. Behind the bar there was a second dead man, a wiry former fighter named Calvin Traviligni, known to most as Trav. Trav had tended bar at Charmaigne's for seventeen years and had taken a bullet to the face, crashed into a rack of bottles, and died in a puddle of broken glass and a potpourri of spilled whiskey, vodka, rum, and gin. No liqueurs. Nobody in this part of town drank that shit.

At the back of the room a fourth uniformed officer sat with a young black girl who wore too much makeup. Old before her time, Jaalisa had been on her way home after a long night on the only job she'd ever known, a job her father had first given her, and heard the shots. Saw a car tearing off down the street. She insisted to the officer that she had seen nothing more.

The stray took all of this in immediately, and it darted across the room and slid along the base of the bar beneath the lazily whirling fans. The beer and cigar smells were ingrained in the wood, but the new scent of blood hung in the air like a fresh coat of Hell's own paint. The cat was skittish at the smell of blood but did not let its instincts turn it away. The plainclothes cop, a detective, noticed it, and the cat noticed him noticing, but they ignored each other.

At the back of the bar the cat went to a corner booth that

was draped in shadows, not far at all from where Jaalisa was being interviewed, squeezed for some vital detail that might make this crime more than a statistic. The stray leaped up onto the bench of that booth and sat down.

And then it changed.

The only sound was a low rush of air, like a man inhaling suddenly. Flesh rippled and bone stretched with impossible fluidity. Where the cat had been, Clay Smith now sat staring at Sergeant John Brodsky, the uniformed cop who had called him down here in the first place.

Déjà vu. Clay had first been in Charmaigne's forty-seven minutes earlier. He and Brodsky had a passing acquaintance based almost entirely upon Clay's reputation. He wasn't a private investigator, but for a wealthy resident of the Quarter he had found himself in the midst of enough murder investigations in recent years—and was invaluable in solving nearly all of them—so much so that some of the members of the N.O.P.D. had come to rely upon him. Other cops, however, detectives in particular, despised him.

Clay didn't mind. It was never about being liked.

A call on his mobile phone from Brodsky had brought him to Charmaigne's before the department had sent a homicide detective down. That was better for everyone, politicswise. He had talked to Brodsky, heard about Jaalisa's 911 call, the deaths of Trav and the kid on the floor, and nodded once.

Then he had gone to work.

Someone had gunned the kid in the doorway while Trav was getting the place cleaned up for business. The bartender always came in early to wash the floor, wipe down the tables, all the things that nobody wanted to do when they were closing up at 3 A.M. The kid—whom no one had identified yet—had obviously run in through the door and then been shot in the back. Trav had been a witness, and witnesses have a very short life expectancy.

Clay had examined both bodies without touching them. He had made a show of considering the crime scene. But that was just for the sake of the cops who were watching him, trying to figure out how he did it.

They couldn't see the tether.

The souls of murder victims never passed on to the afterworld immediately. Always, they clung to their victims for a time, crying out for vengeance, perhaps hoping someone will hear their anguish. If Clay reached the victim within the first few hours after their murder, he could still see the tether, an ethereal trail of ectoplasm that stretched from the hollow shell that had been the victim's flesh all the way to the current location of the soul.

The soul that was attached like a lamprey to its killer.

Clay had followed the tether out the door of Charmaigne's and then on a twisting path through the French Quarter. Eventually, it had led him back here.

The voices of the policemen and the tired, hard-edged words of the prostitute seemed like church whispers as they drifted through the bar. Clay slid from the rear booth and stood up, black shoes scuffing the floor. He wore tan chinos and a simple, V-necked, navy blue T-shirt, and his hair was freshly cut. In this neighborhood he would have stood out, been noticed by everyone he passed. But nobody had noticed a stray cat with copper fur and one white ear.

Clay started toward the front of the bar.

Sergeant Brodsky looked up sharply from questioning Jaalisa, notepad and pen in his hands, and he frowned deeply, then stood up and moved to block Clay's path.

"I didn't even see you come in," Brodsky said.

The man had a round little keg of a beer gut, and he slumped even when standing, but his eyes were bright and intelligent. He only looked the part of the fool. Even now and then there was a tone in his voice that suggested that he knew there was something unusual, even unnatural, about Clay Smith, but he would say no more about it.

"You weren't supposed to," Clay told him with a smile.

Brodsky processed that a moment, eyes narrowing. Then he nodded. "You find anything?"

"Yes. Your perp."

Closer to the front door, the plainclothes detective cleared his throat. "Sergeant, what the hell is this?" He strode toward them, shoes rapping the pitted wood floor. "Where the hell did this guy come from?"

The detective was pale, with dark circles beneath his eyes. He had probably not been drinking yet today, but the stale smell of alcohol exuded from his pores. There were sweat rings forming under his arms, and the white shirt looked rumpled as though he might have slept in it.

"Lieutenant Pete Landry, meet Clay Smith," Brodsky said. "He's here to help."

The lieutenant's nostrils flared and he stared at Clay. "You're him."

"Yes."

"He's got a lead on the perp," Brodsky offered, making a game attempt to defuse the tension.

"Oh, he does, huh?" The lieutenant rolled his eyes and reached into his shirt pocket to pull out a pack of cigarettes. He tapped one out, dragging the moment, and fished into his pants for a lighter. When he snapped it open and set fire to the end of the cigarette, he gazed at Clay through the flame, then clicked the lighter shut.

"So, give, genius. Who killed Travaligni and the kid?"

Clay did not smile. Instead, he stared at the wretched, silently screaming ghosts that clung to Pete Landry, tearing at him with insubstantial fingers. Trav the bartender was there. And the kid. But there were others as well. An attractive, middle-aged woman, a thug with cruel eyes, an old man whose spectral body seemed contorted somehow.

"Come on, Lieutenant," Clay said. "You did. You killed them."

The hand holding the cigarette to Landry's lips shook and dropped away from his mouth.

"Christ, Clay!" Brodsky snapped. "What the hell are you—"

"The kid had something on you, saw you do something else you shouldn't have been doing. Or maybe he was a runner for you. What are you supplying on this block, Pete? Crack? Heroin? He pissed you off, this kid. And the fool bartender, he should've slept in, just this once, but his work ethic wouldn't let him."

The other uniformed officers had begun to slide toward them now, drawn by the words and by the way the air in the bar had grown suddenly heavier.

The lieutenant hesitated only another moment, then put the cigarette to his lips again and took a long drag as his colleagues watched him in confusion and doubt. He let a plume of smoke out the side of his mouth and then glanced around at the uniforms.

"Who the fuck does this guy think he is? Come in here, making accusations like that."

Clay glanced at Brodsky again. "I doubt he used his police issue. But I also figure he's arrogant enough not to have dumped the gun he did use. Check under the seats of his car, maybe the trunk, I think you'll find it. I also think if you check his hands, you'll find residue."

Lieutenant Landry snorted and shook his head, tendrils of smoke rising up to the fan spinning above them. "You got some balls, you. But you watch too many movies."

Brodsky wasn't gaping anymore. The look on his face had gone from incredulous to darkly inquisitive.

"Then you won't mind if Gage and Caleb over there

take a look in your car, right, Lieutenant?" the sergeant asked.

The man laughed. "Damn, boys, y'all can do whatever you want." He nodded toward the two uniforms in question, gestured toward the door. "Go on, boys. Have yourselves a time."

They hesitated only a moment, then glanced at Brodsky, who nodded once. Then the two cops went out the door at a run.

"Jaalisa," Brodsky said, "you want to take a look out the door at the car across the street?"

The prostitute did not seem at all tired anymore. Her eyes were wide and her chest rose and fell as though she were breathing for two. She stared at Pete Landry for a long moment, and he took a long drag on his cigarette, its tip burning red in the darkened bar. Jaalisa shook her head.

"No, sir. I don't think I do."

The lieutenant cleared his throat again, drawing Brodsky's attention. Clay watched as he took a step nearer the sergeant.

"Things ain't never gonna be the same for you after this, Johnny," Landry said, the words a grim promise. "Not ever. And this asshole's not going to find the Quarter real hospitable either. You embarrass me like this? Make a fool out of me? You're the damn fool."

Brodsky's partner, the only other cop still in the bar, had moved toward the door to watch Caleb and Gage. When he spoke, it was so low as to be barely audible, and yet the words resounded through the bar.

"Son of a bitch, John. You might want to look at this."

The moment Brodsky glanced over at him, the lieutenant snapped the strap off his gun and slid it out of the holster with a swiftness borne of years of practice. He brought it up, taking aim at Brodsky's temple. The sergeant was the nearest armed man. It only made sense that

Landry would take him down first, Clay second, the cop at the door third. The hooker likely didn't even enter into his homicidal logic.

Clay moved with stunning speed, putting himself between Brodsky and that gun. The lieutenant fired, the report echoing through Charmaigne's. The bullet tore through Clay's chest and lodged in his vertebrae, trapped there. He winced at the pain, but already he was changing again. This time, however, there was no cat. Not even the human face of the man the people of New Orleans knew as Clay Smith.

Instead, he showed Lieutenant Pete Landry his own face. His real face. His clothes were gone, save for a scarlet ceremonial drape around his waist that hung nearly to his knees. Clay towered over Landry, nearly nine feet tall and as broad as two men across the chest. His red-brown flesh, from hairless scalp to bare feet, was damp and soft and run through with cracks.

"Go on, asshole," Clay rumbled, "shoot me again."

Wide-eyed and hyperventilating, the asshole did.

Clay ripped the gun out of his hand, breaking three fingers, and grabbed Landry by the throat, trying his best to avoid meeting the grateful gaze of the murderer's ghosts. He did it for them, but he could not withstand the sadness in those eyes.

He squeezed the lieutenant by the throat until the man's eyes rolled up to white.

"Step away from him," Brodsky demanded.

Clay glanced over, saw that the sergeant had drawn his own weapon. He let Landry drop, gasping, to the floor and looked down at Brodsky. He smiled, and he knew it was a grotesque smile.

"John, my friend, you want to know how I track killers? I'll tell you over a beer sometime. If you want other answers about me . . ." Clay paused and took a long, calming breath, staring into Brodsky's eyes. "Trust me when I tell you, you're not alone."

With that small, gasping noise he changed again, from towering clay figure to copper-furred cat. Brodsky shouted after him. The uniforms were all cursing, wondering what the hell was going on. Caleb and Gage had just stepped back inside with a small pistol in an evidence bag. One of them stooped and tried to stop the stray as it ran out the door, but he was too slow, too clumsy.

The cat darted into an alley, past a Dumpster, and then along other streets until it came once again to Rue Dauphine. As it passed beneath the shading branches of a tree that grew up from the sidewalk, the cat disappeared and was replaced by Clay Smith once more. He had no bullet wound. Not even a tear in his crisply clean, navy blue T-shirt.

He cut through to Bourbon Street and fell in amidst the swirl of tourists, the loud shouts of hucksters, the jazz band playing "When the Saints Go Marching In" on the corner. Clay hated Bourbon Street, hated the cheap, carnival atmosphere of it, but he had walked that street at least once every day since he had come to live here. It was alive and vibrant and filled with color, and at least for a handful of minutes it could make him forget the things he could not remember.

As he passed by a restaurant that was serving breakfast, he heard people hushing one another inside. There was something urgent about their manner, so he ducked his head into the restaurant and saw that everyone waiting for tables had stopped to watch the newscaster on the television above the bar.

The visual cut away to a scene of the New York skyline. Blood was raining from the sky.

• • •

THOUGH the subway tunnel was abandoned, the roar of nearby trains thundered throughout the underground. The air was dry and chalky, and there on a platform unused for decades, Doyle felt the shimmer of magick, as though their every breath disrupted cobwebs of time. This was a sensation he had felt recently, in the foyer of the brownstone where Yvette Darnall and her fellow mediums had died to keep Sweetblood's secret. This place had been frozen in time, had been hidden away from untrained eyes.

Until now.

"Doyle! Why don't you get what we came for?" Eve snapped.

His gray brows knitted together as he turned to glare at her. Her jacket was torn where the demon's claws had ripped through suede and cotton at her shoulder, and blood was seeping into the fabric. The thing towered above her on the platform, its footfalls cracking the tile floor with every step. Even as Doyle glanced at Eve, the thing Sweetblood had set here to guard his hiding place bent once more and lunged for her. Distracted in that moment by her ire at Doyle, Eve could not avoid its ridiculously long arms, and the demon snatched her by the throat, one of the sharp protrusions on its arm cutting a gash in her face that flayed her cheek to the bone.

She snarled in pain, latched onto its wrist with both hands, swung her legs up and braced them against its body, and then used that leverage to break its arm. The grinding snap of bone echoed across the platform. Eve dropped to the tile and rolled away from the guardian, then turned to glare at Doyle.

"What the fuck are you just standing there for?"

Doyle smoothed his coat. His own wardrobe had thus far suffered only the veil of dust that hung in the air and covered every surface.

"Merely wondering if you might be bleeding less if you concentrated on what you were doing rather than policing my own actions."

He raised an eyebrow as the demon raced at her again, roaring, cradling its shattered arm. Then he turned away, leaving her to the battle. Eve's face would heal, as it always had. All of her wounds would disappear. That was the gift and curse of her immortality. In comparison, his own extended life was merely a parlor trick.

Since the moment they had left Yvette Darnall's brownstone, he had been trying to sense the power of Sweetblood. When they had entered Grand Central Station, he had known they were on the right track. Had anyone but Sweetblood cast the glamour that hid the guardian's true nature, Doyle would have seen right through it. Not that it mattered now. The trail had led him here, to this platform, to the door that now stood before him.

Or perhaps not.

Though to Eve it seemed he was merely standing there, Doyle was searching for the emanations of the magick Lorenzo Sanguedolce had used to hide himself away. At first it had seemed to lead through that door, but now he frowned deeply, knitting those eyebrows once again, and turned to focus upon the tiled wall to his right. A tremor went through him and he felt something tug him, as though he were a fish who had just taken the bait. Quickly he strode across the platform.

Eve hissed loudly and Doyle glanced over to see her on the demon's back, her legs wrapped around it from behind. Its protective spines stabbed into her, but she held on tightly as she tried to reach around to claw out its eyes. For just a flicker of a moment her gaze caught his, but he ignored the continued accusation in her eyes as he approached the far wall.

Doyle felt his skin prickle and the hair rise on the back

of his neck. His stomach clenched and he was forced to pause a moment to avoid spraying vomit all over the floor. With a flourish he crossed his wrists and then spread his arms in front of him, and some of the magickal seepage that had infected the air around him dispersed. Sweetblood did not want any visitors. It was too late for that.

"You must not disturb the mage!" the demon bellowed in its hellish, grinding voice.

Doyle whipped around to see it lunging for him, but in that same instant Eve plunged two long talons into its right eye. The sound was sickening, and a spray of viscous gray fluid spurted across the cracked tiles.

"You're missing the point, Fido. Someone's gonna wake the old bastard up. Better us than the alternative," Eve snarled.

The demon shrieked and tried to reach for her, then threw itself backward, crushing her between its own body and the floor, impaling her on those terrible spines. Eve screamed.

Doyle ignored her.

He reached out toward the tiled wall. His fingers traced lines in the decades of dust and grime that had accumulated there. Despite Sweetblood's magick, this place had not been entirely untouched by time, not like the brownstone. Doyle thought this was all part of the ruse, part of the cover, in case another sorcerer should have gotten this far. He saw through the glamour as others might have, but he was skilled enough also to see past the diversion.

With a glance over his shoulder, he saw that Eve was choking the guardian, though her own blood pooled on the subway platform. He saw the door that he had been about to enter and wondered what lay beyond it, what peril Sweetblood might have placed there to dispatch seekers who came too close to discovering his location.

With a blink of his eyes and a flick of his wrist, Doyle

cast a spell that shattered the tiles on the wall. They showered down in fragments, revealing a stone wall behind them that he doubted had been part of the original plans for this location. A tiny smile passed over Doyle's features, and he laid his palm upon the stone.

"Lorenzo," he whispered. "Can you hear me? Some choices are not yours to make. Your power can't be allowed to fall into the wrong hands." Doyle closed his eyes and summoned magick from a well of power he had accumulated within him over the years. Images like shards of broken mirror glass tumbled through his mind, of family dead and friends left behind, of grief and the wonder of discovery, of a man he once had been, and the trifle his meager efforts at entertainment seemed to him now.

This work, laboring in the shadows between the darkness and the light, was what mattered.

"*Tempus accelerare,*" Doyle whispered, and his fingers went rigid as power surged up his arm. It ached to the marrow and he gritted his teeth. Friction heated the palm of his hand where it lay against the stone wall.

And the stone crumbled away to nothing in front of him.

There was an alcove behind it, a space in the wall perhaps ten feet high and equally broad. Within that recess was a block of amber, like a massive slab of rock candy. It was honey gold with hints of red, and through it Doyle could see a distorted view of the man encased within. Sweetblood's eyes were closed, his expression peaceful, as though he lay in a casket rather than frozen in a trap of his own creation. Though dulled by whatever substance encased him, Sweetblood's magick crackled like electricity in the air within that recessed chamber.

"Time to wake up now, Lorenzo," Doyle whispered. "No matter how reluctant you may be."

The ground shook beneath his feet. He heard the sounds

of Eve and the guardian in combat, the snorting, rasping of their breathing. He smelled Eve's blood and the fetid ichor of the demon. Trains rumbled elsewhere along the New York subway system, their growling echoing in the tunnels. But Doyle had stopped registering any of these things as he stared through that amber slab at the features of his former mentor, the man for whom he had searched for decades. A mage with enough power to scar the face of the world.

It was only when Eve screamed his name that Doyle realized something had gone terribly wrong. On instinct, he manifested a magickal energy charge from his fingers as he spun around to see what had alarmed her. Even as he did so, they were already leaping up onto the subway platform.

Corca-Duibhne. The Night People.

They were lean creatures with taut, ropy musculatures and skin the color of rust, shaped like humans but no larger than a girl in her early teens. The Corca-Duibhne were stealthy and swift, able to merge with shadows and creep along seemingly sheer walls. All of them, male and female, had black, spiky hair and eyes so oily dark that they seemed nothing but pits of shadow in their heads. They had been called the Night People in a time when the only stories about them were told in a fearful huddle around the village fire. Yet now they had adapted to the modern world. They wore human clothing and sported bits of silver in their ears and noses where ordinary people might have piercings.

But the Corca-Duibhne were not ordinary. They were not human.

Doyle began to shout for Eve, but his voice faltered as he saw the Night People overrun her and the demon guardian Sweetblood had chosen to protect his hiding place. Both had been weakened by their combat. The guardian had a shattered arm and had been blinded in one eye. Eve was bleeding from multiple wounds, her clothes sodden with sticky scarlet, and the Corca-Duibhne were strong and fast and far too many. She was ferocious and nearly impossible to kill, but Eve would not be of any help to him at the moment.

"Damn you, Lorenzo," Doyle muttered. "This is your fault."

The Night People lunged for him, first three, then seven swarming over Eve and the guardian to rush at Doyle. But he knew they weren't really racing at him. Their goal was behind him. Doyle placed himself in their path, and he could feel the hole in the wall behind him, the magick that pulsed from the amber slab in which Sweetblood was encased. The Corca-Duibhne gnashed their jaws, baring teeth that were jagged and cruel, and their oily eyes focused on him.

"Don't be an idiot," snarled the one in the front, its voice low and insinuating.

Doyle had waited long enough. He raised both hands, palms outward, and azure light flashed from his fingers, throwing blue shadows on the high walls and a cerulean glow out into the tunnel. A wave of magick traveled with this light, and the force of it slammed into the Corca-Duibhne, cracking bone and ripping flesh, throwing the nearest of them sprawling across the floor in a tangled heap. But there were too many of them still swarming up from the subway tunnel.

The guardian demon was dead. Doyle saw one of the Night People greedily dragging its head away from the others as a keepsake. Eve fought alone, but she was not quite so buried as she had been in those rust-colored bodies. Her talons flashed and throats were torn and skulls crushed.

Still, there were too many.

Doyle inhaled deeply and rose to his full height, glaring

down at the creatures that began to gather in a hesitant circle. They were wary of him now, and he tried to adopt his most imposing air. Sparks still danced from his hands, and his vision was tinted with blue as some of the magick contained within him leaked out his eyes. He focused his will and sensed the power of Sweetblood emanating from the amber slab behind him. *I can feel it,* Doyle thought. *Perhaps I can siphon some of it.*

He clawed the air in front of him, leaving shimmering streaks of light hanging there. The Night People hesitated once more, but only for a moment before they began slowly edging toward him again, closing in.

"Corca-Duibhne. You have no idea who you're dealing with," he thundered, voice booming across the platform, echoing off the walls. "I am the only student Lorenzo Sanguedolce ever taught."

One of them, a female whose form was almost elegant in comparison to the others, shuffled several cautious inches nearer. Doyle tried to count them. There were dozens.

"We're not here for the student, but the master," she said, upper lip curling back, nostrils flaring.

Doyle raised his hands again, quivering as he began to draw on the magickal energies within and around him. "You'll have neither!"

But even as he summoned the power to attack again, he heard a click-clack from far above him. Doyle glanced upward in alarm, but too late. Corca-Duibhne had skittered up the walls and along the ceiling, and now they leaped down at him, limbs flailing so that he could not judge their number.

He released a wave of destructive magick from his hands, and it burst upward, destroying those shadow crawlers who had thought to surprise him. But the distraction was enough. The others on the platform leaped at him, talons tearing his clothing and his skin, preternaturally strong arms driving him down to the platform so that he struck the back of his head on the tile. For a moment he was disoriented, and in that moment one of them pounced upon him. Its fetid breath was in his nostrils and its mouth gaped wide, jagged teeth dropping toward his throat.

"Ferratus," Doyle muttered.

The sound that filled his ears was a keening, static buzz, a nighttime field full of crickets, but it accompanied a crimson glow that enveloped his entire body. The creature attempting to tear at his throat was burned where it touched him. All of them were. And yet the Night People did not stop. Doyle was protected within the magickal shield he had woven around himself, but they continued to attack him, those behind forcing the others to pile onto him, though it burned their flesh. The Corca-Duibhne attacking him began to scream, and though his magick protected him from harm, it did not keep out the acrid stench of their burning flesh.

Doyle slowly focused his will, steadying himself, healing the gashes he had received. He caught a glimpse past his attackers and saw that Eve was up on her feet now, hair and eyes as wild as he had ever seen her, covered not in her own blood but in that of her enemies. She was snarling, having sloughed off any pretense at humanity, and when one of the Night People came near enough, she tore its head from its shoulders.

Then the melee of ancient horrors attempting to kill him shifted, and he could see her no more.

"That is enough!" Doyle shouted.

The burst of magick that erupted from him then incinerated all of the Corca-Duibhne that had surrounded him. Shaken and weak, he staggered to his feet amidst a shower of rusty ash that had once been the flesh of the Night People. For just a moment he looked to Eve, but she was already regaining some of her composure. The handful of Corca-Duibhne who remained were fleeing back into the shadows of the tunnels, slipping along the walls with impossible speed. Eve looked in disgust at her ruined clothes.

Doyle shivered as he saw the last of the Night People creep away across the ceiling of the subway tunnel. But it was not this sight that caused him to shiver. Rather, it was the absence of the tremor in the air he had felt before, the electric presence of the barely contained power of Sweetblood the Mage.

Even before he turned, Doyle knew what he would find.

The recess in the wall where the amber encasement had been was now empty. In the handful of moments in which he and Eve had both been overcome, the Night People had made off with the inert form of the most powerful sorcerer in the history of the world.

Outside the rain of toads had become a bloody drizzle.

4

LEONARD Graves sat on the metal bench in the small, oval park in the center of the affluent Louisburg Square section of Boston's Beacon Hill. Its bow-front 1840s townhouses faced each other across a private oasis of green amongst the brick and still-functioning gaslights.

He had been there since early morning, surrounded by the first signs of spring in New England. The recently mowed grass was a healthy, dark green from April's cool rains. Forsythia buds were just starting to bloom, and crocuses forced yellow heads up from the dark soil at the enclosure's far end. Graves had always loved springtime. It brought a sense of renewal he had always considered poetic, the cycle of life beginning again after a season of death.

If only that was the case with all things.

Dr. Graves gazed through the wrought-iron fence at his current residence. The corner townhouse, which belonged to Mr. Doyle, had been built in 1846, one of the last homes to be constructed in this privileged neighborhood, or at least that was what he had been told by the original architect. With its brick, brownstone lintels, and granite steps, it re-

sembled the other houses on either side of the square, but
there was also something that gave it an air of difference. At
times the townhouse felt alive, as if imbued with a spirit all
its own by the powerful magicks wrought within its walls.
Graves often thought of it as a great, monolithic animal, its
windows open eyes gazing out upon a world in which it believed itself supreme.

Doyle's was the first of a row of seven homes in front of
him, and another six stood opposite them, all of the residents
holding partial ownership to the beautiful park in which he
sat. Graves doubted that Doyle had ever noticed the beauty
just outside the front of his home.

The magician and Eve had gone away late the previous
evening, and he pondered the success of their mission. It had
been this concern that drove him outside to the peace of the
park in bloom. There had been no calls, no attempts at communication; even the spirit realm had been strangely quiet,
and it made him anxious. In the old days, this would have
been a call to action, a chance to strap on his guns and throw
himself full bore into the thick of things, but now . . . There
was no use worrying about it; he would know their accom-
plishments, or lack thereof, soon enough.

He turned his face up toward the murky sunshine. The
clouds were thick today with the slightest hint of gray, as if
soiled, but the sun's beams did manage to break through in
places. What he wouldn't give to be able to feel the sun upon
his flesh again. He recalled how dark his already chocolate
brown skin used to become when exposed to long doses of
the sun's rays. What was it that Gabriella used to say to him?
From mocha to mahogany.

He smiled with the memory of his fiancée; she had loved
this time of year as well. Graves looked down at the translu-
cence of his hands, his smile fading. There were always so
many reminders of the things he missed, simple things that
he had once taken for granted. The touch of a cool breeze

that prickled the flesh, the smell of a garden in bloom, the love of a good woman. The list was infinite.

Irony there. He had eternity to miss infinity.

Graves rose from his seat and strolled through the garden. *Why do I insist on torturing myself?* But he knew full well the answer. He liked the pain and what it did for him.

It made him feel alive.

The sound of a key turning in a lock distracted him from his ruminations, and he gazed over to see an older woman, toy poodle cradled in her arms, letting herself into the park. She was from old money, her family having lived in Number Ten Louisburg Square since the 1830s. Not long ago he'd had a conversation with one of the bricklayers who had worked on Number Ten's construction and didn't have very flattering things to say about the family then, or the generations that followed. Greedy bastards and bloodless crones, Graves believed the laborer had called them. He watched as the woman put the fluffy white dog—Taffy—down in the grass and, in a baby talk, urged the animal to relieve itself. Taffy looked in his direction, sensing his presence, and began to growl menacingly, or at least as menacingly as an eight-pound poodle could. The woman chastised the dog with more baby talk.

Graves looked away from the pet and smiled. What had Eve called the animal when she saw it from the window of Doyle's parlor the previous night? *A ratdog?*

Thoughts of Eve returned his mind to the task that had drawn her and Doyle out of the house. Graves wished he could have accompanied them, but they had little need of a ghost. After sixty-odd years, it still irked him that he had been taken out of action. The great Leonard Graves, explorer, scientist, adventurer extraordinaire, put out to pasture by an unknown assassin's bullet.

Stay and monitor the murmurings in the ether, Doyle had told him as he and Eve departed. Those same murmurings had alerted Graves to the potentially catastrophic situation in the first place, but since his comrades' departure, the voices had grown strangely silent, as if too frightened to speak.

A sudden chill went through him. Graves wasn't sure how it was possible, for he had no real sense of feeling, but he knew, even before looking up at the sky, that something had happened to the sun.

An unusual cloud of solid black, miles wide and thick, was moving across the sky, blotting out the burning orb. He studied the dark, undulating mass and determined that it wasn't an atmospheric condition, but something altogether horrible. A droning hum grew in intensity, caused by the beating of millions of insect wings. Flies blotted out the sun, more flies than he had ever seen. His concerns went to his comrades, and their mission, when a screech cut through the air like a surgeon's knife through flesh, diverting his attentions yet again.

The woman from Number Ten Louisburg Square was screaming, her hands clawing at her face as she looked down upon the grass in the grip of terror, her feet stamping the freshly cut blades as if in the midst of some wild, ceremonial dance.

Graves drifted closer and arrived just in time to see the last of Taffy's fluffy, white fur disappear beneath a sea of glistening, black-haired bodies and pink, fleshy tails. Rats, many of them the size of housecats, had swarmed the dog, the sounds of tearing flesh and the crunching of bone perverse evidence of an unnatural hunger.

The sun blotted out by flies, a dog attacked and consumed by rats. Graves again thought of Doyle and Eve, suspecting that he already knew the level of their success.

It was enough to fill him with fear.

Enough to frighten even a ghost.

• • •

ALL shadows were connected.

A twisting maze work of cold black passages entering into realms of further shadow, or worlds of light.

Squire had parked the limousine, after their five-hour drive back from the Big Apple, inside the townhouse's private garage. Parking was at a premium on the narrow streets of Beacon Hill, and he thanked the Dark Gods that Doyle had the foresight to purchase the property behind his residence and eventually convert it from storage to garage space.

Eve wasn't doing too well. She seemed better than she had when Doyle first helped her into the back of the car after their little scuffle at Grand Central, but still looked pretty much like a stretch of bad road.

"I'll take her up into the house," Doyle told him as he helped the injured woman from the backseat of the limousine.

She had been unusually quiet for most of the drive, telling Squire to shut his trap only once. He figured she must have been hurt pretty badly. There was quite a bit of blood on the backseat's upholstery, and he had made a mental note to have it cleaned when things settled down. *If things settle down,* he cautioned himself.

"Go to the freezer in the cellar and bring her back a little something to help pick her up," Doyle told him.

Leaving the two to make their way up into the residence, Squire found the nearest patch of shadow and disappeared within it. Hobgoblins traveled the shadowpaths. It was their gift and their greatest defense. This day he used them to reach the basement beneath the Louisburg Square townhouse. Squire had his pick of places to emerge, the cellar rife with huge areas of gloom. It didn't matter the size or shape; a hobgoblin could bend and fold himself into just about any position.

The drive had been exhausting, and he welcomed the ease with which he was able to enter the cellar. In Doyle's employ, things were rarely so easy. He emerged into the basement from a patch of darkness beside a shelving unit that held the burial urns of some of Mr. Doyle's closest friends and business acquaintances. *You never know when you're going to need to talk to one of them again,* the magician had told the goblin once, shortly after acquiring another urn for his collection.

"Hey, guys," he said to the urns. "Got another bad one whipping up; you should be thankful that you're all dirt."

The goblin did not need light. His eyes were used to navigating the pitch-black hallways of the shadowpaths. He slipped across the crowded storage room to the refrigeration unit humming in the corner. He tugged open the door, a cloud of frigid air escaping into the mustiness of the cellar. Multiple packets of blood hung within the unit, recently stocked by the boss for just such an emergency. *That's the boss, always thinking ahead,* Squire mused, taking what he needed. He wondered how far ahead Doyle had thought about the current situation.

He also wondered when it was going to be his turn to grab a snack. Sure, Eve was injured. Her health had to come first. But his stomach had been growling since Hartford. A burger and a milk shake would be nice. Even just a bag of fries. Hell, he'd settle for a donut.

Squire sighed. *First things first.*

The goblin made sure that the door was shut tight and quickly turned away. Squire recalled the problems of storing blood in the past. Dry ice had been what they used way back when, but it didn't offer much of a shelf life. He painfully remembered how much Eve would complain when she was forced to drink a batch that had spoiled. He again praised the Dark Gods for advances in technology as he plunged head-on into the nearest patch of shadow.

• • •

"WHAT do you mean, he was taken?" Graves asked, hovering above the Oriental carpet in the formal sitting room of Doyle's townhouse.

The sorcerer had placed pages of the newspaper on the sofa and was gently lowering the bloody and beaten form of Eve down atop them. "We were attacked and Sweetblood was taken." The mage sighed, looking worn and weary. He removed his coat, walking through the spectral form of Graves as if he wasn't there.

Graves spun around, watching as Doyle hung his jacket on a wooden coat rack outside the parlor. "You're one of the most powerful magicians on the planet; at least that's what you tell us. Who could have managed to do that to you?"

Doyle came back into the room, rolling the sleeves of his starched, white dress shirt. "The Night People. The Corca-Duibhne."

The squat, misshapen goblin, Squire, suddenly appeared from the shadows of the fireplace, stepping out into the room with multiple, fluid-filled plastic bags clutched in his arms. "And we should'a let 'em all get wiped from existence way back after the first Twilight War, that's what I say." Squire took care not to track soot from the fireplace onto the priceless Oriental rug. He gnawed on the corner of one of the blood packs to open it.

"They attacked in surprising numbers," Doyle said. He gestured toward Eve, who lay unconscious upon the sofa, bleeding onto yesterday's news. "Eve was occupied with an antagonist of her own. The beasts overpowered us and made off with the archmage's chrysalis. There was nothing we could do." The magician shook his head, gazing off into space.

"There's silence in the ether," Graves told them, crossing his arms. "That can't be good."

Doyle walked to a liquor cabinet in the corner of the elegant room and removed a crystal decanter of scotch and a tumbler. He filled half the glass with the golden brown liquid, placed the stopper back into the bottle, and put the decanter away. "Not good at all," he agreed, helping himself to a large gulp of the alcohol. It was yet another sensory experience that Graves had come to miss since joining the ranks of the dead. He envied the magician's ability to enjoy the twelve-year-old Glenlivet single malt, spirits of a different kind altogether.

A low moan interrupted his thoughts, and Graves saw that Eve was awake. She sat up, wincing in pain, blood-soaked newspaper squelching beneath her. Her hand came up to rub at the back of her head and came away stained with scarlet.

"Shit," she muttered beneath her breath. A clot of thick, coagulated blood dropped from the corner of her mouth to land upon the front of her sweater, torn and stained from her conflict earlier that morning. "What's a girl got to do for a drink around here?"

EVERYTHING hurt. Eve turned her somewhat blurred gaze to Squire, who appeared to be having some difficulty opening a blood pack. The goblin gnawed on the pouch's corner, but the plastic was proving too tough for the creature.

"Give it to me," she demanded, reaching for the bag.

Insulted, Squire handed it to her. "I was only trying to help," he grumbled. But he set the remaining packs in her lap where she could reach them. "All this drinkin' has made *me* a tad parched," the goblin said, ambling from the room. "I'm going to get a beer."

Eve brought the pouch of blood to her mouth, careful to avoid the side that the hobgoblin had chewed. She felt her canines elongate with the promise of feeding, and she tore into the thick plastic container. The blood flowed into her mouth and her entire body began to tingle. Greedily Eve sucked upon the pouch, draining it in seconds, and tossed the empty container to the floor to start another.

"Carefully, Eve," Doyle barked. "Do you know the expense of removing blood stains from such a delicate carpet?"

She finished another of the blood packs, placing the wilted plastic beside her on the stained newspaper. "I think we have a bigger problem right now than soiling your rug. My coat? Remember that coat? I bought it in Milan. My clothes are ruined. Do you hear me bitching about it?"

"Well, now that you mention it—" Squire began.

She stilled him with a dark glance.

Eve could feel the blood working its magick upon her, the cuts and gashes closing, foreign objects trapped beneath her flesh being pushed out from within by the healing process, bruises and abrasions beginning to fade. If it weren't for the fact that the world could very well be going to shit, she'd have been downright giddy.

"These Corca-Duibhne," asked Graves, a cool vapor drifting from his mouth as he spoke. "You've encountered them before?"

Doyle finished his scotch, placing the empty glass on a silver tray that rested upon a wheeled cart beside the liquor cabinet. He glanced around at his allies.

"I've crossed paths with the loathsome breed from time to time." The mage crossed the parlor to wearily lower himself into a high-backed leather chair by a curtained window. "Since the Twilight Wars, the species had been functioning more as individuals, hiring themselves out to the highest bidder. It's been quite some time since I've seen them this organized and working with such purpose." He laid his head back in the chair and closed his eyes. "It does not bode well."

Eve sipped slowly from another of the blood packs, feeling almost one hundred percent. "Something's pulled them together again," she said, a thrum of warmth cascading through her. "Could be the threat that the spirit realm's so agitated about."

Graves furrowed his ghostly brow as he regarded her. Eve smiled.

"Where are we on that?" she asked him. "Any closer to defining what exactly this threat is?"

The specter shook his head. "The restless souls have retreated even further into the spirit realms than usual. I sense that they are afraid of what is coming."

"And we don't have a clue as to what that is?" she asked him, making sure that she hadn't missed anything while she had been unconscious.

"I'm sorry to say, no," answered Graves, a winter's chill from his mere presence spreading throughout the room.

All was silent except for the rhythmic ticking of the large grandfather clock located in the hall just outside the room. Eve shifted her weight upon the newspaper, the sudden lack of activity making her antsy. For days the spirit worlds had been in a tizzy over some impending supernatural threat, and the most powerful magician in the world had just been stolen; things were not looking too good for the home team. Eve looked about the fancy sitting room of the Beacon Hill home, at the wispy form of the ghost Leonard Graves hovering in the air, at Doyle seemingly nodding off in his chair. She had another drink from the packet of blood, for if she didn't she was surely going to scream.

At last, when she couldn't stand it anymore, she rose and glared at them. "So, what now? I'm going to get bored if we sit around here much longer." She gave Doyle a meaningful glance. "And you know what I'm like when I get bored."

Eyes still closed, Doyle slowly raised a hand to silence her rant. "Patience, Eve," he said. "The wheels of fate are in motion."

"What the hell is that supposed to mean?" she snarled.

Far off in the house she heard the trill of the phone ringing, and then the voice of Squire as he answered.

Doyle smiled. "The wheels turn slowly at times, but they do turn." The mage made a spinning motion with his hand even as Squire entered the room holding a piece of notepaper in one hand and a bottle of Samuel Adams in the other.

"Hey, boss, you just got a call from a Julia Ferrick," he read from the paper. "Said she needs to talk to you right away about her son." Squire looked up from the message. "The broad's on a tear. If you ask me, I don't think she's wound too tight."

Doyle's eyes snapped open, a crackle of magick dancing on his lashes. "The Ferrick boy," he muttered, more to himself than anyone else in the room. "How interesting."

A nasty chill spread through her body, and Eve looked to see that Graves had drifted closer.

"You were expecting that call," the ghost said. It was not a question. "Will this woman and her boy play some part in the scheme of things?"

Doyle gazed toward the shuttered windows. "We all play a part in the greater scheme of things, Leonard. Each and every one."

The doorbell rang, echoing through the townhouse, and they all looked at one another and then to Doyle.

"Somebody call for pizza?" Squire asked, taking a swig from his bottle of beer. "God, I could use a pizza. Or two."

"I'm sorry, my friend. I don't think that's the pizza man," Doyle replied.

"Let me guess," Eve said. "At the door now? Another player."

Doyle stood, checking the crease in his pant legs. "Precisely. And the part you will play at this moment, Eve, is to answer the door. Our latest player will be in need of some refreshment before the two of you go to see Mrs. Ferrick and her son." He pulled down his rolled shirtsleeves, buttoning the cuffs.

"Where do you think I'm going, exactly?" Eve asked. "Nightfall's still a ways off."

There was nothing humorous about the wan smile that appeared on Doyle's face just then. "Check the windows, my dear. The darkness comes early today."

Frowning, Eve glanced at the tall windows at the front of the room. They had heavy drapes that Doyle often pulled to shield the room from sunlight for her protection. She had presumed those drapes were responsible for the gloom in the room, but now Eve saw that they were tied back properly, and that while the world outside those windows was not pitch-black, it was a dusky gray. She went to the window and glanced up at the sky. A cloud of blue-black mist, like the smoke from a chemical fire, hung above the city of Boston, churning and widening. There were streaks of red in that cloud as well, and even as she glanced at them, they seemed to spread.

"That damned New England weather," Eve muttered darkly. "Guess I'm going out after all."

Again the doorbell buzzed and then there came the distant echo of a fist pounding upon the front door.

"I'll throw together some sandwiches," Squire said, "maybe make some of those Ore-Ida fries." He slipped into a patch of shadow thrown by a massive oak bookcase. No matter how many times Eve saw the goblin do that, it never ceased to amaze her.

"And my part, Arthur?" asked Graves. "You have some assignment for me as well?"

Doyle wore an expression of regret. "I do. You must go deeper into the land of the dead, Leonard. Whatever is frightening the wandering spirits, we need to know what it is. It may be our best clue as to what threat we face."

Eve wasn't sure, but she could've sworn she saw the

ghost swallow hard. It would be difficult for him. From what she understood of the spirit realms, the deeper one traveled, the harder it was to return to the realms of the living. Leonard Graves still had some serious business to finish here and didn't want to put that in jeopardy.

Then Doyle left the room and Eve followed after him. They went together into the foyer. Doyle started up the stairs and Eve paused a moment to watch him.

"What about you?" she asked on her way to the door. The bell rang again and she scowled. "Going to finish up that nap?"

The magician paused on the stairs. There were so many rooms up there. One of them belonged to Eve, though she rarely stayed there. Doyle glanced at her, and the sadness in his eyes was so dreadful she was forced to look away.

"Sometimes fate requires us to do the most painful things," he said, then continued upward, walking as though he bore some terrible, invisible burden.

Then it dawned on her what he was doing—where he was going—and for the briefest of moments, Eve actually felt sorry for the old man.

Their visitor gave up on the bell and began pounding on the door. Eve scowled as she marched toward it, picking at the bloodstains on her sweater, wondering if there was anything worth wearing in the closet in her room. "Keep your fucking shirt on."

Throwing back the bolt and twisting the lock, she pulled the door open. Clay stood just outside in the gloom. Eve raised an eyebrow.

"Well, well. Look what the apocalypse dragged in."

AT the end of the hall on the second floor was a locked door that no one had passed through in many years. Doyle found it sadly amusing that after all he had been through in his extended years, he could still remember the exact moment when he had locked it, sealing away a part of his life that he hadn't been sure he could live without.

It was the hardest thing he had ever done, almost as difficult as what he was about to attempt now.

Doyle unbuttoned the top button of his white shirt, reaching for the chain that he always wore around his neck. At the end of the chain hung an old-fashioned skeleton key, familiar to all houses of this age. There was a tremble to his hand as he brought the key to the lock. A spark of supernatural release was followed by just the slightest whiff of a scent foreign to this house, the smell of some primeval forest after a drenching rain. He savored the heady smell, taken aback by the powerful emotions it evoked. He turned the key, gripped the glass, diamond-cut knob and turned it.

The door opened with a creak, the light from the hallway eagerly spilling onto an ascending, wooden staircase, illuminating another door at the top of stairs. The door was of solid iron, made for him in 1932 by a smith by the name of Hendrickson who hailed from Erie, Pennsylvania. Doyle had helped the metalworker make contact with his long-dead mother in lieu of payment for his metalwork.

He never imagined that he would look upon that door again. It had been put there as a precaution, to keep things where they belonged. Now, Doyle began to climb, gripping the wooden banister as he ascended. It seemed to take an eternity. On the final step he stopped. There were no keyholes, no sliding bolts, or crystal knobs to turn, just cold and unyielding iron. He placed the flat of his hand upon the metal, sensing contact with the magicks he had placed within it so long ago. His palm began to tingle as a dormant spell came sluggishly awake.

"Open," he whispered.

The door shimmered, a tremor passing through it. A tiny hole appeared and began to grow, the metal now malleable, as if returning to its molten state. The opening expanded, the substance of the door peeling back upon itself as it created an entryway large enough for him to pass through.

A warm, humid breeze flowed out from the expanding portal, and Doyle could hear the gentle patter of a falling rain upon the vast forest beyond the confines of the hallway and door.

It was just as wild and frighteningly beautiful as he remembered it, the lush vegetation every shade of green that could possibly be imagined. The place was older than recorded time, stirring musings about origins of the mythical Garden of Eden, but he had not returned here for intellectual stimulation. Only reasons most dire would have forced him into this place again.

The sorcerer stepped through the doorway. He let the place wash over him, turning his face up to the thick canopy of trees that blotted out the sky. The rain dropped from the leaves upon his upturned face. He opened his mouth, tasting the purity of the world he had entered.

The moss writhed beneath his feet, and he glanced down to see that blades of grass bent to touch the soft leather of his shoes. *What a wondrous place,* he thought, so very sorry that he had ever left it.

The patch of ground before him began to roil, turning over upon itself, and in the blink of an eye, two pale-skinned creatures erupted from the earth and crouched before him. Adorned in armor made from the bark of trees and flat polished stone, the warriors thrust their spears toward him.

Doyle let his hands fall at his sides, tendrils of mystical energy leaking from his fingertips, showing the pair that he was far from defenseless.

"I have come on a matter of grave importance," he spoke in the lilting tongue of the Fey. *"The fate of my world is at stake, and yours as well. Yes, both our worlds . . . and all of the others besides."*

5

CLAY piloted a silver Cadillac through the streets of Boston, holding the steering wheel as though it was fragile and might shatter in his hands. There were very few other cars out on the street, but still he drove slowly, his speed dictated not by traffic but by his fascination with the terrible phenomena that were unfolding in the city. The Cadillac felt like some protective bubble out of which he and Eve could observe the horrors around them.

The sky was tinted the dark crimson of drying blood, and swarms of mosquitoes traveled like terrible storm clouds. Clay had been forced to detour away from the entrance to the Massachusetts Turnpike because manhole covers had blown out of the pavement surrounding it and raw sewage flooded the street. Eve had suggested Route 9 to drive out to Newton, and he'd headed that way only to pause at a place where the road was overrun by rats. But he'd stopped only a moment before rolling the Caddy right over them, hearing them pop beneath its tires.

It wasn't going to get any better. The rats weren't going to clear off of their own free will. Whatever this storm was, it wasn't going to pass without someone doing something about it.

"Pretty unsettling, isn't it?" he said, breaking a long silence in the car.

"I've seen worse," Eve replied.

Clay shot her a hard look. "You're not the only one, Eve. But I'm not talking about this." He waved a hand to indicate the bizarre goings-on in the city around him. They passed a Humvee that was pulled over to the side of the road. The driver had his face pressed against his window, staring up at the sky. "I'm talking about what it means."

She arched an eyebrow and Clay felt his throat go dry. By God, she was beautiful. He was the last person to be taken in by surface appearance; he knew better than anyone that it rarely reflected what was within. Yet there was something so exotic, so ancient about her that she took his breath away. She had taken the time to change out of the blood-soaked clothes in which she had met him at the door and now wore black trousers and an embroidered red camisole that looked both expensive and—with its spaghetti straps baring her arms, throat, and shoulders— more revealing than what Eve normally wore. There was a silk jacket in the backseat that had clearly come from the closet of one designer or another. Clothing was Eve's *other* weakness, second only to blood.

"What does it mean, then?" Eve prodded him.

"That's what's so unsettling," he explained. "This sort of thing is happening all over the Northeast, but it's concentrated here. I've lived as long as you have—"

"And how many can say that?" she whispered.

He ignored her and went on. "—and normally there's some kind of prophecy, isn't there? You'll get the clairvoyants with their visions and maybe some ancient writings, omens, and portents—"

Eve turned sideways in her seat. "What do you call all

this shit, then? Last I heard, showers of blood and rains of toads were considered pretty ominous. And as for portents, there aren't many that can beat red clouds blotting out the sun."

Clay took a long breath and shook his head, but he kept his eyes on the road. "No argument, but normally there's some warning, enough so that people like Doyle, the kind of people who watch for these things, know they're coming much earlier."

A streak of black darted across the road in front of them, and he had to jerk the wheel to the left to swerve around it. As the Cadillac shifted lanes, he caught a glimpse of that black streak, but it was not a streak any longer. It was a dog, maybe a German shepherd, but he could not be at all certain. Whatever sort of dog it was, it was not the beast's fur that was black. It was the crows.

The dog had stopped now in the middle of Route 9, and they had a clear view. Clay slowed down even further and stared. The dog's body was covered by crows, their wings madly beating the air as their beaks plunged again and again at the dog, pecking it and tearing its flesh so that some of the black-feathered birds were splashed with its blood.

"You're right," Eve said softly. "It's unsettling."

Clay found no satisfaction in this admission. His foot felt suddenly heavy on the accelerator and the Cadillac sped up. He had had enough, now, of the signs and portents, had seen far too many people huddled inside their homes and looking out the windows in panic and wonder. Phone lines were out. Cellular communication was no better. Television and radio and cable signals were warped static.

From what Eve had told him, Doyle clearly had some idea what was going on. And if Clay knew Doyle, there would already be some kind of plan in motion. He wanted to know what it was and what his place in it would be. The time for watching it through the windows was over.

"Eve?"

"Yeah?"

Clay glanced at her. "Why are you always snapping at me? I'm not exactly Mr. Sensitive, but I'd like to know what I did to piss you off."

"Nothing," she said. "You didn't do anything."

They drove in silence for several minutes. Clay consulted the paper in his hand upon which directions to the Ferrick house were written in Squire's cramped scrawl. He left Route 9 and took them deeper into Newton, up narrow, tree-lined streets and past wealthy neighborhoods. In time he turned onto a more conventional suburban street and peered at house numbers as they passed colonials and ranch homes. Many of the houses were dark and looked empty, their occupants having remained at the office or stuck somewhere else. But there were lights on in some houses, and the sound of the Cadillac's engine brought faces to the windows.

Clay hated to ignore them, but he had no choice. If they tried to soothe the fears of every person who was afraid, they would lose focus on the larger picture, and the peril would only grow more dire.

At number seventy-two, a sand-colored split-level with dark blue shutters, he turned into the driveway. The garage door was open and a Volvo wagon was inside. That was good. Mrs. Ferrick had called Doyle, but the phones had gone out shortly thereafter, and there was no way to be sure she would stay put when the chaos had worsened.

"This should be interesting," Clay murmured, mostly to himself, as he put the car in park and killed the engine. He opened the door but paused when he felt Eve's hand on his arm.

"Hang on."

Clay turned to her and was surprised to see pain in her gaze. Eve was usually all hard edges and slick smiles.

"It's really nothing you did," she said. "It's me."

One leg already out the door, he held it open and studied her more closely. "How, exactly? How is it you, I mean? We've worked together before, Eve. I've got you and Doyle to thank for setting me straight when my life was a mess. But it's obvious I get under your skin. Why is that?"

Eve nodded slowly, then pushed her hair out of her face and met his gaze. She could be fierce, but at the moment there was a vulnerability he had never seen in her before.

"Think about it. Think about what you are."

"What I am?"

She gave him a look that made him feel incredibly stupid, and then pointed upward. "You're *His* clay. You're connected to Him in a way that nothing else on Earth is. After the suffering He's put me through, you have to ask why being around you hurts me?"

His heart went cold. Clay stared at her, but Eve looked away, opened her door, and stepped out, the soles of her boots clicking on the pavement. She shut the door and started toward the house. After a moment Clay followed her, pocketing his keys. He wore the same face, the same form, he had worn in New Orleans, a persona he had adopted many years before to make himself feel more human. But he had never been human. Sometimes, when he was particularly fortunate, he forgot that.

Eve rang the doorbell. With the buzz of mosquito swarms and the blood-red sky, the utter normality of that sound seemed grotesquely incongruous, and yet for some reason it set him at ease.

They stood side by side on the doorstep.

"You're not the only one He has made suffer," Clay said, his voice low, unwilling to look at her now. "Perverse as it might be, I'd rather be suffering because I was the subject of His vengeance, as you've been, than because He couldn't spare a moment's thought to my fate."

There were noises inside the house, voices and the staccato sound of rushing footsteps on wooden floors. Clay's attention was drawn to the curtains in the bay window upstairs, and he saw the face of a woman appear amidst the bone white, lace-trimmed fabric. She was perhaps forty and might have been attractive without the fear that was engraved upon her features. Mrs. Ferrick, he assumed. She stared at her two visitors for a moment and then gestured to him to be patient, that she'd be right down, almost as if they were ordinary callers at her door and that the city was not being besieged by hellish occurrences fit for the Biblical book of Revelations.

Once more Eve gripped his arm, but this time her touch was gentle.

"You remind me," she said. "But maybe that's not so terrible. Hard as it is, you also remind me that I'm not alone."

Clay smiled, and then there were footsteps on the stairs inside and the sound of the chain being slid off the lock, and the door was pulled open from within. In the woman's hands was a white business card that had once been crisp and new but had now been bent and had its edges made ragged by Mrs. Ferrick's anxiety. According to Squire, Doyle had given her the card years earlier. She had lent him little credence then, but Clay figured recent events had made her more open-minded.

"He sent you? Mr. Doyle?" she asked hopefully.

"Yes. You're Mrs. Ferrick?" Eve asked.

She nodded. "Can you . . . can you help Daniel?"

Clay felt for her. This woman's world had started to fall apart long before the sun had disappeared from the sky.

"We can try. But it might be better if we talked about it inside."

Mrs. Ferrick glanced upward and then looked around her neighborhood, the landscape cast in a crimson gloom, and she nodded. "Of course, I'm sorry." She stepped away from the door. "Please, come in."

DANNY Ferrick lay on his bed, staring at his ceiling with headphones on. His MP3 player wasn't working for some reason, so he had to resort to old CDs. He had a mix on at the moment that he'd burned himself, with the Misfits, Primus, Taking Back Sunday . . . all kinds of stuff, including some old-school Zeppelin. If he could have gotten away with it with his mother just down the hall, he would have dug through his closet to get the small bag of weed he'd scored the previous week and lit one up. He wasn't as into weed as a lot of the guys he knew—he couldn't call any of them friends, really—but the times he had smoked, it had taken away some of the weight that he felt pressing on him all the time. Right now, he would have liked to smoke some weed because he thought it might kill the urge to scratch at his skull, just above his temples. He tried desperately to ignore the feeling, to ignore the way his sickly yellow skin had reddened around the hard protrusions on his head.

Not just reddened. He was just pretending to himself, being a pussy about it. The redness and swelling around those bumps had been just the beginning. Now the skin had begun to split.

His heart beat wildly in his chest, and though he tried to force himself to pay attention to the music, to listen to something, anything else, he could not. He was terrified and excited in equal measure. What the hell did it mean? The sky was turning red. Mosquitoes had eaten the neighbors' cat. Those kids he'd seen throwing up maggots. And it had rained blood. Blood. He knew it was because he had tasted it, just thrust out his tongue and let it drizzle into his mouth.

He shuddered now, there on his bed, the back of his head cradled upon his pillow. Why had he done that? It was disgusting. Completely.

Yet not completely. Not really. His shades were drawn, but he didn't need to be able to see out the windows to know what was happening. He had seen enough. The world was going to Hell. Or Hell was coming to Earth. It wasn't really a long stretch for him to begin imagining that what was going on outside and what was happening with his own body were connected. If that was Hell out there, then maybe Hell was coming out in him as well.

Chillax, he told himself. *Just derail that thought train.* But he could not.

How else to explain the way his skin continued to harden to rough leather, or the way his fingernails had become thick and sharp. Even now he reached up to idly scratch at the dry, cracking skin around the protuberance at his right temple. Before he even realized he was doing it, he had peeled a strip of parchmentlike skin away, and his nail—his claw—had struck something beneath that was hard and marble smooth, like a tooth.

Danny froze.

Shit.

It was one thing to think it. Another to discover the truth.

He sat up in bed and stripped off his headphones in the middle of a Blink-182 tune. Danny swung his legs over the side, hitched up his baggy black pants, and went to the mirror above his dresser. There was a small light on the bureau, and he clicked it on, then plucked off the shade for better illumination. He bent over and stared at himself in the mirror. Sure enough, where the bump protruded from his skull above his right temple, the dry skin was gone. Beneath it, something else had been revealed. Something sharp and enamel hard, black as oil.

A horn.

Oh my God, he thought. Then he gave a laugh that sounded weak and trembly, even to him. *Maybe not my God after all.*

Danny reached up to scratch away the dry skin that encased the horn on the left side of his head and it was like tearing at a scab. It came away with little resistance. His upper lip curled back in disgust, and he saw his teeth, which seemed longer and sharper than ever to him.

"Oh, fuck. Oh, fuck me," he snarled. "This just so completely sucks."

In the mirror he saw motion behind him, and he turned and stared at the woman who had just stepped into his room. She had mocha skin and long, raven black hair, dressed like a fashion model, and wore the most playful smile he'd ever seen.

"I don't know," she said. "I think they're kind of cute."

Storm clouds roil above the city of New York, a thunderstorm pregnant with the promise of heavy rain. It's All Hallows' Eve and the year is 1938. Far, far below, the city is alive with teeming life, hidden within cars and beneath umbrellas, New Yorkers determined to enjoy the night in spite of the storm.

Dr. Graves grits his teeth and his breath comes too fast. His heart hammers in his chest and the torn muscles in his shoulder burn. With one hand he grips the railing of the observation deck, the rest of him dangling over the side, rain sluicing off his coat. The wind buffets the face of the Empire State Building, helping him to cling there. But if it should shift direction, Graves knows he will be dead.

Since birth he has worked to hone his body and his mind, urged on by his widower father, who raised his son to be an example of what their people could accomplish if only they set their minds to it. Anyone else would have let go already. The pain that sears up each finger and along his arm is unimaginable. But Graves refuses to let go. Too many lives are depending on him. He's not going to give Zarin the satisfaction of taking his life.

Dr. Graves feels his fingers slipping. The rain has made the railing even slicker. The air itself is moist and it is hard to breathe. He closes his eyes and slows his breath, forces his pulse to match it. Then, with a grunt, he hauls himself up and shoots his free hand upward, latching on to the railing. With both hands secured, he struggles to pull himself up.

His eyes are squinted against the rain and the wind whips against his back. Exhaustion seeps into his bones. He is stronger than an average man, with ten times the ordinary human stamina. He has worked to make his body the pinnacle of human physical achievement, yet Dr. Graves is not superhuman. He draws a long breath, knowing that should he lose his grip, he will be little more than a smear on the pavement far below, washed into the sewers by the punishing rain.

Thunder shatters the heavens, rolling through the storm clouds above. Lightning strikes the needle atop the Empire State Building, followed by booming thunder even closer than before. He thinks of Zarin and the storm, the pure rain falling upon Manhattan, and he knows that he has no choice but to live. He must live.

Dr. Graves seethes, muscles popping as he drags himself upward until he can get an elbow on the rail-

ing. A sudden gust of wind nearly dislodges him, and
then he is able to throw his upper body over the
edge, and he is sliding over the railing and onto the
observation deck. He tumbles into a wet and heaving
ball upon the floor of the deck, rain still soaking him,
but it takes him only a moment to catch his breath
before he is up once again. Graves stands in a
crouch, expecting an attack, but apparently Zarin
has already presumed Graves has been dealt with,
for he is nowhere to be seen.

Alarm stabs his heart. If Zarin is gone, then it
may be too late to stop him from seeding the storm
clouds with his poison, from having a deadly, toxic
rain fall all over the city. Cradling his right arm, the
torn shoulder muscles throbbing in agony, he rises
and begins to run along the outer edges of the observation deck.

Graves rounds the corner and Zarin is there, a
short, ugly little man bent over a tray of small canisters, each tied in a net and attached to a large balloon. Zarin is filling a balloon with gas from a
portable tank, and Graves knows at once that it is
helium. And now he knows how the madman plans
his attack. The poison canisters must have timers.
The balloons will carry them into the storm where
they will spray toxins into the air, and the rain will
become fatal.

Wiping the water from his eyes, Dr. Graves shouts
Zarin's name and races at the killer.

Fog encroaches at the edges of his vision, en-
shrouding him, and for a moment Graves is lost.
Then from out of the fog he sees a figure emerge . . .
it must be Zarin!

But it is not.

Gabriella is wearing a dress he bought for her

that falls upon her curves in such a way as to make
his heart and lips both stutter. She smiles at him, her
chestnut eyes brightening, and the fog begins to thin.
There is an electric hum around him, and Dr. Graves
feels as though he is awakening from a terrible
dream. He glances about and finds himself in the familiar setting of his Washington Heights laboratory.
To many he is an unwelcome neighbor, but the pres-
tige of his reputation balances out their concerns
about the color of his skin and the fact that
Gabriella's does not match his own.

"Leonard," she says, her voice still thick with the
sultry accent of the little fishing village on the north-
west coast of Italy where they had met. "We were
supposed to meet your friends at Birdland an hour
ago." There is no chastisement in her voice, only
that playful, loving patience. "Come, now. Enough
of science for tonight."

Graves glances down at the beakers on the table
in front of him, at his notebook and the thick black
pencil he has been writing with. A warmth spreads
through him that has been rare in his life, and he
leans forward to shut off the burners beneath the
beakers, snuffing those small flames.

When he looks up expectantly, she is gone.

The lab is gone.

The air is thick with humidity and the buzzing of
flies, and the heat is oppressive. Sweat drips down
his back and stains his shirt at the armpits, his body
so warm that the droplets of it are a cooling relief
where they trace their paths on his skin.

Tangled jungle stretches as far as he can see in
every direction. Things chitter and rustle in the trees
but he pays them no mind. He did not hike all this
way to let the wildlife drive him off. This is the Yu-

catán, where his next step could be into any one of a hundred agonizing deaths. There were far more ways to die here than there were ways to live. But Dr. Graves was not returning to New York without the object of his quest.

And now he has found it. He holds his breath and stares at a cluster of strange, spiny-barked trees in front of him. They twist in upon themselves, branches intertwining as though in a dance. The Xuithla tree was dismissed by most botanists as tribal myth. Yet here it is. The rarest tree in the world, and if its legendary healing properties are more than legend . . .

Voices erupt around him, echoing through the trees, and Dr. Graves spins in search of their origin. He blinks as the branches seem to reach for him, closes his eyes, and lifts his arm to knock them away, and then the sounds of the jungle disappear.

The voices remain.

When he opens his eyes, he is in a movie palace on the Boulevard St. Germain in Paris. All is dark around him save for the constant flicker of light upon the screen. The voices are speaking French, of course, and he strains to keep up with the translation, trying to make sense of the plot of the film. Even so, he can only lend a portion of his attention to it, for his focus is elsewhere.

His contact is supposed to meet him here, in the theater. The French government has suffered a terrible loss, a theft from the Louvre that seems impossible, with the only clue left behind three single drops of blood tainted with liquid mercury. His investigation has begun to point back at members of the government itself, and so this meeting must be clandestine.

"Excuse me," a voice says, and he is startled to hear the words in English.

Dr. Graves glances over and sees an unfamiliar woman making her way into his aisle, people standing or shifting aside to let her move down the row toward the empty seat beside him. He frowns. If she is his contact, the woman knows little about remaining inconspicuous. Speaking English like that was foolish.

She is too pale, this woman, and her hair is pulled back from her face so tightly that it lends a cruel severity to features that might otherwise have been attractive.

She slips into the seat beside him and makes no attempt to focus on the movie screen. Dr. Graves attempts to keep some semblance of secrecy, but it quickly becomes obvious she has no intention of being subtle.

"You're Leonard Graves," she says, as though this should be news to him.

He nods.

"Look at me, Dr. Graves."

Exasperated, he glances around to be sure he has not been followed, but in the darkened theater he can see only phantom faces, flickering silver in the light from the screen. At length he turns to her.

"You might be a bit more—"

"You're dead, Dr. Graves."

Anger rises in him. His whisper is a harsh rasp. "Are you threatening me, ma'am?"

The woman's eyelids flutter with frustration and she sighs. "Simply stating a fact. Trying to remind you. You've been dead half a century. Think. Remember the bullet. You're here for a reason."

Graves begins to shudder and he feels a terrible pain in his heart.

Phantom pain.

For he has no heart.

Grief swells within him and he turns away from her, only to see the faces of the other theater goers again. The flickering light upon the screen is not what has made them look spectral. Rather, it is the fact that they are specters. Ghosts of the dead.

The silver light from the screen passes through them, their bodies having little more substance than dust motes swirling in shafts of sunlight. Their faces are etched with fear.

He turns back to the woman and sees that she too is transparent. Dr. Graves does not look down at his own body, at his hands. He does not like to look at his hands.

"Who are you?" he asks, the illusion of the Parisian movie palace becoming wispy around them, a ghost all its own.

"My name is Yvette Darnall. I am ... I was a medium."

And he watches her eyes, blue ghosts in and of themselves, as she tells the tale of her own death, of her efforts to locate Sweetblood the Mage, of the trap that he laid for any who would dare to search for him.

"The bastard," Graves whispers, trying not to see that the theatre is gone now, completely disappeared, and there is only a kind of river flowing at their feet, a rushing, turbulent stream of souls. Some of them fly past above and around him, but all of them in the same direction, with a fierce momentum, as though drawn on by some inexorable force.

"Oh, yes, he always was," Miss Darnall says. "But I see it now. I understand."

For a moment Graves does not hear her. He is distracted by a tugging at his arms and the current that drags at his ankles, the stream trying to pull him in, to pull him on . . . and he will not look to see what has such power over him. He frowns as her words finally settle into his mind.

"Understand what? Why he murdered you?"

She shudders and glances away in shame, and now she does not seem quite so severe. "I cannot see it all, of course. Only the silhouette of what may be, not the fine details. But this is why I came to find you the moment I sensed you had moved further into the river of souls. Someone has located Sanguedolce."

"We know," Graves says, nodding, feeling the tug of the soulstream on his body now, and shuddering at its touch. It has been so long since anyone has been able to touch him. He feels the urge to sink into the river, to flow with it. "Doyle was there. One of the Old Races, the Night People, have Sweetblood. He's in some sort of protective—"

"They're trying to open it," whispers the ghost of Yvette Darnall, her face thinning strangely. Her hair begins to come undone and her long tresses flutter in the invisible breeze of the soulstream, reaching away from her as though yearning to join the others.

But her eyes are firm and dark. "Sanguedolce has hidden within a magical shell. It must not be opened."

Dr. Graves stands a bit straighter, drags his feet toward her in the soulstream, fighting its pull upon him. "Why? You know something. I don't spend a lot of time here, in the otherworld, but enough to know that a lot of the spirits who linger around the area where all of these omens and strange phenomena are occurring . . . they've retreated. They're hiding deeper here, or slipping into the soulstream and letting go. Why? Is this what they're afraid of? What will happen if Sweetblood is freed? What is he going to do? Why do they want to break him out in the first place?"

Miss Darnall looks terribly sad now. She reaches out toward him but her form is blurring. Her body is succumbing to the pull of the soulstream, streaks of ectoplasm stretching off her, fluttering just as the tendrils of her hair are doing. Bits of her slipping away. Her face grows thinner, becomes warped.

"I don't know what they want him for. Nor what cataclysm will result from his being freed. But when I searched for him, when I found him, I touched his mind and for just a moment before his spell froze my heart, I saw inside him and I realized that he was frightened. Sweetblood felt utter dread and sheer terror at the thought of being released. Beyond that, I know nothing. Only that if it can frighten the world's most powerful sorcerer, it must be terrifying indeed. But that is not what the ghosts are retreating from."

"Then what—" Graves begins, reaching out to touch her as the soulstream is touching him, thinking perhaps he might hold her here with him a little longer. But his fingers pass through her as though he is solid and she nothing but spectral mist. "What are they running from?"

"Another power," says Miss Darnall, her body tearing itself apart, pieces of her whipping away into the stream, or streaking the air, her face pulled taut, warped, mouth twisted. "Something calls to them, trying to drag them back."

"Back to what?"

With a flap like a flag furling in the breeze the rest of her gives way, the ghost surrendering to the river of souls, carried away from him. But as she sails along the stream, Yvette Darnall looks back at him.

"To their bodies," she calls, a thin, reedy voice that disappears after a moment, swallowed in the stream.

For long moments Graves stares after her. There are lights swirling in the stream and flashing past him in the air. The theater has disappeared, the Parisian movie palace had never been there, unless it had been constructed of ectoplasm, or whatever the substance of this realm is. Now, as he narrows his gaze, he sees in the distance two towering objects that thrust themselves up from the stream. To Graves they seem like the tusks of some impossibly huge elephant, ivory spires a hundred feet high.

But he knows what they were.

The gate.

Though he hates to do it, he glances down at his fingers. They blur and stretch and he sees that his own form has begun to run, to streak, tugged along the soulstream, toward the gate.

He grits his teeth.

Leonard Graves is not ready to let the river of souls take him. Not yet. Not until he knows who took his life, who destroyed him. And if that means he must haunt the world for all eternity, so be it. Though he feels the bliss of the soulstream, the peace of surrender a temptation, he turns his back on the gate and begins to trudge back upstream.

6

DOYLE followed the sentries through the impossibly lush forest. At first glance it appeared to be too dense and overgrown for passage, but the primordial wood obliged their needs and parted to let them through. The people of Faerie existed in a symbiotic relationship with their environment, bonded to the land where they had lived forever.

The sentries quickened their pace, one of them turning to give Doyle a cruel smile as they began to run through the wood. The sorcerer kept up with them as best he could, his heart hammering in his chest as if to escape. He knew they did not appreciate his presence and would do everything short of killing him to make sure he was aware of that fact. But there was no time to concern himself with the hurt feelings of the Fey. They were all in danger—this world, as well as worlds beyond it.

The guards came to an abrupt stop in front of a downed tree. It was enormous, easily dwarfing the mighty redwoods of Earth. Doyle welcomed the brief respite, reaching into his back pocket for a handkerchief to wipe his sweating brow. The wood was eerily quiet and he did not recognize this path to the city of Faerie, but that was far from unusual, for the forest often changed its configuration to keep the great home of the Fey safe from danger. It had done this since the Twilight Wars. Many enemy troops, having found their way into the Faerie realm, never reached their destination, eventually succumbing to the elements of the forest world.

One of the sentries rapped three times on the trunk of the felled tree with his spear. Figures and shadows shifted in Doyle's peripheral vision, and then the forest was alive with movement. Fey warriors emerged from their places of concealment around and atop the enormous fallen tree. They had been there all along, but had not allowed themselves to be seen. A chill ran up Doyle's spine as more and more of the armored soldiers made their presence known. Their pale faces were tattooed with magickal wards of protection, the symbols adding to the ferocity of their appearance. Doyle was familiar with the Lhiannan-shee, the elite fighting force of the Faerie army, but he had thought their ranks disbanded after the Twilight conflicts. Something was definitely amiss, and he began to wonder if he had made the journey to Faerie too late.

A Lhiannan-shee wearing the markings of a commander crouched atop the fallen tree and glared at the sentries, and at Doyle.

"Why have you left your post at the gate to the world of Blight?" The normally pleasant tone of the Faerie tongue sounded harsh coming from the commander.

The world of Blight, Doyle thought with sadness as he wiped his brow. How the people of this magickal realm had learned to hate the world of his birth. At one time, the doorways between the two places had been gossamer thin, but humanity's blatant disregard for the environment had disgusted the Fey, and they ceased interaction with man.

"The doorway was opened from the other side," one of

the sentries, apparently their captain, explained. He pointed to Doyle. "And from the world of Blight, he did come."

The commander of the Lhiannan-shee gazed upon them, his eyes lingering on Doyle, and a ripple of disgust went across his face. With a feline grace, the commander leaped almost delicately down from the tree, but Doyle had seen the ferocity of the Lhiannan-shee in battle and knew they were far from delicate. The commander strode toward him, uncomfortably close, his dark Fey eyes shiny and black like polished lake stones.

"You stink of the filth that is humanity, but there is also something of Faerie about you. How can this be?" the commander asked, his long, spidery fingers caressing the hilt of the short sword hanging at his side.

These warriors were young, perhaps unborn when the Twilight Wars were fought. They did not know him, and that served to further drive the point home that he no longer belonged here. Doyle felt an intense wave of sadness wash over him but quickly cast it aside and looked deep into the commander's dark eyes.

"Lhiannan-shee, what was your father's name?" Doyle demanded in the language of the Fey, his pronunciation and intonation perfect.

The commander was taken aback and gripped his sword hilt all the tighter.

"What was your father's name?" Doyle repeated.

"Niamh-sidhel," the commander replied with an air of pride.

Doyle nodded, raising a hand to stroke his beard. "A brave one indeed. He fell during the battle of the Wryneck, but not before one hundred Fenodyree sampled the point of his sword." Doyle paused, remembering a Fey warrior with an unquenchable thirst for human beer. "He is remembered in both tale and song."

Doyle sang a bit of a remembrance song, the first verse telling of Niamh-sidhel's love of his people and his mistrust of the Night People. It had been quite some time since Doyle had sung, and he felt mildly foolish.

The commander's hand left his weapon, his ferocity turning to melancholy. "Who are you to sing of my father with such reverence?" His voice was now just a whisper in the woods.

"I am Arthur Conan Doyle, and once I called this wondrous place my home."

The Lhiannan-shee's eyes widened with the revelation, and Conan Doyle dared to think that perhaps he had not been entirely forgotten in the land of the Fey.

"I have heard this name. It is spoken in whispers here," the commander said. "There is much anger and sadness associated with your name, Conan Doyle from the Blight."

The memory of the day he had departed Faerie was fresh in Conan Doyle's mind, as crisp as if that particular recollection had been minted only the day before. His grief had been like a gaping wound as he sealed the private doorway from his home to the land of Faerie, believing he would never again look upon its abundant wonders. Now he felt that old wound tear open again and begin to bleed freely.

"Believe me, commander, I am aware that I may not be welcome here. And I would never have entered Faerie unless circumstances were dire," Conan Doyle explained. "Allow me to pass into your great city so that I may warn your king and his Seelie Court of the impending danger."

The son of Niamh-sidhel narrowed his gaze, his gleaming black eyes studying Conan Doyle. At length, the commander turned to his soldiers and raised his long, pale arm, bracelets of rock and wood clattering against one another. The Lhiannan-shee tensed, ready to respond to their commander's signal. He showed them a balled fist, and then opened his hand, his incredibly long fingers splayed wide.

They responded immediately, the melodious sounds of Faerie spell casting filling the air. Conan Doyle watched as their hands weaved intricate shapes, each an integral piece of the magick that was being cast. It took but seconds for one of the gnarled knots in the bark of the great tree to begin to grow larger, and larger still. The thick bark moaned and popped as it was magickally reconfigured, and soon they were looking at a tunnel through to the other side.

"My thanks," Conan Doyle said with a bow of his head.

The commander of the Lhiannan-shee responded in kind. "The sentries will escort you the remainder of the way to where you will speak with the Lady Ceridwen."

The mere mention of her name gave Conan Doyle a spasm of pain. He had hoped to avoid any contact with Ceridwen. He had hurt her more than enough and did not want to cause her any further grief.

"I mean no disrespect to the great lady, but my errand here is most dire. It should be brought to the attention of King Finvarra."

The commander gazed longingly through the opening in the tree. "I am afraid that is impossible, Conan Doyle from the Blight."

Conan Doyle felt another spark of panic. The Lhiannan-shee again deployed, the king unable to speak with him, something was very wrong here.

"Then at the least allow me to speak with the one who leads the Seelie Court," he asked, struggling to hide his frustration.

"And you shall," the warrior agreed, signaling to the sentries.

"Many thanks to you, son of Niamh-sidhel," Conan Doyle said as he followed his escorts into the tunnel's entrance. It was damp inside the great tree, the ceiling dripping with sweetly scented moisture. Conan Doyle paused and turned to glance back at the commander. The other Lhiannan-shee were curiously watching Conan Doyle, this stranger to their world, as he moved through the dripping darkness. "And who now leads the Seelie Court?"

"Why, the Lady Ceridwen, of course," the commander replied.

Conan Doyle felt his pulse quicken and his throat go dry. Something fluttered in his gut.

"Oh my," he said aloud as his escorts took him firmly by his shoulders and he was urged deeper into the tunnel.

From the darkness of the tunnel they emerged into the light, and Conan Doyle had to shield his eyes, for the sun of this world shone brightly upon the splendor that was the kingdom of Faerie. He heard the snap and creak of their tunnel passage closing behind them, but could not pull his eyes from the fabulous view that lay before him. Though he had seen the forest citadel of King Finvarra many times, and even lived within its abundant halls, he still marveled at its magnificence.

Nudged from his reverie by his escorts, Conan Doyle left the shadows of the great tree and proceeded down an open hillock to an elaborate suspension bridge that would allow access to the fabulous settlement nestled in the breathtaking valley before them.

Faerie legend claimed that the kingdom, and all its intricate structures, had been made from the desiccated remains of a long-forgotten god. As Conan Doyle and his Fey companions crossed the great bridge and the buildings loomed closer, Conan Doyle could think of no reason to doubt this ancient tale. The citadel of the royal family rose up from the center of the kingdom, its high, pointed spires the color of polished bone. There was an organic look to the place, all straight lines and rounded curves. His memories did not do it justice.

The trio came to an abrupt stop at the end of the bridge, before an intimidating gate that very well could have been made from the ribs of some gigantic deity. Conan Doyle gazed between the slats of the gate to the courtyard beyond and saw that there was no sign of life. If his memory served him correctly, this was highly unusual, for the courtyard served as a marketplace for the citizens of the kingdom and usually thrived with activity.

Conan Doyle turned to his escorts. "Why is it so quiet? Where are the Fey?"

They ignored his question. "Our responsibility is fulfilled," the more talkative of the pair said with little emotion, and they both turned back down the length of the bridge, leaving him alone.

"How will I get inside?" Conan Doyle asked their departing forms.

"That is not our concern," the sneering sentry said over his shoulder.

The sound of a bolt sliding home distracted Conan Doyle, and he turned back to the gate. To its right was a door of thick, light-colored wood, its pale surface marbled with streaks of a darker grain. The door began to slowly open outward, and he watched as a hooded figure, clad in robes of rich dark blue, with golden brocade about the sleeves and hem, emerged.

"I am here to speak with she who leads the Seelie Court," Conan Doyle said formally, squinting his eyes in an attempt to discern the features of the one whose identity remained hidden within the darkness of the hood.

"We know why you have come, Arthur Conan Doyle." The mysterious figure reached up with pale, gnarled hands to pull back his hood. "The land has warned us of your return, and the grim tidings you bring."

From a copse of nearby trees a murder of crows rose into the air, screaming their panicked caws. Nothing remained secret for long in the realm of Faerie. Even before he had removed the hood, Conan Doyle had recognized the voice of the king's grand vizier, Tylwyth Teg.

"Greetings, Tylwyth Teg, it has been a long time." Conan Doyle bowed his head.

The vizier's hair was long, wisp thin and white, like the delicate webs of a spider upon his ancient skull. It drifted about his head and face, caressed by the gentle breezes that rose up from the valley. As always, Tylwyth wore a scowl of distaste. He had never approved of Conan Doyle's presence in Faerie and vehemently opposed any attempt to teach a human the powerful magicks of the Fey.

"The wound has not yet healed from when last you were among us," Tylwyth snarled, his cadaverous features giving him the appearance of an animated corpse.

"I would not have returned, but for the danger that threatens both our realms." Conan Doyle summoned as much reverence as he was able. "Please, I must be allowed to speak with your mistress."

Tylwyth Teg again raised his hood, then turned and passed through the doorway from which he had come. "You come too late, son of man," he hissed cryptically as Conan Doyle followed. "For catastrophe has already struck our kingdom."

The vizier shuffled across the empty courtyard, and Conan Doyle shuddered with the sense of foreboding that permeated the air. Carts that would normally be overflowing with produce lay abandoned in the corner. Booths used to display the finest wares of Fey craftsmen were empty.

"What has happened here, Tylwyth?" he dared ask as they entered one of the outer structures of Finvarra's citadel. "Where are the merchants, and the people?"

"They are in mourning," the vizier croaked, stopping in

the high-ceilinged hallway to remove a ring of keys from within his robes. Even the citadel itself, which normally bustled with life, was deathly still.

"Who, Tylwyth?" Conan Doyle asked, as the vizier produced a key that resembled the petrified branch of some primeval tree and unlocked a heavy wooden gate. "Who do they mourn? Has King Finvarra—?"

The Faerie advisor gestured for Conan Doyle to proceed through the gate, which led into the king's private garden. "Who do they mourn?" he echoed, shaking his head sadly. "The future, perhaps? Perhaps they mourn the future. But it is not my place to explain."

After Conan Doyle had stepped through, Tylwyth Teg pulled the gate closed behind him with a resounding clatter. Conan Doyle frowned and glanced back through the bars of the gate at the vizier.

"Step into the garden and all will be made clear, Conan Doyle."

Knowing he would get little else from Tylwyth Teg, Conan Doyle turned and strode into the garden. Either side of the stone path was adorned with the largest red roses he had ever seen. The faint sound of gurgling water reached him and he knew that he was near his destination. A moment later he caught sight of the top of the fountain in the garden's center. Though he could not see more than its apex, he recalled an intricate ebony sculpture of a great fish, water jetting from its open maw to rain down into the pool that surrounded it.

He passed beneath an archway woven from a flowering vine known only to the world of Faerie, its blossoms welcoming him to the garden of kings with voices like those of tiny children. And then his feet froze and he could not move. Even his breath was stilled in his chest. It seemed to him that his heart paused as well. Laid out upon the ground around the stone fountain were the unmistakable shapes of bodies, covered by sheets of ivory silk.

"Dear Lord," Conan Doyle whispered. Everywhere his eyes fell were bodies, their coverings rippling as the breeze caressed their silken shrouds, tormenting him with glimpses of the corpses beneath. *There must be fifty of them.*

A tremor went through Conan Doyle. He sensed movement behind him and whirled to face the object of his dread, the reason why he had expected never to return to Faerie. He had tried to fashion a ward, some sort of magickal defense that would protect his heart from the devastation he knew he would feel, but there was nothing to save him from this.

Ceridwen was dressed in flowing robes of soft, sheer silk dyed a deep forest green. Her pale skin was accentuated by the dark hue of her garb. When her eyes met his, she drew a gauzy scarf tight about her shoulders as if experiencing a sudden chill.

"My lady," Conan Doyle whispered, his breath taken away. The ache caused by simply being in her presence was bone deep.

"You said that I would never see you again," the Fey sorceress said, her voice the lilt of a gentle spring breeze, still carrying the melancholy of a long winter. "And I had come to accept that."

When she walked across the stone floor, her dark robes billowing about her, it was with such elegance that she seemed to float, carried by the wind.

"You once told me you would never trust the word of a human. Even one that you loved," Conan Doyle said. He tried to search her eyes but there was only ice there. Never had he felt so torn. Part of him would rather have been experiencing the fires of damnation in that moment, and yet another side of his heart felt utter joy merely to be in Ceridwen's presence once more.

She knelt beside one of the bodies, her long, delicate hand reaching to draw back the sheet that covered it. A dead face was revealed to them, a twisted look of pain permanently frozen upon it.

"Why have you come, Arthur?" she asked, her thumb tracing arcane sigils upon the corpse's forehead. It was a ritual he had seen before, during the Twilight Wars, when an ally had been struck down by infernal magicks. It freed what life energies remained within the confines of the body.

"To seek answers, and to warn you of a great evil on the rise," he said, tentatively kneeling beside her. To be this close to her again was almost more than he could bear. "But I fear I have come too late."

Ceridwen covered the twisted features of the fallen Fey, raising her head to look into Conan Doyle's eyes. He would drown in those eyes, and there was nothing that could be done to save him.

"Who did this, my lady?" he asked, ignoring the urge to reach out and touch her face, to caress her alabaster skin.

She tore her gaze away and moved to another of the covered corpses. "I am your lady no longer, Arthur Conan Doyle. As to the hand behind this tragedy, that is a tale almost too sad to tell." She drew down another sheet of silk to reveal the dead beneath. The countenance of this corpse was even more disturbing than the first. "This evil of which you speak has touched our world as well."

"Who is it? Whose hand has done this?"

Ceridwen glanced up from her ministrations, her dark, soulful eyes again touching his. "It was one of our own," she said, a tremble in her voice, and his heart nearly broke as he watched tears like liquid crystal run down her cheeks, to land upon the upturned face of a dead Fey warrior.

" T W O hundred and fifty channels and not a damn thing on," Squire muttered as he aimed the remote control at a thirty-five-inch television monitor in a hardwood cabinet. The goblin flipped past countless images, each of them dishearteningly similar—another apocalyptic vision of the northeastern United States, or static. Whatever the hell was going on outside was interfering with the digital cable signals.

He reached a stubby hand into the bag of greasy potato chips and brought a handful to his mouth. Squire lived for junk food: candy and chips, burgers and fries, cookies and donuts. Especially donuts. He loved food of all kinds, in fact. It was his greatest pleasure. But the sweetest and saltiest were his favorites.

Stopping at one of the all-news channels, the goblin watched a live feed from Virginia Beach, where the ocean had begun to boil and the fish were leaping up out of the water in a frantic attempt to escape death. Somewhere off-camera people had begun to scream.

"That'll help," he said, taking a swig from his bottle of beer to wash down his snack. "Nothing like a good shriek to calm everybody's nerves." Squire belched mightily, flecks of unchewed potato chip speckling his shirt and pants. Bored with watching fish die, he changed the station. *Maybe a nice game show,* he thought, flipping past channel after channel of the world in turmoil. He tried not to think about what was happening outside. Conan Doyle's agents were in the field, and it was only a matter of time before things were wrestled back under control. That was how it always was. If there was anything Squire had learned in his many years working for Mr. Doyle, it wasn't over until the fat lady shit in the woods.

On a pay station that hadn't gone to static, he finally found a movie. A large grin spread across his face. A nice piece of Hollywood escapist fluff was exactly what he needed. His smile quickly turned to a frown when he realized the station was showing the abysmal Keanu science fiction flick that the actor had done before *The Matrix*.

As if Keanu wasn't torture enough, Squire thought, continuing his search for something to amuse him.

He had clicked all the way to the end and was about to start over again when something on one of the local stations caught his eye. He leaned forward on the sofa, crumbs of potato chip raining to the floor. The handheld camera footage was shaky and made his eyes hurt, but he recognized the area. The camera was pointed toward a bunkerlike structure in the midst of a sea of orange brick. It was the exit from the Government Center subway station, not too far away, and there were things not usually associated with public transit pouring from the underground and spilling onto the plaza.

"Corca-fuckin'-Duibhne," he growled, turning up the volume. There had to be hundreds of the coppery-skinned bastards. It was like watching a swarm of bugs emerging from its nest. Whoever was manning the camera was hiding behind a newspaper kiosk, peeking out from time to time for the disturbing footage. For some reason there was no audio, and Squire imagined that it was probably for the best.

Slowly, he brought a potato chip to his mouth, eyes riveted to the television. One of the Night People had seen the cameraman, its mouth opening incredibly wide in a silent roar. The gnarled, twisted, leathery thing sprang across the brick as though in a dance, needle teeth bared for attack. The picture turned to static, and an anchorwoman who usually looked too damn cool for the room came on as the broadcast returned to the studio. Her face was pasty, and she was sweating to beat the band.

"How long ago was that?" Squire asked the set, listening to the woman's trembling voice. The goblin rose from his chair and went to the window. The red, billowing fog seemed to have grown thicker in the square below, practically hiding the park from view. There was a kind of glow about it now that reminded him of weird creatures that lived so far below the ocean's surface that they had developed their own luminescence.

"No more than a fifteen-minute walk from Government Center to here," the hobgoblin grumbled, though his words trailed off as he noticed dark things moving in the blood-red mist. "Shit!" Squire pressed his face against the glass for a better look. Corca-Duibhne darted through the unearthly fog with an uncanny swiftness, converging upon the townhouse.

Conan Doyle's valet stepped away from the window. There was no way that the Night People could get inside the townhouse. Conan Doyle had set up all kinds of magickal wards and barriers so that nothing that didn't belong could find its way into the place. The image on the television screen again caught his attention. The anchorwoman was crying now, mascara running down her face in oily streaks. She was in the process of confessing her sins to the camera.

"I've got my own problems, sweetheart," he said, reaching for the remote and clicking off the set.

A thunderous clamor came to him from the first floor, as if something were pounding on the door to get in, but of course Squire knew that was impossible. *Isn't it? Son of a bitch, it had better be.*

He jumped feet first into a square of shadow thrown by

the entertainment center, becoming immersed in a world of perpetual darkness.

The goblin scrambled through the shadowpaths toward an exit that would take him closest to the front door. Again came the pounding, the violent sound muffled within the realm of shadow. Squire drew himself out of a patch of black behind the refrigerator in the kitchen, the hot coils at the back of the unit pressing against his face as he hauled his body from the shadow and squeezed out from behind the appliance.

Two Corca-Duibhne scouts crouched in the center of the kitchen. He knew they were scouts because the symbol of their rank was carved into the dark flesh of their faces. No stars or stripes on lapels for these guys. Heads tilted back, eyes closed, their noses twitched as they sniffed the air in search of potential danger.

It wasn't an instant before they got a nose full of him.

I knew I should have showered this week, the hobgoblin thought, scrambling across the tile floor to pull open one of the counter drawers.

The scouts began to shriek, a high-pitched, ululating sound that warned others of their stinking kind that there was trouble present.

Squire spun around, glinting metal cleaver in hand, meeting the first of his attackers with relish. It had been a long time since he had killed a Corca-Duibhne, and as he buried the blade in the skull of his adversary, he realized he was long overdue.

"Look at that, a perfect fit," Squire growled, as the creature continued to fight. "What's that? You'd like seconds?" He drove a stubby knee savagely up into the Corca-Duibhne's midsection, yanked the cleaver from its head, and brought it down again. "What a greedy little piggy."

The scout went rigid as the metal blade again shattered

its skull, sinking deep. *Finally hitting the tiny piece of fruit these shitbags call a brain.*

The second of the scouts was across the room. It had been jockeying around, looking for space to attack. Now it pulled back its leathery lips in a ferocious snarl that revealed nasty black gums and needle-sharp teeth. "He was my brother," the creature snarled, its oily eyes shifting from the corpse of its sibling back to Squire.

"Sorry," the hobgoblin apologized, bracing the heel of his foot against the corpse's shoulder and pulling the cleaver from its head with a slight grunt of exertion. "Did you like 'im much?"

The Corca-Duibhne shrugged, its long, clawed fingers massaging the air. "Not especially," it hissed. "But blood is the strongest bond. I will take your life in exchange for his."

"Is that so?" Squire asked, hefting his weapon, stained with stinking black blood. "I guess it's good to have goals, even if they are fucking ridiculous."

How is this possible? the goblin wondered. Conan Doyle's magick was some serious mojo, but these bastards had breached the house's supposedly unbreakable defenses. *Not good. Not good at all.*

The scout began to move and Squire prepared to counter its attack, but it lunged away from him and bolted through the doorway with a hiss, fleeing the kitchen. The goblin swore beneath his breath. *Night People. Buncha pussies,* he thought, hopping over the body of the dead scout in pursuit.

"Wait up," he called, careful not to slip in the blood pooling upon the tile floor. "I've got something special for you."

Squire did not have far to run. The scout had only fled as far as the corridor that led out toward the foyer. It stood, its back against the wall, holding in its spidery hand the crystal knob from Conan Doyle's front door. The Corca-Duibhne looked at him, and smiled an awful smile. Tendrils of crimson fog drifted into the corridor from the foyer. For the first time, Squire felt the draft, the breeze.

The door was open.

He could not see it from his vantage point, but it was clear these two scouts were not alone. Squire brandished his cleaver, ready to do combat with whatever else had invaded his employer's home. From the foyer came the sound of splintering wood, and then the heavy, plodding tread of many feet. There was a solid thump and a muttered, feral curse, and in his mind he could picture a cluster of Corca-Duibhne carrying something massive and heavy.

Squire was not going to let this happen.

Cleaver clutched tightly in his grip, he started down the corridor toward that single Corca-Duibhne, who now tossed the crystal knob idly into the air and caught it as though it were a lucky coin. Squire wanted to tear its heart out. But a moment later he came within sight of the foyer.

"Son of a monkey's uncle," he whispered.

Eight Corca-Duibhne emerged from the red fog, grunting with exertion as they hauled what looked to be a large chunk of jagged rock between them. They looked like pallbearers carrying a coffin at a funeral. The failing light from outside glinted off the object's surface, and Squire saw that it wasn't rock at all, but a kind of amber, for he could see the shape of a man imprisoned within. At that moment, he knew how his enemies had gained access to the townhouse. It was all so frighteningly clear.

"Sweetblood," he said aloud as the Night People let their load drop to the hardwood floor of the foyer.

A part of him wanted to stay, to defend the homestead from invaders, but another part of him, one far more intelligent than that stupid half, suggested that it might just be wiser to get the hell out of there. He began to search for an exit, a patch of shadow through which to make his escape.

"What, leaving us so soon?" came a voice as smooth as silk, speaking the tongue of the Fey.

Squire turned to see a statuesque female emerge from the scarlet fog. The Corca-Duibhne cowered as she passed them, as if afraid she would slap them, or worse. The woman was dressed from head to toe in black leather, her hair covered in a stylish kerchief of red silk, as if to match the fog. Even though her eyes were hidden behind sunglasses, Squire knew her at once.

"Morrigan," he whispered.

"You're going nowhere," she said, a cruel smile gracing her colorless features. "The fun is just beginning."

Fun like a heart attack, Squire thought as the Corca-Duibhne rushed him, and he raised his cleaver in defense. *Fun like a heart attack.*

7

FINVARRA'S kingdom seemed deserted, yet Conan Doyle knew it was not. The scents of a bounty of ripened fruit reached him as he strode amongst the trees and past a burbling stream along which dryads swam. But there were copses that had been burned black, their charred remains a scar upon the land. The Fey were not gone, however, nor were they hiding.

They were in mourning.

There was no music in Faerie this day, only the sighing of the wind in the trees and the flapping of war banners adorned with Finvarra's crest. From time to time as he followed Ceridwen on a winding walk through the forest, he could hear cries of bereavement. She carried in one hand a staff of oak, with finger branches at the top that clutched within them a sphere that appeared to be crystal. Conan Doyle knew better. This was no crystal ball, but a ball of ice. At the center of that frozen orb there burned a flame, flickering as though atop a candle's wick. This was Ceridwen's elemental staff, a mark of her office and her skill.

Within Conan Doyle there were many emotions at war.

He felt sharp regret and giddy excitement at seeing Cerid-wen, and the urge to help the Fey was strong. And yet he was aware that he was needed at home even more than he was needed here. In Faerie, death had come and gone, taking many souls with it. But in Conan Doyle's world—the Blight—the reaper still walked.

Even simply being in Faerie brought conflicting emotions into play. This was the place he dreamed of when he went to sleep, it was the paradise of his heart, and yet there had been much bitterness upon his departure so many years ago, and to return to it now when such grim events were at hand was dark irony.

Ceridwen paused at a door built of three massive standing stones, two upright and one laid across the top. There was no gate to bar it, but no one would pass through that gate without an invitation from a member of the royal family. He had lived beyond that gate, for a time. The memory made him hesitate.

"What is it, Arthur?" Ceridwen asked.

Conan Doyle gazed at her a moment, then glanced away. "Only echoes, lady. Please go on."

When he looked up again, she was still watching him. Ceridwen frowned deeply and turned to stride between the standing stones. Conan Doyle followed, and as he walked through that door, his breath caught in his chest just as it had done that first time he had trodden upon this ground.

The year had been 1920. The London theosophist Edward Gardner had accompanied him to Cottingley, a tiny hamlet in Yorkshire, to visit the home of the Wright family. Polly Wright had approached Gardner at one of his lectures with the most extraordinary story. The woman claimed that her young daughter Elsie and the girl's cousin, Frances Griffiths, had befriended a community of fairies in a glen near their homes. Not merely befriended, but photographed the fairies.

The girls' claims, and more especially their photographs, had brewed a storm of controversy, but by the time it had begun, and the world was scrutinizing the two girls, Arthur Conan Doyle had already found his proof in the glen at Cottingley. For in the glen he had seen the fairies himself, firsthand. Gardner had accompanied the girls and their parents home, and Conan Doyle—who had already been a student of magick and spiritualism for some time—cast a spell of revelation.

The fairies had been wondrous, gossamer things, like lithe, flimsy women with wings like butterflies. Wherever they flew they left a sparkle, streaking the air with all the hues of sunrise. Never in his life had he seen anything so delicate, so ephemeral, and so beautiful. They had made no sound at all, but their motion was music.

Then one of them had hesitated, hovering a moment, and darted across the glen to beat its wings furiously just inches from his face. Its tiny, golden eyes had widened in shock as it realized that its suspicions were correct. He could see them. He had been watching them.

The vicious little thing had clawed his cheek, drawing blood. As Conan Doyle hissed and clapped one hand to his face, they had all darted across the glen to a large tree that lay on its side next to a brook, its roots torn from the ground and jutting like the antlers of a monstrous stag. The fairies had disappeared amongst those roots, and Conan Doyle had taken a closer look, still pressing his fingers against the scratch on his cheek.

The spell of revelation had uncovered more than the presence of the fairies. The crown of jagged roots that circled the felled tree hid a secret. The tree was impossibly hollow.

Conan Doyle had dropped to his knees and bent low to look inside. Deep within that tree he had seen a glimmer of light. And he had crawled inside.

"Arthur!"

Fingers snapped in front of his face. He blinked several times and found himself gazing into Ceridwen's violet eyes. His breath caught in his throat again and he breathed in the aroma of lilacs, the scent that came off her so powerfully it weakened him. She looked as though she wanted to strike him down with her elemental staff. It took him several seconds before he could glance away.

"You are not the magician I thought you were if you cannot enter the House of the King without it beguiling your senses," she chided him.

Yet wasn't there a hint of amusement, even affection, in her gaze and her tone?

Conan Doyle dared a soft smile. "It has been a very long time. Even such sweet marvels as are to be found in Faerie fade when time and distance intervene. I confess I was so overwhelmed, simply being back here that I did not steel myself for the way in which just breathing the air can spin one into flights of fancy . . . or memory."

For a moment there seemed to be a twinkle in her eye, but then Ceridwen's expression hardened, a veil of sadness drawn across her face.

"Yes, well, do not let it happen again. Flights of fancy can prove very costly, of late. If Morrigan returns, such reckless whimsy could cost your life."

Conan Doyle stood straighter and nodded once, matching the severity of his expression to hers. Yet his eyes hid the memories he had, of Ceridwen coming to him as he neared death, of her bringing him back to Faerie, showing him the herbs that would return vigor and youth to him, the same herbs that still kept him young. He had known enough magick by then to cast the illusion of his own death. Anything else would have horrified and astonished the world. He could not have continued to live the life he had before and begin to grow younger, like Oscar Wilde's fancy. And in the end there was nothing he wanted so much as to disappear into Faerie, to see the world of the Fey through Ceridwen's eyes.

There were so many things that he wanted to say to her, but none of them would be appropriate. He had given up his right to say them long ago. So when Ceridwen turned to continue on, her long silken gown and robe clinging to her lithe form, he followed.

Though he forced himself to focus, to avoid being swept away with the magick of the place, the way the air itself seemed to sparkle, he could not help glancing around several times. Ahead the hill rose up and up and the House of the King had been carved from its face. Spires of rock shot from the ground and there were barrows bulging up from the earth. Elegant arched windows seemed out of place in rocky ledge. Flowers bloomed atop the hill in such abundance that they seemed to spill down its sides.

Amongst the flowers there were fairies. Not people of Faerie, like the warriors, scholars, and magicians of the Fey, but the little people, the ferociously beautiful winged creatures he had first met in Cottingley well over eight decades before. Their colors put the flowers to shame, and they flitted about the House of the King as though it were their own home. And in essence it was, for Finvarra had extended his protection to all the races of Faerie who would show their faces to the sun.

Streams flowed down the hill, from trickle to brook to torrent, and the sound of the water joined with the perfume of the flowers to lend Conan Doyle a peace he had not known since the last time he had stepped inside the King's Door.

Surrounding the hill, the House of the King, were seven clusters of large trees, four to a cluster. In each small copse, the branches of the trees reached out to one another, twining together with such design that Conan Doyle could only ever think of them as braided. The braided branches created a basket in each small copse, sometimes twenty, sometimes thirty, sometimes forty feet in the air. And in its midst, gripped in the same way that the head of her staff gripped the sphere of ice, was a dwelling formed of woven leaves and branches and vines, with flowers sprayed across its roof.

For nearly ten years they had lived in one of those tree-top homes, called Kula-keaine by the Fey. Conan Doyle could still remember Ceridwen's caresses and the way her violet eyes gave off the slightest glow in the darkness when only the rustling of leaves and the songs of the night birds kept them company. As they progressed, Ceridwen resolutely refused to look up at the Kula-keaine where they had made their home, where they shared all of themselves, heart and soul.

They strode along a western path and up a winding set of stairs made from thick roots that protruded from the earth to form steps.

"We're not going to see the king?" Conan Doyle ventured.

Ceridwen did not turn to him when she spoke. "Yes, we are."

He said no more after that, only followed along beside her as she led him around to the western edge of the hill, where the water that came from the bowels of the earth fountained out of a hole in the green and gentle slope and became a rushing river that ran for several hundred yards before disappearing into a cavernous hole in the ground.

A black-cloaked figure knelt at the river's edge beside a pile of cut flowers. He wore a hood to cover his face and the daylight seemed repelled by him, as though a pool of night gathered around him. One by one, with a ritual bow of the head, he dropped the flowers in the rushing water and watched them be borne away. Conan Doyle's heart ached to see him, for despite the black mourning clothes and the gathered shadows, he recognized the figure by his stature and carriage and the dignity with which he held his head and moved his hands.

Together Conan Doyle and Ceridwen approached.

"Uncle," the Fey sorceress said.

As though he had not heard, he picked up another flower and dropped it into the river, repeating the motion of his head and muttering quiet words. Only after the flower had disappeared into the gullet of that underground river cavern did he turn. His face was pale and gaunt, but behind a curtain of his long silver hair were eyes alive with fury and grief.

"We have a visitor," Ceridwen said, and there was a softness in her tone that both pleased Conan Doyle and pained him as well.

Conan Doyle sank to one knee. "King Finvarra. Time has passed, but I hope I am still welcome in your Home."

As though floating, the king rose from his spot by the riverside. He drew back his hood and a fond smile creased his face, yet somehow without dismissing the sadness there.

"You have come at a difficult time, Arthur. But I am pleased to see you, nonetheless. There was great disappointment, even bitterness, in the wake of your departure when last we met, yet you are still and always will be welcome in my Home. I only wish you had returned at a time when a celebration would not seem so grotesque."

Still kneeling, Conan Doyle lowered his gaze. "I understand, My Lord. I could not have hoped for such a welcome for a prodigal. You shame me."

A small sound came from Ceridwen, but Conan Doyle ignored it and she said nothing.

"There is no shame in heartbreak, Arthur," King Finvarra said. "It happens with the best of us. You yearned for the world of your birth and my niece would not leave hers. Hearts have been torn asunder by far less. Have you returned under the guidance of your heart?"

Conan Doyle felt his face flush. He looked up, trying not to see the way that Ceridwen turned away at the very same moment.

"My heart has been here since the day I left, My Lord. It has remained among the Fey, in Faerie, and may well be here until I die. But, no, that is not what brings me. I have come with a warning. And, I confess, hoping for some help. Dark power is at work in my world. Terrible omens. Unnatural magick. I don't know what malign intelligence is behind these events, but they have enlisted one of the night tribes to—"

Finvarra stiffened and glanced at Ceridwen, whose eyes narrowed. So taken aback was he by their reaction that he stopped speaking and only studied them expectantly.

The king stared at his niece. "There, perhaps, is our answer."

"What?" Conan Doyle asked. "What is it? What answer?"

Ceridwen's gaze was cold. There were many unformed thoughts and hopes in the back of his mind about his return to Faerie, about Ceridwen herself, but they were extinguished by that one look. There was only war in her eyes now.

"One of the night tribes, you said. Which one?" Ceridwen asked.

"The Corca-Duibhne. They have straddled our two worlds for a very long time, but they have never been more than an annoyance. I've never seen them so organized, so focused on—"

"You have my sister to thank," Finvarra said, gaunt face now cruel and brutal. "For 'tis Morrigan whom the Corca-Duibhne now serve."

Conan Doyle pictured the corpses of the Fey where they lay in the King's Garden. *One of our own,* Ceridwen had said. But even when she had explained that it had been her aunt, Morrigan, he had not put the pieces together.

"But why?" Conan Doyle asked, genuinely mystified. He searched Finvarra's eyes and then looked to Ceridwen. "If Morrigan wanted to rule Faerie, what does she want with my world? What is she planning?"

"You presume that her ambitions are so small as to extend only to ruling in my place," King Finvarra said. "But my sister has danced in shadows for too long. She knows all the secrets of the darkness. You can be certain that whatever she has planned, it is not nearly so mundane."

His brows knitted as he turned to Ceridwen. "Arthur has come for help, and he needs it, no question. You will go with him—"

Ceridwen gripped her elemental staff more tightly and shook her head. The flame that burned within the ice sphere at its head blazed brighter, and a mist of steam rose from its frozen surface. "Uncle, no!"

A deathly stillness fell over the king. Finvarra stared at her. "We have lived for eons with the philosophy that what happens beyond Faerie is not our concern. But we took Arthur into our Home, and he has requested our aid. Even had he not, we cannot allow Morrigan to interfere with the human world. Faerie must be protected. Ritual must be observed. I cannot leave, nor can I send an army into the Blight. The veil between worlds might be forever torn asunder by such an incursion. But you, niece, you shall go as my emissary."

She lowered her head. "Yes, My Lord King."

Finvarra regarded them both. "It appears the fates have conspired to break the stalemate the two of you entered into long ago. Let neither sweetness nor bitterness distract you. If you are not watchful, Morrigan will end up with both your hearts, and she will feed them to her wolves."

The king turned his back on them then and knelt by the river once more. He raised his hood, and in the full light of day the shadows of grief gathered round him. Falling again into the rhythm of ritual, he dropped his hand to the array of cut flowers, lifted one and dropped it into the river, inclining his head as it went along its way. One flower for each of the Fey who had died at Morrigan's hand.

Dismissed, Conan Doyle turned to Ceridwen. "Shall we go, then, lady?" he asked, and he held out his hand for hers.

"It seems I have no choice." She turned away from him and led the way back along the path toward the King's Gate.

THE cleaver wasn't going to do Squire a damn bit of good.

In a fraction of a second a hundred bits of memory and realization came together in Squire's mind. He stood in the foyer of Conan Doyle's enormous, elegant home and stared at Morrigan. It had been a very, very long time since he had seen her last, but even that had not been nearly long enough. There wasn't a word in any language nasty enough to describe this bitch. She was sexy as hell if you were into that goth look, not to mention chicks with claws instead of ordinary fingernails. But in his entire existence he had never met anyone who could make him feel so small with just a glance. He was a hobgoblin, and his kind were small enough as it was. Morrigan might be a queen of the Fey with all of the cruelty in her heart that her people were capable of, but she had none of their nobility, none of their honor. She was a sour, charmless, vicious cunt.

And he had used those precise words to describe her, to her face, the last time they had met.

Now she stood just inside the door, not far from the portrait of Conan Doyle's son that hung on the wall, with a pair of sunglasses dangling from one finger and a smile that could have sliced him open. Her eyes gleamed red and her nails, teeth, and spiked hair all seemed sharper than he remembered.

"Oh, yes," Morrigan hissed, running her tongue across her upper lip. "I remember you, hobgoblin."

Squire felt his knees jelly. He offered a flickering smile that died instantly. He glanced at the Night People carrying Sanguedolce's amber sarcophagus like a bunch of ugly fucking pallbearers.

"Crap."

He turned and ran back the way he'd come, cleaver at his side. Hobgoblins were faster on their feet than most people presumed at first glance, but that was not saying very much. There was a limit to how swift anyone could be with legs that short. The veins at his temples pulsed and his boots shook the floor. Behind him Morrigan released a stream of derisive laughter, and Squire could hear the grunting of the Corca-Duibhne as they gave chase. Some of them were barefoot, and their claws clicked and scraped on the wood floor.

"Son of a bitch, son of a bitch, son of a bitch," Squire whispered under his breath as he ran, knuckles white where he gripped the cleaver in his hand.

He was going to have to leave the house. Conan Doyle's house. The mage's own wards had not held Morrigan out, and there was no way that Squire himself could defend the place. Conan Doyle was going to be more than a little upset, but somehow Squire had the feeling that paintings and antiques and even a little breaking and entering were the least of Conan Doyle's concerns at the moment. The big question was going to be what Morrigan was up to. Squire couldn't answer that question right now. He had other obligations.

The first was to survive.

The second was to do his job.

Barreling into the kitchen, he leaped over the dead Corca-Duibhne. There was a grunt of triumph behind him and he felt claws snag the back of his shirt. Squire spun and buried the cleaver in the creature's chest. It squealed and dark blood sprayed from the wound. The blade stayed buried in its flesh as it backpedaled, slapping at the cleaver as though it were a wasp instead of a cutting tool. For several precious seconds, it prevented the others of its kind from reaching him.

Squire dove across the kitchen toward the sink. He grabbed the handles of the two small doors under the sink and yanked them open. Even with what light there was in the kitchen, the patch of shadow was deep and black. He ducked his head inside the cabinet, but his shoulders were too broad to fit.

"Shit," he whispered, glancing back.

The Corca-Duibhne had thrown their injured brother to the ground and were trampling over him. Even as he looked, Squire saw one of them stomp on the cleaver buried in the creature's chest, driving it deeper. Putrid blood ran in rivulets across the floor. The nearest one laughed as it spotted him.

"Where do you think you go, now, ugly turnip?"

Squire sneered. This guy was calling *him* ugly?

And then he pushed. His bones popped out of their joints, his arms folding in upon his body, and he drove himself inside the cabinet and into the patch of shadows within. One of them snagged at his foot and he kicked its claws away and, with one last solid plant of his boot on the interior of the cabinet, thrust himself into the shadows.

The shadowpaths opened before him. He could feel them, sense each walkway around him. His eyes were open but there was no color, only levels of its absence. Squire felt at home here, much more so than he ever did in the other world. This was where he belonged. He was not small here, not ugly or freakish. He was not a monster. Here in the shadows he was agile, graceful, and strong.

There was no time for him to pause and reflect now upon Morrigan's attack and what it might mean. There was time only to move, to walk the shadows. He had survived. Now it was on to his second priority.

The darkness rushed past him, caressed him, as Squire hurried along the shadowpath to his first stop. He could feel Conan Doyle's house around him, navigating by instinctual awareness of the ways in which the real world entwined with the shadow world. Moments after he had disappeared inside the kitchen cabinet, he reappeared inside another, much larger enclosure on the second floor of the house.

The weapons closet.

Hobgoblins could see better in the dark. Squire looked around and felt a surge of grim pleasure as he surveyed the swords and daggers, the bows and battleaxes, the maces and morningstars, and the more arcane weapons, his favorite bits and bobbles. Poison dueling pistols. Ectoplasm garrotes.

Beyond the doors of the weapons closet, which allowed only a sliver of light to enter, he could hear the thumping of the Corca-Duibhne's incursion. Glass shattered and doors slammed. Morrigan must have been aware that he was a shadow walker, but still they were searching for him, or trying to find out if anyone else was in the house. There were animal growls that went along with the Night People's movements through the house, but Squire was no longer listening. He was in a hurry, now.

He began with his favorites, unbreakable blades and enchanted arrows, others that he had relied on over the ages. As quietly as he was able, Squire filled his arms with weapons and slipped back into darkness, stepped into the shadowpaths, and made his way into Conan Doyle's garage. Nothing was darker than the trunk of the limousine.

Emerging inside the trunk, he paused to listen but heard no grunts nor footfalls nor clattering of vandalism that would have accompanied the Night People into the garage. Still he was careful to be quiet as he laid the first stash of weapons down at the back of the spacious trunk.

Then he went back.

Quiet. Careful. Swift.

Squire made jaunt after jaunt from weapons closet to trunk, slipping along the shadowpaths and retrieving blades and poisons and blunts. He was many things to Arthur Conan Doyle—valet and chauffeur and confidante—but the most vital part of his service was as armorer . . . as squire. It was his duty to care for the weapons, to supply them when needed, to see that Conan Doyle and his comrades were never unarmed. It would have been simple for him to escape the house, to leave Morrigan behind, but he was not going to leave the weapons.

On his seventh trip into the weapons closet, he heard voices.

Squire froze with his hand upon the grip of a scimitar whose blade was engraved with ancient symbols even Conan Doyle didn't understand. He quieted himself, holding his breath, and he listened. They were speaking Danaaini, the language of the Fey. One of the voices belonged to Morrigan and the other, a male voice, to another of her kind.

So the Corca-dweebs aren't the only ones taking orders

from her, Squire thought. He wasn't fluent in Danaaini, but he understood enough to get at least part of the conversation.

"Prepare," Morrigan said.

The other Fey muttered some sort of subservient, bootlicking response that Squire didn't bother working too hard to translate.

"We must be very careful if we are going to open—" Several words he did not understand followed this. And then, "Tell the skulkers to keep an eye out for Conan Doyle. I want to make certain he receives a proper welcome when he—"

"What is that smell?"

Squire grunted in annoyance. Like humans, like the Fey, hobgoblins had their own scent. He couldn't smell it himself, of course, but Eve had often told him he smelled like rotten apples. *And who would know better?*

Silence had fallen in the room outside the weapons closet. The Fey could walk without any noise at all if they wished to, but Morrigan did not bother. Squire had an image in his mind of her sniffing at the air, of her pausing to glare at the doors to the closet. He heard her footfalls on the hardwood as she marched toward him.

With deep regret Squire glanced around at the weapons that remained, trying to choose what he would rescue for his final trip. There really was no question, however. There was a longbow on the wall that had belonged to Ceridwen, a gift she had given to Conan Doyle before he had left Faerie. Squire snatched the bow off the wall just as the closet doors flew open and Morrigan stood silhouetted in the light from the room beyond.

"You should have run further than this, wretched thing," she snarled, the red scarf that had covered her hair now down around her neck. Her nostrils flared. "Go on, hobgoblin. Choose whatever weapon you like." With a flourish she gestured to the armaments that remained in the closet.

The light from the outer room reached deep inside the closet. Morrigan had him trapped. Or so she thought. For the wicked bitch had barely noticed that she cast her own shadow, and it was as black as her heart.

"Sorry, babe," Squire said, taking a single step toward her. "I'm a lover, not a fighter."

And he dropped away into the shadow on the floor, her scream of rage following him down into the darkness.

I N the living room at the Ferrick house, Clay stood behind a high-backed chair with his arms crossed. Eve sat at the edge of the chair, resting her hands on her knees, and when she spoke, she sounded more earnest than Clay had ever heard her. On the sofa, Danny Ferrick stared at her, brows knitted beneath the little nubs of his horns. He was slouched down as though he might sink into the cushions, baggy black pants hanging on his legs like curtains. He was twisting the corner of his oversized T-shirt in his hands. The boy's mother was so pale Clay thought she would either vomit or faint within the next few seconds.

She surprised him. The woman was stronger than she looked.

"You're lying!" Julia Ferrick said, her chest rising and falling quickly as though she was trying to keep from hyperventilating.

Clay put both hands on the back of Eve's chair. "No, Mrs. Ferrick. I can assure you that she's not."

Beside her, on the couch, the boy she had always thought of as her son began to laugh softly. Clay was unsure what to make of that laugh, and he narrowed his eyes as he studied the boy, who kept rubbing the soles of his red Converse high-tops on the carpet. Danny Ferrick shook his head and reached up to run his fingers over his small horns again. He sighed, glanced at Clay, and then focused on Eve. He was a teenaged boy and Eve was every teenaged boy's dream of a woman, so he trusted her.

"Seriously. You're not just messing with me?"

Eve shook her head. "No, Danny. No way."

The kid frowned again, narrowing his eyes. "So who is this Doyle guy again?" He turned to his mother. "How did you meet him?"

Mrs. Ferrick gazed at her son as though another word from him would shatter her like a China doll. She fidgeted with her hands again, and for the first time, Clay noticed how short her fingernails were. A couple of them were ragged. The woman had clearly been stressed even before all this lunacy had come into her life. She gnawed her lower lip.

"I don't suppose either of you has a cigarette?"

No one responded. Mrs. Ferrick shook her head. "Just as well. I quit." Then she lowered her eyes. "Mr. Doyle came to see me a few years ago. Just showed up on the doorstep one day while you were at school. Your . . . your condition had already started to show up. Your skin. But only just. I . . . I'm not even sure you had noticed it yet, but I had, just at the back of your neck one morning at breakfast.

"Mr. Doyle rang the bell. He was so polite, and so well dressed, I thought he must be selling something or . . . or trying to convert me or something." She uttered a tiny laugh of disbelief that sounded very much as though she were choking on unshed tears. "He said—"

The woman shook her head. Clay wanted to go to her, to sit with her and comfort her, but he knew there would be another time for that. For now, the truth was what mattered, and he did not want to interrupt the telling of it.

"What did he say, Mom?" Danny asked, trying to get

his mother to look up at him. "Did he tell you . . . what Eve just said?"

"No," Mrs. Ferrick said, catching her breath. "All he said was that . . . that someday I would want to ask him some questions about you, and that when the day came, I should call. And he gave me his card and he . . . he just left. I thought he was some nut. Some . . . some asshole, thinking he knows something about my son that I don't."

Eve sat back in her chair and lifted her chin, appraising Mrs. Ferrick. "But you kept his card."

The look the woman shot at Eve was full of venom. "Yes. Yes, I kept the card. He's my son. I brought him up myself. Everything I've ever done has been for him. I'd do anything for Danny. So, yes, I kept the card. Now you come telling me he's some . . . some demon child, some changeling baby, whatever the hell that even means."

"I explained what it—" Eve began.

"I don't want your explanations!" Mrs. Ferrick said, voice on the edge of hysteria. She brought one hand up to her mouth, gnawing a bit on her thumbnail, oblivious to their attentions.

"Mom," Danny said, his eyes revealing his pain, and he touched her arm to try to calm her. She grabbed his hand and held on tight.

"Now you come telling me that he isn't my son? That Danny isn't my boy at all? To hell with both of you and your Mr. Doyle, too." Mrs. Ferrick glanced at Danny. "He's all I've got."

Eve began to say something more, but now Clay leaned down and touched her on the shoulder and she closed her mouth. For a long moment the Ferricks, mother and son, just sat there holding hands, both of them staring at their unwelcome visitors. They were a strange sight, the woman in her suburban mother uniform of khaki trousers and white blouse, and the boy in his sloppy, unbuttoned shirt with the bright orange surfing tee underneath. Clay focused on Danny. The boy seemed not to want to look at him, but at last he did. Clay nodded gently. Danny swallowed and licked his lips, baring his needle teeth, if only for a moment. He took a deep breath and turned to his mother.

"Hey. Mom. Look at me."

Mrs. Ferrick studied his eyes.

"No. I mean look at me."

Defiantly, she continued to stare into his eyes.

"It's killing me, what I see in the mirror, y'know?" Danny said, and the anguish in his tough-guy voice was enough to force Clay to glance away a moment. "But, well, what they say makes sense. Sucks, but it makes sense. And if it's true . . . God, if it's true, I'm sorry, 'cause that means the kid you had in the hospital . . . he's somewhere else. I don't know where. But you're my mother. And you're the best. Seriously. You are.

"But if it's true . . . and I can't lie to you, it *feels* true. If it is, it means I'm not a freak. I'm not some fucked-up kid who doesn't fit in anywhere, 'cause I don't have to. I'm not one of them. One of the nasty little pukes I go to school with. If it's true . . . and I think I want it to be. That would be better, I think. Better than the way things have been."

Mrs. Ferrick recoiled from her son, stood up, and turned her back on the sofa, on her guests. She was quivering and hugging herself, and when she turned again, there were tears streaming down her face, and she had bitten her lip hard enough that a small trickle of blood went down her chin.

"How can you . . . how can you say that?" she whispered, sniffling, wiping away tears and blood. Then she shook her head again, with finality, and stared at Eve and Clay. "I don't believe it. I won't believe in it. I've never believed in angels and demons, no Heaven or Hell. That's all bullshit. None of it is real."

Eve began to stand, but Clay was faster. He moved around the chair and strode toward Mrs. Ferrick. She flinched as though afraid he might attack her. Clay passed her and went to the window, then quickly drew back the curtain.

"Have a look, Mrs. Ferrick. You've seen what's going on out there. Are you telling me none of that is real?"

She hesitated a moment, then joined him at the window. Clay looked with her, and together they gazed out at her neighborhood, overrun with a crimson fog, at the sun blacked out by an eclipse, at a swarm of mosquitoes that clung to a car as it careened down the street, tires squealing, only to bump up over the sidewalk and crash into a minivan parked in a driveway just a few houses away. The shattering of glass and crump of metal upon metal made the woman flinch.

"There are . . ." she began weakly, "there are explanations for it. All of it."

Clay sighed. He stepped in front of her, forcing the woman to look at him. "All right. All right. Give me an explanation, then, for this."

He reached out and touched her hand, and in an instant of painfully shifting bones and flesh that flowed like mercury, he *became* Julia Ferrick, right down to her gnawed fingernails and her crisp white blouse. The woman blinked and gasped for air, breath hitching in her throat as she stared at the mirror image of herself that he had become.

And then she fainted, tumbling so quickly toward the floor that Clay did not have a chance to catch her. He was only grateful that the living room was carpeted.

"Mom!" Danny called, running to her, kneeling beside her. The kid twisted his face up into a terrible grimace, and when he spoke again, it was in a rasping whisper. "I'm sorry. Sorry I'm not what you wanted."

Clay decided to give the boy a moment to collect himself. He stepped back, then looked over to where Eve was unfolding from her chair.

"That went well," she said.

Before Clay could respond to her sarcasm, he heard the squeal of tires yet again from outside the window. He turned, peering through the glass into the darkness beyond, and saw the limousine barreling through the suburban neighborhood. Its brakes screamed as it skidded to a halt in front of the Ferrick home and then slowly turned into the driveway.

"Eve," Clay said. "Trouble."

8

T O M Stanley stood above the grave of his recently departed mother and wept, hot scalding tears streaking his round, cherubic features. It was this way every time he visited, a deluge of sorrow for the woman who had meant the world to him.

He crouched upon his mother's grave and used the elbow of his jacket to rub imaginary fingerprints from her gray marble headstone. It had been set in place earlier that week by the groundskeepers of the Mount Auburn Cemetery, and Tom could not escape the certainty that they had marred it somehow. He paused, studied the gleaming marble, and then shook his head, buffing the stone again. His mother had been gone for a little more than two weeks, and already it felt like forever.

Strange shadows moved across the ground and Tom gazed up from his routine of sorrow, troubled by something he could not put a name to. The cemetery was strangely deserted this day, perhaps because the weather was so odd. Far off in the distance he heard what could have been the faint rumble of thunder. He wished that he had bothered to listen to a weather report before leaving the house. The sun was partially obscured by weird, shifting, gray clouds, and a strange reddish fog drifted just above the grave sites.

Like the red tide in the ocean, he thought. *What the hell is this? Biological warfare in the city of Cambridge?* He chuckled to himself, a bit giddy, a razor edge of hysteria bubbling just under the surface, as it had since his mother's death.

His gaze shifted back to the headstone. *Loving Mother,* he read through teary eyes and couldn't have agreed more with the simple inscription. He doubted there had ever been a mother more dedicated to her child's happiness than Patricia Stanley.

Tom removed a silver flask from his coat pocket and had another jolt of whiskey. He had been indulging more since his mother's passing, to help ease the pain of her loss, and was beginning to worry that a problem was developing. *That's all I need,* he thought, helping himself to another large swig before screwing the cap back on and returning the flask to his pocket, *another problem.*

Widowed not long after his birth, she had always been there for him, playing the role of both mother and father. He could still hear her voice as she defended her only son from accusations that he had been responsible for the deaths of some neighborhood cats and dogs. These were echoes of a past that seemed only yesterday, but in truth was so very long ago. That was the nature of time, though.

Time was a teasing bitch, and he wished that he could treat it like all the other teasing bitches who thought they were better than him.

How dare you accuse my Tommy! his mother had wailed. *To think my little boy could be responsible for such a thing is a sin!*

He was sure she had always known that he had killed

the pets. But she wasn't about to let them ruin her son's good name. And besides, they were only stupid animals; what harm had he really done?

Tom wished that she had been as understanding about the other killings.

Once again tears filled his eyes, and he wondered if he would ever feel happy again, or if there would only be grief for him now, forevermore. He had been coming here every day since her burial, hoping to experience some sense of closure, but all he felt was the gaping hole left by his loss.

He stared at the ground beneath his feet, imagining the fine mahogany coffin nestled in the grave below, and the peaceful countenance of the elderly woman at eternal rest within. How he hated to think of her down there, alone, without him to take care of her. She had been rather fragile in her last years and had needed more of his attention, but it had been the least he could do after the years she had devoted to him.

"Why did she have to die?" he asked aloud, dropping to his knees, the moisture from the dewy grass seeping through his pants. But it was a foolish question. He knew the answer. Tom leaned in and pressed his forehead against the cool marble of the gravestone.

She had to die because she was going to tell.

Animals were one thing, but people were another altogether. He wasn't exactly sure how she had found out about his nasty little avocation. Maybe she'd discovered the trophies he kept hidden in the footlocker beneath his bed, or even watched one of the special videos he'd made. He didn't know for sure, which was why it came as such a surprise when she ordered to him to stop or she'd inform the police.

"You made me so angry, Mom," he said, bringing a

beefy fist up to gently pound the marble. He fished in his pocket for his flask again and had himself another drink.

Tom had been doing his thing for years. The pets had been nothing but a warm-up to bigger and better things. He'd developed a real knack for zeroing in on the losers of the world, ones who would never be missed. Over time, he'd actually begun to think of himself as a kind of public servant, making the world a better place to live, one loser at a time.

How did she think he could just stop? Or that he would *want* to stop, for that matter?

The flask was empty, and he let it fall to the ground. "Why couldn't you understand?" he slurred, alcohol making his mouth a bit numb. He recalled her horror as he tried to explain why he did what he did, the immeasurable joy he received when he watched the light of life go out of their miserable eyes. But his mother didn't understand. She had begged him to stop, begged him to be the good boy that she always imagined him to be. But what his mother had asked of him was impossible.

Why? he asked again.

Tom pushed the troubling recollections from his mind and replaced them with thoughts of happier times—his memories of each murder—and immediately he felt soothed.

It was darker now, as if the sun had decided to pack it in early. The red mist continued to swirl about him. He wasn't sure he'd ever seen a fog so unusual. It was kind of creepy. Gripping the tombstone, he pulled his powerful bulk up, the bones in his knees popping in protest. It was times like these that reminded him there might come a day when he wouldn't be able to do what his mother so desperately wanted him to stop, that he would be too old. Just thinking it was enough to stoke the fires of his urge. It was as if a switch had been flicked inside his head, and he knew what he wanted to do—what he *had* to do.

It had been a little over two weeks since the desire was last satisfied. The memory of it flashed before his mind's eye. His mother was crying and carrying on, telling him that what he was doing was wrong, that he would go to jail, and who would take care of her then? She had been upstairs in the house they had shared since forever, changing the sheets on his bed, as she had every Tuesday for as long as he could remember. Dirty bedclothes in her arms, she had pushed past him, saying that he had left her no choice. She had to tell someone what he was doing, that it was all for his own good.

Tom had never thought of her as one of them—the losers that wanted to hurt him, to keep him down, but for a brief moment she had become the enemy. As she prepared to descend the winding staircase, he had thought about how dangerous it could be for an old woman to be performing the duties of a household. One terrible fall, and that would be that.

His left hand tingled with the memory of the act, and he brought it slowly up to his face, flexing his fingers. It had been the gentlest of pushes that sent the woman he had loved most in all the world tumbling down the wooden steps. She had landed in a twisted heap, her face covered with his dirty laundry.

She had still been alive. He'd gently pulled back the sheet that covered her face and found her wide-eyed and gasping, her neck bent in a most unnatural way. But the look in her eyes told him that death would soon claim her. He had seen that look many times before, and when it finally did come, the first tears of mourning had fallen from his eyes.

A horrible accident, the neighbors had whispered, and he had almost started to believe it was true.

Almost.

Tom wiped his eyes on the sleeve of his sports jacket and reached out to retrieve his empty flask. He slid it into a pocket and told his mother that he would be back again tomorrow. The urge to kill was growing stronger. He placed a kiss upon his fingertips and touched his mother's headstone.

As he turned away from the grave, he noticed movement in the fog. It was a woman, slowly walking amongst the graves. Tom squelched the murderous hunger that began to urge him on. *This is not the time or place,* yet he continued to watch the woman who moved stiffly toward him.

And then he noticed the others. They were all heading toward him, walking through the eerie red mist. It was a strange sort of exodus from the cemetery, and he wondered if anything was wrong. Puzzled, Tom fished through his pockets for the keys to his car and turned down the winding path that would take him to the parking lot.

A grave at the left of the path exploded, and Tom stumbled backward, reeling, as cold muddy earth and pieces of rotten wood pelted his face. The heel of his shoe caught the edge of a marker, and he went down on the grass.

The crowd was closer now and he prepared to yell to them, to ask for help. The words had almost left his mouth when he became distracted by motion in the darkness of the now open grave.

There was something, somebody crawling up out of the dirt. He guessed that it had been a woman, but only because it wore the tattered remains of a navy blue dress, and he could see a string of pearls still adorning the dry, leathery, brown skin of her throat. The woman hauled herself up out of the hole, rose stiffly to her feet, and shambled toward him with a gaseous gurgle.

He knew, then, of course. Knew exactly what he was

looking at. But that did not stop his mind from attempting to rationalize. The poor woman had somehow been buried alive and had managed to free herself. That was the only explanation he would allow.

"Are you all right?" he asked, as she lurched closer.

The mist cleared. And he *saw* her.

Her hands were covered in loose flesh like gloves two sizes too big. She had no eyes, just two empty sockets that squirmed with life uncomfortable being above the ground.

Tom Stanley began to scream, just as his victims had done.

All around him graves exploded, and he scrambled to his feet, lashing out at the decaying woman who blocked his path. The animated remains of the woman fell sideways, her skull striking a stone marker and shattering. He did not want to see what was inside the corpse's head and was thankful that the red mist obscured it from his view.

He screamed for help into the fog. There had to be other mourners nearby. From the corner of his eye he saw movement upon the ground. Hissing things clawed their way up from other graves and dragged what remained of themselves across the grass toward him.

A powerful hand came down upon his shoulder, skeletal fingers digging into his flesh. He spun out of its grasp and turned to see that it was the woman he had first noticed in the red mist. He tried to flee, hopping over the things crawling on the ground in the swirling fog. But she grabbed him again and he was forced to push her away, to *touch* her.

Her flesh was like wet clay.

"Bitch," he snapped, stepping back as she reached for him. Savagely, he slapped her hand away as the others slowly emerged from the crimson fog, all of them decayed and covered with grave dirt.

Part of him wanted to cry, to lay down upon the ground

and curl up into a ball, begging for his mother's protection. But he knew he couldn't. He had to get away or they would get him for sure. It had to be the mist, something in the weird fog that made them come back from the dead.

They surged toward him, the noises they made horrible. He turned to run, but the ground erupted beneath his feet and he felt his ankle clutched in a powerful grip. He fell hard to the ground, the wind knocked from his lungs in an explosive wheeze. Tom rolled over, gasping for air, trying to free himself from the grasp of the pale hand that had reached up through the dirt and grass.

The dead were closer now. He could see their horrible faces and knew them all. They had come for him—all the losers he had killed over the years—and they had brought along friends. They shuffled closer, smiling, mocking him as they always had done.

Tom lay back upon the moist earth, overwhelmed by their number, throwing his hands over his face, curling himself into a tight little ball. "Mommy!" he shrieked, his eyes clamped shut against the horrors bearing down on him, and he felt a cold, gentle caress upon his cheek. Opening his eyes he saw that they still loomed above him. He knew them all, each and every one.

But one he knew better than all the rest.

She knelt at his side, her head bent oddly to the left as she smiled at him.

"Mommy?" he asked, certain that his prayers had been answered and she had come to save him from the monsters that wanted to make him feel so small. He reached up and pulled her into his arms. "I missed you so much, Mommy," he said. He felt the cold flesh of her face press tightly against his cheek, and she moved her head to plant an affectionate kiss upon his lips.

He tried to pull away but her lips pressed firmly against his, and her teeth, so incredibly sharp, had found his tongue. She tore it from his mouth. Tom could no longer speak.

He couldn't even scream.

DR. Graves fought his way back into the world of the living, his spectral energies forcing through the membranous covering that separated the physical plane from the realm of the dead. *Like being born again,* he thought as he materialized in the room designated for him on the second floor of Conan Doyle's Beacon Hill townhouse. The insistent tug of the afterlife was severed by his manifestation in the material world.

The room was filled with mementos of the many adventures he had undertaken during his life. Souvenirs were displayed about the room, multiple framed newspaper headlines a reminder of what he had been to the world. His ghostly eyes scanned the objects and headlines, remembering the details of his achievements. It had been a good life—a full life—and a familiar, bitter question rose in his mind. *Would it be so bad to let go? To finally succumb to the pull of the stream?* Each time he visited the afterworld, it was harder to return, to fight against the current of the gate, and the reality of what lay beyond it. The ultimate mystery awaited him there, one that had baffled the human species since they had first walked erect, and one that he hungered to solve.

But there was another more personal mystery that required his attentions first, before he could even think about giving himself to the stream. Graves' eyes fell upon a particular headline, and he felt the same insatiable rage, the same desire for justice that filled him each time he read it. *"Dr. Graves Dead! Famed Adventurer Shot! Identity of Killer Still Unknown!"*

It was a comfort, surrounding himself with memories,

and a tether to his past, but it also served to fuel the rage and frustration he still felt at his inability to solve the mystery of his own murder. He would find the one who killed him, the one who stole away his life. But until that time came, Dr. Leonard Graves would do as he had always done, fight to keep the world safe from harm.

The ghost returned his attentions to the case at hand. He had to speak to Conan Doyle. In his mind's eye, he again saw Yvette Darnall as she was pulled away by the soul-stream. *What was it she said about the fears of the dead, just before the gate drew her in?*

Something calls to them, trying to drag them back . . . to their bodies.

Graves was startled from his musings by a clamorous din. He presumed it was only Squire beginning yet another of his frequent home-improvement projects, but this was hardly the best time for such endeavors. Walking was an affectation for a specter, of course, but still Graves preferred it when inside the house. He found it unsettling to simply propel his ectoplasmic form along by the force of his will, and he was certain others did as well. So though he did not bother with the door, passing instead right through the wall, he did so by striding from his room into the corridor as though he were an ordinary, flesh and blood man.

At the last moment, the oddness of the clamor he had heard troubled him further. What if that noise was not Squire's doing? As he emerged into the hall, he willed himself to be unseen.

And then he froze. What he saw there in the corridor filled the ghost with dread.

The enemy had invaded their headquarters.

Coppery-skinned creatures moved about the hall, excitedly speaking to one another in a harsh, guttural tongue as they kicked open doors in a search for the townhouse's occupants. *Corca-Duibhne,* he thought. Based upon Eve and Conan Doyle's description, these could only be the Night People. Graves watched as four of the leather-clad creatures emerged from the bedroom Conan Doyle always kept ready for Eve. The creatures had an article of her clothing, a silk blouse he'd seen her wear on more than one occasion, and were tearing it into pieces, each taking a swatch, bringing it to their upturned, piggish noses, and inhaling her scent.

How is this possible? Graves wondered. The protective wards Conan Doyle had placed around the house should have been more than sufficient to prevent the infestation of these lowly creatures. But here they were, moving freely about the premises.

The Corca-Duibhne finished with Eve's scent and began cautiously moving toward the door to Dr. Graves' own bedroom. Because they could neither see nor scent him, they would pass right by him. He debated whether or not he should confront them and decided that it would be wiser, for the moment, merely to observe. He had no idea, after all, how many of them there were, and whether or not his comrades were in the house, or if any of his friends had been injured.

The obvious leader of the quartet motioned for his brethren to step back, preparing to kick open the door to his room.

Bastards, Graves seethed. *They don't even have the common courtesy to see if it's locked.*

Since meeting his death, Dr. Leonard Graves had grown more cautious, but it didn't mean that the reckless instincts of the adventurer were completely gone. He couldn't help himself. Still invisible to the creatures, he drifted up behind the Corca-Duibhne and slid his spectral hand into the back of their leader, ghostly fingers plunging into the thing's flesh.

The creature froze, a violent shudder passing through its thin body. Then the Corca-Duibhne whipped around with a ferocious snarl, lashing out at its startled teammates, and they began to fight amongst themselves.

Graves smiled, but his amusement was disrupted by the oddest sensation, like a tremor passing through the very fabric of the world.

Magick.

The heavy wooden door at the end of the hall, which hid the entrance to Faerie, exploded violently open, crashing into the wall behind it. Graves floated back, his spirit pummeled by powerful, magickal emanations flowing from the open door. The Corca-Duibhne cowered.

A woman of obvious Fey descent stepped from the doorway, supernatural discharge crackling about her statuesque form. She was dressed in black leather and moved with a casual predatory grace that informed Graves that here was the real enemy. Two men, also bearing the physical characteristics of Faerie, flanked her, listening intently to her every word.

"That is the last of the passages to Faerie. With that path sealed, there will be no interference from the Fey," she announced, a smile slashing across her severe countenance. "I do so get a thrill when a plan comes together."

Though he had no flesh to feel with, a chill went through Graves. He had no idea if this witch knew it, but Conan Doyle was in Faerie even now. If she'd closed all the doors between the worlds, Conan Doyle would be trapped there. *This is not good, not good at all.* He was debating what to do next when he noticed that the woman was staring in his direction. The Night People, still cowering in front of his bedroom door, dropped to their knees under her withering gaze.

"What is that behind you?" she asked, eyes sparking

with menace as she pointed a clawed finger in his direction.

The Corca-Duibhne leaped to their feet and spun around, unsuccessfully searching the air for his presence.

Is it possible? Graves wondered. *Can she see me?*

With a sound like grease on a hot pan, thick strings of magickal energy erupted from the woman's fingertips, and Graves knew that the answer was yes. The putrid yellow tendrils tore through the Corca-Duibhne in their path, leaving them squealing and writhing upon the floor.

With the speed of thought, Graves shot up toward the ceiling, avoiding the attack. Though he was dead, ectoplasm did exude a kind of spirit energy. Somehow, this sorceress could see that energy. He made a mental note to ask Conan Doyle about the visual range of the Fey for future reference.

"Come to Morrigan, little spirit," the Fey sorceress whispered, manipulating the tendrils of magickal power as an extension of her grasp.

Morrigan. Graves was certain he had heard the name before, but he didn't have time to search his vast memory for all the facts. Best to simply get out of there, try to find out what had happened to the others. He floated upward even further, beginning to pass through the ceiling. One of the mystic tendrils snagged his ankle, and pain the likes of which he had not imagined possible in the afterlife engulfed his lower leg and began to spread. The air around his captured limb began to shimmer and wave, and he saw that where he had been touched by the witch's magick, he was becoming visible.

"There you are," Morrigan hissed, manipulating more of the energies to take hold of him.

Ghosts were insubstantial, often unable to influence the physical world at all. But the supernatural was something else entirely. Graves sometimes had trouble touching a human being, or anything of the human world, but monsters and magick . . . he could combat them. Unfortunately, this meant that he was vulnerable to their touch as well.

Graves tried to block the pain, a trick he had mastered in life and never expected to need in death. He was tugged toward the floor. More tendrils converged upon him, sensing the air for his whereabouts, using his gradually materializing foot for reference. He didn't have much time. For a moment, he ceased his struggles. The string of magick that gripped his ankle loosened, just slightly. With every ounce of his will, he tore himself away from its grasp and darted down through the floor to the level below.

The foyer swarmed with invading Corca-Duibhne, and they began to panic as Morrigan shrieked from the floor above them. Graves flowed through the amassed Night People, who stumbled about the townhouse lobby, banging into one another in alarm. Then he was through the battered front door and out into the freedom of the night.

The neighborhood was deathly quiet except for the wails of a dog howling in the distance. The animal was afraid, and Graves did not blame him in the least. Things had grown worse since his departure to the spirit realms. A thick, rolling fog, the color of dried blood, covered the ground and blotted out any light from the sky.

The ghost rose above Louisburg Square, the pain pulsing through his leg just starting to fade. He hovered above the rooftops and gazed in awe at the city below him. The unnatural mist seemed to hold it captive, and shapes that even at this distance he could tell were not human shambled upon the streets. He dove down toward them for a closer look and recoiled at the sight. Corpses in various stages of decomposition were making their way through the streets, all moving in the same direction, as if being drawn to something.

Graves could sense the turmoil of the souls trapped

within the moldering remains, and then he understood the final words of the psychic Yvette Darnall. Something had dragged the spirits back to their putrefying bodies, intent on using them for some insidious purpose that he had yet to fathom.

Graves rose again into the air, watching the dead march down Beacon Street through the blood-red fog. Conan Doyle was gone. He knew he had to find his other allies, but first he needed to learn more about what was drawing the dead back from the afterworld. *At the very least,* he thought, as he watched them all streaming in the same direction, *I want to find out where they're headed.*

"BLAST!" Conan Doyle bellowed above the shrieking winds that had abruptly torn through the quiet of the forest. He planted his feet firmly upon the moss-covered ground, fighting the sucking void that attempted to pull him in. He had been trying to reopen the doorway from Faerie to his home, but it was no longer there. In its place was a swirling vortex, a churning vacuum that tugged at him, a magickal trap that would consume him and anything else within the reaches of its voracious hunger.

Fighting the pull of the maelstrom, he threw himself backward, landing hard on the forest floor.

"Arthur!" Ceridwen screamed, her voice barely audible over the mournful wail of the vortex.

Struggling against the pull of the current, Conan Doyle turned onto his stomach and sunk his fingers into the soft earth, trying to drag himself away from that sucking hole in the fabric of Faerie. He saw Ceridwen now, anchored to a nearby tree with one hand. In the other, she still held her elemental staff. The flame within the sphere of ice that capped that length of wood glowed like a miniature sun, aroused by the presence of dangerous magicks.

The strength of the maelstrom increased, and for every inch of progress he made toward Ceridwen, he felt himself pulled back by three. The two sentries that had escorted him earlier cowered nearby, holding on to one another for dear life. One had managed to grab hold of an ancient vine beneath a cover of loose dirt and leaves and was using it to secure them against the inexorable pull.

It had happened so quickly. They had decided to return to his townhouse in the world of Blight and had used the magick of the ancients to open the door. He had not even considered the possibility that a threat might be present, not even taken basic precautions. *Arrogant fool! Bloody amateur,* he fumed, even as the screaming void dragged him closer. *Walked right into that one like some novice.*

The sentries cried out in fear, and Conan Doyle lifted his gaze to see them sail above his head, still clinging to one another, broken vine trailing behind them like the tail of a kite, as they were consumed by the hungry whirlpool. Spells and incantations flooded Conan Doyle's mind, but he could not concentrate long enough to cast one. Then, as if some powerful beast had grabbed hold of him, he was violently torn from his purchase upon the ground, and he knew that his time was up.

He thought he heard the voice of Sanguedolce mocking him for his arrogance, but realized that it wasn't the voice of the archmage that he heard at all, but that of his former lover.

"Is being sucked into the abyss part of your plan, good sir?" Ceridwen called to him over the din that filled the wood.

A tether of magickal force engulfed his body, suspending him in the air before the hungry void. His body crackled with an icy blue corona of supernatural energy.

"If it be so, I question the soundness of your judgment," the Fey sorceress yelled, as she emerged from her place of safety behind the great tree, her staff extended. She had changed clothes for traveling to the human world and now wore a hooded blue-green cloak and handwoven trousers the color of sand. In the swirl of the vortex, her cloak fluttered and the effect created in her attire the illusion of the ocean crashing on the shore. The sphere of power at the staff's end glowed once more, ice and flame combined by Faerie magick into a cold blue fire, providing him his lifeline. She fought the pull of the trap, struggling to keep her footing.

The maelstrom increased its pull upon the forest, and he listened to the creaking moans of the trees as their tenacity was tested. Ceridwen fell to her knees, sliding across the forest floor, but still she held her elemental staff high, maintaining her concentration and preventing him from being drawn into the spiraling hole.

Conan Doyle cleared his head and found the invocation that would suit his needs. He spun around to face the insatiable gyre and uttered a string of powerful words. The mage extended his arms and felt the might of the ancients flow through him. The countering magick streamed from the tips of his fingers, and his spell began to knit closed the rip that had been torn in time and space.

The portal to chaos fought him, screaming and howling, but his magick was stronger. Sensing imminent victory, he roared the last of the incantation. The swirling maelstrom imploded with a thunderous clap of sound that knocked him and Ceridwen through the air, back across the ravaged clearing.

An eerie stillness came over the forest and Conan Doyle slowly rose, checking for breaks and injuries. He glanced up to find Ceridwen standing where the vortex had been, passing her staff through the air, verifying that the rift had indeed been closed completely.

"I'm fine," he said.

She turned and narrowed her gaze, looking at him coldly. "Plead your pardon?" she asked, confused.

"I said I'm fine." Conan Doyle brushed dirt and debris from his clothing. "Just in case you were concerned with my well-being." He knew he was being curt, but at the moment, her total disregard for his welfare was maddening.

"I see," she said, expressionless. Emotionless. She turned her attentions back to the spot where the maelstrom had been. "All trace of the entryway to your home, to your world, is gone. The last of the known gateways between Faerie and the world of Blight is no more."

Conan Doyle felt a tremor of something akin to fear in his heart. If Morrigan had been inside his home, the situation in his world had become most dire indeed.

"We shall have to build a new one," he said. The process was time-consuming, but there was simply no choice. "We'll return to the kingdom immediately and—"

"No," Ceridwen interrupted. "There is no time for that."

Conan Doyle glared at her. "What else do you suggest? If that was the last entryway, then we have to conjure another."

Ceridwen turned her back to him and began to walk away. "It was the last of the *known* entrances," she said, striding deeper into the dark wood.

"But I know of another."

9

GRAVES needed perspective.

Insubstantial, he nevertheless felt some resistance as he floated high above the city of Boston. The unnatural darkness caught at his ectoplasmic form with a million tiny claws, and the red fog seemed to slow him. From high above he tried to peer through the mist, and he knew he had to get closer to the ground.

It took a moment for him to make sense of the city's topography, only the shapes of the buildings visible to him from this height. He had fled from Conan Doyle's Beacon Hill home, but not gone very far. As he descended, he could make out Boston Common below, and turning, he saw the Massachusetts State House, a grand old building capped by a massive golden dome, the beacon of Beacon Hill. Graves chose that as his destination.

In a handful of seconds, no time at all for the dead, he alighted upon the State House's golden dome and steadied himself. All of that was illusion, of course, solidity imagined into reality by his own desire, but it was comforting to him to hold on to the tangibility of the world that had been lost to him for more than half a century. Others could not feel his presence, but he could touch them.

Leonard Graves could still feel.

Atop the golden dome he paused to collect his thoughts, and he gazed at the city that spread out from the base of Beacon Hill. In the decades since his death, he had been witness to three other uprisings of the dead, none of them on a scale even close to this one. Dr. Graves was an analytical man. His mind had made the connections between Morrigan, the strange red mist, and the resurrected dead immediately.

Now, as he peered through a nightmare of darkness and bloody fog, he could see a number of forms shambling across Boston Common and others on Tremont Street. Though it was impossible to know for sure in the fog and the dark, logic dictated that they must be the dead. No sane living human being would be out on the streets now.

The dead were walking south.

Graves frowned, wondering why, and then he pushed the question aside. He was not going to have an answer quickly, and there were other priorities. He had to locate Conan Doyle and the others. Eve and Clay had been sent off on some errand or another, but he did not know to where. That was his only lead.

Another question lingered in his mind.

Why not me?

The spirits of the dead were being drawn back into their bodies, but Dr. Graves was a specter himself. A ghost. Some terrible power was dragging those souls who were still floating in the ether back to their rotting corpses, even to their moldering bones. He had seen some torn from the river of souls itself. Yet he did not feel the slightest tug upon his spirit.

Why? The red mist is expanding, ballooning outward. Perhaps only those who died here, upon the grounds

*touched by the mist, are affected. Or perhaps wandering
ghosts, the restless dead, those like me who refuse to be
drawn into the soulstream, are not affected. Or perhaps
there is simply not enough left of my body, now, for even
magick to put into motion.*

Graves did not know what, precisely, was going on. He
did not have answers to these questions. But he would find
them. And to begin, he knew there were places he might
investigate that could lead him further along both of his
lines of inquiry.

He pushed himself off the State House dome, its golden
surface a dark, hellish orange as it took what little light
was available and reflected the red mist. As he passed over
Boston Common, drifting just above the trees now, he confirmed one of his suspicions. He was not the only ghost
unaffected. The lonely shades of several homeless men
wandered the park, resting on park benches and picking
imaginary garbage out of trash cans, acting out the routines
of their lives.

They had died there on the Common, these men. Unless
they had been cremated, it had been recently enough that
there would certainly have been enough left of their remains to make an effective zombie. That was possible, but
the more he considered, the more he began to think that
one of his other theories was more likely. These homeless
men had been lost souls long before they were dead. As
ghosts, they walked the paths that had been familiar in life
and seemed not to feel the pull of the river of souls at all.
They were kept here by the infirmity of their minds, even
as Graves himself was anchored to the mortal plane by his
obsession with the mystery of his own murder. He felt certain his theory was correct, that ghosts who still haunted
this world were immune to this magick as long as they remained here and did not slip into the soulstream.

Dr. Graves left the Common and propelled his spectral

form along Tremont Street past the Park Street Church. Tucked in amongst buildings to the left and right, and abutting it to the rear, was the Old Granary Burying Ground. It was a strange cemetery, located in what some might have taken to be an empty building lot left behind by a demolition crew if not for the low wrought-iron fence. The burial ground was a tiny plot of land where eighteenth-century headstones thrust from the ground, and a recitation of the names read like a litany of American history.

Paul Revere was buried there. A short way further along a narrow path that weaved beneath shade trees was the grave of John Hancock. Samuel Adams had been interred at the Old Granary as well, along with all of the victims of the Boston Massacre and the parents of Benjamin Franklin. It was a quiet place of reflection in the center of the city, a piece of its history. Graves always thought it shameful that throngs of admirers visited the edifices left behind by the great hearts and minds of any generation, and rarely their graves.

It was no wonder that none of their ghosts had lingered on this plane.

That did not mean the Old Granary Burying Ground was devoid of ghosts, however.

Dr. Graves passed through the black wrought-iron fence and alighted upon the ragged lawn, pretending to himself that he could feel the ground beneath his shoes. The walls of the buildings that rose up to block in the other three sides of the burial ground were imposing, but with the red-black sky and the scarlet fog, they lent a sense of security as well. He glanced up, and then over his shoulder, but he was alone.

"Christopher?" Graves ventured, his voice drifting amongst the headstones with the fog.

"Hello, Leonard."

The voice was close by, almost in his ear, and Graves

darted away even as he spun around in surprise. Decades
of phantom life ought to have made him immune to being
startled in such fashion, but clearly they had not. And the
ghost of Christopher Snider knew it.

"This is hardly the time for games, Chris," Dr. Graves
chided him.

The spectral boy was lanky, yet handsome, his appearance precisely the same as it had been on that day in late
February of 1770, when he had been shot by a British soldier, just eleven days before the Boston Massacre. The wry
grin on the ghost's face, however, revealed that though his
shade mimicked the body he'd had in life, his mind had
continued to grow. He was no boy. He was a specter. Centuries old. Yet there was still something of the child in him.
An enigma, then, this phantom boy. Graves had never been
able to discover just what anchored Christopher Snider to
the mortal plane. Perhaps one day, he thought, the boy
would feel enough at ease with him to tell him. For now, if
not friends, they were at least allies in the battle against the
despair that threatened all the lingering, wandering dead.

"My apologies, sir," Christopher said, giving Dr.
Graves a small bow. The ghostly boy was grimly serious
now. "You are right, of course. It was only that I was
pleased to see you. I know of your penchant for involving
yourself in calamitous situations. I was certain you would
be at the center of whatever is causing this horror."

Graves nodded, glancing toward the street. "I plan to
be. But to do that, I need to find Eve. And to find Eve, I
need your help."

A ripple went through the ectoplasm that made up the
shade of Christopher Snider. His upper lip curled back in
distaste. The ghostly boy seemed to withdraw, but he did
not actually retreat from Graves. Rather, his spirit thinned
and became less defined so that the red mist flowed
through him and nearly obscured his features.

"You know my feelings about the Children of Eve," Christopher said.

"I do," Graves confirmed. "That's why I ask. You hate them. But you always know when there are vampires in the city. You've got some sort of ethereal grapevine going, tracking them. I know you've helped Eve with her hunt in the past."

"Look around, Chris," Graves said, gesturing with translucent hands toward the city around and above them. "It's safe to say there's no time to waste. I need to know if there are any of them in the city right now. And where."

The ghost drifted away, toward the wrought-iron fence where he could look down upon Tremont Street. Graves followed him and lingered just at his side. A car was parked up on the sidewalk, locked and abandoned in a hurry. Along the road were others in the same condition. Graves thought he saw silhouettes inside one of them, people who had simply pulled over when the chaos had begun and now were likely too afraid to venture on, no matter how badly they wished to be home.

"Christopher?" Dr. Graves whispered, his voice a ghost itself.

"I know," the spectral young man replied, nodding. He glanced at Graves. "I apologize. To search for any of Eve's Children without intending to kill them is difficult for me to grasp."

Dr. Graves had always suspected that vampires had something to do with the boy's death, despite the story about the British soldier. Either that, or he had seen loved ones murdered by the monsters. But now was not the time to pry.

"If it helps, I can assure you the creature will come to no good end."

"Of course it helps," replied the ghostly boy with a hollow laugh. "As much as anything will."

Graves waited for more, for an answer to the question he had posed, doing his best to feign patience he did not feel. When he felt he could not wait any longer, he spoke the ghost's name. "Christopher—"

"Do you know what my favorite memory is, Leonard? It was in 1831, right here. Or, rather, there in the Evangelical Church. The children's choir sang beautifully in those days, but on that particular day they sang a new song, freshly written. The song had never been sung before, not publicly. It was 'My Country, 'tis of Thee.' Do you know it?"

Startled by this turn in the conversation, Graves frowned and stared at him. "Of course I do."

Christopher smiled in remembrance. "Yes, yes. Of course you do." Then he turned to Graves, and there was nothing at all of the child in his spectral features any longer. "That is my most precious memory, Leonard. And it happened more than sixty years after my death. The irony is painful sometimes."

He sighed and looked around the fog-enshrouded cemetery before glancing back at Dr. Graves.

"I'm told that one of Eve's Children has made its nest in the Regency Theatre on Charles Street. There was a fire there last year, you know. The owners have promised to rebuild, but so far nothing has been done."

"You know so much about this city, but I've never seen you further from your grave than this gate."

"I listen," the ghostly boy said. "They walk by, the living, and they don't know anyone's here. They talk. And I listen."

Dr. Graves was reluctant to leave. Christopher had never been so open with him, never seemed so willing to talk about his haunting of the burial ground. But the red mist churned around them and the sky was dark and the dead were walking out on the streets of Boston.

"Thank you, Chris. I'm sorry I have to go. Maybe—"

"Go," the other ghost said, waving him off. "Perhaps you and your friends can stop all of this. Come back when you can. I'm not going anywhere."

With nothing more to say, Graves began to rise, floating away from the burial ground. He traveled quickly now, the buildings little more than a blur around him. There were several churches nearby, and it occurred to him that the people who had abandoned their vehicles might well have fled to those edifices of faith. Hopeful voices would be raised within. Prayers would be sung or spoken.

Dr. Graves had wondered all his life—and thereafter—whether anyone was listening.

He drifted through the scarlet fog, following Tremont Street for a while and then climbing above the buildings. Graves did not like to pass through structures unless they were his destination. There was something unsettling about it, but also it felt to him as though he were intruding upon the privacy of whoever might live or work within them.

Charles Street had a string of old theaters and play-houses, some still used for traditional theater and others as comedy stages. The Regency had once had a beautiful facade, but it had faded over time, as such things did. Then at the twilight of the twentieth century, it had been restored, not only outside, but within. The stage and the curtains and the beautiful art on the domed ceiling inside the theater had all been brought back to their original beauty and luster.

And then the blaze had ruined it all.

Firefighters had been able to stop the flames before they had completely gutted the building, but the elegance of the place had been eradicated, charred beyond recognition. As the weeks and months had gone by, the hope that insurance would allow the owners to start anew began to dwindle. A police cordon still blocked the entrance to the Regency Theatre, but such things do not keep out homeless people searching for a place to shield themselves from the elements and willing to risk the dilapidated architecture crumbling on them.

Nor did such cautionary postings keep out vampires.

Insubstantial as the red mist—perhaps even more so—Dr. Graves passed through a boarded-up window and was inside the shadowy skeleton of the theater. The place still reeked of burnt wood. Graves drifted above the balcony and looked around at blackened remnants of a once grand structure, and he thought how fortunate it was that the place had been empty when the fire had started.

The vampire had made its nest in the orchestra pit.

For the most part, ghosts were intangible. But Graves had quickly learned that while it took phenomenal effort to touch a human being, he had no difficulty laying hands on supernatural creatures.

It was a male vampire, a thin, filthy thing in stolen clothes with long, greasy blond hair.

"Child of Eve," Graves said, floating down toward it.

The vampire looked up quickly, startled, its jaundiced yellow eyes glowing in the dark. It tried to fight him.

Tried, and failed.

FOR perhaps the hundredth time since the sky had gone dark, Katherine Matthews picked up the phone and listened to the hiss of dead air. There was no dial tone, nor any of the other signals the phone company sent when there was trouble on the line. No fast busy. Not even that annoying beeping it made if she left it off the hook. The first few times she had picked up the phone, she had spoken up, asked if there was anyone else on the line. But there was no one there. Just that hiss.

Yet if she listened for half a minute or so, couldn't she make out something inside that hiss? A kind of pattern, like the gusting of the wind. The hiss seemed tremulous, as though the dead air on her phone line was laughing at her.

Katie Matthews had owned Lost and Found Books for seventeen years. It was not merely her business, however. It was her home. The shop was on the first floor of her house in Cambridge, just north of Boston, and she lived alone in a quartet of rooms in the second story. But for now she sat behind the checkout counter near the front door of the bookshop, where she had been ever since the darkness had fallen and the bloody mist had rolled in.

She was used to being by herself in the store. As silly as it sounded, she always told people she could never really be alone there, not with all the books. Lost and Found was overflowing with hardcovers and paperbacks, new and used, of all types of genres. In the back there was even a section of antiquarian books. The typical customer never bothered to even wander into the rear of the shop, but there were always those discerning clients who knew precisely what they were looking for and would peruse those shelves.

Katie had been tempted at first to retreat to the antiquarian section, but the only windows were at the front of the shop, and the idea of being unable to see what was going on outside terrified her even more than the view beyond the windows. If anything worse happened, she would be trapped back there. From here she could at least run up the stairs to her apartment.

Only to be trapped *there*.

She didn't want to think about it anymore, but there was no one to call, no one to talk to. The only escape she could think of was the one she had been using her entire life. Once she had hung the phone up, she picked up the copy of *Cold Sassy Tree* she had been delving into. It wasn't the sort of thing she usually read, but it was the first book she had laid her hand upon when she had reached for something to hang on to, somewhere to escape.

Outside the mosquitoes were gone. All of them, as far as she could tell. And that was something, at least. But now . . . there were figures moving through the red mist. At first she had thought about unlocking a window and calling out to them, asking what was going on. The radio did not work and neither did the small TV behind the counter.

But there was something off, something more than a little odd, about the way those figures were walking. They moved in a kind of rhythmic stagger that felt like a warning to Katie. So she kept the windows closed and locked, for all the good the glass would do if someone really wanted in. And she kept quiet, and she read, and after every few pages she glanced up and hoped the mist would be gone and the sun returned, and she picked up the phone and prayed for a dial tone.

Only to have the dead air laugh at her again.

Her skin prickled with awareness that all was not right, and her pulse raced, but she forced herself back into the book. She was past the halfway mark but knew she had only registered a fraction of what she had read. Much as she wished to get completely lost in those pages, she knew she was fooling herself. There might not be a book in the world that was powerful enough to help her escape from this.

Katie read a few pages further when there was a creak in the old boards of her house. It was a familiar sound, and late at night it gave her comfort. An old house moved with the wind. But there was no comfort in it this day. She glanced up at the sound, and her eyes were drawn to the window once more. The bloody fog rolled past the glass, thick and damp, leaving a red film on each pane.

With a sigh she reached out and lifted up the phone again, cursing herself for doing it even as she raised it to her ear. It was foolish to keep doing this. Obsessive-compulsive idiocy. But she could not help herself, though she knew what she would hear.

Nothing.

She told herself it was nothing.

Another creak drew her attention, but this one was followed by a thump and a rustling noise, from deeper inside the shop.

Katie could not breathe. Her lungs were frozen. Her eyes were open almost too wide as she hung up the phone and moved around the counter. There were only dim overhead lights at the back of the store, in the antiquarian section, but now a brighter light pulsed there, a blue-green glow that cast the entire section in its oceanic hue.

Soft thumps issued from the antiquarian section.

Katie's chest hurt from holding her breath, but she felt as though she could draw no air. Her shoes scuffed the wooden floor as she shuffled past shelves overflowing with books. The musty smell of old paper filled her nostrils. That aqua glow pulsed, turning her clothes and her hands that same color, even as she moved deeper into the store.

She paused a moment and closed her eyes. With all the concentration she could muster, she focused on taking a breath, and soon she was shuddering as she inhaled sharply. She kept her eyes closed, trying to steady her breathing. When she opened them, she glanced at the front of the shop again, saw that the view from her windows had not changed, and nodded to herself.

Once again she began to move toward that glow, that rustle and thump.

Katie felt a soft breeze caress her face and she gasped again, blinking in surprise. There was a scent on that breeze, the smell of earth and flowers and trees ripe with fruit. She shook her head and reached up to touch her face where the breeze had whispered past her.

She was just at the arch that led into the antiquarian section when there came another small thump. Her gaze was drawn instantly to the left, to the third shelf from the top, to a leather-bound book that seemed almost not to belong here. Most of the books in this section had bindings that were dried and cracked and faded, but the leather covering this tome was fresh and supple so that it seemed almost new. It gleamed in that blue-green light, and the way it sat on the shelf, it jutted from its place, as though someone had pulled it out several inches.

And it moved. Ever so slightly, it moved.

The book seemed to jump in its slot, there on the shelf, edging further out from the other volumes.

It tilted, and then it tumbled, end over end, and struck the floorboards, falling open with a ruffle of pages. Katie let out a small cry and put a hand over her heart as if to warn it to slow down.

That blue-green light flashed more brightly than ever, and she had to shield her eyes. In that moment the breeze that had caressed her swirled around her again, tousling her hair, and the scents it carried were so delicious she thought she had been carried away, finally given the escape that she had longed for.

Then the light retreated and she blinked away the shadows behind her eyelids.

Two figures stood with her in the antiquarian section of Lost and Found Books. Once again Katie Matthews felt as though she could not breathe. One of them was a dignified-looking man with a graying mustache and a wrinkled suit. Katie thought she recognized the man from century-old photographs.

The other was a stunningly beautiful woman of imposing height, clad in a cloak the color of evergreens in winter. She clutched in her hand an oaken staff, topped by a sphere of ice, with a flicker of flame inside. An elemental staff. Her eyes were a bright violet.

Katie's hands fluttered as though she had forgotten what to do with them, and a lightness came over her heart that nearly made her faint. Almost giddy, she went down on one knee and lowered her head. Once upon a time, years before, she had read the wrong book and opened the wrong door, and it had been Ceridwen who had closed it for her. She had pledged her loyalty to the Fey on that day, like a handful of others she had met in the ages since. But she had never seen Ceridwen in the flesh again.

Until today.

"My Lady Ceridwen," she said, her voice cracking, shaking with emotion.

Ceridwen touched her head.

"You've done well, Katherine. You are our loyal friend."

Katie took a deep breath and looked up at Ceridwen, at the power in those eyes. This woman was everything she had ever wished to be, and yet rather than making Katie feel small, somehow Ceridwen lifted her up, gave her pride in herself.

"Something terrible is happening outside," Katie said, forcing her voice not to tremble.

"We know," Ceridwen replied, already striding toward the front of the shop, her companion hard on her heels. "Do not worry yourself, Katherine. You have done just as we asked, for so very long, kept that book safe and our secret in your own heart. I can do no less than keep you safe in return."

At the door, Ceridwen turned and stared at her, and Katie felt blessed.

"We will weave protections around the house. Do not step outside this door until the sun returns to the sky."

Then Ceridwen and her companion went out the door, closing it tightly behind them, leaving Katie with only the delightful scents of Faerie floating in the air to mark their passing. After a moment she sighed happily and picked up the book from the floor. Its leather was not scuffed at all from the fall. She held it in her hands and then allowed herself a bittersweet smile before sliding it back onto the shelf.

She would have given anything to reverse Ceridwen's trip, to travel through the pages of that book through to the other side, to Faerie. One day, she prayed that Ceridwen would grant her that wish. And she knew that if that day ever came, she would never want to come back.

10

A tiny ember of fury burned in Morrigan's black heart. She had not expected to find an errant phantom in Conan Doyle's home, but even had she known, she would not have wasted a moment thinking on it. What was a ghost, after all, to her power? They were fragments, figments, the echo of a spirit. But whoever this ghost was, he had knowledge that he should not have, and Conan Doyle might well have other allies. The damned specter had escaped her, thwarted her, and Morrigan was not pleased.

She was not concerned about it raising opposition to her. Nothing could stand in her way now. But just the idea that a damnable figment had escaped her was infuriating.

No, she told herself. *Enough.* With great effort, she forced thoughts of the ghost from her mind. Triumph was at hand. Elation. Divinity. She was not about to allow a minor annoyance to spoil that. She had other, far more thrilling matters to attend to.

Several of the Corca-Duibhne vermin under her thrall scattered from her path as she strode down the corridor of Conan Doyle's home to a room whose broad double doors stood open to receive her. Morrigan swept into the high-ceilinged chamber and surveyed the room. It had once been used as a ballroom but now appeared to be a storage place for pieces of mechanical equipment that she imagined Conan Doyle and his lackeys used to keep their fragile forms physically fit. The exercise equipment had been pushed out of the way, up against the mirrored walls, to make room for the amber-encased body of Sweetblood the Mage.

The chrysalis rested in the center of the room, and though that strange magickal sarcophagus stifled the mage's power, Morrigan could still feel it emanating from within. She had stationed several Corca-Duibhne around the chrysalis as guards, but they kept their distance from Sanguedolce. Inert or no, he was so powerful a mage that their entire race feared him.

Morrigan laughed softly, amused by their furtive glances toward the chrysalis. Their nearly primitive brains were incapable of realizing the potential that lay before them, the power that could be drawn from the ancient fool. But, of course, this was best. Such power was never to be wielded by the likes of these twisted little barbarians.

Fearful eyes upon her, she approached Sweetblood's cocoon and stared through the amber encasement at the still features of the mage. The energy that radiated from Sanguedolce was intoxicating, and she fell to her knees beside him, a collective gasp going out from the Corca-Duibhne around the room. His magick, the wards around this chrysalis, were trying to repel her, but she held her ground, letting it wash over her, becoming almost drunk with its potency.

Morrigan lay her hands upon the imperfect surface of the chrysalis and was jolted by a surge of magick that struck her, coursing through her with the burning power of a lightning strike. She shuddered and moaned aloud, but did not remove her hands. Her teeth gnashed, pain spiked through her flesh, pushing up into her head. She bit her lip and blood dripped down her chin. Through the amber surface of the cocoon, she stared down into Sanguedolce's frozen visage.

She remembered the first time that she had ever laid eyes upon the magician, ages past, in Faerie. During the Twilight Wars the forces of the righteous had fought valiantly to stem the flow of darkness into the world of the Fey, and the worlds beyond it. She and her brother, Finvarra, had stood together at their father's side. The daughter of the king, she had been his trusted advisor and his personal bodyguard. In the midst of battle, Sweetblood had appeared, hovering above the battlefield, observing the conflict with a cold, unwavering eye, as if attempting to determine whether he should bother to become involved.

This memory awakened others in Morrigan. Clearly, now, she remembered her physical response to the sight of Sweetblood on that day, the warmth that had tingled in her belly, the pulse of arousal that had begun to throb inside her. Now, as then, she felt a ferocious heat thawing the deep chill that normally enveloped any such urges within her. She had felt his potential for power then, as she did now, and it inflamed her lust.

Sweetblood had not taken part in the Twilight Wars. Upon discovering the presence of Conan Doyle among the ranks of the virtuous, he had returned to the world of Blight in a flash of magickal exhibitionism. There were those among the Fey who thought Sweetblood had a rivalry with Conan Doyle and would not fight at his side. Morrigan, however, had felt certain that Sanguedolce had simply deemed the conflict to be beneath him. She had never forgotten him, or the power he wielded; it had haunted her always. Here was the key to everything that she desired. With that power, her darkest dreams could be made real. She had sworn to have it for her own, at any cost.

Now here was the power, beneath her very hands. Morrigan brought her face closer to the surface of the chrysalis.

"You can't keep me out forever, my sweet," she whispered, running her fingers sensually across the jagged surface of the amber encasement, pressing her supple, leather-clad body against it, as if attempting to arouse the sleeping figure within.

She began to mutter beneath her breath, words that were ancient before man had dropped from the trees to walk erect.

"Moggotu sandrathar," Morrigan hissed. *"Memaritus gosov iknetar shokkar-dos fhinn."*

Arcane power snaked from her clawed fingertips, flowing across the surface of the chrysalis, attempting to find a weakness to exploit upon its unyielding exterior.

"Tann-dissarvar, Bottus, Nava-si, Tiridus valkinsu!"

Morrigan spread herself across the cocoon. There was a flaw. She knew it. She sensed it. The chrysalis was damaged; otherwise she would not have been able to feel Sweetblood's power leaking out. Already she had been able to use some of the magickal radiance thrown off by the chrysalis to strengthen her own sorceries, to shatter the wards Conan Doyle had set up around his home. Ironic, that the power of the master should be used to destroy the sanctum of the student. Morrigan had a taste of Sanguedolce's magick. But it wasn't enough, for she knew the full extent of what awaited her once the enchanted shell was breached, and she wanted it all. She lay atop the cocoon, letting her own magick flow outward, sensing, probing, searching for the flaw so that she might permeate the chrysalis.

She writhed atop Sweetblood's amber sarcophagus, ancient incantations issuing from her mouth as she rubbed her body against its unyielding skin. Her magick slipped across its surface, hungrily searching for a way inside, and for a moment, she thought she had succeeded.

The chrysalis shuddered, and Morrigan exerted even more of herself, eagerly grinding her sex against her prize in an attempt to coax the magick from the entrapped sorcerer within. If she searched for the flaw from without, and she could cause Sweetblood's own power to search for an exit from within . . . she sensed the power building within the amber and called to it sweetly in the voice of the ancients, urging it to burst forth from its confinement.

The chrysalis shook yet again and she cried out with passion. Morrigan was riding the crest of everything she had ever hoped for. The renegade Fey sorceress could see it all before her mind's eye as it came over the rise, glorious to behold. Her enemies vanquished, the world of Blight and then Faerie bowing to her every whim, with so many others to follow.

And all in the name of her true love. Her true passion. *All that I do and all that I am, I dedicate to you,* she thought. For though she had desires of her own, they existed solely for the glory of another. She would have all that she craved, but what she craved the most was the glint of loving approval in the eyes of the Nimble Man.

It is all so close, and coming closer. Close enough to touch.

Morrigan suddenly cried out, not in pleasure, but in excruciating pain. The chrysalis lashed out at her defensively, a pulse of arcane energy that repelled her, sent her sprawling across the room with such force that she struck the wall, cracking the mirrored glass, and fell limply to the floor.

The Corca-Duibhne were terrified, but for the moment their fear of the mage was overwhelmed by their loyalty to their mistress. Or, perhaps, their fear of Morrigan was simply greater. They swarmed around her, concerned for her safety, but none daring to put a hand upon her.

She lay upon the wood floor, her body smoldering. Morrigan had known that it was unlikely she would be able to breach the chrysalis so simply, even with its flaw, but still her blood burned with rage and humiliation. She wanted Sweetblood's power *now*.

Fury consumed her, and she gave herself over to it willingly. Morrigan sprang to her feet, lashing out at the Night People that huddled about, concerned for her. Her claws tore into their dark flesh and stinking blood spattered off the ballroom's mirrored walls. Rage contorted her features, surged through her veins, and magick would not satisfy her. She used her hands to tear at them, to break their bones, to eviscerate them. It had been some time since she had let herself go, giving in to the bloodlust that had been with her since birth. It was ecstasy.

Dead Corca-Duibhne lay at her feet, their blood collecting in shimmering dark puddles as Morrigan wrestled the rage back under control. The stink of new death around her, she took several long breaths before she felt capable of looking once more upon the object of her desire and her fury. The chrysalis stood unchanged, untouched, in the center of the room. But not for long. She would have the power she desired.

"Mistress."

The word was spoken by two voices in concert, and Morrigan turned toward the broad double doors of the ballroom. There stood Fenris and Dagris, the twin Fey warriors who served as her lieutenants. Each of the brothers held in his arms a struggling human child. The twins were freaks amongst their own kind, psychically bonded, one unable to exist without the other. They had some skill with magick, and great skill in battle, and their loyalty to her was the only emotion either of them felt that was not clouded with insanity.

The twins entered the room with proud smiles upon their gaunt faces. They had done precisely what had been asked of them, as always. As she had many times before, Morrigan congratulated herself on the decision she had made to free them from their imprisonment in Finvarra's citadel. She could not have found dogs more loyal.

The children wailed in terror, beating at their captors. Morrigan motioned for Fenris and Dagris to approach. The twins stepped forward, each of them holding out his terrified package. The babes were young, a boy and girl, each no more than four years of age. *Perfect,* Morrigan thought, reaching out with a single claw to prick each of the children's mottled cheeks, drawing beads of blood. The babes screeched all the louder, and she brought the taste of them to her mouth.

"Yes," she said, satisfied with what she had sampled in the blood. "They should do nicely."

Morrigan smiled, her pleasure gradually returning. She had been impatient. Attempting to breach the chrysalis with only her own power had been vain and self-indulgent. Now, though, her hopes and dreams were only a blood ritual away.

"DO you have any sour cream?" the twisted little man with the strangely pointed ears asked her, even as he helped himself, yanking open the refrigerator to peruse its contents.

Julia Ferrick couldn't bring herself to answer. It was as if she were trapped in some bizarre fever dream, aimlessly walking around familiar dreamscape locations as the horrors continued to unfold. The odd, dwarfish man was but the latest addition to an equally strange cast of characters that had taken up residence in her home. Sitting at the marble-topped kitchen island, she gazed toward the window above the sink and saw the thick red fog swirl ominously about outside. The usual view of the trees in her backyard was completely obscured by the bizarre weather that had supposedly engulfed the city and its suburbs; at least that was what her visitors told her.

"You got some old milk in here . . . Christ, it's got the Lindbergh baby on the carton!" Squire turned toward her, wide-eyed. Then he gave her a terrifying smile, something out of *Grimm's Fairy Tales*. "Just kiddin'. Heh. But seriously, the sour cream gives it that little bit of extra somethin'," the man . . . *I think he is a man* . . . said as he pulled himself out of her refrigerator, arms filled with ingredients.

Julia went over to the oven and opened the cabinet above it. She pulled down a bag of Oreos and set it on the cooktop, then fished behind a jar of peanut butter to grab an unopened box of Winston Lights. Her fingers quivered as they retrieved the cigarettes. Then, quickly, she dug through a drawer for matches. It was her emergency pack, her fallback, held for a time when it wouldn't matter anymore what Danny's reaction would be to her smoking again. She imagined it stenciled with the words, *In Case of Apocalypse, Tear Plastic*.

There were no matches, so she turned on one of the gas stove's burners and bent, shaking, to light the cigarette. The first intake of carcinogens was harsh relief. Her fingers stopped quivering. She gnawed her lower lip, then took another puff before blowing out a plume of smoke. Her back was to Squire.

"Feel better now? You needed a smoke, huh? I know the feeling. Not that I smoke but . . . Oh, hey, Oreos!"

When Julia spun to look at him again, Squire had already picked up the bag of Oreos and was helping himself. The package crinkled as he drew out a pair of cookies and popped them in his mouth like they were dog biscuits. She expected him to throw back his head and gulp them down, but instead he stared at her and then spoke up once more, talking with his mouth full.

"So. Sour cream?"

"What?" Julia asked him. "The sour cream . . . for what?"

Squire rolled his eyes, snatching another Oreo from the pack and then going back to the open fridge. He retrieved a couple of items from within and then closed the door with a bump from his hip. "For the omelets we're making for the hungry troops? Remember?"

She smiled nervously. "Right. Sorry." Eyes darting away, she took another long drag on the cigarette, no longer caring if the house smelled like smoke. She leaned back to look through the doorway into the living room, where the others had gathered. "My head is spinning."

"That's all right," Squire said, returning to the refrigerator. He yanked open the door again and helped himself to some eggs. "Gotta admit, this business has even got me seeing stars, and that's sayin' somethin'."

He asked her for a large frying pan from the rack that hung over the kitchen's center island. She doubted that he could have reached it even with the added help of a stepping stool. Julia retrieved it for him.

"Best thing to do is keep your head and keep thinkin' the good thoughts." He looked at her as he doused the pan with no-stick cooking spray. "That's what I do, and it hasn't failed me yet, except for that business with the Beast of Gevaudan. That shit was just bad news from the start."

He rattled on a bit more, and she nodded her head and smiled politely, but deep inside she could feel it building, the urge to scream and throw them all out of her house, her son included. If, at that very moment, she had been given the choice to crawl back inside her mother's womb, Julia

Ferrick would have done so without so much as a second thought. She felt as though there was an electric current passing through the floor and into her body.

She found herself gnawing on the nail of her left index finger, even as she tapped the ash from her cigarette into the stainless steel sink. Great. She'd given in to temptation, and now she had two habits to kick instead of one. But, God, the cigarette was a comfort. Just holding it helped to steady her.

Squire was using a whisk to beat the eggs inside a bowl, humming busily to himself, seemingly content to ignore the fact that the world was falling apart all around them.

"That's quality," Danny said as he came into the kitchen.

Julia thought for a moment about trying to hide her cigarette, but it was too late. He looked disappointed for a moment and then just sighed. She gave him a small shrug. What could she say? In a situation like this, the kid should understand. She thought about putting it out, but he'd already seen her anyway, and she needed that cigarette.

Averting her eyes from his gaze, she took another drag and let the smoke trail from her mouth. Then she did her best to smile. She put on a brave face for her son—and he would always be her son, no matter if she had given birth to him or not, no matter if he was not even human. The tiny black horns that had burst through his skin and now protruded, just above his temples, made her shudder, but she did her best to hide her revulsion.

"What's up, kid?" she asked him.

"I wanted to know more about this Doyle guy. Dude took an interest in me, but how does he know all the stuff he knows? I asked Eve what his story was, but she said to ask Squire." Danny focused on the ugly little man, and Julia was grateful he wasn't going to fight her about her smoking. "Says you've worked for him the longest."

Squire abandoned his cooking for a moment to snatch a few Oreos from the package. He popped one into his mouth and went back to whisking eggs. "You want the short version or the long version?"

Danny sat on the edge of the table and crossed his arms. "Let's start with the Cliff's Notes. Mom says I have a short attention span."

"Mr. Doyle. The boss. Aka Arthur Conan Doyle. Learned a bunch of magick. Tries to keep the nasty shit from bothering normal people. End of story."

"Come on. There's got to be more to it than that."

Squire shrugged. "Lots more. But you wanted the short version."

"Hold on," Julia said. "Just . . . just hold on." The cigarette dangled from her fingers, nearly forgotten. Her brows knitted as she stared at Squire. "Arthur Conan Doyle. His parents gave him the same name as the creator of Sherlock Holmes?"

Danny shot them a confused look, his Converse Chucks squeaking on the linoleum. "What, you mean that cartoon? Sherlock Holmes in the thirty-something century?"

Squire snorted, but it wasn't derisive. Danny amused him. "Kid, Sherlock Holmes is one of the greatest fictional creations ever. People around the world know who he is. Like Mickey Mouse and Superman. He was created in the 1800s."

Then the leather-skinned, ugly little creature turned on a burner and started to heat a pan in which to cook omelets. He didn't even look up as he responded to Julia's question. "And, no, the boss ain't named after Sir Arthur. He's the real deal. The one and only. You see the way he dresses? He's not old-fashioned. He's just *real* old-school."

"No shit?" Danny asked, a strange grin spreading across his badly scarred features. "That's just so fucking cool."

"Watch your mouth," Julia snapped, glaring at her son. It was such a maternal thing to do that she had a moment of dislocation, as though none of this was happening. It was all impossible. This latest news was only the most recent in a string of impossibilities. But the tip of her cigarette burned and the smoke warmed her throat. She was awake and alive. Julia knew the difference between a dream and a nightmare.

Everything that was happening to them was real and true. Danny was . . . what he was. But just with those few words, with the rush of instinct she had to chide him for his foul language, a part of her mind snapped back into place. He was her little boy, still. No matter what. She had raised him, put Band-Aids on his scrapes and cuts, comforted him when he had a nightmare. How could she possibly think of him in any other way?

"Sorry, Mom," he mumbled, averting his eyes.

She reached out and ruffled his thick, curly hair, and gasped when a handful of it came away in her fingers, floating to the floor. "Dear God," she muttered, staring at the bald spot that she had created.

"It's okay," he reassured her. "It's been falling out pretty steadily for the last few days." He moved the hair around on the floor with the toe of his sneaker.

She felt the tears well up in her eyes. It took every ounce of her self-control not to break down sobbing.

Clay and Eve entered the kitchen, their focus on Squire.

"How are those eggs coming?" Clay asked.

Julia gazed sadly at her son and slid down into a chair at the kitchen table. Danny kicked at her chair lightly, playing with her, being a brat, but only to remind her of who they were, to let her know he was still there and still himself. She nodded, smiling weakly.

"Eggs?" Squire barked at Clay, flipping a golden brown

omelet with a spatula in the frying pan. "When have I ever merely prepared eggs, compadre?"

Clay laughed pleasantly, and Julia trembled again as she recalled how the handsome man had somehow changed himself into a mirror image of her, her exact doppelganger. How such things were possible she did not know. All she did know was that she was not going to be getting used to them at any time soon. She took another drag of her cigarette, now smoked almost down to the filter, and chose to focus on the kitchen conversation. She was becoming fairly adept at preventing herself from losing her mind. It seemed she had no other choice. What was that old saying? *Adapt or die.* Her version was a little different. *Adapt or lose your marbles.*

"A repast fit for a king," Squire said, flipping another omelet on the burner beside the first.

"If it's anything like that goulash you tried to pawn off on us last fall—" Eve chimed in, drawing a glass of water from the tap.

"That was no fault of mine," Squire protested. "I was assured by the butcher that the meat was of the finest quality." He broke one of the omelets in half with the spatula, flipped it onto a plate and handed it to Clay. "How was I to know that dog meat was considered a delicacy in his particular dimension?"

Clay sniffed the food on his plate suspiciously and wrinkled his nose as if smelling something foul. Danny burst out laughing beside her and she jumped. Laughter had become a foreign sound in this household of late, and she had almost forgotten it existed.

"Are you partaking?" Squire asked, turning to offer Eve a fresh omelet on a plate.

The woman threw up her hands to ward him off. "I'll pass." She leaned her head forward and sniffed around the offering. "Is that . . . is that garlic I smell?" she asked him.

The ugly little man smiled mischievously. "Chopped up nice and fine, just how you like it."

"Asshole," Eve spat, and Squire cackled.

Julia didn't understand the joke, unless it was simply that Eve didn't care for garlic. After she'd stubbed out her cigarette in a coffee mug, Squire brought plates for her and Danny and she thanked him, but could not bring herself to eat. Her son, on the other hand, ate his own portion and then helped himself to hers as well.

"How long do we give Conan Doyle to find us?" Clay asked as he brought his empty plate to the sink for Squire to wash. The little man now stood atop a chair and was cleaning up, the sink full of hot soapy water.

Eve leaned in the doorway between the kitchen and living room, drinking her water. Danny could not take his eyes from the attractive woman, Julia noticed, and in a way, she could not blame her son. Eve was one of the most strikingly beautiful women she had ever seen, with the body and the fashion sense of a supermodel. In an ordinary woman, it might've made Julia envious. Yet there was something about Eve that made the hair at the back of Julia's neck stand on end. She wondered what her story was, what bizarre secret she kept in order to be associated with the likes of Squire, Clay, and Mr. Doyle.

"We give him as long as it takes," Eve said, a dangerous edge in her voice. It was clear in her tone that she neither expected, nor would accept, an argument. "I'm sure he's figured out what's going on by now. We wait for him. Then we'll make a plan."

Clay stood on the other side of the island across from her and folded his muscular arms. "And if he doesn't come back? If this Morrigan woman who's taken over the house gets the better of him?"

"I forgot what a bundle of joy you could be." Eve scowled at him.

"Conan Doyle will come back, don't you worry," Squire said as he scrubbed a plate clean with a sponge and placed it in the strainer to dry. "It'll take more than that nasty Faerie bitch to put him down for the count." He turned atop the chair at the sink to look at Julia. "Pardon my French."

She was about to tell him that it was all right when there was a thump on the front door. Julia jumped, placing a hand against her chest. She could feel her heart racing.

Eve was the first to react, moving into the living room and toward the door.

"Could it be Mr. Doyle?" Julia asked, hoping it was. She had met the man, and whether or not she had to think about their claims as to his true age and identity, his presence would be welcome. At least he seemed human enough. But she wasn't sure if she could stand another bizarre stranger the likes of her current guests.

"It's possible," Squire said, jumping down off the chair, drying his hands with a dishtowel.

Clay remained very quiet and still, positioning himself so that he could watch Eve as she went to the door. None of them moved out of the kitchen, however. Not yet. It took Julia only a moment to realize that Clay and Squire had remained where they were as protection for her and Danny. Yet for some reason, this made her even more frightened.

There came another thump, only this one was much more violent, as if someone or, Heaven forbid, some*thing* was trying to get inside.

"If it's the Jehovahs, tell 'em to screw!" Squire yelled, and Eve slowly turned to fix him in a menacing stare.

"She doesn't like you very much, does she?" Danny said to the little man.

"It's all a show," Squire told him. "She'd be lost without me."

They all watched as Eve took hold of the knob, slowly turned it, and pulled open the door. Something growled at her from within the shifting red mist outside.

Then it erupted from the bloodstained night, bursting through the doorway.

THE vampire lurched into the Ferrick house, arms pinwheeling, trying to regain its balance. It seemed more like the leech had been thrown into the house than it had planned any focused attack. Not that Eve cared. The thing was filth. She grabbed hold of the slavering, mad-eyed blood bag and threw it to the floor, then dropped upon it, placing one knee in the small of its back. She grabbed a handful of filthy hair, yanking its head back toward her.

"Hey, Julia, ever seen this asshole before?" she asked as the leech screamed and thrashed beneath her.

The Ferrick woman emerged from the kitchen practically hiding behind Clay. Squire and the demon boy came out after them. Julia shook her head, staring wide-eyed at the vampire. She kept shaking, like at any minute she was going to lose it completely.

"Watch her," Eve said, eyes narrowed, gesturing to Clay. He nodded.

Eve focused on the leech again. Its stink filled her nostrils.

"Goddamned vermin," she muttered as she twisted its head around so she could look it in the eye. "So nobody invited you inside. Must be hurting you pretty bad to be in here," she whispered in its ear, leaning in close. "Breaking the rules and all." Eve felt the bone structure within her hand begin to shift and change, fingers lengthening, nails elongating. She didn't need a wooden stake to slay the vampires of the world. Everything she required was at her fingertips.

Her fingers became long talons, their tips like razors. With a flick of her wrist her claws could end a vampire's existence with dreadful swiftness. Just one of the perks of being mother to them all.

Eve sliced a single talon across the leech's parchment white throat, slitting the skin and teasing out a slowly descending curtain of blood that slid down its neck. She was careful not to get it on her clothes. This whole crisis had already ruined one outfit, and though she didn't care much about her pants, the top was nice. Expensive. And she'd never be able to get bloodstains out of it.

"Mother's going to put you out of your misery," she whispered.

The vampire shrieked and bucked with such force that Eve was thrown from its back. She rolled to her feet, snarling and cussing, but it was already up and fleeing toward the still-open door. Eve started after it. Its speed was unnatural, but she was faster. Impossibly fast.

She stopped three feet from the door.

The filthy leech was trapped on the threshold of the house. It was lifted off the ground by invisible hands and dangled there, hissing and lashing out. But Eve could see the terror in its eyes. She arched an eyebrow in curiosity, for it was not her that the leech was afraid of.

Beyond the door there was only the crimson fog, yet the vampire hung there, several inches off the floor, feet kicking as though it actually needed to breathe. Slowly, a figure began to coalesce on the front stoop of the Ferrick house. The eyes were first, dark and mysterious, like tarnished copper pennies. Then handsome, angular features, and muscular arms. A hand, clutching the vampire's throat.

"Eve," said the new arrival, "let's not have this pathetic animal running loose, all right? But make it fast. I owe it that much, at least, for being my hound, for leading me to you."

The voice was warm and low, and yet a blast of frigid air churned up from the place where the ghost of Dr. Leonard Graves appeared.

Eve smiled. "Of course, Leonard. A pleasure to see you, as always."

She tore the vampire from his grasp and raked her claws across its throat, nearly severing its head from its neck. There was a moment where the thing's flesh crackled like damp wood in a fire, and then it exploded in a blast of cinder and ash, its dying embers drifting down to the carpeted entryway like gray snow.

"That rocked!" Danny Ferrick said, only to have his mother shush him, her tension obvious even in that simple utterance. A package of cigarettes had appeared in her hands, and she was tapping one out.

"So how is it out there?" Eve asked, as Dr. Graves drifted into the house. "As bad as we think?"

The ghost glanced around the living room, frowned as he noted Julia and Danny, and then paused just inside the doorway, apparently not wishing to cause the woman even more of a fright. "I wish I could put your fears at ease," he said, turning to gaze out into the night of swirling red fog. "But I've never been much of a liar."

"Oh, Jesus. I'm in Hell," Julia Ferrick muttered to herself. The pack of Winston Lights seemed to explode, showering cigarettes onto the floor. She started to shake as though she was going to fall apart entirely.

"No, hey. Julia, listen. Listen to me. It's all right," Clay said.

Eve turned to find him shooting her a dark look, and at first she did not understand. Then she became aware of her talons. She nodded slowly, willing her hands to resume their normal shape, their elegant human form. She strode across the room to Julia and held up both hands. The woman stared at her, shaking her head, mouthing some denial or other.

"Mom, didn't you hear him? It's okay," Danny said, trying to reassure her.

Eve felt sorry for the kid. But none of them could afford to have the mother fall apart. They didn't have the luxury of looking out for her at the moment. "Julia. Hey, Julia!" Eve snapped.

The woman's eyes went wide, her nostrils flaring, and she glared at Eve.

"We're a motley crew, aren't we?" Eve said, almost succeeding in keeping the amusement out of her voice. Almost, but not quite. "Yeah. A motley crew. You've picked up enough already that none of this is a surprise to you. Conan Doyle's a sorcerer. A mage, we say. Clay's a shapeshifter, but that's only the easy explanation for that. The same way 'vampire' is a convenient way to describe me. You won't believe me, but trust me when I tell you the rest of my story would fuck you up much worse than that one word. Dr. Graves, here," she said, hooking a thumb to point out the new arrival, the tasty-looking man with dark bronze skin that seemed translucent at times. "He's a ghost. But he's a friend. May be hard for you to take, but we're the good guys. We're on your side. Deal with reality, or don't. Up to you."

Julia did not look up at first, and Danny was at her side. "Mom?"

Then the woman actually laughed. It was a dry, sort of unhinged little chuckle, but it was something. "A ghost," she said. "He'd have to be. I remember my father telling me stories about Dr. Graves when I was a little girl." Her gaze shifted toward Graves. "You were his hero."

The specter nodded once. "I'm honored."

"Honored," Julia said. She closed her eyes and shook her head. Then she dropped to her knees and began to collect her cigarettes. Danny got down and helped her, concern and regret in his eyes. When he handed her several of them, Julia sat back on her legs and looked up at Graves again, her hands full of cigarettes. Her eyes seemed somehow clearer than before.

"You're honored," she said, gazing at Dr. Graves. Then she looked around at the rest of them and dropped all the cigarettes but one, which she tapped nervously against her thigh. "What a circus. I should have rented a tent. You're all monsters, then, right? All of you, monsters of one kind or another. My son . . . my son is a demon. Or something like that. But whatever you are . . . I know you don't mean me any harm. I know you're trying to stop this . . ." she gestured toward the window, where the crimson fog had begun to glow, just slightly.

"Just tell me what I can do to help." Julia climbed to her feet, taking a long breath. She put a hand on Danny's shoulder and then glanced at the others again, holding up her lone salvaged cigarette. "And please, for God's sake, somebody get me a light."

Eve had to hand it to the woman, she'd seen stronger people reduced to dribbling idiots over lesser things than this.

Pleased that they weren't going to have to deal with Julia Ferrick losing her mind, Eve turned to the ghost. "All right, Leonard. Tell us something we don't know."

Dr. Graves had a quiet dignity that seemed to make them all stand a bit straighter. "The townhouse has been overrun with—"

"Know it," Eve interrupted.

The ghost scowled. "A sorceress of unimaginable power—"

"Know that, too. Her name is Morrigan and she's blood kin to our own Ceridwen."

The air around the ghost became increasingly colder as

his annoyance grew. "Perhaps you should be filling *me* in as to what's going on."

"Is that all you have?" Eve asked him.

"Are you aware that the souls of the dead are being pulled back to their remains, that they're being driven from their graves, and all of them seem to be drawn toward the same location in the city?"

"Finally," she said. "Something I didn't already know."

"Nor did I," said a voice from the depths of the night, from the folds of the bloody mist.

"Jesus Christ, what now?" Julia whispered.

Two figures emerged from the fog, stepping in through the door. Arthur Conan Doyle glanced around the room approvingly. Lady Ceridwen, elemental sorceress of the Fey, gave them each an icy stare. Eve admired her cloak, but the pants were completely without style. Ethereally beautiful she might have been, but her fashion sense was for shit. Earth tones, browns and greens, no patterns, nothing especially bright. No sophistication at all. But what pissed Eve off was that Ceridwen was still stunning, no matter what.

"Excellent, you're all accounted for," Conan Doyle said.

"Nice to see you're still amongst the living," Eve replied. She shot an amused glance at Graves. "No offense."

"None taken."

Conan Doyle stepped further into the living room, the stoic Ceridwen at his side. "It appears that the situation is most dire," he said gravely, making eye contact with them each in turn.

"Now let us set the wheels in motion to effect a remedy, as swiftly as we're able."

THE lights were out, now. The fog had stolen them.

The Ferrick woman had been kind enough to allow him the use of her home office for his ruminations. Conan

Doyle sat in the darkness upon her black leather chair and attempted to relax, letting his mind wander. It was times such as this, when the tensions were high, that Arthur Conan Doyle felt the effects of his nearly century and a half of life. His back ached, and his bones creaked with only the slightest of movements, and he wondered quite seriously if he still had the inner strength to deal with problems of this magnitude.

His agents—his Menagerie as he liked to call them—had seemed to breathe a sigh of relief upon his arrival, so he kept his doubts and fears to himself. He would do as he had always done. In the midst of chaos, he would find the skeins of order and attempt to weave them together once more.

This was the first time since early that morning that he'd had a chance to sit and collect his thoughts. In his mind he catalogued the data he and his agents had gathered. Nothing was too small or inconsequential. He analyzed the events of the previous days, considered the entire history of Sweetblood the Mage, and how Conan Doyle himself had come to dedicate himself to a search for his former mentor. The incident in New York, when he had failed to procure the amber-encased body of the mage, was a moment he examined thoroughly. Conan Doyle replayed every conversation, reviewed every action, but no matter how he tried, a discernable pattern had yet to emerge.

Frustrated, he rose from the chair and began to pace. *Is this the time?* he wondered. *The time when all of my resources will prove not enough, when my own ingenuity will result only in failure? Will this be Reichenbach Falls, for me? How many years can one man fight the darkness before the universe demands an accounting, before the pendulum must swung in the other direction?*

Conan Doyle pushed the thoughts from his mind; he was tired, not having slept since the brief catnap he'd managed on the recent drive to New York in pursuit of Sweetblood. He needed to sleep, but time was of the essence. Rest could wait; he needed to think. He might not yet have a plan of action that would halt the horrors going on in the streets. But that was because there were still too many questions in his mind. He was going to need to find some answers. His Menagerie was depending on him. The world was depending on him.

"Think, blast you," he muttered beneath his breath as he stared through the slats of the office window. Outside he could see nothing, the world totally obscured by that red mist. His thoughts had become like the whirling maelstrom left by Morrigan in place of the entrance from Faerie to the world of his birth, fragments of information swirling furiously about inside his mind.

There came a knock upon the door.

"Yes?" Conan Doyle called, turning his attention from the red-tinted night.

The door came slowly open, a beam of light from outside cutting through the darkness to partially illuminate the room. "Didn't know if you'd still be awake," Squire said sheepishly as he entered.

"And now you do," Conan Doyle said, turning his attentions back to the window and the unnatural conditions beyond it. "What can I do for you, Squire?" he asked, annoyed that he had been disturbed, but at the same time grateful for the distraction.

"Before leaving the townhouse, after I loaded up the weapons and shit, I made a stop in your study."

Conan Doyle paused, raised one eyebrow, and turned toward the hobgoblin again. Squire stood at the center of the office holding something in his hands, a familiar red velvet case.

"It was the last thing I thought of before I flew the coop. Thought you might need it," he said, holding it out to Conan Doyle. "Y'know, to help you think and all."

Squire placed the velvet case on the desk in front of the leather chair.

"Thank you, Squire," Conan Doyle said warmly, touched by the gesture, and by the loyalty of his faithful valet. "That was most considerate of you."

"Don't mention it, boss," the hobgoblin said, making his way to the door. "Least I could do, considering you're the one that's gonna be responsible for saving our asses." Squire grinned as he went out into the corridor. "Goodnight, Mr. Doyle," he said, closing the door gently behind him, plunging the room again into red-hued shadow.

"Goodnight, Squire," Conan Doyle said under his breath, leaving his place at the window to approach the case left for him on the desktop. Conan Doyle reached down and took the velvet case in hand, slowly opening it to reveal its contents. He removed the briar pipe, its rounded, ivory bowl giving off the faintest aromatic hint from the last time he had smoked, and a pouch of his favorite tobacco blend. Many a problem had been hashed out over a smoldering pipe.

Conan Doyle lowered himself back down into the leather chair and began to fill the pipe, stuffing the tobacco into the bowl with his index finger. Finished, he brought the stem of the pipe to his mouth as he uttered a simple spell of conflagration to ignite the briar's contents.

The mage puffed upon the pipe, filling the room with the rich scent of the burning tobacco. He leaned back in the chair, a halo of smoke drifting about his head, already beginning to feel the soothing effects of his pipe, and attempted again to make sense of the swirling maelstrom that his thoughts had become.

You're the one that's gonna be responsible for saving our asses, Squire had said. Crude, but not entirely inaccurate.

Conan Doyle only prayed that after all this time, he was still up to the challenge.

11

THE air inside the study was thick and redolent with the aroma of Conan Doyle's tobacco. He drew it through his nostrils in long, slow breaths, lips holding his pipe tightly. His eyes fluttered slightly as he sketched in the air with his fingers. Yet these were not sigils or runes, not symbols of power he was using to draw hexes. His hands were not spell casting; they were choreographing. There was much to be done, and all of his Menagerie would be called upon. It was up to him to determine how best to utilize them.

Conan Doyle opened his eyes. The study—he was amused by the modern fashion of calling such a room a home office, as if it were some new invention—was dark, and beyond the windows the crimson fog drifted along the streets. The sky was still black above the fog, but it was no longer merely that the sun had been eclipsed. Real night had long since fallen.

And what of the morning? Will dawn come at all?

He wished he could tell himself that the question was rhetorical. If he had spoken the words aloud and been overheard, that was precisely what he would have said.

But these were his secret thoughts, and he could not lie to himself. Morrigan was powerful, and the forces she had brought to bear showed him he had underestimated her. The Corca-Duibhne, the dead, some of the Fey, and who knew what else had joined her cause. And Conan Doyle still had not a single clue as to what that cause was.

Power, you fool, he thought. *Of course, it's power. Morrigan tires of being the sister of the king. She wants something of her own to rule, to control.*

Conan Doyle frowned, taking another breath of pipe smoke. Could it really be that simple? Perhaps. History was riddled with those whose only lust was for power. Yet something about that did not ring true for him. Morrigan had never been so bold, never acted out her malice in so conspicuous a manner. For her to take such a risk, to close the door on ever returning to Faerie as anything but a captive, he was certain she must have some other motivation. But no amount of rumination would provide him with a reasonable solution to that problem.

More information was required.

He exhaled a plume of smoke, and as it clouded in front of him, a flash of self-recrimination went through him. Yes, he had needed time to deliberate the next step, but undead horrors still marched across the city and he had no doubt that bizarre, apocalyptic phenomena continued to erupt throughout the region.

The time for thinking was over.

Mr. Conan Doyle rose from the armchair in Mrs. Ferrick's study and plucked his pipe from his lips. He inclined his head and blew a breath across it, a breath that contained the tiniest of spells, and the ember glow within the pipe died. He returned it to its case and left the study.

The hall was dark, but a glow of candles flickered upon its walls. The power had been unreliable at best, so Julia Ferrick had unearthed quite a collection of wax substitutes for electricity. Whatever Squire and Danny's mother had been up to in the kitchen, it had been the last time they'd depended on the electrical power in the house. Conan Doyle started toward the living room, where he had left most of his comrades, his agents, only to realize that the candlelight now illuminated both the living room and dining room, and that the low voices he heard were coming from the latter.

Curious, he stepped into the living room. There in the silence, in the dim, flickering glow of burning wicks, Julia Ferrick lay sideways on the sofa, legs drawn up beneath her, sleeping fitfully. She muttered something and shifted, her anxious heart afflicting her dreams, but she slept on. Several feet away, Danny sat on the floor with his knees drawn up under his chin, watching over his mother. He still dressed the part of the rebellious child, but circumstances had brought them closer, it seemed, than they had been for some time. Danny's eyes glowed orange in the candlelight.

Conan Doyle and the demon child watched one another for several moments. Danny made no sign that he had seen the old mage, but Conan Doyle knew the boy was aware of his presence. At length he beckoned with an outstretched finger.

"Come," he said. "We have a great deal to discuss."

Danny frowned at him and glanced at his mother again.

"She will be all right," Conan Doyle assured him.

Then he turned and went into the dining room, knowing that the boy would follow. The room was a surprise. Though the house was pleasant enough, it was decorated with the casual laissez-faire attitude of most modern American homes. The dining room, however, was all dark wood and silver behind glass, and the small chandelier was black iron. It had the atmosphere of another age, and Conan Doyle immediately felt more at home here.

The others were all gathered there. Squire had opened a

liquor cabinet and discovered a bottle of Talisker scotch, which Conan Doyle presumed had been there since the house had a *Mister* Ferrick within it. The goblin presided, now, over a pair of shot glasses that were set upon the dining-room table. One was his own, and the other belonged to Eve, who had tilted her high-backed chair away from the table and propped her boots upon its surface. Conan Doyle frowned, displeased by her lack of courtesy, but this was typical of her. Eve was long past taking lessons in propriety from anyone. He also chose not to mention his distaste at the idea of the pair of them doing shots of finely aged scotch.

Ceridwen was seated across from them. She held her elemental staff across her lap, cradling it as though it was her child, and she gazed into the ice sphere atop it, watching the dancing flame therein with the manner of a descrier. Conan Doyle knew this was not far from the truth. There were things she had seen in the ice there that had come to pass. For now, though, the ice was clear save that flame.

At the far end of the room, Clay stood with his arms crossed, speaking with Graves. The apparition of the dead man was as solid as Conan Doyle had ever seen it, and he thought perhaps it was the setting that inspired Graves to such focus. He was in the ordinary house of a more or less ordinary woman, and in such close quarters he felt awkward about appearing as what he was . . . a ghost.

Clay wore the face that had become his most common visage, and he was the first to glance up when Conan Doyle entered the room.

"Well, well," Eve said, taking her boots from the table and reaching for her newly filled shot glass. She stood and raised it as though in a toast. "I'm going to guess we've got a plan."

"We do indeed," Conan Doyle replied.

Eve threw back the shot of Talisker and knocked the

glass loudly onto the table. "About time," she said. "I'm so bored I've got spiders in my brain. The goblin was starting to seem like a scintillating conversationalist."

"Hey!" Squire protested. "I've got oodles of personality. I'm a catch!"

Eve laughed. "If I spend enough time with you, I'm sure to catch *something*."

Conan Doyle appreciated the fact that Clay and Graves, at least, seemed appropriately grim. He glared at Eve, but Ceridwen spoke up first.

"That will be enough," the Fey sorceress commanded.

Eve flinched, eyes narrowing at the presumption in Ceridwen's tone, but that was all right. The women were equally formidable. Ceridwen was royalty, but Eve was royalty of a sort herself. A matriarch in her own right. Still, there were times when angering her was the only way to remind her of what her priorities ought to be.

"I apologize for the wait," Conan Doyle said, "but it is time, now, to get to work." He gestured around the table. "Please, all of you, be seated." The old mage turned toward Danny Ferrick, who waited behind him in the arched entry of the dining room.

"Danny, come in. Join us. This is your house. You have a right to hear what we plan to do."

The teenager nodded, the nubs of his horns gleaming sharp and black in the candlelight. He passed Conan Doyle and took a seat beside Ceridwen, though he fidgeted and glanced at her several times, distracted by either her beauty or her power, both of which were palpable. Conan Doyle took note of this, and of the way the boy stole glances at Eve as well. A teenaged boy between these two women . . . Danny was unlikely to hear a word he said.

Conan Doyle sat at one end of the table and Clay at the other. Squire and Eve pulled their chairs in closer. Graves did not sit at all. Ever. Regardless of how solid he might appear, he was, after all, merely a shade.

"Now, then," Conan Doyle said, surveying his Menagerie, "let us be clear about this. Thus far, our efforts have been less than useless. We have learned little of value. The first order of business is to improve our position in that regard."

He turned the plan over in his mind, wishing there was more to be done. Conan Doyle opened the case for his pipe, finding comfort in it. Once more he blew lightly on its bowl and it was rekindled. He took a long pull upon it, let out the smoke, and then merely held it in his hand.

"Ceridwen will infiltrate my home. Morrigan has the Corca-Duibhne at her disposal, as well as a handful of Fey warriors. In order to discover what her intentions are, subtlety will be more effective than force. For now. Morrigan wants access to Sweetblood's power, and we must know why. It cannot be to release him, for Lorenzo Sanguedolce could easily destroy the tainted sorceress. The only way she could have breached the magickal defenses around my home is if Sweetblood's chrysalis is already leaking. But he has not been released, or the world would know it. If we rush to battle without answers, it might cost more than our lives. It might lead to catastrophe."

Conan Doyle nodded at Ceridwen. He was aware of the magnitude of what he was asking, sending her alone into the lair of their enemy. But such was his faith in her. And if anyone was to combat Morrigan alone, her niece had the best chance of surviving such a conflict.

"For my part, I will remain here. I hope that Mrs. Ferrick will be kind enough to watch over me whilst I meditate and attempt to reach Lorenzo. Our minds touched once before, when I first discovered his strange sarcophagus, and now I must try to communicate with him again. We must know why he hid himself away. From our brief contact, it is clear that Sweetblood believes that there will be cataclysmic consequences if his chrysalis is opened. The signs and portents might not all be Morrigan's doing. Some of them could be a result of the natural and supernatural worlds reacting to the prospect of Sweetblood's release ... or whatever Morrigan plans to do with him. There are too many questions. I hope Sweetblood can be made to provide some answers."

A strong wind had begun to blow and the storm windows rattled in their frames. The red fog seemed to undulate as it swept past outside. Conan Doyle took his pipe firmly between his lips and drew a long puff into his lungs. Outside, the wind screamed. Danny Ferrick muttered under his breath, and even Squire glanced uneasily out into the bleeding night.

"Yes. It is almost as if the malign powers of the universe sense us here, within these walls, plotting against them," Conan Doyle said, sitting back in his chair and regarding them.

Ceridwen gazed at him, her eyes so clear and bright that he could not help but recall the days in which he had lost himself within them. Conan Doyle's heart ached. He wished for all of this to be over so that he might have just a handful of moments to speak with her in peace, to let her know that his time with her was so cherished that its memory alone had given him the strength to endure terror and hardship. But, if ever, that was for later, when this parade of horrors had come to an end.

"That may be truer than you know."

Conan Doyle turned his gaze upon Eve. Her tone was often so cavalier that it was easy to forget her age, her significance to the worlds of men and monsters. Now her voice had altered, however. Her words were weighted with knowledge as ancient as human thought.

"Speak your mind, Eve," he said.

Squire turned to look at her, the expression on his face reflecting a kind of disappointment, perhaps because the woman who had been his drinking companion moments earlier had now been subsumed by her true self. Eve pushed her raven hair away from her face and stared at Conan Doyle.

"There are those of you who dislike any discussion of true evil, of Heaven and Hell as anything other than random dimensions, worlds folded upon worlds not unlike this land of men or Faerie, Lemuria or Asgard. You don't want to hear about God, about angels and demons."

Dr. Graves floated behind her chair, his arms crossed. "With all we have experienced, the Judeo-Christian myth is a bit too exclusive to be believed. One thing negates most of the others."

"No," Eve said, glancing at him. "No, it doesn't. I'm not talking about the doctrine of any one church. I'm talking about the reality. The truth. The beginning. Out there in the universe, there are powers beyond your imagining, and powers beyond *their* imagining, and one power beyond them all."

Clay had been silent during this, but now he sat up a bit straighter in his chair and gazed first at Graves and then at Conan Doyle. "Eve is correct, of course. You know my story, Doyle. You're the one who helped me discover it. Yet you doubt it? There are things that are evil in form and thought, in blood and flesh, not merely by intent."

Danny Ferrick bared his sharklike teeth in a dubious grin. "Hold up, you guys. Seriously. All of you."

The Menagerie turned, as one, and stared at the boy. Conan Doyle was surprised that their scrutiny did not deter Danny from continuing. It boded well for the boy. Clearly he had begun to accept what he was, and that the world held the darkest of secrets.

"Go on, Danny," Conan Doyle said.

The teenager drummed clawed fingertips upon the table, saw what he was doing, and stopped. "Okay, look, no offense, but you guys need to shut the fuck up and get this posse in motion. Yeah, there's evil. I mean, duh. Sorry, but any asshole can look out the window. This Morrigan, is she powerful enough to be doing all of this, making it rain toads and blood, resurrecting an army of *Resident Evil* rejects, blotting out the sun, making little kids puke up maggots?"

Conan Doyle raised an eyebrow and turned to Ceridwen. As one, they both shook their heads firmly.

"No," Ceridwen said. "My aunt has never had that kind of power."

"So, other options, then?" Danny asked. "I'd come up with a few, but if you can't play it on GameCube, I'm guessing none of my thoughts are gonna help out."

None of them responded. At length, Conan Doyle cleared his throat. "Simply this," he said. "Either the dark powers in the world are being exacerbated by Morrigan's actions, and all of this is merely a by-product . . . such phenomena are not uncommon, though the scale of this outbreak is tremendous and—"

"Or?" Graves interrupted. The ghost still had his arms crossed, a forbidding expression on his face. "You said there were two options."

"Or Morrigan is not our true enemy and is merely serving a greater darkness, something powerful enough to cause all of this to happen."

Squire snorted derisively. "Oh, wonderful. What's the bad news?"

Conan Doyle shot him a withering glance and the goblin fell silent, looking appropriately penitent.

"The boy's right," Clay said. "We're wasting time. We know what you and Ceridwen are going to be doing, Doyle. What of the rest of us?"

The glow of candles flickered across Clay's face, and for a moment Conan Doyle could not focus on his features. It was as though he could see, in that moment, every face Clay had ever worn. He hesitated a moment before turning his attention to Dr. Graves.

"The time has come for us to speak of the dead," Conan Doyle began. "I do not believe that Morrigan is directly responsible for this mass resurrection. It is likely yet another supernatural portent. However, given what Dr. Graves has told us about the walking dead he observed in Boston— that some of them seem to be traveling toward a single destination with a great deal of purpose—the only logical conclusion is that Morrigan is attempting to use them to her advantage, as her servants. Given their course, I believe they are being directed toward the Museum of Fine Arts, and that they are being sent to retrieve something for Morrigan that she cannot retrieve for herself.

"That object would be the Eye of Eogain."

They all stared at him. Squire threw up his hands. "All right. I give. How the hell do you know that?"

Conan Doyle smiled. "Why, it's—"

"If you say 'elementary,' I quit," the goblin cut in.

The old mage puffed on his pipe once more. "Very well," he replied. "Let me tell you a story." He watched them all over the bowl of his pipe. "Before the Romans laid claim to the British Isles, magick roamed there unchecked. Chief among its practitioners were the druids, sorcerer priests who performed the correct rituals and sacrifices, and made certain that the hungry dead, the mischievous spirits, and the peoples of Faerie kept away from their tribes.

"This was no simple task. There were powerful demons that saw this as a challenge, and some of the dead were vengeful if their mischief was disrupted. But worst of all for the druids were the arrogant Fey. There were those in

Faerie who were not at all appeased by the druids' offerings, and though the king forbade them from interfering with the human world, still they looked for opportunities to bedevil the druids. The worst of these, a trickster sorceress, cast her cruel eye upon Eogain, perhaps the most powerful druid in all the isles. He was an archmage with skill unmatched in that age.

"Eogain had tapped the magick of the universe, but he feared that his will would not be sufficient to control it, to focus such power. So he turned to a different skill, and from silver he fashioned an orb, etched with runes that would channel magick. His left eye had been lost in battle with a child-stealing goblin—"

Squire cleared his throat. "No relation."

Conan Doyle ignored him and went on. "Eogain replaced his left eye with that silver orb. From that moment on, every black-hearted beast and dark spirit feared the Eye of Eogain, for with only a look he could destroy them.

"His mere existence, however, was an affront to that Fey trickster, and she came upon him as he slept and murdered him, dumping his body in a peat bog, silver eye and all."

He saw confusion upon the faces of the Menagerie and would have liked to lead them to his conclusions, to show them the logic through which he had arrived there. Conan Doyle felt it was more instructive to cause others to think than to do their thinking for them. But the time for such indulgences was over.

"This tale is more than legend, my friends. Seven months ago, outside the English village of Windling, workers cutting blocks of peat from a local bog discovered a human skull, mummified by the peculiar conditions of having been put to rest in the bog. There was some skin left upon the skull, and wisps of hair, and in the scored left orbital cavity, a silver sphere marked with runes."

Even the wind had quieted outside the house. It was Clay who spoke.

"The Eye of Eogain," he said.

"Indeed," Conan Doyle replied, taking a long breath. "I have been following the progress of this story since I first learned of it. Those who are studying the skull have been unable to remove the Eye without damaging the skull, and are reluctant to do so. For now, they have chosen to leave it intact, and for the last several months, Windling Man, as they refer to the skull, has been touring America with an exhibit bearing the crude title, 'The Bog People.'"

One by one, Conan Doyle watched as understanding lit their faces. They all seemed intrigued, but Ceridwen looked genuinely surprised, even a bit angry. Conan Doyle had dealt with such reactions from her before. Even when they had loved one another beyond reason, she had felt that he kept his thoughts too much to himself.

"And you think that Morrigan is also aware of the Eye," Dr. Graves ventured, his spectral form shimmering in the candlelight.

"I'm certain of it. All of her actions of late have been timed to coincide with the arrival of Eogain's skull in Boston, at which time she would have access both to a power locus, the Eye, and to a place where the walls between worlds has been worn thin. Namely, my home. All she needed then was Sweetblood, and, of course, she's found him."

Ceridwen lifted her chin, and when she spoke, it was with the regal bearing she had learned as the niece of King Finvarra. "Why have you not mentioned this to us before?"

Conan Doyle frowned. "Until Dr. Graves gave me his report a scant hour ago, I was not aware that Morrigan had an interest in the Eye. I admit I ought to have at least suspected she might desire it, but we have had several other things to keep us occupied."

"Okay," Squire said, "but how did Ceridwen's bitchy aunt know about the Eye in the first place? Far as I know, she hasn't set foot in this world since the Twilight Wars. And even before that, she always talked about 'the Blight,' didn't like hanging around here much."

"Ah, but once upon a time she liked it very much," Conan Doyle said. "This was two thousand years ago, Squire. And Morrigan knows very well the tale of Eogain and the power of his Eye, for she was the one who murdered him, who left him to rot in that bog in Windling."

"Why didn't she just take it?" Eve asked. "I mean, she's an evil twat, but she isn't stupid. An item like that is exactly the kind of thing you magicians collect, just in case. Why leave the Eye in his head, at the bottom of some bog?"

"The Fey hate silver," Clay noted, "but still—"

"I told you Eogain was powerful. The runes he etched into the silver eye were not only to absorb and channel magick. There were others as well. Defensive marks. He enchanted the eye so that if it is touched by hands not human, it will simply destroy itself, disintegrate."

Danny slapped the table enthusiastically. "I get it! She's controlling some of those zombies, sending them to the museum to get the Eye for her because she can't touch it."

"Precisely," Conan Doyle agreed.

Clay stood up quickly, troubled. "Which means we've got to get to the museum right away. We have to get the Eye before the undead can retrieve it."

"Or, at least, before they can return it to Morrigan," Conan Doyle said.

Eve scowled as she rose. "Well, what are we waiting for?"

Conan Doyle frowned. "You *were* waiting for our few clues to be evaluated, and for a plan to be set in motion.

And now they have, and now it is. By all means, don't let me keep you, Eve."

He shot a glance at the goblin, who had his glass of fine scotch slightly tilted, pressed against his lips, but paused now as Conan Doyle spoke his name.

"Squire. Take Eve, Clay, and Dr. Graves to the Museum of Fine Arts. Provide them with weapons. After you have obtained the Eye, we shall all regroup here. By then, I am quite certain we will know exactly what it is that we face."

They all began to rise, heavy with the weight of purpose. For too long they had simply been reacting to the horrors that were unfolding in the city. At last they were going on the offensive. Conan Doyle sensed that each of them shared his satisfaction that the time had come. All save one.

"Wait," Danny Ferrick said, idly stroking one of his small horns. "Wait a second."

Everyone paused and regarded him curiously.

"What about me?" he asked.

Conan Doyle stiffened, nostrils flaring, and his eyes narrowed as he studied the boy who was not a boy at all. He had felt the boy deserved to know what was happening, and that it might help him to accept the truth about himself to know what other sorts of creatures existed in the world. But his intentions ended there.

"You're to remain here with your mother and myself," Conan Doyle said.

"Bullshit," Danny snapped. "What's that about? I can fight. Look, obviously I'm not just some kid. I'm strong, and nearly fucking impossible to hurt. I want to help."

"Admirable," Conan Doyle said. "But there is something I want you to understand. Ever since I learned of your existence, I have kept watch over your development, checking in from time to time. I did this, Danny, not because I hoped to recruit you to fight on my side of this war, but to make absolutely certain you did not fight for the *other* side."

The boy's mouth hung open in astonishment, little rows of fangs glinting in the candlelight. He looked as if he had just been slapped.

"That's so . . . that's totally unfair. You don't even know me. Where the hell do you get off saying shit like that?"

"I think I've been more than fair," Conan Doyle replied, giving him a hard look. "There are those who would have killed you in infancy, just to be safe. We shall see what your destiny holds, Danny Ferrick. But not tonight. Not tonight."

He turned and left the room, and the Menagerie followed.

In the hall they were met by Julia Ferrick, who had overheard at the very least the last few moments of their conversation. She had woken from her sleep and wrapped herself in a blanket. Her face was etched with sadness and she held one hand to her mouth as if to block a scream. When Danny emerged from the living room, his mother went to him. Though he tried at first to push her away, a moment later he relented, and she held him in her arms and whispered a mother's love into his ears and kissed his hair, careful to avoid scratching herself upon the points of his horns.

THE crimson mist churned, a sea of red clouds that drifted across streets and lawns and swayed trees, a dread wind rustling branches and killing leaves, which fell and were carried away in the fog. The night sky above was obscured by the blood mist, swirls of scarlet against the black heavens. Somewhere in the night, not far off at all, dogs snarled and let out unnatural cries as they tore at one another.

All along the street where the Ferricks lived, doors and windows were closed. Some homes had electricity still, though it flickered unreliably. Others glowed with the light of candles. But most of them were dark, and things shifted in the shadows behind the windows. It might have been people that moved within those homes, or it might have been something else.

Conan Doyle smoothed his jacket, then raised one hand to brush down his mustache. His fingers crackled with static, and with magick, for though his hands performed these idle tasks, his eyes were alert and he scanned the red fog around the Ferrick house for any sign of attack. The way that supernatural events were rippling across the area, there were certain to be other enemies than Morrigan out there in the dark.

He spared a glance to his right. Ceridwen clutched her elemental staff and stood at attention, the breeze ruffling her cloak. A soft blue glow emanated from the ice sphere at the top of the staff, and a cold mist seemed to furl up from it, untouched by the bloody fog that swept around them.

The two of them stood guard while Clay and Eve checked the interior of the limousine and Squire looked beneath it. There was no sign of anything sinister, so the goblin hitched up his pants and slid into the driver's seat. Graves's ectoplasmic essence rippled as he passed through the door and took the passenger's seat.

Clay held the door for Eve, who slipped on a dark red coat she had retrieved from the trunk of the limo and then climbed into the backseat. Hesitating a moment, Clay looked across the roof of the limo and locked eyes with Conan Doyle. The two men nodded at one another, and then Clay got into the car beside Eve.

Conan Doyle and Ceridwen waited silently as the limousine pulled away. When its red taillights blended with the mist, they retreated together to the door of the Ferricks' home.

"I'll take the living room," she said. "You'll take the dining room, I assume?"

"Fine," he agreed.

Danny and his mother were waiting in the living room. When Conan Doyle and Ceridwen entered, Julia Ferrick drew in a quick breath, as though she had to summon her courage or her self-control, or perhaps both. When she spoke to him, her tone made it clear that her opinion of him had suffered greatly these past few minutes.

"I understand you need my help," she said.

"I'm not sure I need it," Conan Doyle answered truthfully. "But it is always wise to have someone watching over me when I place myself in a meditative state. If there is an attack here, you could wake me, and the same if I seem unduly troubled in my trance, if I convulse or wounds begin to spontaneously appear upon my flesh."

Ceridwen sighed, and the two females exchanged a meaningful look. "In other words, he does need your help. He simply wouldn't choose to phrase it that way."

"He must be loads of fun on a date," Julia muttered.

Neither Conan Doyle nor Ceridwen responded to that. After an awkward moment, Conan Doyle simply nodded to Ceridwen and then gestured toward the Ferricks to proceed with him toward the dining room.

But he found he could not leave Ceridwen to her work without pausing. He stood at the arched entry that led to the house's main corridor and looked back at her. Her fingers had begun to scratch at the air, to dart and weave and paint sigils. The ground rumbled and shifted slightly beneath the foundations of the house, and the temperature in the living room dropped twenty degrees in a matter of seconds, and continued to go down.

The ice sphere upon her staff glowed more brightly, and the blue mist that wreathed it began to spin around it in a pulsing ring.

"Ceri," Conan Doyle whispered.

She started at the sound of his voice. Slowly, she turned to face him, her features sharp as shattered glass, eyes bright with magick and pain.

"Don't call me that," she said.

Conan Doyle nodded in apology and regret. "I just wanted to tell you to be careful."

"I don't need you to worry for me, Arthur," Ceridwen said coldly, snapping off each word. Instantly, she seemed to regret it. She went back to preparing her spell, lips moving soundlessly, fingers sketching at nothing. Then, without looking at him, she half turned and she spoke again, and this time her voice was intimate with the memories they shared.

"But I . . . I am glad that you do."

JULIA Ferrick had stepped into a dream.

That was untrue, of course, and she knew it. Even so, that thought ran through her mind time and time again. How many times had she heard the expression, *It was like a dream.* Hundreds? Thousands? It was funny in a nauseating way because there was nothing remotely dreamlike about the things she had experienced in the previous twelve hours.

There were monsters in her house. A vampire woman whose name and comments implied she might be so much more. A man who could be anyone or anything, wear any face. A goblin with a foul mouth, crass and yet somehow comforting. An elf or fairy or—and here an insane little giggle threatened to bubble out between her lips—whatever Ceridwen was. Conan Doyle . . . a magician. A real magician, who also claimed to be Sir Arthur Conan Doyle, a man who had been dead as long as Julia's grandmother had been alive.

And her son. Her own son.

Daniel. Oh, sweet God, Danny.

According to Conan Doyle, he wasn't even remotely human. And yet he *was*. He was her son, damn it.

Again that mad giggle tried to escape her lips, and she raised a hand to cover the smile it brought, not wanting it to be misinterpreted. This wasn't a dream or a nightmare; it wasn't Julia through the looking glass. She was wide awake, and there was no doubt in her mind that her senses were reporting accurately. The things she saw and heard and smelled and touched were real. All of her assumptions about the world—taught to her by generations of human society—were wrong. Were lies.

Her mind wanted to reject it all, wanted to retreat to the protection of ignorance. But the contents of Pandora's Box could never be returned to their place. The truth could not be undone.

Julia blamed Conan Doyle for that. She knew it was absurd, knew that the man was trying to combat the dark forces that were at work upon the world. But he was also aloof and distant and had known the truth about her son for years, yet kept it secret from her. And the way he had spoken to Danny in the dining room . . . Julia was glad Conan Doyle wouldn't allow Danny to accompany the others; he was safer here. But Conan Doyle didn't know her boy. As tormented as he had been in recent years, dealing with the physical changes they had initially thought of as some kind of affliction, Danny was a good kid. Conan Doyle's suggestion that Danny was not to be trusted because of what he was infuriated her. What mattered wasn't what he was, but *who* he was.

Conan Doyle sat at the far end of the dining-room table. He had done away with the filthy pipe he had been smoking and now simply steepled his fingers beneath his chin, leaning back in his chair. He almost seemed not to notice her, his eyes closing, his chest rising and falling in a rhythm that gradually slowed.

"Mrs. Ferrick?" he said, sounding disoriented.

"Yes?"

"I wish things could have been different for you," he said, barely above a whisper, so that she was not at all certain if she had heard him correctly.

And then, "Wake me at any sign of trouble."

Julia stared at Conan Doyle as his breathing slowed further. His face seemed almost jaundiced in the candlelight. Soon he inhaled only once or twice a minute, and his eyes were partway open, revealing only the whites beneath.

He was gone. And Julia found herself feeling more charitable toward Conan Doyle than she had previously. For though his body was here, his mind was clearly elsewhere, and without him the walls seemed closer and the crimson mist more ominous. She was more aware than before that out there on the streets of her city the dead were walking. Without Conan Doyle's reassuring presence, she felt afraid.

It made her hate him all the more.

"Mom?"

Startled, Julia turned to see Danny standing in the corridor, just outside the room. He had been silent since they had joined Conan Doyle for this meditation, or whatever it really was. She smiled wanly at her son, wanting to believe his assertion that the truth had made him happy. Plainly there was more to it than that. To know that she and her bastard ex were not his biological parents had to have hurt

Danny, but she could understand that it helped him to know that he was different for a reason. That he might have a purpose beyond being the freak the other kids stared at in the high school hallways.

"You look tired, honey," Julia said. "Why don't you get some rest? Nothing else is going to happen until they come back."

"That's what I was going to say," Danny told her. "Yell if you need anything, or if anything, y'know, happens." He gestured at Conan Doyle.

"I will," she promised.

Then Danny was gone from the doorway and she was left alone with the hollow husk of Arthur Conan Doyle and the flickering glow of candles.

12

CERIDWEN was taken aback by how much it still pained her.

Standing in the center of the Ferricks' living room while attempting to establish communications with the elemental forces of this withered world, the sorceress was forced to deal with emotions she had thought to be callused over long, long ago. They were feelings buried so deeply that she had underestimated their devastating strength, believing that after all this time, she had surely grown stronger than they, the overwhelming sadness and fiery anger that had come as a result of Arthur Conan Doyle leaving her life.

But she knew she had been wrong, feeling the effects of seeing him again as if the decades that separated them were but the passing of a season. Ceridwen had hoped she would be stronger than this and, at that moment, wished in hindsight that she'd had the wisdom to partake of some spell or magickal elixir that would have dulled the painful memories of what she and Arthur Conan Doyle once shared.

The hurt of their lost love was a distraction, and that was something she could ill afford at this time.

Ceridwen hissed aloud, suppressing the rabid emotion that now bled from the newly ravaged wound of feelings, and forced her attentions fully to the chore at hand. There would be time later to deal with the trivial pains of her failed relationship, when the fate of worlds did not hang so precariously in the balance. Right now, she had to concentrate every facet of her consciousness upon communicating with the elemental spirits that composed the world of man—the world that the Fey had come to call the Blight.

With her staff, upon the parchment of open air, the Faerie sorceress wrote the intricate spells of elemental calling that had been passed down from generation to generation, as far back as the Fey could remember. The forces of nature had always been at their beck and call, a symbiotic relationship built upon a strong mutual respect.

The air grew steadily colder, her breath clouding from her mouth as she uttered the names of the primordial spirits that made up the world. As she spoke the last of their names, she felt the frigid air around her become charged with an eldritch energy that had existed since the explosion that was the birth cry of creation. The floor beneath her feet thrummed as the chilled air began to swirl. The flames of the candles, strategically placed about the room for illumination, stretched, growing taller, leaning toward the coursing air. She could feel the presence of those whom she had called, weaker than the last time they had communed in the world of man, but still a force to be reckoned with nonetheless. Sadly Ceridwen wondered if there would ever come a time when the elemental spirits would be too weak here to answer her call, but that was a concern for another time.

"You have summoned and we have answered, child of

the Fey," said the elements, their wispy voices speaking in unison. *"What task would you ask of us?"*

Ceridwen bowed her head in reverence to the forces that bound the universe. "Great and wise elemental spirits, this world in which you reside is in grave danger, and I ask of you only one thing, to transport me quickly and stealthily to my chosen location so that I may deal with this threat." She raised her head to see that a vortex composed of the elements swirled about her: earth, wind, fire, and water. "Will you aid me?" she asked of them.

The spirits did not answer and Ceridwen began to wonder if the distraction of her feelings for Arthur Conan Doyle had affected her far worse than she had first imagined.

"Spirits?" she questioned. "Have you heard my plea?"

They were still silent, whirling about her, and she was about to ask them again when at last they spoke.

"Perhaps it would be best if this world were to die," they said in unison, and Ceridwen found herself stunned by the response.

Long had the forces of nature on this world been under constant assault, the dominant species of the planet having no respect for the heavenly body on which they thrived. Mankind's arrogance and blatant disregard for its environment were maddening, and she could not help but entertain the thought that perhaps the spirits were right. Every time that she had set foot upon this accursed world, she found it in worse condition than the last. Humanity was killing this place that had once been second only to Faerie in its lush beauty.

The outcome was surely inevitable. Does it really matter if this place is to die now or later? she pondered. Ceridwen could not even begin to understand how Arthur could have left the world of the Fey for such a tainted place, but he loved this world of his birth and had made himself its protector. It was not her place to encourage its demise.

"No," Ceridwen said forcefully to the elemental manifestation that surrounded her. "This is not the time or place for such discussions. There is much life still left in this world and I, as well as others who share the same thoughts, are not yet ready to allow it to pass."

The elements were quiet, dwelling upon her words.

"Perhaps we were too rash," the spirits hissed. *"Your faith momentarily restores our hope. We shall watch further before this world's fate is decided upon."*

"A wise decision," Ceridwen answered, again bowing her head in respect. "Will you then grant my request?"

The whirlwind began to swirl all the faster around her, the elements blurring together as one powerful force. *"Take us into yourself, and in your thoughts, show your destination."*

Her former lover's home took shape within her mind as she inhaled, allowing spirits of nature access to her body.

"Yessssssss," they whispered all around her. *"We know this place."*

And the winds spun all the faster, shrieking and moaning as the forces of nature readied to do the sorceress's bidding.

"A traveling wind," Ceridwen said, clutching her staff of power to her chest, the icy ball adorning it pulsing with a cold, blue light, the combination of the frozen water and the fire within. "That is what I ask of you. A traveling wind to take me to the home of Conan Doyle."

"It is but the least we can do for you, child of the Fey," the elements said as they took her within their embrace, lifting her up from the ground.

"The least we can do."

• • •

DANNY Ferrick stared with awe into the living room.

The boy had had every intention of going up to bed, to lie down and attempt to understand what he had learned about himself, as well as the world in which he lived. In his mind he saw his life and the world in which he lived represented as a gigantic rock, its dark, jagged surface covered in patches of lichen and moss, undisturbed and untouched for perhaps hundreds of years. But then that rock was flipped over, and something else entirely was exposed—something terrifying, and yet absolutely fascinating. That was the real world for him now—the world in which he belonged.

His foot had just touched the first step that would take him up to his room when he'd felt it. It was like a gentle tug, as if there was an invisible rope wrapped around his waist and somebody at the other end, pulling—drawing him toward the living room.

Danny turned. He knew that Ceridwen was in the living room performing some kind of magickal spell that would take her to Conan Doyle's house. *Is that what's pulling me?* he wondered as he moved quietly down the hallway, clinging to the shadows. *Is Ceridwen's magick somehow calling to me?*

He heard voices coming from the room, and by the sound of it, the woman was not alone. Danny pressed himself against the wall before the doorway and listened. Ceridwen's voice was beautiful, like the singing of a song every time she spoke, but the other voice—multiple voices really, speaking as one—made the dry skin around his new horns itch like mad and the hair at the back of his neck stand on end.

Danny carefully peeked around the doorframe, not wanting to be seen. He was going to have his look and, with his curiosity satisfied, go right up to bed.

At least that was what he had intended.

All that he had seen recently, all he had experienced, it paled in comparison to what he was seeing at that moment.

"A traveling wind," the Faerie sorceress said aloud, her voice filled with authority. The air in the room, seeming to have become almost solid, spun around her incredibly fast, but she remained calm in the center of the maelstrom. "That is what I ask of you. A traveling wind to take me to the home of Conan Doyle."

The unnatural wind conjured within the living room of Danny's home screamed and moaned like twenty cats in heat, and it became more difficult to see the Faerie sorceress at its core.

"It is but the least we can do, child of the Fey," came the voice that set his nerves on edge, and Danny realized that it was coming from the body of the storm itself, that somehow the whirlwind was alive.

"Awesome," he whispered, transfixed by the sight. His body shook with the wind, his pants so baggy that they fluttered behind his legs.

"The least we can do."

And with those final words, the traveling wind spun all the faster. Furniture and knickknacks, anything not nailed down, were tossed about the living room by the powerful winds. Then the woman was lifted up from the center of the room and carried within the belly of the unnatural storm toward the ceiling.

Danny could not take his eyes from the sight, watching in awe as the manifestation of the sorceress's magick began to grow smaller, collapsing in upon itself. Ceridwen was leaving, being taken away by what she had called a traveling wind, and he felt the unnatural pull again—the tug that had brought him to this room grow all the stronger. He gripped the doorframe, his clawed fingernails digging into the hard wood as he fought to keep himself from entering the room. There was a part of him that wanted to go, to throw himself into the whirling vortex and accompany Ceridwen on her mission, but that was not his place. According to Conan Doyle, it was not his time.

The pull upon him was incredible as he watched the twister compress in size, Ceridwen nothing more than a dark stain at its core. It would be gone soon, transporting the woman to Conan Doyle's house where she would gather information to help them take down those responsible for what was currently happening to the world. And where would he be? Daniel asked of himself. He would be here, doing absolutely nothing, even though he knew that he was more than capable of helping.

The boy heard Mr. Doyle's hurtful words again echo within his skull *We shall see what your destiny holds, Danny Ferrick. But not tonight. Not tonight.*

"Then when?" he asked aloud, knowing very well if Conan Doyle's people—his agents, were not successful, things would be getting mighty hairy for mankind, and he might never be given the opportunity to show them what he knew he was capable of. This was his chance to truly belong, to prove that he was one of them.

Danny let go of the doorframe and allowed himself to be drawn into the room. He felt the drastic change in temperature, and he could see his breath. He stared up at the dissipating whirlwind, now less than half its original size, and still he struggled with the idea of what he should do.

Not tonight, the voice of Conan Doyle said again, warning him away from the thoughts of what Danny knew he should not be doing. And in his mind he saw himself leaving the room, climbing up the stairs to his bedroom where he would wait for the others to return from their chosen missions. This was what he *should* do.

"Fuck that shit," the boy growled, tensing the muscles in his legs and leaping up into the air at the magickal maelstrom. And he was pulled inside the final vestiges of the diminishing vortex, carried away from his home upon a traveling wind, eager to confront his destiny.˙

I N the dream, the world of man was hers to command.

Wearing robes of elegant silk, she walked in the garden of bones, the remains of those who challenged her, as far as the eye could see. They were arranged in the most beautiful of patterns, sticking up from the poisoned earth and hanging from barren trees, twirling amusingly in the fetid winds. The artisans of the Corca-Duibhne had outdone themselves, she thought, admiring the artistry of the Night People's work, creating sculptures both pleasing to her eyes and filled with meaning. This place would serve as a reminder to any who would dare to challenge her supremacy. A place to show them that any hopes of insurrection would be met with punishment, swift and terrible.

The mournful winds shifted ever so slightly, carrying the plaintive wails of the humans left alive to her ears. They were used as cattle now, a food source for her voracious army. A fate they most assuredly deserved.

And beneath the now eternally nocturnal sky, the sun forever blotted out by the undulating mist of scarlet red, Morrigan leaned back her head and basked in the misery that she had wrought. It is only a matter of time now, she thought, her body beginning to tingle with anticipation, only a matter of time before the world of Faerie fell prostrate before her, and she began to cry tears of thanks for what her master had given her.

"It is all I've ever dreamed of and more," Morrigan said, her voice trembling in emotion as she
gazed up into the sky. And something moved there
above her, something great and terrible that glided
through the mist-filled air, the pounding of its mighty
wings like the heartbeat of a world in peril.

Morrigan lay upon the king-sized bed of Arthur Conan
Doyle, her naked body still covered with the sticky after-
math of the recently performed blood ritual, still gripped
within the fantasy of dream. The spell that she had woven
had been extremely taxing, and she often found that a brief
nap was exactly what was needed for her to retain that
much-needed edge, and what better place to rest after the
exhausting job of sacrificing two innocent children, she
thought, than upon the bed of your vanquished enemy.

Her eyes came suddenly open, awakened from her
blissful respite by a disturbance in the ether. It was like the
vibrations felt within the silken threads of a spider's web,
an alarm of sorts warning that something could very well
be amiss. Morrigan raised herself up on her elbows, gazing
about the darkness of the master bedroom.

The two boggarts, large doglike beasts lying curled and
content at the foot of the bed until that moment, raised
their blocky, black-furred heads and sniffed at the air. The
animals growled, a horrible gurgling sound, the loose flesh
around their mouths rippling back to reveal angry red
gums filled with razor-sharp teeth.

"What is it?" she asked the demonic beasts, conjured as
a precautionary measure to watch over her while she slept.
The two unnatural animals tilted back their large, square
heads, sucking whistling lungfuls of air into their eager
nostrils. They sensed it the same as she, the faintest hint of
a magickal disturbance in the air.

"Come." Morrigan beckoned the animals to her as she

left the bed, and they slunk from atop the mattress to the floor, their short, triangular ears flat against their skulls in submissiveness as they stood on either side of her naked form, licking the dried blood of the children from her hands.

She concentrated upon the ripple in the ether, attempting to discern its purpose but, much to her frustration, could not read it.

"Who would dare such a thing?" she asked aloud, padding naked across the bedroom to the door, taking some satisfaction in the knowledge that the two who could challenge her were not present upon this world; she had seen to that.

Morrigan flung the door wide, startling a band of Night People who had set up a kind of encampment outside the bedroom door. The creatures quickly averted their eyes, not wanting to incur their mistress's wrath.

"Did you feel it?" she asked them. "A spell has breached our defenses."

The boggarts started to whine, eager to track the scent of the invasive magick.

"Go," she commanded them with a wave of her taloned hand, and the beasts bounded down the upstairs hall, powerful muscles rippling beneath jet-black flesh, scattering Corca-Duibhne and their belongings in their fury to hunt that which did not belong.

Morrigan followed close behind, fearing the worst as the eager boggarts descended the stairs, their claws scrabbling across the hardwood floors for purchase as they made their way toward the ballroom, and her most treasured possession.

Disturbing images flashed through her mind, scenarios that rendered all that she had planned moot. She first imagined finding the chrysalis of Sweetblood shattered upon the ballroom floor, the powerful mage now free and filled with fury, and then the equally horrific thought that the chrysalis was gone, stolen, not a piece to be found. She quickened her pace, catching up to the doglike creatures sniffing and digging eagerly at the bottom of the closed ballroom doors.

Filled with anticipation, she gripped the knobs in her eager hands, turning them and pushing the doors open. The boggarts bounded into the room, howling and snapping at the air as if it were filled with prey.

A deadly spell of defense danced upon Morrigan's lips, crackling arcane energies ready to lash out at any enemy present, but the room was as she left it.

The twins, Fenris and Dagris, looked startled as they stood above the sarcophagus of solidified magick that held the body of Sweetblood the Mage.

"Mistress?" Fenris asked, his voice filled with concern.

They were still doing as they had been instructed, maintaining the spell that would hopefully allow them greater access to the magickal forces imprisoned within Sanguedolce's cocoon.

The boggarts continued to pace about the room, howling and carrying on. Something had been there; of this she was certain. Morrigan strode naked toward the chrysalis, wanting to see with her own two eyes that her means to victory was still very much within her grasp.

She felt the twins' questioning eyes upon her bare flesh, but she paid them no mind as she reached down to wipe away the blood of the sacrifice that covered the mage's containment vessel, hoping to gaze upon the visage of the one whose power she had so come to desire. The blood had partially coagulated, and it sloughed off, plopping to the floor as she ran her hand across the cocoon's chiseled surface.

Morrigan actually breathed a sigh of relief as she caught sight of the form of the mage, still trapped within, but that relief quickly changed to concern as her eyes studied the frozen countenance of the archmage all the closer. Something was different. If she was not mistaken, Sweetblood's expression had somehow changed.

And he appeared very angry.

THE sleek black limousine cut through the billowing red fog like a surgeon's knife through diseased flesh. In the driver's seat, the hobgoblin Squire sat quietly, piloting the vehicle through the impenetrable mist with an expertise that Clay found uncanny.

The shapeshifter gazed out his side window. Though morning, he could see practically nothing other than the undulating clouds of crimson. Even with the structure of his eyes changed, giving him the best possible vision, he could still not make heads or tails of where they were, or where they were going.

"How do you do it?" Clay asked Squire from the backseat.

The goblin started, grabbing hold of the rearview mirror and manipulating it so that he could see into the backseat. "You talking to me?"

Eve shifted in the seat beside Clay, hugging herself as if cold, leaning her head against the glass of her window. "No, the other little twisted freak driving this car," she growled sarcastically. "Of course he's talking to you."

Clay shook his head. Squire and Eve certainly shared an interesting relationship. He was never quite sure if the two actually despised one another, or it was all some kind of act to deflect attention from the fact that they truly cared for each other.

"Hey, Eve, got a box of native earth in the trunk, why don't you lay in it?" barked Squire.

"Miserable shit," she grumbled, slumping lower and closing her eyes.

But then again . . .

"The driving," Clay said before Squire could launch his second, venom-filled volley. He moved forward in his seat to speak with the hobgoblin. "How do you manage to actually navigate through this stuff?"

Squire shrugged. "It's really instinctual," he said. "Kind of like traveling the darkness of the shadowpaths." The goblin explained further. "I can feel where I need to go inside my head. It's weird, and hard to explain."

The vehicle suddenly banked to the left to avoid something in the middle of the road. Clay got a quick glimpse through the side window as the car sped past. If he wasn't mistaken, it looked to be nothing more than a rotting human torso and head, writhing maggotlike across the center of the road. Yet another of the pathetic things responding to the siren song that drew the dead to the Museum of Fine Arts. Their destination as well.

"You see that?" Squire asked him as he expertly steered the car back to the center of the road.

"Yeah," Clay answered. He could now see the shapes of other animated corpses shambling through the thick fog of crimson, in the road and on either side. Squire managed to avoid them with ease.

We must be getting closer, Clay thought.

"Hey, you know what that guy in the road would be named if he were hung on a wall?" the hobgoblin asked.

Clay wasn't quite sure what the diminutive chauffeur was talking about. "What?" he asked. "I'm not sure I . . ."

"Art," Squire answered, stifling back a guffaw. "Get it? His name would be Art. He would be hanging on a wall? Art? It loses a lot if I gotta explain it."

Graves was sitting in the front seat, and now the ghostly figure turned to look at the driver. "Maybe it would be wise if you just concentrated on your driving and ceased all attempts at humor," the ghost said coldly, the first words he had spoken since pulling away from the Ferricks' home in Newton.

Squire shook his gourdlike head in disgust. "Jeez, try and lighten the mood a bit, and suddenly I'm treated like the friggin' bastard child of Carrot Top."

Clay leaned back in his seat, letting the uneasy silence again hold sway over the inside of the car. It was obvious that Graves did not appreciate Squire's attempts at levity, preferring the somber silence. Over the years, Clay had seen the different ways in which soldiers prepared themselves for battle, no two warriors doing it in quite the same way. He'd always preferred a little quiet reflection before the war, reviewing the multitude of shapes that he could possibly manifest in order to combat and defeat the threat he was about to face.

Clay gazed at the back of Graves' head, able to see right through it to the windshield in front of him. He didn't know the adventurer all that well, having worked with him only a handful of times, but he had been a man of science in the days when he was still amongst the living. Clay could only imagine how disconcerting it must have been for the man to be confronted with the existence of the supernatural. *How do you prepare for something that you spent your entire living existence believing didn't exist?* Clay understood why the spirit would have no patience for Squire's stupid jokes.

"I'm just pulling onto Huntington Ave," the hobgoblin said from the driver's seat. "It's only a matter of time now."

The road had become dense with the reanimated dead, and the chauffeur continued to do as well as could be expected to do avoiding hitting them, but the closer they got, the harder it was becoming. Clay flinched as the front of the vehicle struck the body of a woman, the impact spraying a shower of thick milky fluid across the expanse of windshield.

"Whoa, that's gonna leave a mark," Squire said beneath his breath, hitting the button to cover the windshield with cleaning fluid before turning on the wiper blades.

Squire dealt with his tensions of the coming conflict with humor. It was something that Clay was familiar with. In an age he now recalled only through the veil of time, he had known a great Sumerian warrior called Atalluk, who would gather his fellow soldiers the night before they were to wage war against their enemies and tell humorous stories about his childhood and his ribald adventures with members of the opposite sex. Clay smiled with the ancient memory. The men loved those tales, the stories helping them to relax and to relieve the tensions they were most likely experiencing in regard to the approaching combat.

Atalluk had been a gifted warrior, but gifted with wit as well. Clay still carried a certain amount of guilt for killing the Sumerian upon the battlefield, but there had been no choice. It was what he had been paid by the opposing forces to do.

The limousine hit a slow-moving cluster of ambling dead, their dried flesh and bones scattering like dusty tenpins. "Strike!" Squire roared, shaking a gnarled fist in the air under the disapproving gaze of Leonard Graves.

Clay glanced at Eve, who still appeared to be resting. Here was someone that he had fought beside on numerous occasions, who understood and embraced the meaning of calm before the storm. She was a creature of infinite patience in dire circumstances, Eve was, and there wasn't another warrior that he would rather have fighting by his side. When it was time to fight, she would be ready; he had no doubts about that.

The dead had become even more numerous. Their horrible faces crowded around to peer into the limousine as it began to slow.

"We're almost there," Squire said, gunning the engine, plowing through the mass of decaying flesh and bones. "I want to get you close enough so you're not bogged down. They can be a real pain in the ass, these dead guys."

The goblin leaned on the horn, as if that would make a difference. "Outta the way, you stinkin' bags of bones. Can't you see we're trying to get through here!"

Clay felt his respiration gradually begin to increase, the beating of his heart quicken. It was as it always was for him, the response of his body to the battle that was sure to come.

"Are we ready?" he asked.

Graves turned in his seat to look at Clay, his death-pale features nearly transparent. "As set as I'll ever be when dealing with things of this nature," the ghost said, apparently perturbed that he was again forced to face the facts that he had so vehemently denied in life. Graves drifted up and out of his seat toward the limo ceiling, his head passing through the roof.

"I got your backs," Squire said, his large eyes reflected in the surface of the rearview mirror, and he cracked the door on the passenger side, ready to exit.

Clay looked to Eve, the woman scrunched down in her seat, seemingly still in the embrace of sleep.

"This is it, Eve," he said, reaching to shake her awake.

The woman responded in an instant, gripping his wrist in her powerful grasp before his hand could fall upon her.

"I'm awake," she told him, and he could see by the look in her deep, dark eyes that she was more than ready for what they were about to face.

"Then let's do what we came here for," he said, pulling his wrist out of her grip and preparing to open his passenger door.

As he did this, he heard the surprising sound of laughter, a pleasant sound, and one that he did not remember hearing too many times before. Clay looked across the backseat to see that Eve was giggling as she too prepared to exit the car.

She must have felt his eyes upon her and turned her head to meet his gaze.

"What's so funny?" he asked, completely in the dark as to what could have tickled her funny bone at that particular moment.

"Yeah," Squire reiterated, a breathless tension in his voice. Even he did not see any signs of the humorous at the moment. "What's the joke?"

"Art," she said and again began to laugh. "The guy with no arms or legs hanging on the wall. His name would be Art."

Eve opened her door, stepping out into the billowing crimson mist that hid an army of the dead. "That's pretty fucking funny," she said, just before slamming the door closed behind her.

And as Clay also left the vehicle, his body pulsing with the potential for violence that was to follow, he was forced to admit that the woman was right; it was funny.

When you looked at it from a certain way, it was all *funny.*

13

Kingsley is dead.

Conan Doyle, for that is how he is known to all
and sundry, sits in the foyer of the Grosvenor Hotel
with an unlit pipe propped between his lips. His eyes
glaze as he gazes across the elegant foyer at ladies
and their gentlemen, bustling to and fro. It is the
middle of November, yet already the spirit of Christ-
mas is in the air. Conan Doyle spies a small boy, perhaps five, running circles round his Ma'am's legs as
his Da has an angry word with a bellman.

The father often loses patience with the boy.
Conan Doyle can see bruises on the child's inner
arms, dark purple marks where his father's thumb
and fingers have gripped too tightly. The mother
loves her husband, but she holds her breath, hoping
his temper is satisfied by berating the bellman and
quietly trying to calm her boy so that he does not
draw his father's attention.

The bellman is new to the job. Conan Doyle can
see this from his shoes. The uniform is new, the but-

tons polished, but the shoes are badly scuffed, heels worn. The man had not been working at the Grosvenor long enough to have saved money for new shoes.

And Kingsley is dead.

The bellman has no money. The boy's father is far too rough with him. But Conan Doyle's own son, the pride of his heart, had been taken by the influenza. The wounds that Kingsley had received at the Somme had not killed him, but they had weakened him.

Kingsley is dead, and now a fortnight later Conan Doyle sits in the foyer of the Grosvenor Hotel and frowns as he glances up at the woman who has just entered through the revolving door. She is a large woman, stern featured and well dressed, and she carries in each hand a tiny Union Jack, the flag of Britain. As if in a dream, she waltzes silently and alone, waving these small banners, and then she disappears through the revolving door once more, returning to the street.

Moments later, a roar begins to build. Voices. Weeping. Dancing feet.

Armistice. The war is over.

Kingsley is dead.

"Peace," a voice says, dry and cold. It is not a greeting, but an observation, and even then it is more cynical than celebratory.

Conan Doyle taps his pipe on his knee and glances up into the face of Lorenzo Sanguedolce, his olive skin, fancy mustache, and Italian accent marking him as a suspicious character in these times of war.

"Kingsley is dead," Conan Doyle tells him.

Sanguedolce nods. "Yes. But he has not gone far,

Arthur. Not yet. You may still be able to speak with him for a time."

Ice forms around Conan Doyle's heart and he cannot meet Sanguedolce's eyes. "I think not."

"No?"

"No. If I speak with him, I may become too fond of the idea of joining him."

When he looks up, they are no longer in the Grosvenor Hotel, these two men. Conan Doyle stands on Wandsworth Road, looking up at the face of the Three Goats' Heads pub. The name of the place is repeated on three signs, two on the building itself and one on a post in front of it, along with a faded reminder that one might also find Watney & Company's ale inside. The windows are filthy. Gathered in a small circle are a quartet of rough-looking men in dark derby hats.

The war has not yet begun, will not begin for years yet.

Conan Doyle enters the Three Goats' Heads. Ale spills from glasses as the barkeep slides them along a table. The air is choked with smoke, a fog that obscures his vision.

In the center of the pub there is a table that is clean, save for a single pint of ale. Despite the crowd, no one goes near. Impossibly, there is a circle of clear air around and above the table, as though the wafting smoke is kept out by some invisible wall. Conan Doyle has come to Wandsworth Road this evening in response to a note, a summons signed by Lorenzo Sanguedolce. He has heard of the man, of course, the one they call Sweetblood the Mage. He has dismissed much of this talk as merely that. Talk.

One glimpse of Sanguedolce's eyes, like bright pennies, and the way he seems to exist separate from *the world, even in the din and dirt of a public house, and Conan Doyle knows there is more to the man than talk.*

He sits across from Sanguedolce. He says nothing by way of introduction. They have never met, but still they know one another.

"You're a fool," Sanguedolce says, voice dripping with venom.

"What?" Conan Doyle demands, taken aback.

"Languishing in memories, in the comfort of the past," Sanguedolce explains. "You can't afford the luxury."

All other sound in the Three Goats' Heads is abruptly silenced. The smoke thickens, becomes a wall of gray, and their small table is nearly in darkness. Beyond the table, things move in the smoke, and Conan Doyle is certain that they are not the patrons of the bar, not thick-necked men in dark derbies, but others. Things that move in shadow, thrive in it, even consume it.

He has been drifting inside himself. Lost. Sanguedolce is right. He is a fool. But somehow, despite it all, he has found the archmage's mind, touched him. Even now Lorenzo's face shimmers and blurs. Morrigan's power interferes, as do the spells Sanguedolce used to hide himself, so long ago. Conan Doyle brushes a hand through the air, clearing some of the strange ash that hangs there, and he can see Sanguedolce more clearly.

For the moment.

"Quickly, then," Conan Doyle snaps, angry at himself, angry at Sweetblood. "Talk. What is Morrigan's plan? What does she want you for?"

"Idiot," Sanguedolce says. "I was hidden for a reason."

The archmage draws back his hand to strike, but it never touches Conan Doyle. The smoke and ash coalesce around them, and Sanguedolce seems a part of it now, gray shadows enveloping him, erasing him.

"No!" Conan Doyle cries. "Wait!"

"This is not my doing. There is too much darkness between us, too much power."

But his voice sounds distant, muffled, and diminishing with each word. Then . . .

"Here." And a hand thrusts out of the smoke gray shadow, a fingertip touching Conan Doyle's forehead, a light tap just between the eyes.

Slivers of pain lance through his head. His eyes burn. Bile rises in the back of his throat. Images erupt in his mind. Flashes of color, accompanied by the shrieking of children and the agonized wail of mothers. A city on fire. A highway lined with the dead. A barricade built of rotting, festering corpses. Charred flesh falling like snow from a dead black sky. Holes in the world, craters where entire nations had once been. A small, grinning girl with a bloody mouth and sharp teeth, looking up at her father with a knife in one hand and her mother's eyes in the other.

Armies, marching.

Disease on the wind. Red welts and yellow blisters, a crowd dropping one by one, like wheat beneath the scythe.

And from the darkest corners of the world, hideous beasts begin to emerge. Demons. And worse.

"My Lord," Conan Doyle whispers. "Morrigan doesn't have this kind of power. What does she call?"

Now he feels himself choking on the smoke, the gray shadows sheathing his eyes, smothering him, crawling up his nostrils. Conan Doyle passes a hand before him and the gray withdraws only enough that he can see the outline of a face in the smoke. The lips move, but Sanguedolce's voice is in his head, not in the smoke.

"You don't listen. This isn't Morrigan's plan. But she has already corrupted the sorcery of my chrysalis. My power is already seeping, drawing attention. It must be sealed again. The things you have seen . . . they are inevitable unless you can stop her. If I am freed, this is the fate of the world."

Conan Doyle is cloaked in gray smoke again. Once more, furiously, he waves it away, but this time when it clears he is at his table at the Three Goats' Heads, and he is alone.

And he awakened.

The wind whipped Danny Ferrick's face with such ferocity that tears stung his eyes. It tugged at his clothing like ghost fingers, and he felt himself spun around, feet dangling uselessly beneath him, a scarecrow in a hurricane. It was all blackness and wind, save for brief glimpses through the dark, eyeblink windows on the world, none of which offered the same view as the last. He squeezed his eyes closed.

A hard gust blew him upward, and as he floated downward again, he felt solid ground beneath his feet. A spiral breeze kept him from stumbling. He opened his eyes upon a dark room. The curtains fluttered in the traveling wind, and his hair was ruffled a moment longer, and then the breeze died, and all was silence in the room save for the settling of dust upon the wooden floor.

The canopy of the four-poster bed was the same ivory

as the curtains. The carved wood of those posts was bone white. A long bureau was against the far wall and a fireplace, dark and cold, was set into another. Other than these, the room was featureless, with no sign of any occupant. There were no lamps, no mirrors, no books or handbrushes, and only a single pillow on the bed.

Unless something had gone wrong, this was Mr. Doyle's house. Danny figured it was a spare bedroom because it certainly did not seem as though anyone lived here. *But* . . . He frowned, glancing around the room. The door was firmly closed. He had followed Ceridwen here, let himself be swept along in the wake of her magic. *So where the hell is she?*

The darkness of the room felt comfortable to him, as though it was a robe he had slipped on. His eyes had always adjusted well to the dark. Danny moved soundlessly across the room and opened the door just wide enough to peer through, and pressed an eye to the crack. The room he was in was at the end of the hall, and the corridor outside the door only a wing. There were five other doors, two on the left and three on the right, and then a left turn. It was dark, but where the corridor turned there was a glimmer of distant light, perhaps from a room around the corner.

Ceridwen's shadow was on the wall at the end of the corridor, thrown by the glow of that dim light.

With no sign of anyone else, Danny slipped out of the room and pulled the door softly shut behind him. His nostrils flared and he smelled blood in the house. Somewhere. And it wasn't human blood. His forked tongue slid over sharp rows of teeth, and he felt his lips pull up into a kind of smile, as if he had no control over his response to that scent at all. Then he realized that it wasn't a smile. It was a snarl.

Danny moved in silence through the dark corridor, still wrapped in shadows. He felt invisible. He had always been good at hide-and-seek as a child, always had an uncanny ability to sneak up on others unawares. For the first time he realized this was not an ordinary thing. He cloaked himself in darkness and slipped quietly down the hall, and this time when he smiled to himself, it was genuine.

At the end of the hall he peeked around the corner, remaining out of sight, and when he saw Ceridwen, he caught his breath.

This new corridor was far longer, and halfway down its length was a balustrade and a stairwell that came down from above and continued on toward the first floor. Danny had no idea what floor they were on now. The dim light upon the walls was from somewhere below. At the landing, just beside the stairs, were two creatures unlike anything Danny had seen before. They were stooped, hands twisted into claws, long talons dangling by their knees. Their skin was leathery brown and rutted with lines that might have been scars or wrinkles or grooves in tree bark. And yet he had the idea that if they stood up straight and hid their faces, they might have been able to walk the daylight world and pass as human.

Just the way Danny did.

But he would have seen them for what they were. He would have smelled them. They had the stink of raw meat and sewer on them, these things. Danny had heard enough from Conan Doyle and the others to know they had to be the Night People. The Corca-Duibhne. Seeing them made him tremble, but not with fear. He shook with the urge to kill them.

Ceridwen was in the hall as well, only ten or twelve feet from the Night People. The ice blue sphere atop her staff glowed softly. Danny could not help but notice the way her long limbs moved. She was breathtaking. Her whole self seemed illuminated by the same ice blue light that glowed within that sphere.

Magick, he thought. For even as he watched, she moved nearer the two hideous creatures, and neither noticed her.

With an elegant flourish, Ceridwen spread her arms and glided toward the Corca-Duibhne; to Danny it almost seemed as though she were dancing. It was a strange moment of ballet that ended with Ceridwen reaching out to touch the nearest of the two Night People. A blue light blossomed from her fingertips, blue-white mist leaked from her eyes in streams that floated on the air, and the sphere atop her staff flared with a moment of brilliance.

The monstrous creature froze, leathery skin turning that same ice blue. A wave of chilling cold swept up the corridor and Danny shivered, staring at the scene that played out before him.

The second Corca-Duibhne turned, shivering at the blast of frozen air, and its eyes widened. It opened its mouth, flashing yellow razor teeth, but before it could sound an alarm, Ceridwen's free hand flashed out and gripped it by the throat. Her muscles were taut, but even in profile Danny could see her face was expressionless. Her eyes were as cold as the ice of her magick. The creature let out a single groan, but no cry of alarm came.

The ice formed first upon its yellow fangs. Then its eyes froze in its head. Moments later it was little more than an ice sculpture, just like the other.

"Holy shit," Danny whispered from the shadows.

Ceridwen swept her staff around in an arc that shattered them both. Thousands of shards of ice cascaded along the floor of the corridor. Then she stood still once more, as though she had not even moved, and she held her staff before her in both hands.

Danny felt a warm breeze begin to ruffle his hair. A wind sprang up in the corridor. One moment it was gentle, even pleasant, and the next it whistled in his ears and nearly knocked him off his feet, a tropical blast of heat that seared his lungs when he inhaled. His claws dug into the wall and he clung to the corner, knowing if he fell he would give himself away. He watched in awe as the frozen remains of the two Corca-Duibhne swirled and eddied in the hot wind.

They melted away to nothing, leaving not a drop of condensation on the floor.

Gone.

The wind died and Danny held his breath, staring at Ceridwen. The Fey sorceress went to the stairs and glanced upward, and then leaned over the balustrade, getting her bearings.

Then she turned her icy eyes upon him.

Danny shuddered. He had cloaked himself in darkness, had felt sure that his stealth was part of what he was, one of the few benefits of his supernatural genesis. If this was to be his life—the life of a monster—he'd thought at least there might be something good to come of it.

"Come here," Ceridwen said, and though she spoke in a whisper, her words carried to him.

Abandoning any effort to hide himself, Danny hurried down the corridor to her. He glanced around at the many doors along the hall and at the stairs, worried that at any moment more of Morrigan's followers might discover them.

As he approached, Ceridwen grabbed his wrist and drew him up to her. Her fingers were ice upon his skin, and that frozen mist still leaked from her eyes. She towered over him, and he had not realized before just how tall she was. A shiver went up and down his spine, but it was not the cold that made him tremble. Ceridwen was indeed beautiful, but it could be a terrible beauty, a cruel flaw-lessness.

"What do you think you're doing?" she demanded in a terse whisper.

"Helping," he said. "I wanted to help."

"Arthur told you to stay behind."

Danny had no response to that and so he said nothing. He felt his brows knit, felt his upper lip curl into another snarl, but could not prevent these reactions. They were instinctual. As much as he feared her, if Ceridwen did not let go of his wrist, he thought he might try to hurt her.

His ears twitched. Voices reached them from the stairwell. Someone was coming up from below. Ceridwen turned toward the stairs and raised her staff, but this time it was Danny who grabbed hold of her wrist.

"No," he whispered. "We're here to learn. To do that, we listen."

She glared at him a moment, and then she nodded. Danny moved swiftly and silently to the nearest door. It was unlocked, and he led Ceridwen inside. He left the door open several inches and knelt to put his eye to the crack. The room was dark, and once more he gathered the shadows around himself, hoping Morrigan's followers wouldn't be as perceptive as Ceridwen, hoping the darkness would keep them from noticing him spying.

He knew Ceridwen was behind him. Even now she would be standing above him, trying to peer into the hall. Danny could feel her there, could feel the cold. And that was the two of them. Ice and shadows.

Together they waited, and they listened, in the cold and the dark.

THE glass was shattered in the doors of the Museum of Fine Arts. The broad stone stairs in front of the building's grand facade were swarming with the dead. Corpses crawled over one another, trying to get to the doors. The red mist that enveloped the entire city churned and rolled in clouds that obscured the horror surrounding the museum for a few seconds before thinning once more. Flags beat the air, jutting from the brow of the building, and banners advertising the latest exhibitions covered part of its face.

There were walking dead who were crumbling with every step, who were clothed in tatters. Some of them had lost arms or hands, even lower jaws, and what skin remained was parchment stretched across their cheeks or sunken eye sockets. Muscle tore as they walked, but the magick that propelled them was merciless.

Eve moved through the dead with her long sword like the reaper with his scythe. Yet this was a bloodless harvest. The blade Squire had provided from Conan Doyle's armory hacked into them with the pop and dry cracking noise of snapping kindling. Her coat flowed around her like a toreador's cape, but she did not need any red flag to draw their attention. The restless dead had been sent to the museum for a reason, but presented with targets, with vibrant, alive creatures to kill, they deviated from their mission.

She felt the blood race through her, her mind descending into a primitive rage that often enveloped her in combat. Her mouth opened and she howled a cry of battle that echoed out across the empty street. Her heightened senses brought to her the scent of Clay nearby, but he and the specter, Dr. Graves, were lost in the mist and the sea of staggering dead.

Cold fingers clutched at her jacket and snagged in her hair. Eve spun, bringing the sword around with both hands upon its grip. This time, however, the blade met more resistance. Some of the walkers were freshly dead, their flesh and muscle more substantial, their bones harder. Two hands grabbed her head and a pale, fat man in a three-piece suit dipped his jaws as though he might tear out her throat.

Eve gave a cruel, rasping laugh as she thrust her sword point through his midsection. With her preternatural strength, she hoisted the fat cadaver off the ground and dumped him on top of several others. A dead woman, her face painted in the garish makeup of morticians the world over, seemed to grin as she reached out and twisted her fingers in the fabric of Eve's blouse, tugging at the spaghetti straps as though intent on tearing it off. Eve hacked her hands from her wrists.

It was a perverse death dance, a black tie event, every corpse dressed in its Sunday best. But Eve wasn't getting anywhere. The limousine was back at the curb and she had made some progress, but not enough. She was at the bottom of the museum steps, and cutting through the dead was taking too long. There were just too many of them. The sword was too slow.

"Squire!" she roared into the sky, into the red mist.

Off to her right was a statue of a man on horseback. She heard the goblin replying even as she spotted him emerging from the dark shadow beneath the statue.

"What can I do ya for, darlin'?" he called.

Eve sheathed her sword. A pair of dead walkers, one only days dead and one rattling with every step, tried to take advantage of the moment. She lashed out at the fresh one, grabbed it by the face and yanked it toward her. With her left hand she dug her talons into the flesh at the back of its neck, plunged her fingers in around bone and gristle, and tore out its spinal column. The other, the crumbling, brittle one, she shattered with a single kick of a designer boot.

"This is taking too long!" she called to the goblin. "I need something that's going to clear a bigger path."

Even through the mist she could see Squire grin. The goblin slipped back beneath the statue and disappeared in the darkness there. Squire could fight when necessary, but that was not his purpose among Conan Doyle's agents. He drove, yes, but only because he enjoyed it. Squire was the armorer, the weapons master. As long as there were shadows for him to pass through, Eve knew she would never be without a weapon when she needed one.

The dead continued to grab at her, but now Eve was less concerned with fighting them. Destroying each one would take forever and was a waste of time. Getting through them, past them, that was the priority. She felt her rage begin to subside. Had these been living enemies, bodies humming with fresh blood, she would have found it much more difficult to sublimate her fury and her bloodlust.

But they were dead, hollow things.

Obstacles.

Eve tore through them, picking up one dead walker and tossing it at the others. With a single swipe of her hand, she tore the head off the corpse of a teenaged girl. Her gaze swept the crowding dead, and she saw a skull-faced cadaver, a man who had been extremely tall. She pulled the arms from the withered corpse and drove it down in front of her. It fell across several others and they scrambled to get up, to get free, to get at Eve. Planting a boot solidly on the dead man's chest, she launched herself over the heads of a dozen of the staggering zombies.

Eve landed in the midst of another horde and began to fight them as well. She was halfway up the stairs when she heard Squire call her name. She turned to see him slip from the darker shadows up against the wall of the museum.

"How about this?" Squire asked.

He raised a pump shotgun in one hand. Eve grinned and raised her own hand, and Squire threw the weapon to her. She snatched it from the air.

"I could kiss you."

"Don't flatter yourself, babe," Squire replied, and then he was gone again, lost in shadows.

Eve turned the shotgun and aimed in the general direction of the museum's front door.

"All right, numbskulls. Now the fun starts."

She pumped the shotgun and fired. The blast tore the torso out of a corpse right in front of her, ripping through two others behind it, and knocking down several others that were clustered with them in a tangle of clawing arms and twitching legs. Tiny bits of human gristle spattered her top, but at last she was beyond caring about her clothes. There were always more shops, always something pretty to wear. But she didn't get an evening like this very often.

Again she pumped and fired, racing forward, leaping up stairs. She found her footing where she could, crushing bones under her boots, darting in amongst the dead. The shotgun boomed in her hands and she neared the top of the stairs.

Then the shells were spent, the shotgun smoking. Eve dropped it to clatter on the stone steps and drew her sword once more. The museum doors had been torn open and they hung off-kilter in their frames.

"In," she snarled.

CLAY could be anyone. He had met warriors in his long, long life who were terrifying in every aspect. Some of them were unnaturally strong, some large enough that ordinary men would have called them giants. Some were like gods to the simple people who worshipped them. But he could also be anything. A tiger. A grizzly. A snake. Even some things that had only existed in the imagination of the Creator, things that had never walked the Earth but that He had considered.

The dead were quicker than they looked, jerking and lunging and clawing. But Clay did not need swiftness or skill, did not need agility to deal with these mindless abominations. All he needed was power and an appetite for destruction, and he had both in quantity today.

Once outside the limousine, and away from the eyes of his comrades, he changed. There were times when he felt awkward about his nature, about the malleability of his body. He wanted them to see him as Clay, to have an identity in their minds, and experience had shown him that anyone who saw his flesh run like mercury and his bones reshape often enough could lose track of who he was.

He hated that, for there were times when the only way he could know himself was to see how he was reflected in the eyes of others. That was the fundamental truth of what he was.

He was *Clay*.

Now his hot breath snorted from his nostrils and he felt his muscles ripple in his chest. Black fur stood up on the back of his neck, and he felt the crimson mist caressing the tip of each hair. He was a five-hundred-pound mountain gorilla, a silverback. Clay marched forward, trampling the walking dead beneath him, feeling their bones crushed to dust under his feet. Seconds passed as he cleared the area around him of zombies. His massive hands closed on the heads of the corpses. Some of their skulls shattered in his grip. Others he tore away from their shoulders.

"Having fun, big boy?" a voice asked.

With a grunt, the massive gorilla turned and stared as a slit appeared in the undulating darkness beside him. Like some grotesque birth, Squire slipped through the womb of shadows and stood before him, holding out a huge Turkish battle-axe, a weapon almost as large as the goblin himself.

"Fun," Clay replied.

He snatched the axe from Squire in one enormous gorilla hand. The goblin took two steps backward into darkness and was gone, even as the walking corpses tried to grab him. Clay swung it with such power that he cleaved the heads from two of the dead and in the same blow cut a freshly dead man completely in half, the divided portions of his corpse striking the paved sidewalk with moist weight.

He threw back his head, free hand pounding his chest, and let out a gorilla roar that echoed back from the enveloping mist. The dead surrounded him and Clay began to trample them again. The axe swung out, clearing a path, and with his free hand he slapped others down to the ground. He reached the stairs, huge feet cracking the stone beneath him. The dead fell before him. His progress was slow, but inexorable.

Then, with another snort of hot air, the mountain gorilla paused. There were times when Clay transformed that he lost himself in his new shape. It took him a second to clear his mind, to make sense of what he was seeing.

Just ahead, the ghost of Leonard Graves walked toward him down the stairs. The walking corpses sensed the phantom of the dead adventurer. They could feel Graves' presence. But they could not touch him. Their fingers, sometimes little more than bones, snatched at the spectral form of Dr. Graves, tried to tear his flesh, to grab hold of his clothes. But there was nothing there. It maddened them, and some of the mindless dead seemed somewhat less mindless now, their faces etched with a vicious frustration.

"Clay," Dr. Graves said calmly as the decaying corpse of a woman in military uniform reached through his ghostly flesh and grabbed hold of another of the dead.

With a shudder and a grunt, Clay twitched and transformed back into the human form he most often wore. There was something in Graves' tone and bearing that made him feel foolish. And now that he no longer wore the body of an animal, he thought he knew what it was.

"There are too many to fight," Clay said.

He swung his axe, not to cut but to batter, and knocked away three of the dead who were clutching at him.

Graves could not be touched, but his expression revealed his frustration. Abruptly he tore his gaze from Clay and reached out to the two zombies nearest him. His hands, pure ectoplasm, reached inside the rotting corpses, disappearing within. Their spirits had been forcibly pulled from the afterlife, restored to dead flesh, to rotting brains and madness. Now, with a single tug, Dr. Graves ripped those souls back out of their bodies.

The ghosts screamed in torment, eyes wide with unspeakable agony. But in the moment before they shimmered and dissipated like smoke on the breeze, they gazed at Dr. Graves with profound gratitude.

"You're wasting time out here," Graves told him.

Clay frowned. "Eve?"

"Already inside," said the specter.

"Shit," Clay said, kicking a zombie in the chest as he started toward the stairs to the museum. "It's just second nature. Something like this happens . . . you know once they're done here, these deadheads are going to look for more populated areas. That's what they do, zombies. They kill. I've never understood if they're hungry or just angry, but that's what they do. It doesn't feel right, leaving them walking around."

Graves floated beside Clay, ignoring the carnage as the shapeshifter tore and hacked through more of the dead. "There are already too many of them for us to stop them. It would take hours. Maybe days. We don't have that kind of time. It's not why we're here. And if we do the job—"

"There may be another way to stop them," Clay finished.

Even as his lips formed the last of these words, they were not lips anymore. He opened his beak and cawed loudly, and he spread his falcon wings wide and thrust himself up into the air.

Dr. Graves kept pace. The ghost flew beside him. Clay stretched out his wings and glided in through the front doors of the museum. The huge foyer echoed with the shuffling footsteps of the dead. There were shattered corpses on the floor, unmoving, and it was easy to follow the path that Eve had taken. She had blazed the trail for them.

Up through the main hall Clay flew, the ghost of Dr. Graves keeping pace with him. They turned and passed through arched passages, and soon they were moving through the collection *Art of Ancient Africa*. An exhibition of Egyptian burial jars, sarcophagi, bracelets and necklaces, and many other objects was ahead. Though the museum held some of the most beautiful and most celebrated paintings in the world, it was these wings that had always fascinated Clay. Paintings were only that. Art, yes, and some of it breathtaking. But the objects that people held in their hands and lived with thousands of years ago . . . those were memories.

The European collection was ahead. Signs announced an exhibit called *Life in the Middle Ages*. The skull would be there, kept behind glass so that spectators could view the oddity that was the Eye of Eogain, the silver false orb with ancient words scrawled in the metal.

An artifact. Nothing more than that, or so the curators thought.

Clay reveled in the form of the falcon, in the interplay of air and wings, in the feeling of flight. He zipped lower across a vast hall, through another arch, and then dipped his right wing to turn again.

Around that corner, none of the dead were still walking.

Eve marched toward him across a floor strewn with fallen cadavers and the still-twitching parts of the resurrected. She had cleared herself a path, but now she was retracing her steps.

"This doesn't bode well," Dr. Graves whispered, words reaching him as though the ghost had whispered in his ear.

Clay beat his wings, stretched out his talons, and even as

he alighted upon the tiled floor, he transformed once more. Any reticence he had to do so in front of his comrades was gone, sacrificed to the needs of the moment. Bones creaked and shifted, and his flesh undulated and pulsed as it expanded. It happened with such speed that Eve took a step back and brandished her sword toward him.

"Watch where you point that thing," Clay said.

Eve rolled her eyes and lowered the blade. Her gaze lingered on Clay a moment, even as Dr. Graves' ectoplasmic form coalesced alongside them.

"What happened, Eve?" Graves asked. "You couldn't find it?"

She snarled, baring her fangs at the specter. "I found where it's supposed to be, Casper. They got there first. These fuckers are brainless. Morrigan's got to be controlling one of them directly enough to make it her puppet. One of the dead took Eogain's skull, and the Eye along with it."

"Damn it!" Clay snapped. "We've got to get it back! We've got to find the one that took it!"

At this, Dr. Graves raised an eyebrow. Eve stared at him in disbelief.

"Look around, Clay," the vampire said, gesturing toward either end of the hall, where the dead had begun to gather again, staggering toward them. There were dozens, just in this hall alone. There must have been hundreds in the museum and in the streets around it. "How are you going to figure out which one took the Eye?"

"Split up," Clay said, already moving away from them. "You find the one that moves with purpose, the one that's moving away faster and more directly than the others, you'll find the Eye."

"Where are *you* going?" Dr. Graves demanded.

Clay gave them one final, grim look. "There might be another way."

14

MORRIGAN ascended the staircase, her voice as she called to her acolytes like the shrill cry of a carrion bird drifting over the fields of war. Hidden in the darkness of that side room, it took every ounce of restraint Ceridwen could muster not to explode into the corridor to attack. Her mind was filled with images of what Morrigan and her followers had done to the Fey as they attempted to topple the ruling house, and her blood was afire with rage and hatred. The ice sphere atop her elemental staff glowed more brightly, responding to her fury.

Daniel Ferrick squatted before her, peering into the hall through the narrow gap they had left between door and frame. He glanced up at Ceridwen, his demonic features illuminated in the icy blue light of her staff. The voices of their enemies drew closer, and it was clear that Danny was worried that the glow from her staff might give them away. Before she could respond to his concerns, the boy acted, reaching a clawed hand toward the pulsing orb.

Ceridwen watched with wonder as the substance of shadow within the room responded to some unspoken command from the boy. Strips of writhing umbra flowed from the gloom, wrapping themselves around the body of the orb, diminishing the light, like storm clouds blotting out the sun.

And suddenly she understood why Conan Doyle had shown such interest in the young man. *There is enormous potential here,* she thought, watching as the boy, satisfied that his action had guaranteed their safety, turned back to the crack in the door. *Potential for good, but if not properly nurtured, for great evil instead.* If they survived this current threat, they would need to be vigilant, for while Daniel Ferrick and his place in the greater scheme of things was currently undetermined, it would be up to them to prevent him straying into the embrace of shadows. But that was a worry for another time.

Morrigan passed by their hiding place with nary a glance. She was clothed only in a cloak of scarlet, her lieutenants—Fenris and Dagris—nipping at her heels. Ceridwen recalled the council meeting where the fate of the twins was to be decided, and how it had been her merciful vote that had prevented the insane brothers from being put to death for their murderous actions against the citizens of Faerie. Seeing them here, serving the likes of Morrigan, was enough to ossify what remained of her once compassionate heart.

At the end of the hallway, Morrigan and her lieutenants stood before the door so familiar to Ceridwen. Painfully, she remembered the numerous times she had used the passage from Faerie to Earth and back again. She found the memory of that final pass through it, her lover sealing it up behind her for what was supposed to be forever, particularly unpleasant.

"I have to be certain," she heard Morrigan say, motioning for one of the twins to open the door. "I have to be sure that Conan Doyle has not somehow found a way to reestablish a passage between Faerie and the Blight."

Obediently, Fenris pulled open the door, filling the upstairs with the screaming wails of the yawling abyss.

Ceridwen could feel Daniel's eyes upon her, as if he were looking for someone to validate what he was seeing. She had to remind herself that despite the boy's appearance, and blossoming talents, he still perceived the world as a human would, and sights such as this were still far from the norm. She reached down and squeezed his shoulder reassuringly.

The shrieking void pulled hungrily at Morrigan and her lackeys. Fenris and Dagris used the open door as a kind of shield, hiding behind it to avoid being sucked inside. Morrigan, however, stood defiantly before the doorway, staring into the maelstrom. Seemingly satisfied that her hex was still intact, she gestured for her lieutenants to seal it up again.

The mournful cries of the maelstrom ended abruptly, the hallway plunged into silence as the twins succeeded in closing the door.

"Do you see, mistress?" Fenris asked, breathing heavily from his exertion. "Your fears are unfounded."

Dagris nodded. "Your magnificent agenda proceeds as planned."

Morrigan drifted away from the door and her lieutenants, pulling the cloak of scarlet around her. "And so it does," she agreed, looking about as if searching for something to satisfy her suspicions. "But I did sense something, and when things as important as this are in motion, one cannot afford to be complacent."

Ceridwen drew Daniel further back into the darkness.

Fenris and Dagris left their place, moving to eagerly stand beside their mistress.

"He'll be here soon, won't he?" Dagris asked, an idiot's grin forming on his pale, angular features.

Morrigan smiled dreamily, reaching out to stroke his cheek. "Yes, he will."

Daniel turned to Ceridwen, confusion in his eyes. He was looking to her for some kind of explanation, but she had no more idea what they were talking about than he did.

Then, as if in answer to her silent question, Fenris spoke again.

"The Nimble Man," the madman whispered in reverence. "The Nimble Man is coming." And he then began to giggle, clapping a pale hand over his mouth.

Ceridwen felt a searing pain in her lungs and realized that she had stopped breathing. She and Conan Doyle had known the situation to be dire, but this . . .

Danny flinched away from her, tugging his shoulder from her grasp. Ceridwen realized that in her shock she had tightened her grip enough to hurt him. She cast an apologetic glance toward him in the darkness, but all the while her real focus was on the conversation that continued in the corridor.

Morrigan spoke about the Nimble Man with a passion that barely fell short of arousal. "Trapped between Heaven and Hell," the witch said. "But now I have the power to set him free. And when he is delivered into this world, he will build a kingdom of his own and make war upon all of those who betrayed him, angel and demon alike."

The twins bowed their heads and then dropped to their knees before her. "And you will be his bride," Fenris whispered, his grin hideous.

"No," Morrigan snarled, a cruel smile snaking across her face as she shook her head. "Not his bride," she corrected her lieutenants with a waggle of a clawed index finger. "I shall be his queen."

Razor-sharp fragments of the puzzle floated about inside Ceridwen's troubled thoughts, beginning to come together. She shuddered. The Fey sorceress left Daniel by the door and moved deeper into the shadows of the room to stand before a window, its shade drawn against the darkness. There was more to learn, but first they had to escape this room undetected.

Daniel watched her curiously, but did not dare break the silence to ask what she was doing.

Ceridwen brought the head of her staff near her lips, whispering to the darkness that still enshrouded the orb. The shadow Danny had summoned dissipated. The sphere pulsed with restrained power, and then a single tongue of flame emerged from its icy surface to dance in the air before her. Ceridwen asked of it a favor. The fire obliged her, sensing the severity of the situation, flowing between window and sill, out into the crimson mist.

She closed her eyes, concentrating on the world beyond the house, guiding the fiery elemental spirit upon its mission. And through the bond she shared with it, the sorceress found the distraction that was needed.

The car was parked haphazardly on the side of the street, its driver lost to the evils of the bloody fog. Ceridwen directed the flame, urging it to crawl up inside the vehicle's belly, to seek out the fuel that powered its internal mechanisms. Finding what it sought, the fire bit into the fuel tank, puncturing the metal.

The explosion was a clap of thunder, the flash and flames cutting through the scarlet fog to briefly illuminate the unnatural darkness.

Ceridwen silently thanked the fire elemental for its assistance and returned to Daniel at the door.

Morrigan and the twins were already on the move, bounding down the hallway toward the staircase.

"It came from outside," Fenris snarled, drawing a curved dagger from a scabbard at his side.

Dagris's fingers crackled with a spell of defense as he looked about nervously.

Morrigan remained eerily calm, pulling the red cloak tighter about her as they rushed to investigate this disturbance.

"Quickly now," Ceridwen whispered in Danny's ear, pulling open the door and stepping stealthily out into the hall. "We'll need a cloak of shadow," she told him, peering over the banister. "Otherwise we might be discovered before we can reach him."

"Reach who?" Danny asked, even as he did as she asked, drawing the darkness around them. "Shouldn't we be thinking about getting the hell out of here?"

Ceridwen ignored the question. She ushered him into the hall, the shadows coalescing around them. It was dark in the townhouse, and they merged with the gray gloom as they went quickly along the hall and then down the stairs into the foyer. There was pandemonium in the house, Corca-Duibhne responding in panic to the explosion outside. Ceridwen and the boy waited at the bottom of the steps, a shroud of darkness concealing them from their enemies. The front door was open and the red mist swirled eagerly over the threshold as the Night People swarmed out to investigate.

Unnoticed, Ceridwen led Danny down the corridor toward what had been a ballroom in long-ago days. She could feel the pulse of the magick of Sweetblood in the air. It beckoned to her.

The doors to the ballroom were open, but once they were inside, Ceridwen closed them quietly.

"We won't be needing this anymore," she said, using her elemental staff to burn away their cover of shadow.

"Are you sure this is a good idea?" Danny asked.

But she was no longer listening. Her focus had been captured entirely by the crystalline sarcophagus lying in the center of the room. That, and the fact that they were not as alone as she had thought.

"Oh, shit," Danny whispered.

A trio of Corca-Duibhne sentries dropped from the ceiling, and two large boggart beasts emerged from behind Sweetblood's magickal chrysalis and charged toward them.

"Morrigan cannot be allowed to tap into Sweetblood's power. No matter what the cost," Ceridwen said.

There was no time for prolonged conflict, and again she called upon the elementals, summoning the spirit of the air for assistance. The atmosphere grew very still, and then a primordial roar filled the room. The Night People and their fearsome pets were tossed away by screaming gusts of wind like so much chaff, their bodies striking the walls with a chorus of snapping bones.

"Remind me never to make you mad," Danny said, staring awestruck at the broken and twitching bodies of their enemies scattered about the room.

Ceridwen rushed to the chrysalis and knelt beside it. Already there was a breach in it, a tiny crack, yet enough that Sweetblood's magick was seeping out, emanating from that bizarre shell. Yet there was other magick here as well. Ceridwen waved her fingers, dragging ripples in the air, and she could feel what had been done. A spell had been cast—by Morrigan, she presumed—a hex that utilized the blood of an innocent. Morrigan had tried to break the chrysalis open. Ceridwen felt her stomach roil with disgust. The atrocities Morrigan would perform in the name of her dark faith knew no boundaries.

I shall have to move him, Ceridwen thought, glancing around. If she had the time, she might be able to remove Sweetblood from the townhouse, to bring him to Conan Doyle. If she could manage it, they would have the advantage over Morrigan. First, though, she would have to try to seal the breach in the chrysalis. She did not have the power to permanently restore the encasement created by Sweetblood's magick, but she could perform a temporary repair.

Ceridwen raised her staff. The orb glowed with the ferocity of a white-hot star, and the sorceress began the process of undoing what her aunt had begun.

"Can I help?" Danny asked, standing nervously by her side.

Ceridwen felt the magick build, flowing from the center of her being up through her arms to be channeled through her staff.

"Just watch the door," she whispered. Then she bent closer to the strange chrysalis, peering at the figure frozen within. "But if *you* can hear me, mage, I could use your assistance."

Sparks of magick leaped from the ice sphere atop her staff, fingers of power that caressed the bloodstained chrysalis, seeking out imperfections—cracks upon its surface. The scent of the spilled blood permeated the room as the chrysalis was cleansed.

"Aid me in repairing that which contains your power, that prevents your might from being used for ill. Time is short and—"

A crackling sound filled the air. Ceridwen glanced up just in time to see Danny tumble through the air and crash on the floor, clothes smoldering. She spun to see Morrigan framed in the doorway, elegant features made ugly by a hideous sneer. One of the doors had been torn nearly from its hinges.

"Time?" her aunt asked. "You have run out, I'm afraid."

Arcs of power erupted from her fingers and struck the surface of the chrysalis, creating a backlash of magick that whipped at Ceridwen. She cried out in pain as her connection to Sweetblood's magick was violently severed.

"Ceridwen?" Danny called as he began to rise.

Morrigan paid no attention to the demon boy, and that was best. Ceridwen did not want Danny hurt more than he already had been. The taste of her own blood filled her mouth, mixing with the bitterness and rage that she felt as she stared at Morrigan, and at the twin Fey warriors who now stepped with her into the ballroom.

"You won't believe this, but I'm actually quite happy to see you," Morrigan told her.

Ceridwen shot a glance at Danny. "Prepare yourself," she said, though she doubted that he understood the full meaning of her words.

The boy crouched down, a fierce gleam in his eyes. "Ready when you are." His voice was a rumbling growl, in tune with his bestial nature.

Morrigan and the twins moved further into the room, proceeding with caution. "I knew that something wasn't right; I could feel it in my bones, so to speak, but I just couldn't put my finger on it." She smiled, and Ceridwen wasn't sure if she had ever seen Morrigan's teeth look quite so sharp. "I thought that I might actually be going mad."

"Too late for that," Ceridwen spat.

With her free hand she wove a spell, and a wall of fire blazed up from the floor, with Ceridwen, Danny, and the chrysalis on one side, and Morrigan and her lackeys on the other.

Danny was at her side, then, nostrils flaring as he tried to see through the flames. "Nice!" he said. "But I don't think that's going to stop them."

"It's not meant to," Ceridwen said, and she bowed her head, holding her elemental staff before her. A wind began to swirl around them and her cloak billowed behind her like the surge of an ocean swell.

"What are you doing?" the boy asked, as the whirlwind buffeted him. "Hey, you can't—"

"A traveling wind. Go to Conan Doyle," she interrupted. "Tell him what we've learned."

He started to protest, but his words were drowned out by the roar of the flames Ceridwen had summoned. The two of them glanced at the blaze, only to see that Morrigan was stepping through the fire. Her mouth was open wide and she was consuming it, eating the flames.

The traveling wind wailed around the boy, taking him back to where he had come from, and not a moment too soon.

Morrigan and the twins crossed the charred floor.

"All right, then. It's time, now. Time for us to settle family business. I promise you, it's going to hurt," Ceridwen said, extending her arms, the sphere atop her staff beginning to glow with menace.

Her aunt grinned, black smoke drifting from her mouth.

"I wouldn't have it any other way," she growled.

And the twins began to giggle.

CONAN Doyle came awake with a gasp, as if during his trance he had been holding his breath. His lungs burned, and his heart beat against his ribs like a caged bird. It was like awakening from a deep winter's sleep, his thoughts a jumble. He breathed deeply in and out, attempting to calm himself, to gather his wits.

His face felt strangely damp, and he reached up to touch his cheeks. There were tears running from his eyes, and he recalled the dream he'd had of his son. Conan Doyle took a handkerchief from his jacket pocket and dabbed at his eyes. He couldn't remember the last time that he had dreamt of Kingsley, or the last that he had cried, for that matter.

Images from his psychic communication with Sweetblood flashed through his mind. The pictures in his head of what the future held in store if Morrigan succeeded were nearly more than he could bear.

"Dear God," he whispered, returning his handkerchief to his pocket with a trembling hand.

Yet amongst that jumble of images, certain facts surfaced. If he had understood correctly, some of the horrors he had been shown were not Morrigan's scheme, but a secondary result of her actions, unforeseen even by the Fey witch herself.

Footsteps marching across the floor above distracted him from his ruminations, and Conan Doyle realized that during his trance, Julia Ferrick had taken her leave.

He listened to her footfalls on the staircase. All that he had asked was for her to stand watch over his body while he was in his trance. "Blasted woman," he growled, indignant that she had left her post.

Julia raced around the corner into the dining room, a look of absolute terror upon her wan features.

"Was it too much to ask that you adhere to my wishes, or is that—"

"He's gone," she said, ignoring his reproach. "Danny's gone."

Conan Doyle stood, wincing as the bones in his spine popped. It wouldn't be long before he had to partake again of the Fey elixir that staved off time's ravages. "Are you certain? Where would he have gone? I forbade him from involving himself with my operatives' assignments."

Julia laughed, a disdainful barking sound. "You forbade him," she said with a shake of her head. "Like that's going to mean anything to a sixteen-year-old boy. You forbade him. Give me a break."

Conan Doyle recoiled as if slapped. "Madame, please." He knew that he now lived in an age far different from that in which he had been born, but he was still taken aback when such language was unleashed by a member of the fairer sex. "Get hold of yourself."

"You get hold of yourself!" she screamed, starting to pace. "My son is missing, Mr. Doyle, and if you can't understand why I'm upset, I suggest you take a look outside the window."

He considered a spell of tranquility, but decided against it, choosing instead to steady the woman's nerves with words. "Losing your wits will not help you find your son, Mrs. Ferrick."

Conan Doyle reached out a comforting hand, and the moment he laid it upon her shoulder, she seemed to collapse into him. All her fury disappeared, leaving only her fear for her son. She shuddered and began to cry.

"When was the last time you saw Daniel?" he asked.

Julia wiped at her leaking eyes, stifling the sobs, trying to compose herself. "It was right before you went into your trance. He said he was going up to bed."

Conan Doyle pulled thoughtfully at his gray beard. At that point, the four had already departed on their mission. That left only Ceridwen, but he could not imagine that she would even consider allowing an inexperienced youth to accompany her.

"I . . . I know he's . . . different," Julia Ferrick stammered, "but he's still just a kid." Her eyes began to tear again, and she pressed a fist to her mouth as if she might stifle the emotions that threatened to overwhelm her.

Conan Doyle wanted to tell her otherwise, to explain what little he knew about the creature that she had raised as her son, but he erred on the side of sensitivity. He could be a callous man, at times. He knew that. But he never meant to be.

"Mrs. Ferrick. Julia," he began. But his words were interrupted by a sudden roar that rattled the windows in their frames and caused the pressure in the house to change so dramatically that his ears painfully popped.

"What the hell was that?" Julia asked, blinking, wincing as she opened and closed her mouth to relieve her own discomfort.

Conan Doyle was already in motion. The sound was familiar to him, and he knew that it signified answers. A traveling wind had arrived, but it would never have created such a thunderous roar unless it had been conjured quickly and carelessly.

"What was that?" Julia demanded as she pursued him from the dining room. "Doyle, answer me!"

He did not want to get her hopes up, choosing instead to lead her to the answer, and hopefully the relief of her distress.

Danny Ferrick knelt in the center of the living room, a puddle of vomit on the carpet before him. Conan Doyle glanced around the room, but to his dismay, Danny was alone. Ceridwen had not returned with him.

"Danny," his mother cried, kneeling at his side, throwing her arms around him. "I was so worried! Are you all right?"

The boy struggled from her embrace, pushing his mother away as he climbed to his feet. He lunged at Conan Doyle, gripping the man by the lapels of his jacket, staring wildly into his eyes.

"Danny?" Julia said, her voice hollow, crushed by his rejection.

"Ceridwen," the boy croaked, his breath stinking of spoiled milk. "She sent me away to tell you." The boy's legs were trembling, barely able to hold his weight.

"Then tell me," Conan Doyle urged, icy dread running along his spine. "What have you learned?"

"The Nimble Man," Danny said, wavering on his feet, a shudder passing through him. "She wanted me to tell you that Morrigan is trying to free the Nimble Man. I wanted to stay—to help her—but she made me come back to warn you."

Conan Doyle nodded wordlessly. The boy was about to fall down, so he steered Danny to the sofa and helped him to sit.

"Is it bad, Mr. Doyle?" Julia asked as she settled on the arm of the sofa, fussing over her son. She glanced up at him expectantly, waiting for an answer. "Is it bad?"

He wondered what he should tell them, just how much of the truth this woman in particular could stand. But Arthur Conan Doyle was not a man who minced words.

"Worse than you could imagine."

THE smell of decaying flesh made her angry.

Eve wasn't sure why exactly, other than the fact that once the smell got on her clothes, it was hell to get out.

A rotting, undead executive type in a navy blue suit hissed at her, baring jagged jack-o'-lantern teeth that jutted from blackened gums. She and Graves had cornered four of the walking dead in the museum's gift shop, but this asshole was the feistiest.

"You can hiss all you like, Gomer," Eve snarled. "None of you are going anywhere until you tell me something useful."

A chill washed over her as Dr. Graves moved closer. He stood with his arms crossed, and she imagined how formidable he must have been when he had been a man of flesh and bone.

"You don't think they'll just volunteer the information, do you?" Graves asked, hovering weightlessly in front of the gift shop doors.

"Sure," Eve said with a shrug. "They look like a reasonable bunch of dead guys. Why not?"

The executive lunged with a gurgling scream, hands hooked into claws and mouth open to bite.

"Then again," she said, driving her fist into the cadaver's face. It felt as though she had punched through a rotting melon. The corpse danced horribly at the end of her arm, its face and skull collapsed around her hand.

"That's just fucking gross," she spat, yanking her fist free with a wet, sucking pop. Further disgusted, she snapped a savage kick to the dead man's chest, hurling him backward into a T-shirt display. The corpse seemed to break upon impact, what was left of its head lolling obscenely to one side as it crumpled to the floor in a twisted heap.

"Quite effective," Graves said, slowly nodding his head. "Perhaps if you were to break them up into smaller pieces."

Eve flicked her hand at the ground, spattering the linoleum with rotting brain as she tried to shake off the gray matter on her fist and arm. "Look, I didn't say I was an expert. I said that I've been known to be pretty good at getting information out of guys who didn't feel like talking. Obviously my technique doesn't work so well on dead folks."

The three remaining corpses began to circle around them, as though they had gained courage—or at least motivation—from the destruction of the fourth.

"If you'd like to give it a try, be my guest," Eve said, turning toward the shambling corpse of a woman so withered she seemed almost a scarecrow. Eve snatched her up by the front of her dress and hurled her into the others, knocking them all to the floor.

"Perhaps I will." Graves drifted from his place at the door to levitate above the undead that thrashed upon the floor, trying to stand. "I doubt I could do any worse."

One of the corpses untangled himself from the others.

He had been a middle-aged man, obviously cut down in the prime of his life, his white shirt soiled from the grave. In his recent activity, the buttons had been lost, revealing the pale flesh of his chest and stomach. Eve noticed the serpentine stitching that writhed vertically from esophagus to navel.

The zombie leapt up at Graves with a hungry snarl, but his fingers passed harmlessly through the substance of the ghost.

"You'll do," Dr. Graves said.

The specter plunged one of his hands into the corpse like a magician reaching into his magic hat. The zombie froze, its decaying form snapping rigid. Graves pulled his hand free, withdrawing a white, writhing shape from inside the dead man's remains.

Eve watched, fascinated. "What is that, its soul?"

"Near enough," Graves replied, holding on to the squirming ectoplasm as its rotting shell collapsed like a marionette whose strings had been cut. The two other corpses grew still, staring at the ghost, as though they understood what he had done.

Eve was not sure if they were frightened, or envious.

The amorphous thing in the spirit's grasp writhed, vaguely taking on the shape of the man it had once been.

"Listen to me," Graves said.

Eve smiled. The man's voice just oozed control. It was damned impressive that even dead, the guy could still exude that much authority. She remembered how the world had been captivated by this man when he was still amongst the living, never really understanding the attraction. But as Eve watched him now, she began to see what she had not taken the time to notice before.

The ectoplasm retained the shape of a man, reaching up to the ceiling, but Graves prevented it from flowing to where it yearned to go. The soul moaned, not so much a sound that was heard, but one that could be felt, a low bass vibration that she could feel in the center of her chest.

"You will talk to me," Graves told it. "What was it that you sought here?"

"The Eye," said the soul, what passed for its head staring toward the ceiling.

"Did you find it?"

The spirit made another futile attempt to escape Graves, but the ghost held fast. *"Want to go,"* it pleaded. *"Need to be away from this place."*

Graves yanked it down further toward him. "I asked you a question," he roared. "Did you find it?"

"Please," the soul begged, stretching toward the ceiling.

With a grunt of frustration, Dr. Graves drifted to the floor, pulling the ectoplasmic remains of the dead man behind like a child holding a balloon. The soul fought him, but to no avail.

"I will put you back in here," Graves growled, forcing the soul toward the rotting husk that it had been extracted from.

"No!" it shrieked, the intensity of its psychic cries causing Eve to wince.

Graves would hear none of it, pushing the panicking soul stuff closer to where it had been imprisoned. "Did you find it?"

"I searched," the man's soul answered pathetically. *"But I did not find the Eye."*

Graves floated toward the ceiling, letting his prisoner have a taste of where it wanted to go. But just a taste.

"Do you know who did?"

"One of the others," it responded. *"One of the others found the Eye."*

Graves yanked the soul down again, pointing to the restless corpses who lay on the floor below.

"Was it one of these?" he asked.

"No, it was not," it answered immediately, afraid of what Graves could do to it. *"One of the others has the Eye . . . one of the others out there."*

With one of its willowy appendages, the soul pointed outside the gift shop, out into the museum.

Graves turned his attention to Eve.

"Oooh, scary," she said. "But what the hell. It worked better than my approach."

The ghost released that tormented soul, and they both watched as it hungrily swam toward the ceiling, passing through the white tiles, and then disappeared into the ether.

"Not really," the ghost replied despondently, drifting down toward their remaining zombie captives. "We don't know any more than we did before."

Eve watched as the ghost tore the imprisoned souls from their cages of decaying flesh, releasing them to the ether as well.

"We can only hope that Clay has been more successful," Graves said, drifting closer.

"So what do you think?" she asked him. "Should we grab a couple more and hope we hit the jackpot?"

Graves folded his arms across his chest. "I suppose it couldn't hurt," he said.

"So many dead guys," Eve sighed, moving toward the glass doors, looking out into the museum at the straggling corpses that still meandered about outside. "So little time."

15

THE red mist that swirled outside the Ferrick house had its own strange luminescence. A crimson glow came in through the windows, and though they were closed, from time to time the house whispered with a breeze, a draft from nowhere, and the candles in the living room flickered and threatened to go out.

Danny did not want the candles to go out. There were very few things he was certain of this night, but that was one of them. Without the candles there would be only that red glow, and he would have to wonder a little harder what was causing it.

He sat on the sofa in the living room with his mother beside him. She clutched his hands for comfort, but he wasn't sure which of them was comforted the most by this contact. It was weird to him. All the shit that he normally cared about—his skateboard, his tunes, his room, the latest video games, even the way he looked in the mirror—it all seemed so small now. What good was that new shirt from Atticus he'd wanted now? Little things had always been part of his mother's stress, too, but she'd always seemed to know the difference. Danny guessed they were both learning more about the big picture now than they ever wanted to.

Together they watched Arthur Conan Doyle pacing the length of the room. The man—the mage, Danny had heard him called—barely seemed to notice them.

From the moment Danny had returned to the house, magically transported here by Ceridwen, Mr. Doyle had been lost to them. Danny had been impressed by the guy in general, but he had not thought very much about the magick he supposedly wielded. Mr. Doyle seemed grim and courageous, but not really very intimidating.

That had changed.

Conan Doyle paced the room with his teeth ferociously clenched, prowling back and forth as though each step was some small victory. His eyes gleamed with dark purple light that coalesced into tears and then evaporated, trailing tendrils of lavender smoke behind him. The jacket Conan Doyle had been wearing was draped over a chair and his sleeves were rolled up. In the moments when he paused at one end of the room to turn and pace the other way, he reached up to run his fingers over his thick mustache. It was a pensive action, the unthinking gesture of a man readying himself for a fight. His whole demeanor, the marching, the rolled-up sleeves, contributed to that image.

He looked mean.

They weren't friends, the Ferricks and Mr. Doyle. They had not known each other long enough to be friends. But they were allies. Even so, Danny would not have interrupted him, even if the hordes of Hell were crashing down the door. In the reddish glow from the mist outside and the flicker of the candles, Conan Doyle looked like a demon himself.

But he's not the demon, is he? That'd be me. His pulse quickened.

His mother leaned on him a little. He could sense her fear, practically taste it, and he understood. All she wanted to do was curl up with her baby boy, close her eyes, and pretend that the nightmare world that was seeping in through her windows and under the door, the monsters she had invited into her home, would just go away. But they weren't going to. And her baby boy was one of them.

No matter how she yearned to shut her eyes to what was happening, however, Danny knew she would not. Julia Ferrick was not that kind of woman. The world had thrown some real shit in her path in the last few years, and she had never let it stop her.

His fingers gripped her hand and he gave her a squeeze. "It's going to be all right," he whispered, his voice a rasp, almost menacing, even to his own ears. With the grotesque and malevolent atmosphere that had enveloped the city, he was becoming *more* of what he was. He knew he should be frightened, but it felt right to him. Even his thoughts were changing. His mind . . . he felt more adult, in a weird way. Smarter, even. It was more than a little fucked up.

When she glanced at him, there was a storm in her eyes almost as intimidating as the fury in Mr. Doyle's.

"You shouldn't have gone, Danny. You should have stayed here. When I think about where you were . . . the danger . . ."

Again his fingers tightened on hers. He narrowed his gaze and cocked his head, wanting to make sure their eyes were locked, that she would not turn away.

"No, Mom. It was the right thing to do. No matter what . . ." he glanced nervously at Conan Doyle, who had instructed him not to go. "It was the right thing. If I hadn't gone, Ceridwen might never have been able to tell us what Morrigan was up to. And besides . . ."

He took a breath, then closed his mouth. His tongue brushed against the backs of his jagged teeth. The skin his horns had torn through still itched and flaked, but he resisted the urge to scratch it.

"Besides what?" his mother asked warily.

Danny let out a breath through his nostrils, plumes of hot air as though from a furnace. "It felt good. For the first time, it felt like I was part of something."

Her expression was crestfallen, as though he had just broken her heart. But Danny could not run away from what he was, and neither could his mother.

Mr. Doyle stopped his pacing in the precise center of the room.

Danny and Julia Ferrick stared at him.

"Mrs. Ferrick, I am sorry to have taken advantage of your hospitality in this way. Rest assured, Squire will make an appearance shortly, after which I and my agents will no longer be a burden to you."

The words were simple enough, but Danny didn't like the sound of it. It sounded as though Conan Doyle was going to shut him out of it again. A flutter of anger went through him and another blast of hot air came from his nostrils. It burned coming out, as though he was some dragon boy, but he doubted that fire breathing was going to be one of the abilities his demonic nature was going to give him.

"Where are you going?" Danny asked. His mother said nothing. He figured she was just relieved to be quit of Conan Doyle and all of his friends.

Mr. Doyle rolled his sleeves back down and began to button them. He did this as though there were nothing at all in the world that ought to be worrying him at the moment. There was a fussiness about him as he smoothed the fabric and then took his jacket and slid it on again. He truly was a man of another age.

When he glanced up again, that purple glow steamed

from the corners of his eyes, and another glimpse of his fury flickered across his face.

"Where? To war, of course. To battle. There's nothing to be done for it now. If Eve, Clay, and Dr. Graves succeed, it will be helpful, but even if they do not, we must do our best. No matter the consequences. The alternative is unthinkable."

"The alternative?" Julia Ferrick asked.

Danny glanced at her, squeezed her hand, and nodded at Conan Doyle. "Come on, Mr. Doyle. We've been through enough of this with you. I think we've earned the right to know. Who is the Nimble Man? What's this all about?"

For a long moment, Arthur Conan Doyle peered down his nose at the Ferricks, frustratingly aloof. Danny wanted to hit him, but then he remembered the rage burning just inside the man and knew he shouldn't push. At length, Conan Doyle's expression faltered, and now Danny saw tragedy in his eyes, catastrophe in the twist of his lips.

"I made a mistake," Mr. Doyle said roughly. He cleared his throat and raised his head a bit, meeting their gazes with more assurance. "I made assumptions, you see."

"No. We really don't," Danny told him.

Conan Doyle nodded. "All right. Plain as can be. Morrigan has always been cruel and calculating. She rejoiced at the pain of others and schemed to get what she wanted. This was her nature. Arrogant cruelty, deceit, betrayal.

"When I learned from Ceridwen and her uncle Finvarra that Morrigan had turned upon her own people, had made a gambit for control of Faerie, I assumed she had simply reached the inevitable point where her spite and jealousy and her lust for power had eliminated what little caution and patience she might have had. Upon her defeat, she came into this world, and I thought all of this was about power, for her. About destruction and bloodlust and the pleasure she receives from others' pain, yes, but mainly about power. Having someone to rule. To subjugate.

"But it wasn't about that at all.

"It's about faith for her. She's a religious fanatic, not a dictator. And that is, oh, so much worse."

Danny had been following him, at least for the most part, up until now. He shook his head. "I don't understand. What do you mean?"

Julia Ferrick sat a bit forward on the sofa, peering at Mr. Doyle with keen interest. "This Nimble Man. She worships him? He's . . . some kind of god?"

Mr. Doyle smiled at her as though he had seen her in a new light, and his expression revealed a newfound respect. Danny found himself oddly proud of his mother.

"Precisely," Conan Doyle said. "Or near enough. The myths of Heaven and Hell speak of the Fir Chlis, the angels who rose up against the Creator. They were defeated and banished, cast out of Heaven and forced to build a new order for themselves in damnation.

"All but one. None of the myths record the name of this once angel. They refer to him only as the Nimble Man. Somehow he escaped the full brunt of the Creator's wrath, but though he avoided Hell, he could not return to Heaven. He became trapped in stasis in the ether between those realms. Neither of Heaven nor Hell, he nevertheless could see both, could hear and sense them. He had the gifts of the Creator, and the fires of Hell at his command, but also the desires of the damned, and the guilt of the sinful. Emotion shredded his mind.

"I've been misreading this situation all along. The omens and portents we've seen have been happening as harbingers of his arrival. The Nimble Man has the powers of Heaven and Hell at his command, but he is utterly and completely insane. And Morrigan is trying to bring him to Earth."

• • •

RED mist had started to gather inside the museum, seeping in through broken windows and shattered doors. Clay raced through the museum with an ancient battle-axe in his hand, hopes and suppositions coalescing in his mind. The dead had not deviated much from their purpose here, so most of the exhibits and corridors were untouched. He ignored those undisturbed places. But where there were broken display cases or other traces of the passing of the dead, he paused to look around.

But he did not pause for long. He had an idea that he would find what he searched for back in the grand entry hall of the museum. Behind him, he heard Eve and Graves coming along. There were still some of the walking dead in the gift shop, of all places. Clay thought that perhaps they had gotten themselves stuck in the aisles or in a corner and were confused, like rats in a maze.

The dead could not think clearly. Their minds were muddled, their souls numbed by being forced back into flesh that was rotting. They were able to understand Morrigan's commands—go to the museum, retrieve the Eye of Eogain, and return to her—but little more than that. And some of them could not even retain that much thought.

As he raced into the grand hall he heard shouting.

"No! Get away from me!"

Beneath the final few steps of a circular stairwell that went up to the second floor, a night watchman had tucked himself away, hiding from the dead. Six or seven of the shambling dead, these so rotten that bits of flesh flaked off them as they moved, had begun to encircle him. Their bodies were too far gone, their minds too dessicated, for Morrigan to continue to control them. Now they fell into the instinct of the walking dead, the hatred of the living, the hunger for supple flesh and hot blood, for life.

Even as Clay raised his battle-axe and rushed across the

room, one of the dead fell to its knees and tried to reach beneath the steps. Its skeletal fingers clawed the watchman's navy blue uniform pants, and the man began to shriek, kicking out with both feet. Black shoes cracked dead fingers, and when the watchman saw this, he began to curse loudly again, fear replaced by fury. He slid out a little, landing a solid kick in the zombie's face that collapsed its skull like papier-mâché. But now that the man had moved, the others were able to get hold of his legs, and they began to drag him out.

"This is becoming tiresome," Clay muttered to himself.

With all of the zombies on the ground, trying to grab at the watchman, he waded into them, kicking and stomping. The axe was idle in his hand as he crushed the spine of the nearest creature. He swung his heavy boot and kicked the head off a second. Clay stomped another skull to powder, but by then they were rising and he stood back, brandishing the axe.

"Oh, my Lord," the watchman whispered as Clay went at the withered corpse of a woman in a blue cocktail dress, hacking off her head. "Is this real? Is it the End Times? I . . . I thought I'd be saved. I've been faithful."

The axe fell, cleaving a skull in two, then Clay swung it low and cut the corpse of a uniformed soldier in half at the midsection.

"Good for you," Clay said.

He finished off the last of the zombies in the lobby, their mouldering corpses sliding to the ground with the thunk of bone and the rustle of autumn leaves. One of them continued to moan, voice like storm winds raging outside a lonely cottage. Clay stamped a foot upon its head, cutting off the eerie sound, and freeing the soul within.

The watchman flinched when he looked up.

Clay raised both hands, including the one with the axe. "I just saved your life, friend. A little gratitude."

The man's jaw dropped and he nodded quickly. "Yeah. Yeah, of course. Thank you. Th-thank you so much. But . . . you didn't answer me. Is this it? The End Times?"

The shapeshifter studied the man for a moment and then shook his head. "Not if I have anything to say about it. Look, you couldn't have been the only one on duty."

The watchman shook his head. He pulled himself out of his hiding place and stood. With a shaky hand he pointed into the darkness on the far side of the massive hall. Clay frowned as he followed the man's trembling finger. Sprawled on the floor beside a statue of a man and a woman locked in a romantic embrace, with a child seated at their feet, was another figure. This one was as unmoving as those in the statue, but it was flesh, not stone.

"Hank, you idiot," the watchman whispered, grief in his voice. "You idiot."

"What happened?" Clay asked, studying the man intently. "Tell me exactly what happened."

The watchman was not a small man, but he trembled as he spoke, and he shook his head, still not quite believing what he had just survived.

"We . . . we were trapped in here. With that fog and the power out and, well, we were arguing. He didn't want to leave his post. I wanted to go home, be with my wife, if this was really it. When we saw . . . when we saw them coming . . ." His eyes went wide and he laughed, more than a little hysterical. "Zombies! When we saw them coming, we hid behind the counter."

Clay glanced over. It was a long marble counter where visitors could get information and buy tickets. He had passed it on his way in. The watchmen must have been hiding behind it even then. If he had known . . .

"It got quiet for a bit, but I made Hank sit tight. Then . . . we heard them coming out. The moaning, the sounds they made, I felt like I couldn't breathe just listening to them. But Hank, he had to look, had to raise his head, see what they were up to. Idiot.

" 'Dave,' he says, 'I think they're stealing something.' And he starts to get up! Can you believe that? He starts to get up. I drag him back down, practically wetting myself. I'm a good Christian. I never thought I'd still be here when the Beast took hold of the Earth. 'Who cares?' I say. 'Let 'em take whatever they want! This is the Last Days.' But Hank's not going for that. His eyes got all crazy. He always took the job too seriously, like it was an honor, working here, like the exhibits were the Shroud of Turin. He loved all this stuff. He started shaking, just out of control, and then he was gone before I could stop him. At first there were only five or six of them; and maybe he thought he could take them; they didn't look real fast. He grabbed the nightstick off his belt and went in swinging.

"The fool."

Clay nodded, putting it all together. Time was wasting. He couldn't spare another minute with the watchman. Not if he was going to stop Morrigan from getting the Eye. He grabbed the watchman by the wrist and pulled him toward his friend's corpse, but when the man held back, not wanting to see what had become of his friend, Clay relented and continued on his own.

Hank had been torn apart. His nightstick was fifteen feet away, droplets of blood all around it. The dead man had been eviscerated. He was so badly damaged that he would not be coming back from the dead. If Clay looked closely enough, he knew he would find that there were things, organs, missing. Eaten by the dead. But he did not care to investigate. He turned quickly back to the survivor.

"The thing that the dead were taking. What was it?"

The man looked as though he might collapse at any moment. His flesh was as pale as that of the dead. "That's the thing. It was a head. This preserved thing, from a bog. I don't . . . I don't know more than that. Hank could have told you. He knew every piece in every exhibit. He loved this place."

"Yes," Clay whispered, and he knelt by the ravaged corpse and put his hand on the man's chest. He twitched several times and his eyes fluttered, and for just a moment his features might have blurred.

"Hey!" the watchman called. "Hey, what are you doing to him? He's dead! He's—"

His words stopped short. Clay assumed it was because he had just remembered the battle-axe, and what it was capable of.

When Clay stood, he could see a trail of ectoplasm, a pale stream of spirit energy, a tendril of smoke that extruded from the body of the dead man, off into the darkness on the far side of the museum. The zombies who had killed this man were also the ones who had the Eye of Eogain. And the trail of ectoplasm that linked a corpse to its killer would lead Clay right to them.

"Stay here," Clay told the watchman. "I doubt they'll be back, but it's not safe outside. Stay until the mist is gone."

"Or until the devil calls my name," the watchman muttered.

Clay shook his head. "It's not the end, my friend. Just a taste of it. A sneak preview. You just stay here until it's over."

"How long do you think that'll be?" the man ventured, his moment of swagger gone and his horror and grief returning.

"Hours. A day. If not by then, then maybe never."

The watchman stared at him. Obviously the man had been expecting some words of comfort. But Clay had none to give.

Axe gripped tightly in his hand, he plunged into the shadows of that grand entry hall, heading off into the far corner, away from the front doors, following the tendril of ectoplasm as though it were a leash at the end of which he would find his goal. At a wall the trail turned left, and ahead he saw damp, luminescent, crimson mist clouding inside, rising up toward the high ceiling. There were tall windows there. Shattered.

Shattered outward. The soul tether led him out through the broken windows, glass crunching under his boots.

An instant later, there were no boots. In the space between one footfall and another, he dropped to all fours and his hands and feet had become massive paws. His flesh flowed, bones shifted, and now his head was heavy and he shook his lion's mane as he raced after Morrigan's undead servants.

Clay threw back his head, felt his chest expand, and roared, the sound echoing off the faces of buildings and sliding through the bloody fog. He roared a second time and a third, and then he paused to glance back at the museum.

The ghost of Dr. Graves appeared in the red mist beside him as though grown from the darkness. Graves stared at him, nodding in approval.

"Remarkable," the ghost said.

Clay swung his massive head toward Graves. "Eve?" he growled.

"Coming," Graves replied, pointing to a second-floor window.

It exploded outward in a shower of jagged glass and Eve dropped through the air in a neat somersault, legs tucked beneath her. She landed in a crouch beside him.

"You roared?"

"Follow me," Clay growled.

He set off at a run, retaining the lion form. The others did not ask questions. They could not see the soul trail that led him on, but the three of them were allies, now.

Amongst them was a sense of purpose. They all knew what was at stake.

"Where did Squire get off to?" Eve asked.

Neither Graves nor Clay responded. The goblin would have to take care of himself, for now. Mr. Doyle had given them an assignment. It was time to fulfill it.

Claws scraping pavement, Clay followed the tendril of ectoplasm around a corner and saw their prey. There might only have been a small number that had left the museum through that shattered window after killing the watchman, Hank, but now there were dozens of them spread out across the road, shambling at different speeds. Some dragged a leg behind them, injured. Others crawled on their bellies, responding to Morrigan's command and unable to stop.

Through the crimson fog they moved, and when the wind blew, Clay could hear their moaning.

In their midst, right at the center of the road, four of the dead were clustered close together. One among them held something in its arms. From behind, Clay could not see what it was, but he could guess.

"Destroy as many as you can. I'll get the Eye."

Eve was preternaturally quick. Faster, even, than a lion. She raced ahead of them, leaped onto the back of a gleaming new BMW, and launched herself into the air. From the scabbard slung across her back she drew her sword, and even as she landed in the midst of a crowd of the dead, she swung the blade. It whistled through the air and the carnage had begun.

A ghost could move with unreal quickness, stepping through space instead of across it. Dr. Graves appeared instantly amongst the dead. A man in a gray suit walked between a woman in a dark green dress and a small boy, all three of them holding hands. A family.

Graves plunged his fists into their rotting flesh and tore their souls loose, set them free. It was a mercy.

The lion, the shapeshifter whose name sometimes was Clay, bounded toward the quartet of walking dead who were escort to the Eye of Eogain. He drove the first down beneath his weight, cracking its bones. One massive paw lashed out, and with a single swipe of his claws, he tore away part of the second shambling corpse's spine.

He began to change. But this time he slowed that metamorphosis. It was painful, letting the flesh pause in between forms, bones not set correctly, muscles half formed. Clay grasped a dead woman by the shoulders and opened huge leonine jaws, then snapped them closed upon her head.

The lion-man spat bits of skull and dessicated brain onto the pavement.

Then he morphed again, and now he was just Clay. Just Joe. Just a piece of the connective tissue of the world, touched by the Creator and attached to the heart of every living thing.

The zombie holding the skull of Eogain continued shambling in the general direction of Beacon Hill, toward Morrigan, as though the carnage around it had not happened at all. Clay reached for its head, clutched it around the neck with one hand, shoved his right hand into its mouth and tore off the top of its head.

Eogain's skull—silver eye glittering in its socket—tumbled toward the ground. Clay caught it before it struck the road. He raised it up and stared at it, saw the symbols engraved in the silver, and wondered what Morrigan would do without it.

"Eve!" he shouted, turning toward her. "I've got it."

But the raven-haired beauty was otherwise engaged. More dead had appeared. They came along the side streets. A manhole burst open and clanged onto the road, and several cadaverous figures dragged themselves up from the sewer. Clay stared at them, wondering where they were all coming from.

Morrigan, he thought. *She's sensed what we're up to. And she's not giving the Eye of Eogain up without a fight.*

Dr. Graves and Eve were surrounded, but holding their own. Eve was tearing out their throats, and Graves their souls. But Clay shook his head. There was no way to know how many walking dead Morrigan could bring against them, and he had the Eye. There was no reason to fight.

"Forget them!" Clay called. "Let's go!"

"Good idea!" Eve shouted back at him, tearing open the torso of a dead man. "Where are we going? You've got somewhere there aren't any dead guys?"

Clay looked around, searching for the best route of escape. Even as he did, he saw that he was a target again. At least a dozen of the dead were beginning to encircle him, slowly, as though ruled by one mind. And perhaps they were.

"Hey, big boy!" a familiar voice called.

Squire crawled out from the darkness beneath the BMW fifteen feet away. The goblin looked tired.

"Where the hell have you been, munchkin?" Eve snapped at him.

Squire shot her the middle finger. "Busy. Now, listen. I just shadow walked back to the Ferricks. Conan Doyle wants us all to meet up with him in front of the State House, as soon as we can get there."

"Glad to hear it," Clay called, turning round and round, ready to tear into the zombies that surrounded him. "How did you plan to get us there?"

The goblin put his hands on his hips, the ugly, twisted little beast looking almost comical. "The limo's right around the corner, smart-ass," he said, pointing just up the street. "I've got to get back to Conan Doyle."

And then Squire dove back into the darkest of shadows beneath the BMW, barely avoiding the grasp of a dead girl who could not have been more than eighteen when she breathed her last.

Clay glanced around at the zombies that were closing in on him, clutching the skull of Eogain in one hand.

"Wonderful."

MR. Doyle buttoned his jacket, smoothed his mustache with fingers crackling with magick, and gazed down his ample nose at Danny Ferrick.

"I think not, Daniel."

Anger flared in the demon boy's features. His chapped, leathery skin flushed with color, and tiny embers burned in eyes turned to charcoal. Then he shook his head, and despite his devilish features, Conan Doyle could see the boy in that face again.

"Listen, Mr. Doyle, I know what you're worried about. I know what you think. My mother . . ." Danny glanced over at Julia, at the woman he had always thought of as his mother, and there was sadness and apology in his gaze. "My mother doesn't want to accept it, but I know what I am. You're not wrong about that.

"But you're wrong about *me*.

"Maybe my blood is a demon's blood. Maybe I'm not human. But this is my world. This is my house. I'm still Dan Ferrick. I still . . . I still love my mother, and my friends." He glanced at Julia again, but then he turned his tumultuous eyes upon Conan Doyle.

"I can feel the darkness in me. It's in my head sometimes. And it's in my heart. I laugh at things I shouldn't. Sometimes I want to . . . hurt people. But I know it, Mr. Doyle. And I keep it reined in. The darkness. That's got to count for something. I'm not going to let it control me.

And if I'm going to be able to fight it, you have to give me the chance to do it for real, not just on the inside. You don't have a clue what it's like to be me. To live now. Yeah, you're alive, but you grew up so long ago, you might as well be from Mars for all you know. You know all this stuff about magick and other worlds. Whatever. You don't know much about this one. So you can't know *me*, or what I've got going on in here." He pounded a fist against his chest.

"I'm not gonna let the darkness win. Not inside, or out. So I need to be part of this. To remind me, all the time, what I'm fighting against."

Mr. Doyle took a long breath and let it out slowly. He pulled his pocket watch out by its chain, glanced at the time, and then slipped it back in. They had to go. There was no more time for discussion.

Julia must have seen it in his face, for she began to shake her head, her breath coming faster, in sharp hitches. "No. Not my boy," she said. Then she turned to her son. "You're wrong, Danny. Maybe part of you is what he says. But there isn't . . . I won't believe there's some kind of evil in you."

"That's just your mouth talking, Mom," Danny said softly. "You know what's true. I know you do."

The two of them were gazing at one another, Julia's heart breaking, when there was a soft whisper of noise, like the ocean in the distance. It ceased as abruptly as it had begun, but Conan Doyle glanced around, recognizing the sound.

Squire emerged from the shadows beneath the coffee table into the flickering candlelight.

"Brought them the limo, and the message," he reported.

"Thank you, Squire," Conan Doyle said. Then he nodded toward Julia. "Now, if you'll keep Mrs. Ferrick company, young Daniel and I have an appointment to keep."

16

EVE drove wildly down Beacon Street, wielding the limousine like a weapon of war, running down the bothersome dead, crushing them beneath its wheels. She couldn't have even begun to describe the satisfaction she felt.

"Tell me again why we let you drive?" Clay asked from the backseat, as the corpulent body of a naked man suddenly covered the windshield, pale rolls of decaying flesh pressed against the glass, obscuring what little they could see of the road ahead.

"Think of it as a reward for the good job you did in finding the Eye," Eve said, swerving the car in an attempt to dislodge their passenger. The zombie held on, its nubby, yellow teeth scraping the glass as it attempted to bite its prey.

"Fat son of a bitch," she growled. "How am I supposed to see what I'm hitting?"

Graves did not precisely sit, but rather lingered in the passenger seat beside her. Now the ghost leaned forward and reached through the windshield, his ectoplasmic arm easily passing through the glass and then through the chest of the obese man on the hood of the car. The animated corpse went rigid as Graves tore out its imprisoned soul, the spiritual essence writhing and wailing in his grasp. Graves let the soul swim free, but the corpse remained on the windshield.

"Great," Eve barked. "First I had a living dead guy blocking my view, and now it's just a dead guy. That's such an improvement." Steering the car with one hand, she fumbled for her seat belt. "This calls for drastic measures," she said, as she snapped her restraints into place. She shot Clay a glance in the rearview mirror. "Buckle up."

"What are you going to do?" He knitted his brows, clutched the mummified head of Eogain protectively beneath his arm, and struggled to strap himself in.

Eve pressed down on the accelerator, rocketing down Beacon through the blood-red mist. She watched the speedometer climb past eighty, feeling the car shimmy and shake, listening to the bumps and thumps, as it obliterated the obstacles in its path.

"Eve?" Clay asked again.

"That oughta do it," she hissed, squeezing the steering wheel in both hands.

She could feel Graves' cold, spectral stare upon her. "Perhaps you should slow down before—"

Eve stomped on the brake. The abrupt stop at that speed threw her forward. In the back, Clay grunted as he, too, was caught by his seat belt. Graves was entirely unaffected. He studied her with cold detachment as the brakes screamed and the car fishtailed, spinning them completely around. But Eve had accomplished what she'd set out to do. The fat corpse flew off the hood of the limo, a missile of decaying flesh that collided with other shambling dead walkers, clearing a path through them.

"Extreme, but effective," Graves said, unruffled, floating just above the passenger seat.

Eve grinned as she banged a U-turn in the center of Beacon Street, crushing more of the dead beneath the wheels. "That's me in a nutshell."

THE dead staggered through the blood-red fog. Some of them sensed the presence of the living and began to move toward the State House. On the steps of that grand structure, Conan Doyle tugged out his pocket watch and checked the time, wanting nothing more than to begin their attack, to get back into his home and discover whether or not Ceridwen still lived. He cursed under his breath and clicked the watch cover shut, then glanced out across Boston Common, ignoring the dead.

Danny Ferrick stood beside him on the stone steps. "Holy shit. Zombies," the boy said. "Real zombies. I mean, you did notice the zombies, right?"

The boy's voice cracked fearfully, but he held his ground as the walking dead began to ascend the steps toward them.

"Yes. I noticed them," Conan Doyle replied. He allowed himself a small smile. Danny was a brave boy. The rotting carcasses of these decrepit creatures had been returned to life against their will. Conan Doyle thought that perhaps when his own time came, at last, when the herbs and magicks of Faerie would no longer keep him alive, it might be best to be cremated.

The scent of the dead, the stink of grave rot, assailed his nostrils as they moved closer. Close enough that Conan Doyle could see the maggots that squirmed in their decaying flesh.

"Stand close to me, boy," he told Danny, and he extended his arms, pointing his open palms toward the advancing cadavers.

The spell flowed from his lips in guttural Arabic. Symbols etched in purple fire swirled up from his hands, increasing in number and size, flowing in a crackling wave toward the dead things upon the stairs.

One moment they were ascending and the next, as the fiery sigils touched them, they were no more, their decaying flesh and bone turned to trails of oily black smoke that became lost in the churning, scarlet mist.

"Damn, Mr. Doyle. That is wicked cool. Do you think I could ever learn to do something like that?" Daniel asked with admiration.

"Could you learn?" Conan Doyle repeated. "Yes. Will I ever teach you? I seriously doubt it."

"Why not?" the demon boy asked. "Afraid I'm going to use my superpowers for evil or something?"

Conan Doyle simply stared at the boy. He could feel the arcane energies still coursing through his body, leaking from his eyes. And within Daniel Ferrick, he could sense an altogether different brand of arcanum. "There is nothing at all amusing about that, young man. Do not make me doubt my decision to include you in this endeavor. We'll discuss your place in the greater scheme of things another time."

The boy avoided eye contact, choosing to look everywhere but at him. Conan Doyle watched as Danny's gaze grew wide and he pointed down the steps at the sidewalk below.

"There're more of them," the boy said.

Conan Doyle saw that he was right. More of the dead were appearing out of the mist, approaching the steps.

"Lots more," Danny added, his voice a rasp.

The corpses ambled out of the concealing fog, up onto the sidewalk, and through the open gate in the fence that encircled the State House steps. One of the dead, little more than dirt-covered bones, tilted back its eyeless head and opened its mouth in a silent scream. Rich black earth, rife with squirming life, spilled from its gaping maw, and Conan Doyle prepared to summon another incantation to defend against this latest incursion.

He never released the spell. Just as he was about to raise his hands again, there came the shriek of rubber on pavement and the roar of an engine, and his limousine erupted from the bloodstained night, riding up over the curb onto the sidewalk, colliding with the zombie horde, splintering bones and scattering bits of their decaying corpses.

"Sweet," Danny said as the limo came to a screeching halt in front of the gate.

The driver's door swung open and Eve emerged. Clay exited the backseat and Dr. Graves floated out through the roof.

Conan Doyle clasped his hands together behind his back. "I was beginning to worry."

"We would have been here sooner," Eve said, slamming her door, "but traffic's a bitch."

"Where's Ceridwen?" Clay asked, shifting the mummified skull of Eogain from one arm to the other as he came around the car.

Conan Doyle studied the faces of those who had gathered beneath the banner of his cause, his Menagerie. Denizens of the weird, but warriors, each and every one, sharing the common goal of staving back the encroaching darkness. It was a precarious battle, one that might as easily tip the scales toward shadowy oblivion as to the embrace of light. But it was a war that he had sworn to continue, one that he believed was worth fighting, even if it meant the deaths of those loyal to his mission.

No sacrifice was too large, for it served a greater good.

"Ceridwen, I'm afraid to say, has been captured."

The words hurt him, each of them barbed, sticking painfully in his throat as he struggled to speak. The others appeared taken aback, knowing only too well the level of power the Fey sorceress was capable of wielding, as well as his emotional involvement.

"Here's an idea," Eve said, sweeping her raven black hair away from her exotic features. "How about we go get Ceridwen and kick Morrigan's Faerie ass? That sound like a plan?"

Conan Doyle looked out over the heads of his comrades. The dead were still out there, but now they seemed loathe to come closer—some primitive survival mechanism had been stirred to life in them, though he did not know if it stemmed from his own magick, or from the arrival of his Menagerie.

"If only it were that simple," Conan Doyle replied. "We now know why Morrigan has sought the power of Sweetblood. She wishes to free the Nimble Man."

He waited a moment, allowing them to digest the severity of the situation.

"Which, from your tone, I guess should have me shaking in my boots. And maybe I will when you tell me why," Eve said, obviously unfamiliar with the legends.

It always amazed him how a creature as ancient as Eve could sometimes be so oblivious.

Clay stepped closer to the rest of the group, red mist swirling around his malleable features. "A fallen angel," he said, his expression grim. "But not like Lucifer and the others. He escaped the Almighty's wrath but was trapped between Heaven and Hell. In my wanderings, I've encountered entire religions based upon him, with the ultimate goal of freeing him, but no one has ever had the level of power needed to accomplish this—"

"Until now," Eve finished, the situation becoming clearer.

Conan Doyle nodded. "With her own witchery and Sanguedolce's power, Morrigan has enough magick now to tear a hole in reality. If she knows what she is doing, she could free the Nimble Man."

Dr. Graves was a strange sight in that fog. His own ethereal form was a mist of its own, churning in upon itself, but a breeze blew the red fog so that it caressed him. He was a cloud standing still in a tempestuous sky as the rest of the storm moved on.

The ghost was troubled, and his form solidified a bit as he moved toward Conan Doyle. "You said that Morrigan needed the Eye of Eogain to focus Sweetblood's magick if she was going to try to leech it, to use it. And as you can see, we did not return empty-handed. How can she release the Nimble Man now? Haven't we already won?"

"A fair assumption, Dr. Graves," Conan Doyle agreed, "but another wrinkle has been added to the cloth." The mage rubbed at his eyes, the continued exposure to the unnatural fog causing them to itch and burn. "Without the Eye, Morrigan will most certainly decide to forge ahead with a physical locus to channel Sweetblood's magickal energies. An ordinary human would wither almost instantly with such power coursing through them. We have kept the Eye from Morrigan. And because we have, I believe she will have no choice but to attempt to use Ceridwen herself to channel that power."

"Could that be done?" Graves asked.

Conan Doyle sighed, the consequences of this act of desperation on Morrigan's part too horrible for him to bear. *No sacrifice is too large, for it serves a greater good.* The words reverberated through his thoughts.

"It will most likely kill Ceridwen, as well as release Sweetblood from his self-imposed imprisonment," Conan Doyle said. "But the answer is yes. With Ceridwen as the . . . well, as the circuit breaker if you will, Morrigan will be able to free the Nimble Man."

Ceridwen is back in Faerie, and her mind is at peace.

The warm winds caress her face as she walks hand-in-hand with Arthur through the royal gardens. She notices her mother sitting on a stone bench in the distance, and Ceridwen can not help but smile. Everything is as it should be, not a detail out of place.

Upon seeing them, her mother stands, waving in greeting. But Ceridwen's smile falters when she sees that her mother's clothes are tattered and stained with blood. It is then that she remembers her mother was taken from her long, long ago. A shiver of grief goes through her and she turns to Conan Doyle for comfort, for some explanation of the dread she feels.

But it is no longer Arthur who holds her hand, and the grip on her fingers has turned cold and constricting.

Morrigan smiled and pulled her close, teeth as sharp as a boggart's. "Fight all you like," she snarled, "but it will not alter the outcome."

Her fantasy shredded, Ceridwen returned to reality. Pain suffused every inch of her flesh, and her eyes burned with unshed tears. And now she remembered what had happened, the confrontation in Conan Doyle's ballroom with her aunt, the savage Morrigan. She had sent Danny away on a traveling wind and turned to face Morrigan and her lackeys alone. The battle with them had been swift and brutal, and she had been defeated.

Now she lay draped upon Sweetblood's chrysalis. A surge of the ancient mage's power rushed through her, and she cried out in excruciating pain. They had bound her atop that strange encasement, the sorcerous energies leaking from the cracks in its surface filtering through her body to be collected by the eagerly waiting Morrigan. Her cloak was in tatters, burned through, almost nothing left of it, and her tunic and trousers were smoldering.

"Do you see how wonderfully it comes together?" her aunt asked, manipulating the distilled power of the archmage and sending it back into the sarcophagus, causing the size of cracks in its surface to increase. With each splinter of that amber glass, more of Sanguedolce's magickal potency tore through Ceridwen, more power at Morrigan's disposal.

"Fortune smiles upon me this day. It is unlikely that you will live long enough to witness my triumph, but let me assure you, it will be glorious."

The magick coursed through her, the pain continuing to grow. The mage's power was overwhelming. Ceridwen had heard tales of Sanguedolce's prowess, but never imagined a mortal might be able to wield such might.

Morrigan droned on and on about her plans, but Ceridwen was no longer listening. To escape the pain, she fled to the past, remembering what it was that defined her, what had shaped her. There was pain in the past as well, but it was that pain that had strengthened her, as though in a blacksmith's forge.

From her earliest days, sadness had been her companion. She could barely remember a day when it had not walked by her side. Her mother had been slain in the early days of the Twilight Wars, the victim of a troll raid upon their forest home. She had been but a mere child, forced to watch her mother's fate from a hiding place within the draping boughs of an ancient willow tree. In that moment, she had sworn never to be helpless again.

There were times when the night was deathly silent, and in those quiet snatches of darkness she could still hear her mother's screams. She would awaken filled with righteous fury only to find that there was absolutely nothing that she could do.

Ceridwen cried out now, agony wrenching her back to the present. Pain assaulted her as more fissures formed in the mage's sarcophagus, allowing the flow of magick through her to intensify.

Morrigan laughed, amused by Ceridwen's suffering, but this was nothing new; her aunt had always reveled in the torment of others.

Once more, to escape her anguish, she allowed her mind to drift into the past. Ceridwen recalled with perfect clarity that day, fifteen seasons after the murder of her mother, when the sorcerers of Faerie had taken her into their care, training her in the ways of elemental magick. They had sensed within her a certain fire, unaware that it was an inferno of rage and an unquenchable thirst for revenge. What an excellent pupil she had been, absorbing the intricate teachings as the forest drank the rain.

She saw the battlefield in her mind as it had been so very long ago, littered with the bodies of both friend and foe. The Twilight Wars were in full swing, and a battalion of Corca-Duibhne was continuing to advance on their position. That was when they had first set her loose, allowing her to use her fury over her mother's murder to conjure up the forces to destroy the enemies of the Fey.

Her magick had been fearsome.

Ceridwen had reveled in their suffering, as the spirits of the wind tossed the enemy about the battlefield like children's toys, stealing the breath from their lungs before the earth swelled up to swallow them whole. Those who did not meet their fate from earth or air were washed away by angry torrents of relentless rain, or burnt to cinders by lapping tongues of hungry fire.

Morrigan had laughed that day as well. Gazing out at the carnage that Ceridwen had wrought, her aunt had found the level of devastation and death absolutely joyous. There was no doubt that she would find the fate of the world beneath the ministrations of the Nimble Man amusing as well.

Ceridwen could feel the surface of the chrysalis splintering beneath her, the magick burning up into her body. She began to convulse, the sorcery too much for her weakened body to contain, and at last she found solace in a memory that brought bliss that was the equal of its pain.

She would never have imagined herself capable of the love she felt for Arthur Conan Doyle, a mere human. Their lives had become entwined, their love for one another blossoming soon after the closing horrors of the war. For a while, with him, she had almost been capable of forgetting the trauma of her mother's murder—of the many lives she had taken in wartime. It had been as though she had been given another chance at life, an opportunity to wipe the past away and begin anew.

How foolish she had been to think that the fates would ever allow her to be truly happy. Happiness, she had learned, was the most fragile and ephemeral of things.

Sweetblood's magick roiled inside her. Ceridwen opened her mouth in a silent scream, sparks of magick leaping from her mouth to dance about with dust motes in the air of the ballroom. She did not think that she had ever experienced pain so intense, but her sorrow when Arthur had abandoned her had been near enough. If pressed, Ceridwen would have had difficulty deciding which torment had hurt her more deeply.

She had wanted him to stay in Faerie with her forever, but that was not to be the case. He had tried to explain why he had to return to the world of man, that he was needed there, to protect it from harm. Ceridwen had pleaded with her lover, telling him that she needed him far more than those of the Blight, but her pleas had fallen upon ears made deaf by his commitment to the world of his birth.

Ceridwen felt her anger surge. Only her fury at Arthur had given her the strength to move past her sorrow. Her sadness had turned to bitter rage, and it had made her all the stronger.

But evidently not strong enough.

The sound was like the cracking of glacial ice. Shards of the chrysalis fell away to shatter upon the ballroom floor.

EVE guided the limousine through the tight, winding streets of Beacon Hill with a reckless skill, and Conan Doyle breathed a sigh of relief when they arrived at their destination without plowing into something in the damnable red fog.

"This is close enough, Eve," he told her, from his place in the rear of the limousine, where he sat opposite Daniel and Clay.

Eve immediately brought the limo to a shuddering stop, driving up onto the curb to keep from completely blocking the road. Conan Doyle silently applauded. Despite the supernatural horrors out on the streets this damnable, impossible night, he was sure there were police and fire emergency crews out and about. They might need to pass.

"As good a spot as any," Eve said as she put the car in park. "Don't forget to lock your doors, gentlemen. This neighborhood has gone to Hell."

They exited the vehicle. Louisburg Square was down the street a ways, on the left. Up ahead, an SUV was burning, the flames and black smoke billowing from the wreckage starkly visible through the shifting crimson fog.

"We'll approach on foot," Conan Doyle told them, leading the way.

They slowed their pace as they passed the burning vehicle, all of them casually glancing inside the blackened wreck to see if there had been anybody inside.

"Ceridwen did that," Danny said, motioning with his chin. "We needed a distraction to get Morrigan and her freaky henchmen off the floor we were on so we could get downstairs. She summoned some kind of fire spirit to blow it up."

Conan Doyle said nothing, sublimating his fear for her, concentrating on the task that lay before them. When they reached the edge of the square, just outside the fenced park in its center, they all paused.

"So, how are we doing this?" Eve asked, casually picking the lint from the arm of her jacket, as if what they were about to attempt was no more important than choosing a restaurant.

"The time for subtlety has come and gone," Conan Doyle said, searching the fog for a glimpse of his home. There had been a dramatic change in the sinister energies in the atmosphere just in the minutes that had passed since they had left the State House. If they had any hope of stopping Morrigan, it had to be now. "We hit them from every side, and all at once."

"Clay and Dr. Graves," he said, turning his attention to the shapeshifter and his spectral houseguest, "the two of you shall enter the house from below, through the basement, and ascend accordingly."

He felt a hand grip his arm and turned to face the demon boy.

"What about me?" Danny asked. "You're going to let me help—aren't you?"

Conan Doyle knew that the boy's mother would not approve, but there came a time when the concerns of doting parents had to be set aside and matters of the world taken into account. This was such a moment.

"Daniel and Eve shall enter from above," the mage instructed. "The rooftop door should provide you with access."

The boy smiled, glancing toward Eve. "It's you and me," he said, clenching and unclenching his hands. "We got the roof."

"You don't say," she teased.

"What about you, Conan Doyle?" Graves asked, his voice like the whisper of the wind through the dead leaves of autumn trees. "Will you be going inside?"

Conan Doyle was taken aback by the question. His home had been invaded and Ceridwen held captive inside. The fate of his world was in the balance.

"Of course I'm going inside, old friend," he answered incredulously, stepping from the street to the cobblestones of the square. "But I shall enter just as I always have. Through the front door."

CLAY watched as Eve whispered something to Danny that he could not hear. Then she led the demon boy off into the thick fog. Just before it would have obscured his view of her completely, she glanced back at him.

"Meet you on the inside," she said.

He nodded. The two of them had certainly had their share of conflict, but it was always reassuring to have her around. She was the only thing on the face of the Earth that was as old as he was. Or nearly so, at least.

Now he glanced at Dr. Graves. The ghost hovered above the street, and he was strangely reminded of the balloons of cartoon characters that were pulled down the streets of New York on Thanksgiving Day. For all of his eternity spent on this world, Clay loved the little things, the odd little details that had become such a part of humanity.

Parades, for instance. He loved parades. He hoped the world survived so that he could see more of them.

Graves started toward Conan Doyle's townhouse, and Clay set off after him, swift and sure, his boots all but silent on the cobblestones. The ghost paused beside the old house.

"So, we start from the bottom and work our way up," Clay said.

The ghost nodded and began to sink into the street.

"Hey, what are you—"

"I'll meet you there," he said, just before his head disappeared into the ground. Then the ghost was gone, leaving him alone in the street.

"Son of a bitch," Clay muttered, closing his eyes and thinking of a form he would need to take in order to get into the basement. He hated to be the last one into a fight, and he wondered, as he began to change, if the ghost somehow was aware of that.

Clay doubled in size, his body becoming powerful and squat. He was now covered in a fine, shiny fur, his domed head nestled firmly between brawny shoulders. Lifting his short, muscular arms, he looked down upon the four railroad-spike claws that adorned each paw.

The creature he mimicked was not a mole and not a bear. It was not anything human eyes had ever seen. For though the Creator had put upon the Earth a great many wondrous things, there were beasts he had imagined with his Clay, but then abandoned. Things no one in the world had ever seen. Unless they had seen Clay in action.

Happy with the shape, he dropped to his bony knees and began to dig, the claws making short work of the cobblestoned street and layers of heavy stone beneath. It took him no time at all to burrow a tunnel down under Louisburg Square, through a wall of brick, and into one of the sewers that ran below the townhouses.

The air in the sewer was thick with gases other than oxygen—most likely a mixture of nitrogen, natural gas, and methane—and he altered his lungs so that he could breathe down there. His vision in this shape was poor, but his sense of smell was heightened to the extreme. Clay could smell the distinctive scent of the Night People.

He loped down the partially flooded passage, splashing through the filth until the aroma of the enemy was so strong that he knew he must be just beneath them. Clay dug into the wall, beginning a new passage that would take him into the basement of Conan Doyle's townhouse.

Moments later he exploded up through the concrete floor into the room. His poor eyes located the drifting, translucent shape of Dr. Graves floating in the air.

"Thanks for waiting," Clay rasped as he shifted back to his human form.

Now that his vision had returned to normal, he saw that Graves was focused on one particular corner of the room. At the same time, he noticed the stink in the basement, a smell he had become all too familiar with of late. He had been so focused on the Corca-Duibhne, he had all but completely overlooked it. But in the cellar, it was overpowering. Choking.

The smell of blood.

"Good God," Clay whispered as he looked upon the bodies stacked up against the wall like cordwood, and others hanging by their ankles from hooks on the ceiling. "What is going on here?"

"Isn't it obvious?" Graves asked him. "They're storing food. Using the basement as a larder."

DANNY'S eyes had become accustomed to the fog.

Bizarro, he thought, following close behind Eve as she made her way down one of the small alleys between the homes on Beacon Hill. It unnerved him, in a way, that he could make out the shapes of things through the thick, roiling mist. His vision was changing along with the rest of him, adapting to his environment. Which made him wonder what other surprises his body had in store for him.

He could make out a small wooden fence at the end of the alley ahead of them and was about to point it out when Eve quickened her pace, vaulting over the obstruction with ease and grace. Danny clambered over the fence as quickly as he could, fearful that his companion would leave him behind. He landed in the small yard on the other side in a crouch, his new eyes scanning the fog.

"Keep up, slowpoke," he heard her say, her voice carried on the breeze and swirled with the mist. He caught sight of her fluttering coattails as she went over another fence across the yard. It was sort of a shame that she'd put the coat on at all. The top she had on was nicely clingy and he liked to watch her move. Even with the coat, he could appreciate her . . . but without it . . .

Chill. Keep your mind on staying alive. Danny bounded across the small patch of grass, tensing the muscles in his legs as he prepared to scale the next obstacle. The power in his jump took him by surprise, and his arms pinwheeled as he tried to keep his balance while hurtling through the air. He cleared the fence with feet to spare and landed on all fours, unable to prevent the smile from blossoming across his face. Danny immediately thought of Mr. Davis, the track-and-field coach at his high school, and how the man would have shit his pants if he'd ever seen any of his track team make a jump like that.

"Decent," Eve said, leaning against a brick building.

"Where are we now?" he asked, rising to join her. They appeared to be in another small yard.

"We're at the back of Conan Doyle's place. Figured we'd get less attention if we got to the roof from the back."

Danny stepped back, looking skyward, up the rear wall of the building. Though no taller than four stories, the top of the townhouse disappeared into the crimson mist.

"And we get up there how, exactly?"

Eve pressed herself flat against the building, sinking her long fingernails into the mortar between the bricks. "Silly rabbit," she chided, beginning to climb. "As if there was any other way."

The way she crawled up the wall, Eve reminded him of some kind of lizard, barely making a sound other than the faint scrape of claw upon brick.

"Wait," he whispered, on the verge of panic. He didn't want to be left alone. Danny desperately wanted to be included, to belong. For the first time in, oh, so very long, he felt as though he were part of something, that he truly mattered. He did not want that feeling to end.

Eve stopped midway and maneuvered her body around so she could look down at him.

Not a lizard, he thought. *A spider.* She reminded him of a really big spider.

"What are you waiting for?" she asked.

He couldn't believe she was asking the question. "I can't do that," he told her, growing angry.

Eve righted herself and began to climb again. "Bet you didn't think you could make a six-foot leap over a fence either," she said as she disappeared into the mist.

She was *right about that,* he decided, approaching the wall and doing as he had watched her do. Danny placed his hands against cool brick, digging his fingernails—no, they were claws; his fingernails had fallen out months ago—between the bricks, as Eve had done. He attempted to pull his weight upward.

And succeeded.

Much to his shock and surprise, Danny was climbing

the wall. *Would you look at this,* he wanted to scream, increasing his pace to catch up with Eve.

Fucking Spiderman ain't got nothing on me.

CONAN Doyle stood at the bottom of the stairs that led up to his front door and cleared his throat. He knew they were there, crouching in the shadows, waiting for the opportunity to strike. He removed the pocket watch from his coat and saw that more than enough time had passed for his operatives to get themselves into position.

Taking the first step, he placed one of his hands upon the wrought-iron railing.

"Who is this, my brothers?" came a hissing voice from somewhere in the shadows.

Conan Doyle stood perfectly still, gathering his inner strength.

"A fool, I'd wager," responded an equally sibilant voice. "For who else but a fool would dare approach our mistress's lair?"

The Corca-Duibhne sentries emerged from their hiding places on either side of the steps, weapons crusted with the blood of their victims.

"Poor little fool," said one of the advancing Night People. "Does he even know whose dwelling this is?"

Conan Doyle stepped back from the stairs, letting his hands dangle by his sides. There were eight, all of them wearing variations of black leather. Their faces appeared oily, shining in what little light was available. He was reminded of how much he despised this species, and how the Twilight Wars never should have been declared over until each and every one of the foul creatures had been exterminated like the vermin they were.

One of the Corca-Duibhne came forward, waving a fierce-looking knife before him. "Do you know, foolish little man?" it asked, a cruel, humorless smile upon its oily, black features. Conan Doyle noticed that one of its eyes was missing. "Do you know whose house this is?"

Conan Doyle casually adjusted his shirt cuffs, matching them to the sleeves of his jacket. "Of course I do," he said, returning his hands to his side. His fingers twitched eagerly.

The Night People began to laugh, converging, forming a circle around him.

"Do you hear, brothers?" asked the creature with the missing eye. "He knows full well whose house this is."

"Tell us then," hissed another, this one wielding a kind of axe. Again they all laughed.

Conan Doyle raised one hand, sparks of blue fire dancing from the tips of his fingers.

"Why, it's mine," he told them, and then those cerulean flames arced out from his hand, engulfing them. The Corca-Duibhne cried out in a pathetic mixture of surprise and agony as the magick took hold of them, the smell of their burning flesh filling the air.

Conan Doyle closed his eyes and breathed deeply, taking the heavy aroma of charred flesh into his lungs. *Just like the good old days,* he thought, images of the war cascading through his thoughts, and the mage slowly climbed the steps to his front door.

"And now I've come home."

17

IT would have been wiser, perhaps, for Dr. Graves to lead. He might have gone right through the basement door and into the main house, done a bit of reconnaissance, and returned to give Clay the lay of the land. But Clay was not the sort of man—not the sort of creature—to wait while others put themselves at risk. Graves admired that about him. It might not be the wisest course of action for the two of them to rush headlong up those stairs, but Graves did not feel it appropriate to judge Clay by the standards of human wisdom. He was unique in all the world. Touched by the Creator. Immortal. It was obvious that to Clay, strategy was necessary only when the lives of others were in peril. When it was his own life at stake, it was full steam ahead, and the consequences be damned.

And Dr. Graves, well, he was already dead, so what the hell did he care?

"Do we have any plan at all?" Graves whispered.

Clay had adopted his fundamental form, the one Graves assumed was his true self. He was a formidable figure, at least seven feet tall, with dried cracks in his flesh as though he were made of arid, hard-packed desert. The Clay of God. Someday, Graves would like to hear the story of this remarkable being's life.

But that was for another day.

"A plan? Of course we have a plan," Clay said, hurrying up the stairs, which creaked beneath his bulk. "We kill or incapacitate everything that tries to stop us from freeing Ceridwen, and we make sure Morrigan doesn't set either Sweetblood or the Nimble Man free."

Graves did not bother to pretend to walk. He drifted up the stairs behind Clay. He had willed his appearance to change, somewhat. Now he was the younger Leonard Graves, in the early days of his adventuring. Heavy boots covered his feet and suspenders crisscrossed his back. His sleeves were rolled up, his huge fists prepared for a fight.

"It lacks a certain finesse," Graves told his ally.

Clay laughed as he reached the top of the basement stairs. He glanced back at Graves, eyes twinkling in the gloom. "Leave the finesse to Conan Doyle. It's going to come down to magick. You know it, and I know it. I resent being the muscle as much as you do. In our time, we've both led armies, you and I. But this isn't about who can outsmart Morrigan. It's about who can destroy her."

The words struck close to home. Graves had been a man of science as well as a man of action during his life. It was with a certain reluctance that he took the role of foot soldier. Yet with myriad worlds hanging in the balance and time of the essence, he knew that all that remained was to fight. And so fight he would. With all that remained of his soul.

"Let's get to it," he told Clay.

The shapeshifter turned toward the door. He reached for the knob, but his hand paused an inch away from it. Clay sniffed the air.

"What is it?" Graves asked.

The door rattled and the stairs trembled with the pounding of footfalls beyond that door.

"Boggarts," Clay said.

Graves hissed under his breath. "Son of a bitch."

Then the door exploded inward. Two enormous, hideously ugly boggarts crashed through the splintering wood and leaped upon Clay, jaws gnashing and claws tearing flesh even as the trio tumbled down the stairs in a tangle of limbs.

Graves darted into the air, soaring near the ceiling of the basement. *Boggarts.* He shivered. The Night People could not hurt him, nor could the walking dead. Morrigan had been able to do so with magick. But boggarts were different. Boggarts ate ectoplasm. They could tear him apart, gulp down bits of his spectral body as if he were still flesh and blood. They could tear his soul apart, and eat it, and then there would be no eternal rest for Leonard Graves.

The things attacked Clay, but already one of them had scented him. It must have been how their presence was noticed in the first place. One of the creatures raised its heavy head and turned burning yellow eyes upward. Graves could have fled, but he would never have left Clay there alone. For the boggarts were not the only threat to come through that shattered door.

The first Corca-Duibhne poked its head through the doorway, and it grinned, exposing razor fangs. It scrambled down the stairs after the boggarts, and then another appeared, and another, until there were six, no, eight of them.

And at the last, behind them came another figure, so tall it had to stoop to get through the shattered doorway. It was a woman. Or a nightmare contortion of what a woman might have been. Nine feet tall, the hag had only opalescent orbs where her eyes ought to have been. Her hair was filthy and stringy and hung over the shoulders of the rags she wore, belted with a chain of infant human skulls. Her teeth were long and yellow, her lips crusted with dried blood.

"What the hell is it?" Dr. Graves asked aloud.

On the concrete floor, Clay hurled a boggart across the basement to crash into the burner. The other was still focused on Graves himself. But both ghost and shapeshifter stared at the new arrival.

"Black Annis," Clay said. "It's a Black Annis."

EVE had spent eternity paying for her sins, both those she had committed, and those to which she had given birth. Vampires. Her children. The bastard offspring of an archduke of Hell and the castoff queen of Eden. The Lord might have made her, but the demon had *remade* her. Many times she had thought of giving herself over to the sun, letting its light purify her, end her damnation. But she would not.

She would not stop fighting the darkness until she had expunged her sins. And she would not know when that time had come until the Lord Himself whispered the words in her ear.

Come home.

Until then, she would fight, and she would fear nothing. The Lord would not allow her to die until she had done her penance.

Her knees scraped the house as she scaled the back wall. Another pair of pants ruined. Her talons dug into brick, and she raised herself up quickly, her body as light to her as if her bones were hollow. Such was the strength damnation had given her. Eve could have quickened her ascent by using window frames, but she avoided them, not wishing to be seen until a time of her own choosing.

A glance downward told her the boy was keeping up.

THE NIMBLE MAN 305

She smiled, and as she did, her fangs slid downward, extending themselves. The crimson mist swirled around her, the breeze rustling her hair. Eve ran her tongue over the tips of her fangs as she watched Danny Ferrick climb.

If he lived to see another morning, the kid might actually turn out to be worth having around.

Eyes narrowed, she began to climb again. Talons split mortar. Her knees and the toes of her boots gained purchase against the brick. She was nearly there now, just a few more feet. Despite her speed, Danny was catching up. She sensed him, just below her.

Eve reached up to grasp the edge of the flat roof of Conan Doyle's brownstone. With a single thrust, she pulled herself up with such force that she sprang into the air and landed on the roof in a crouch.

The red mist rolled across the roof, pushed along by the breeze. It eddied and swirled around chimneys and vents and the tall boxlike structure that contained the door that led into the building. Eve took several steps toward it, and then froze.

From the mist, from the shadows, from the night they came. Of course they did. Morrigan would not have been so foolish as to leave the roof unguarded. The Corca-Duibhne moved slowly, slinking across the roof, taking their time to circle around her, like hyenas stalking prey. She counted at least nine, but there might have been more, deeper in the bloody fog, or in the shadows.

"You don't want to do this," Eve warned them.

"Oh, yessss we do," one of them hissed. "You're the traitor. The hateful mother of darkness. There isn't one among us who wouldn't give his life for a chance at tearing out your throat."

"It's been done." Eve grinned, baring her fangs. "I got better."

Danny scrambled up over the edge of the roof behind her.

The Corca-Duibhne hesitated.

"You ready, kid?" Eve asked.

She did not have to see the smile on his face. She could hear it in the tone of his voice.

"Oh, yeah," Danny Ferrick told her. "I was born for this."

The strangest thing happened then. The Corca-Duibhne began to laugh. It was an eerie susurrus of giddy whispers that carried to her on the mist. Slowly, they began to pull back. Eve narrowed her eyes, trying to figure out what they were up to.

And something moved atop the nearest tall chimney. Something large that crawled, lizardlike, up the brick and perched on top. Its wings spread, just a shadow in the scarlet night.

Then it burst into flames.

With unfolded wings, its entire body was consumed by the blaze.

A plume of fire jetted from its snout.

"What is it?" Danny asked, a tremor of fear in his voice.

Still, Eve did not look at him. Her gaze was on the creature, this thing that could incinerate her, could end her life. "A firedrake," she told him. "And it's all yours, kid."

"Get the fuck out of here," Danny snapped.

"Sorry. I've got the dweebs. The big burning motherfucker belongs to you."

MORRIGAN threw her arms upward, the power coursing through her, and she shook in ecstasy. It was like the caress of a thousand lovers. Her nipples hardened and her sex burned with the heat of her passion, wet as though to welcome a lover. And nothing was ever more true, for the only lover she would ever accept would arrive at any moment.

"Yes!" she wailed, tears of joy streaking her face. "Come to me!"

The ballroom was blindingly bright. The magick spilling out through Sweetblood's chrysalis flashed orange and yellow and red, an inferno of color that played off the mirrored walls and the chandeliers above. And upon that chrysalis, seared by the power as though by scalding steam, Ceridwen arched her back and screamed as she had not done since the day of her mother's slaughter, that day when Morrigan had held the girl in her arms and pretended to care.

The young sorceress screamed again, eyes wide with the madness of her agony. Welts had risen on her blue-white flesh, and then blisters, which had burst. Pus ran from her legs and back where the magick seared her. Her mouth opened again but nothing came from it now but magick, power that spilled from her in a torrent of sparks and embers and a silver mist wholly unlike the red fog that had enveloped the city.

Morrigan danced across the room, twirling, stepping over the human sacrifices that her Corca-Duibhne had brought. Their bodies were flayed, their chest cavities opened, their viscera strewn about the floor and shaped into the patterns and sigils that focused the magick she now siphoned from Sweetblood. Ceridwen was the key, though. The filter. Without her, Morrigan might have died calling up the Nimble Man. Now Ceridwen would die instead.

The Fey witch reached her niece.

"Ah, sweet girl," she said. "You with your elemental magick. Your heart was with nature. You never understood that the true power is in the unnatural."

Morrigan ran her hands over Ceridwen's body, even as

her niece bucked upward again, shrieking, crying tears that fell as water but struck the ground as crystals of ice. Her violet eyes misted. Her suffering was exquisite.

Then, abruptly, Ceridwen's eyes focused and shifted to Morrigan. "You'll die."

"Yes, darling. But, first, I'll *live*."

Morrigan bent over her and brought her lips to Ceridwen's. They tasted of mint. Her tongue slid into Ceridwen's mouth, and when the young sorceress bucked again, the magick spilling from the mage erupted into Morrigan's mouth. The Fey witch felt her knees weaken with the pleasure of it and she staggered back. Just a taste of Sweetblood's power was intoxicating, arousing. But soon, she would have that and so much more.

She wiped a bit of spittle from her mouth. "Oooh, that's nice."

"Mistress!"

The Corca-Duibhne hated the bright light. It hurt them. They were terrified enough of Sweetblood, but with his magick coalescing in the room and the glaring illumination, they had fled to the corridor. Morrigan did not care. They were useless to her now except as a shield. All she needed them to do was see that she was undisturbed.

Yet now here was one, a pitiful thing it was, too. A runt. A lackey's lackey. It had called to her, and now it was pointing into the room, pointing at something behind her. Morrigan's instinct was to break it, to shatter the Corca-Duibhne. But then she saw the wonder in its cruel eyes and she turned, holding her breath.

Ceridwen screamed her throat ragged, choking on her own blood. She whimpered, and cried for her dead mother.

Behind her, on the other side of the chrysalis, a slit had opened in the fabric of the world. The magick that Morrigan had leeched from the mage had begun to seep into that hole as if carried by some unseen current. It was a wound in the heart of the universe, and its edges were peeling back like curtains torn aside, or the folds of a new mother's offering.

Within that slit all was gray and cold and still. It was a limbo place, a nothing, a flat and lifeless void.

Yet in the gray, Morrigan could see a shimmering figure, a silhouette gilded with red. And it was growing more distinct, moving nearer to the passageway between worlds.

Morrigan could barely breathe. She could not speak. For here at last were all of her dreams. Here, at last, was her salvation, her happiness, and now she would drive all the souls of creation to their knees even as all of those who had thwarted her were forced to bear witness.

All of the worlds in existence would now be as they were *meant* to be. To Morrigan, her deeds were not cruel, but a mercy. She was not destroying benevolence and beauty, but shattering the illusion that they existed at all. She was setting things right.

The Nimble Man had once been denied. Now her destiny was entwined with his, and all would be as it should be. The Nimble Man would be free.

All strength left her and she collapsed to her knees, her heart near to bursting with bliss.

And inside that portal, the Nimble Man moved closer to this world.

CONAN Doyle straightened his jacket and brushed ashes from his sleeve, then stepped over the charred corpses of a trio of Corca-Duibhne. He closed the heavy oak door behind him and then glanced around the foyer of the brownstone.

He was home.

The Night People came from the parlor, several of them trying to squeeze through the door at once, clambering over one another to get at him like dogs on a fox hunt. Others appeared in the corridor that led to the kitchen, their clothes and faces smeared with blood, one of them holding a chunk of meat in his hand, two bones jutting from its end. Conan Doyle recognized them as the ulna and radius, splintered. It was the lower arm of a human being.

Others appeared on the grand staircase. Two, then a third. A fourth hung from the light fixture above.

There were eleven or twelve of them, all told.

Conan Doyle lifted his chin, nostrils flaring, and stood waiting for them to come. He narrowed his gaze and thought again of war. Not merely the Twilight Wars, but others as well, the conflicts that devastated Europe, that took his brother and his son, that crushed the hearts of so many mothers and fathers and young brides. So much of his early life had been spent in the exercise of his imagination and of his intellect. He respected the mind and the heart, the use of reason. But even then, he had known that there came a time when the basest nature of his enemies would prevail, and the time for reason was over.

"This is my home," he said, biting off each word with grinding teeth. "And I want you out!"

The Corca-Duibhne raced at him, their claws scoring the wood floor. Some of them capered like beasts, others swaggered in their leather, modeling themselves after the darker impulses of mankind. Yet they were all nothing more than cruel, stupid animals.

Conan Doyle threw his head back, summoned the magick up inside himself, and felt it surge into him as though he had been struck by lightning. A blue mist spilled from his eyes like tears of azure steam. The Corca-Duibhne from the parlor were almost upon him. With a twist of his wrist, he lay his hand out toward them, palm upward, and a spell rolled off his fingers. He barked a phrase in Macedonian, and the floor erupted beneath them. The slats of the wood floor became roots that reached up and twined around their ankles. Shoots split off from the roots and sunk into the Night People's flesh, and their bodies began to change. To harden. Bark formed upon their skin, and they screamed as tiny branches grew out from their flesh, sprouting leaves.

They made ugly trees, those four, rooted there in the foyer.

"*Caedo tui frater,*" Conan Doyle sneered as he turned toward the trio rushing in from the kitchen. He drew a gob of phlegm up from his throat and spat it at them. It hit the ground not far from the nearest of them, and a red line snaked from that yellow spittle across the floor, touching the creature's foot.

It turned on the others with obscene savagery, claws raking another Corca-Duibhne's face, slashing its eyes, which burst with a splash of acidic fluid that scored the floor. The red lines on the floor touched the other two as well, and soon they were ripping one another apart, fang and claw, shredding flesh and clothing in a widening spatter of their own blood.

The trio on the stairs paused, hesitating now. They were capable of speech, but in battle and in fear, they rarely spoke. Now the rearmost among them took a step backward, and the others noticed and began to retreat as well.

"*To haptikos Medusa,*" Conan Doyle muttered.

He widened his eyes and felt the blue mist that swirled there pour from within him. It furrowed the air and shot toward them, enveloped them, and when it dissipated, they were only statues. Frozen stone.

Only the one hanging from the light fixture remained. He stared up at it with disdain. It clung there, eyes closed, praying he did not see it. Conan Doyle ignored it, starting for the stairs.

On the second-floor landing he saw the mad Fey twins, Fenris and Dagris, waiting for him.

Conan Doyle started up toward them.

The twins drew swords from scabbards that hung at their sides, mirror images of one another. Conan Doyle held his palms together in front of him as he walked up the stairs. When he opened them, a shaft of razor-sharp, shimmering blue magick grew from the palm of his right hand. This would be his sword. But he would not need it for long.

Dagris moved first, stepping delicately down the stairs to meet him. Fenris came after, more cautiously. They had some skill with magick, these two, but Conan Doyle was pleased they had not chosen to attack him as sorcerers. It would have taken more time than he wished to waste with them.

"There are those who would argue that madmen cannot be held responsible for their actions," Conan Doyle said as he continued up toward them. "Perhaps. Perhaps."

With a lunatic gleam in his eyes and a sickening smile, Dagris swung his sword. "For Morrigan! For the Nimble Man!"

Conan Doyle parried his attack. Dagris deftly maneuvered his weapon again and again, and each time Conan Doyle turned it away. The azure blade crackled, the air redolent with the scent of cinnamon and other spices, the smell of magick.

Dagris thrust his sword. Conan Doyle knocked it away and slammed the Fey warrior into the banister, knocking him over the rail. He fell to the floor with a crack of bone, and did not move again. Seeing his brother killed, Fenris rushed in, but Conan Doyle was ready. He had choreographed this bit in his mind. Dagris was the madder and more dangerous of the twins. Fenris swept his blade down. Conan Doyle tried to dodge, but was only partly successful. The tip of the sword cut his arm and he felt the sting and the flow of hot blood.

But his own azure blade was buried deep within Fenris' abdomen.

Yet there was no Fey blood spilt. Fenris fell to his knees. His eyes were wide as he stared up at Conan Doyle, and his face lost its mask of lunacy. His features grew younger. His body smaller.

"This is the Sword of Years," Conan Doyle told him. "It is not a weapon, but a spell. It is the magick of second chances. Without the cruelty of your brother, we shall see what becomes of you."

The blade had drawn from Fenris nearly all of the years of his life, so when Conan Doyle withdrew it from his flesh, he was only an infant. The Fey child opened his mouth and wailed, a baby's cry. There was a thin line seared upon his belly where the sword had been, but he was otherwise unharmed.

"We shall see," Doyle repeated.

He carried the infant to the second-floor landing and left it there, knowing the Corca-Duibhne would catch the scent of the Fey upon it and leave it alone.

And he moved on.

THE teakettle began to whistle. Julia twitched, startled by the noise. For a moment she felt frozen to her seat, as though even the simple act of making tea was beyond her. She gazed across her kitchen table at Squire, who sat with a gallon of chocolate chip ice cream in front of him, eating right from the container with a soup spoon. When he wasn't talking, or following the instructions of his employer, he was eating. It ought to have been repulsive, but there was something oddly charming about it.

From the first moment she had seen him, she had

avoided looking directly at him, or allowing her eyes to linger. He was ugly. His nose too long and too pointed. His face was long and angular as well, and his mouth was too wide, as though its corners had been slit, so that when he spoke or smiled, it seemed his head was about to split in two. His teeth were jagged and yellow. An animal's teeth. His hair was brittle and unkempt.

But his eyes were kind. It had taken her this long to notice that. The little man—she refused to think of him as a goblin or hobgoblin or whatever Danny had said he was— watched her with the gentlest, most expressive eyes. Squire cussed like a sailor and obviously enjoyed his verbal sparring with the others. And yet despite his appearance and despite his cutting wit, there was something tender about him.

"Want me to get that?" he asked, licking the ice cream from his spoon and nodding toward the teakettle. Its whistle had become a shriek.

"No." She stood up. "No, I'm sorry. I was just . . . I feel a little numb. Just . . . preoccupied."

"Can't say I blame you," Squire said.

Julia went to the stove and took the kettle off. The whistle died to a low hiss, like air leaking from a balloon. The kitchen was lit only by the tiny flames that flickered atop a half dozen candles she had set about the room. There were other places in the house that would have been more comfortable, but she felt the safest in the kitchen. How odd was that? She did not want to think about the answer. She only knew that it felt like a refuge. Like a sanctuary. Like a place she might be busily toiling when her little boy came home to her.

Her lips pressed together in a tight line and she squeezed her eyes shut, refusing to cry. As she gripped the kettle and began to pour the steaming water into the two cups she had taken from the cabinet for herself and Squire, her hand trembled. She set the kettle down. In her mind she saw the next steps that were necessary. Get the tea bags from the cupboard. Milk from the fridge. Some cookies to go with the tea. Anyone else would have been happy with a gallon of ice cream, but she doubted Squire would say no to the cookies.

She leaned against the stove to keep from collapsing.

"Mrs. Ferrick," Squire said, his voice a harsh rasp in the flickering shadows. This little man . . . this little monster in her kitchen.

Her shoulders shook.

"Julia."

Slowly, she turned to face him. His eyes were wide and she saw such caring and intelligence there that she immediately regretted having thought of him as a monster, not to mention the dozens of other uncharitable thoughts that had crossed her mind.

"He's going to be all right," Squire said, planting his spoon back in the ice cream container. It jutted upward like a flagpole.

Julia stared at him, slowly shook her head. "How . . . how can you be so sure?"

His gaze was intense. "I'm *not* sure. But you believe me, don't you?"

Her pulse slowed. She took a deep breath and let it out. A strange peace came over her. Amazed at herself, she began to nod.

"Yes. Yes, I do."

Squire grinned and leaned back in his chair, throwing up his hands. "See that! I've just got one of those faces, y'know! My work here is done."

Julia could not help but laugh. It lasted only a moment, but Squire had lightened her heart, and she was grateful for that. Also, the truth was that she did believe him. He seemed so certain of it. The little man believed with his whole heart that things were going to turn out all right. She knew she had to do the same, that she had to have faith.

Without it, she would never survive the night.

THE Black Annis caught Clay by the throat as he was defending himself from the Corca-Duibhne. He had one of the Night People in his own hands, its chest crushed, its eyes bulging as it breathed its last. But then the hag appeared, far swifter than he would have expected. She was a thing of legend, one of the dark creatures that prowled the shadows of Faerie. It was no surprise that Morrigan had enlisted her aid, and now the corpses in the basement made more sense. The Black Annis fed on human children. Morrigan had promised her a lifetime's supply.

The hag lifted Clay by the throat, sickening glee in her eyes. She stank like vulture's breath, a fetid carrion stench that billowed off her with every move. Her claws could carve stone or bone, and she was only one of a family of sisters. Clay hoped there were no others in Morrigan's employ.

One, though . . . one he could handle.

With a single swipe of her free hand, she tore his stomach open. In the same moment, Clay changed. He *shifted.* Now the Black Annis saw not a seven-foot earthen man, but a mirror image of herself. One of her sisters. Just as hideous, just as rank. The simple creature's eyes went wide, and she threw Clay to the ground and knelt by his side, holding her hands over the wound in his gut.

Even as he retained the shape of a Black Annis, he felt his abdomen knitting together, healing. He was not flesh and blood, after all. Not really. He could only mimic it.

He was Clay.

With one Black Annis hand, he reached up and grabbed

the hag by her filthy, matted hair. He flexed his right hand; claws that could carve stone or bone. With a single swipe, he tore her throat out, all the way back to the spinal column.

Shifting once more to himself, to the face he knew as his own—not the human one he wore so often but the earthen body that had spawned the legend of the golem— he stood to fight the Corca-Duibhne. The boggarts were after Graves, now, howling and snarling as they tried to reach the ghost. Only a few Corca-Duibhne remained. Clay did not bother to alter his form again. One leaped at him and he drove it down to the concrete floor and crushed its skull with his fist.

The other two paused. They were staring upward, at Dr. Graves.

Clay followed their gaze. The boggarts were snarling, gnashing their teeth.

Dr. Graves floated in the air above them, a look of utter disdain upon his face. He wore suspenders and a heavy shirt with the sleeves rolled up. But now something else had been added to his attire. The specter now wore a pair of pistol holsters, one under each arm. They had not been there before.

Clay stared in amazement as Graves crossed his arms over his chest and drew the guns from those holsters. Phantom guns. Ectoplasmic manifestations of Graves' own soul, his own spirit energy. Ghosts had control over their appearance when their souls remained anchored to this world. Many times they could change their appearance, not the way Clay could, but in age or attire.

Yet Clay had never seen anything like this.

"Boggarts are a damned nuisance," Dr. Graves snapped. "You want a taste of me, dogs? I don't think so. You soul eaters may be able to hurt me, even kill a man who's already dead. But it works both ways. If you want little shreds of my soul inside you, all right. But it's going to be my way, not yours."

Graves pulled both triggers again and again, spectral bullets tearing into the boggarts. The impact made their bodies shudder and jerk and drove them back, and then fall over dead, gray blood oozing from their wounds. The bits of soul stuff that had composed the bullets lost their shape, became streaks of ectoplasm that shot back across the room and coalesced around Dr. Graves, reattaching themselves to him.

"It works both ways," Graves said again, holstering his guns.

Clay gave him a quiet round of applause.

The two remaining Corca-Duibhne stared back and forth between the ghost and the shapeshifter, and then ran for the stairs.

Clay and Dr. Graves raced after them.

BEFORE Danny could argue, Eve had abandoned him. She rushed off to attack the Corca-Duibhne, and he was left alone on Conan Doyle's roof, four stories above Beacon Hill. The crimson mist blanketed the building, blotted out the night, and it seemed as though the brownstone was all that remained of the city of Boston.

Atop the chimney, the firedrake spread its blazing wings and rose up into the mist, into the bloodstained night. Danny had no idea what to do. The thing was like some bizarre combination of dragon and phoenix. He could not fly after it, could not defend himself from it. Eve was smart to get out of its way. She was a vampire. The thing would incinerate her in an instant.

Now it dipped one wing and started down toward him.

Danny wanted to run. He wanted to cry. He didn't have time to do either.

The firedrake opened its mouth and a stream of liquid

fire erupted from its gullet, engulfing Danny Ferrick. The flames licked at him, roaring in his ears. It burned. God, how it burned. He threw his head back and screamed, thinking of his mother, thinking what it would do to her to know that he was dead.

The stink of burning skin and hair was in his nostrils.

Danny blinked. His skin was hot and it stung as though he had a terrible sunburn. But the flames were subsiding and he was still alive. The red fog caressed him, cool and moist. When he glanced down at himself, he noticed his feet first. His clothes were gone, nothing but black ash now, eddying in the breeze. His toes had black claws instead of nails. Unable to breathe, Danny looked at his legs, at his chest, looked at his outstretched arms, and saw skin tough as leather but soft as silk, the color of burgundy wine.

He reached up with both hands and felt his head. His hair had been falling out, his skin flaking. Now his scalp was smooth, save for the viciously sharp horns above his temples.

The firedrake let out a grunt, and he looked up to see it circling, ready to attack him again. The flames that made up its body fluttered in the mist and the dark. Danny smiled up at it.

"Bring it on."

The monster attacked again. This time, when the fire engulfed him, Danny did not even close his eyes. As the firedrake flew by, he crouched and leaped upward a dozen feet to snatch it by the throat with both hands. The demon boy dragged the firedrake from the sky, fell to the roof on top of it, and roared with pleasure as its flames licked at his legs and arms and torso.

He slid his hands into its gullet and broke its jaws, tearing its head in two. It felt incredible. It felt good.

In fact, Danny was terrified to discover exactly how good it felt to kill.

18

Ceridwen burns with fever. There is a cool breeze in the trees above, but it offers no comfort. The water diverted from the river into the stone bath is icy cold, flowing down from the mountain, and she can feel it sting her skin, yet her blue-tinted flesh is now flushed with a rich pink, so that her naked body seems painted with the colors of sunset.

That is not right. No, not at all. Her skin should not look like that. She is ill. So very ill.

Her eyelids flutter and she lolls back into the stone basin, the water flowing over her bare flesh. Her nakedness concerns her not at all. She is still young. It will be some time before she has blossomed enough for the men of the Fey to notice her. She is old enough that she has begun to notice the boys, but even so, there will be no intruders here. This is the citadel of her uncle, King Finvarra. Ceridwen's rooms are nearby. And her mother—

Mother, she thinks.

As if summoned, her mother leans into her view,

*her smile, her concerned eyes, blotting out the sky.
The woman's features are severe, her hair cropped
closely to her scalp, but there is a gentleness in her
that most others will never see as she gazes down
upon her daughter.*

*"Ceridwen. The fever has touched you. But do
not fear. I will remain with you, here at your side,
until it has passed."*

*A calm passes through her. The fever still burns.
Her bones ache, her eyes are seared, her throat is
swollen near to closing, her breath rattles in her
chest. But her mother is with her. Ceridwen lets her
eyes flutter closed as a soothing hand begins to
brush her damp hair away from her face. Her
mother's touch caresses her cheek, and the agony of
the fever recedes just slightly. For the first time,
Ceridwen feels as though the icy water in the stone
bath is cooling her, its chill sinking into her flesh,
and the blazing fever abating.*

*Her chest rises and falls in steady rhythm, and
she searches for a peaceful place within . . . only to
discover that she is already there. She can hear the
breeze in the trees, the rush of the river, and the song
of birds, and yet they are all distant compared to the
beat of her heart, the sound of her breathing. She is
deep within herself.*

*The stone bath is rough against her back. The
water envelops her, flowing over her, and its sting
disappears.*

"Impressive."

*Alarmed, Ceridwen opens her eyes and stares in-
credulously at the man standing over her. He has
dark skin and hair as black as raven's feathers. His
chin is covered by a short beard, and he peers down*

at her with eyes the blue of the deepest, most tumultuous river.

Confusion takes hold of her. Where is her mother? Who is this stranger, this intruder into the king's citadel? She glances down at herself, at her body, and sees that she is in full blossom, her body ripened to an age where men might do more than appreciate her. In her shame she tries to cover herself, and the pain sears through her again. Her skin is blistering with the fever, her breathing ragged.

Ceridwen frowns. There is no fever. Somehow she knows this.

"I was not speaking of your charms, lady, significant as they are," the dark man says, gesturing toward her bare breasts. "I refer to your endurance. I always admired you, Ceridwen. Now I see my interest was well-placed."

"Who are you?" she manages to rasp.

The water in the stone bath is no longer cold. It seems, in fact, near to boiling.

"Don't you know?" His smile is thin, a surface thing, so fleeting, hurried away by the grimness of his nature.

And she does know. "Sanguedolce. Sweetblood."

He executes a courtly bow. "Indeed." The twinkle in his eye lasts only a moment. "The damage is done, now. The evil, the darkness . . . it will come no matter what you do. I should let you all die for your part in this foolishness. But there may come a time when I need you. So a word of advice, sorceress.

"You are a channel, a conduit. She's using you to tap my power. Your pain is that you are fighting it. Stop fighting. Take some for yourself."

Sanguedolce crouches at her side. He bends to

kiss her. His lips are soft, but hers are dry and cracked and they burn.

Not with fever, but magick.

"Wake up," he whispers.

Ceridwen woke hissing air in through her teeth, filling her lungs hungrily, and a part of her knew that she had momentarily ceased to breathe. Her eyes opened wide, and though the light inside Conan Doyle's defunct ballroom was brilliant, she did not turn from it. Her teeth gritted, the pain in her back and neck and down her legs excruciating. Blisters burst as she moved. Shards of the chrysalis beneath her cut her skin.

It was striped with cracks, fissures through which the mage's magick spilled. Morrigan's ritual had locked the two together, married Ceridwen's flesh to Sanguedolce's crystal sarcophagus. The agony had blinded her, shut down her mind. But now there was the pinpoint spark of knowledge in Ceridwen's head. She could feel more than pain. In the magick that seared her, that burst from her flesh and raced through her veins, she could feel power.

She could taste it.

Like bile, it rose in her throat again. Previously she had let her jaws gape and vomited up that power, that magick.

This time she clamped her mouth shut with a clack of teeth. Her lips curled back and she sneered. The magick surged up within her.

But Ceridwen did not let it go. She caught it. *Take some for yourself,* Sanguedolce had said in her fever dream. And so she did.

The face of her mother was clear in her mind. The sound of the river that rushed down from the mountain citadel of her uncle, King Finvarra, in the heart of Faerie, was in her ears. She brought both memories into her heart. Words in the ancient tongue of the kings of Faerie formed silently upon her lips and her pain receded. Her flesh healed. The magick of Sweetblood the Mage spilled into her, just as it had before. But Ceridwen was no longer the conduit.

She was the vessel.

With a sneer, she broke her bonds and sprang up from the chrysalis. It popped with the sound of ice breaking on the lake in springtime, and the fissures deepened and widened. She could see Sanguedolce's face deep within the amber encasement. His eyes were still, and yet she was sure he was watching her.

Tensed to defend herself, she found that Morrigan had not even noticed her. The cunning bitch was on her knees in front of a shimmering portal, a slit in reality. Even as Ceridwen took it all in, realizing what it was, she saw a tall, lithe silhouette reach the dimensional doorway from the other side. Cloaked in clouds of gray, it put one foot through, into this world.

The Nimble Man, Ceridwen thought, her heart racing with panic, her mind whispering the doom of all creation. But she would not have it. With Sweetblood's power coursing through her, she held out a hand and in an instant, a sphere of ice coalesced in her palm. A finger pointed at the floor, she summoned the spirits of the wood, and in the space between heartbeats a new staff grew up and into her free hand. Its tip spread into fingers to receive the ice sphere, she set it into place, and blue-white mist began to swirl around the orb. Then a tiny spark ignited within, becoming an ember, becoming a flame. It started to glow.

Morrigan had taken or destroyed her elemental staff. Ceridwen had created another.

As the elemental magick pulsed from the staff, Morrigan seemed to sense it. She twitched, obviously reluctant to turn away from the spectacle of the Nimble Man's arrival. Then she did turn, and Ceridwen was pleased to see the look of fury and wretched hatred on her aunt's face.

"Your brother, my uncle, always underestimated you, Morrigan," Ceridwen said, her words clipped, her magick streaming from her every pore, spilling off her just as Sweetblood's had from the chrysalis. "But you, aunt, always underestimated me."

Morrigan laughed. "Perhaps. Perhaps, Ceridwen. But no matter. The time has passed for your presence to be of consequence." She smiled, and for the first time Ceridwen understood the full extent of her madness. "The Nimble Man is here."

Ceridwen had been about to attack, to destroy Morrigan and attempt to disrupt the flow of magick from the chrysalis to the doorway. But Morrigan was correct. It was too late.

The Nimble Man had come.

Ceridwen had never seen a being more beautiful, nor anything more terrible. His skin was golden and smooth as glass, but shot through with scarlet traces as though his body was tainted. Infected. His form was flawless, and yet unsettling. His hands were too long and tipped with curling claws. Jutting from his back were the tattered remnants of black-feathered wings, only strips of muscle and cartilage now. They had been torn from him, and as he stepped into the ballroom, into the world, three black feathers fell from the vestiges of his wings and drifted to the floor.

His hair was as black as those feathers and fell around his shoulders, and his face was breathtaking. Simply stunning. Angelic, of course.

Until he noticed Ceridwen. Then his lips parted and he smiled, revealing hooked black fangs and a mass of coiling serpentine stingers where his tongue should have been.

The Nimble Man did not speak to her. Instead, he simply hissed.

Morrigan stood and clung to him, and he gazed at her with inhuman, slitted eyes and caressed her.

All the strength Ceridwen had felt restored to her now seemed to slip away.

"Well, it appears I'm just in time for the festivities to begin."

Ceridwen's heart leaped at the familiar voice, and she glanced over her shoulder to see Conan Doyle stride into the ballroom, long coat unwrinkled, every hair in place, as gallant as ever. Tendrils of magickal energy streamed from his eyes and his fingers, and he paused, ten feet inside the door, prepared to fight.

A moment later, one of the windows on the far wall shattered and Eve leaped into the room, landing in a crouch. Behind her, outlined within the window frame, was a wiry, powerful-looking demon hybrid that must have been Danny Ferrick. The air beside Ceridwen shimmered, and the ghost of Dr. Graves formed itself from nothing. One of the mirrored walls exploded inward, and in the dust rising from the rubble, she saw the massive form of Clay.

The Menagerie had arrived.

"Yes, come!" Morrigan cried, turning to face them as she rose to her feet. "You have all saved me the trouble of finding you."

Her face was filled with rapture. Behind her the Nimble Man stretched as if waking from a heavy sleep. His ravaged wings caressed the open edges of the dimensional doorway behind him. He surveyed the room, the individuals arrayed there, and he smiled. But when his gaze touched upon Sweetblood's chrysalis—shot through with cracks from which magick issued in radiant waves—he flinched.

"Now, my friends, keep him still!" Conan Doyle shouted, pointing at the Nimble Man.

They reacted immediately. Eve leaped at the Nimble

Man, more feral than Ceridwen had ever seen her, fangs and claws extended. She landed upon him, clung to his back, and raked her talons across his throat, barely scratching his flesh. Clay was upon him in almost the same instant, but in between one step and the next, he made a transformation that was breathtaking. His arid, fissured flesh shifted, smoothed itself, and began to glow. Wings sprouted from his back, but his were perfect, with feathers of pure white. His skin was alabaster, and his face glowed with such warm light that it was difficult to look at, and yet almost impossible to look away from.

An angel, Ceridwen thought. Arthur had told her about such things. *This is what an angel looks like.*

The ghost of Dr. Graves flitted across the room, taking up a defensive position at the door. Most of the Corca-Duibhne were likely destroyed or had fled in terror, but this had obviously been Conan Doyle's preventive measure, in case any of them should muster the courage to return.

Morrigan uttered a mad little laugh. "Are you all that stupid? Or has Conan Doyle mesmerized you? Are you really that anxious to die? Why don't you run?"

"Run from you?" Ceridwen asked. "I think not."

With both hands she held her elemental staff before her. With a single, guttural sound, she called a frigid wind that churned across the space separating her from her aunt. Ice formed in Morrigan's hair and over her eyes, and for just a moment she stiffened. Ceridwen still felt some of the power of Sweetblood inside her. It did not give her power she had never had, but it amplified her own magick tenfold. With a grunt she banged the base of the staff on the floor and sketched the air with her forefinger.

Lightning crackled from the ballroom ceiling and struck Morrigan. The Fey witch trembled as it raced through her and then she fell to her knees again, but this time it was in pain rather than supplication. She raised her hand to retaliate, but quickly spun to her left and barely succeeded in throwing up a ward before Conan Doyle's spell struck her. It dissipated harmlessly, but she was off balance.

"I'll leave the family squabble to you, shall I?" he called across the ballroom.

Ceridwen nodded grimly and advanced upon her aunt, blue-white mist spilling from the sphere atop her staff.

CONAN Doyle left Ceridwen to deal with her aunt. Even as he passed them, Morrigan was struck by a spell that seared the air between the two Fey sorceresses, and she stumbled backward. So much of her power had been used to summon the Nimble Man, Conan Doyle hoped that it would give Ceridwen the edge.

The Nimble Man was also not at his full strength. The process of being born into this world, of escaping the pull of his limbo prison, had drained him. Conan Doyle had no idea how long it would take for the damned one to recover, but while he was weakened, there was a chance the Menagerie could stop him. If he was given a moment's respite, time enough to muster his strength anew, the world would pay the price.

Clay and Eve grappled with the Nimble Man. Despite his sluggishness, he seemed almost amused at their attack. A low, chuffing laughter came from deep within his chest as he struggled against them, but his lips peeled back and that mass of serpentine things in his mouth danced and writhed there, and Conan Doyle thought that his patience had worn thin.

Some of his strength returning, the Nimble Man began to grow. With a sound like a field full of crickets, the damned one stretched, sprouting in seconds to a height of nine feet, then twelve, with no sign of stopping.

No, Conan Doyle thought. *I need more time. Just a few moments.* It was up to his comrades to buy him that time.

"What the fuck is this?" Eve snarled, trying to hold on to her prey. As if she thought she might shrink him again, she opened her mouth, jaws distending, and tore at the Nimble Man's throat. She slashed her talons down and tore at one of the Nimble Man's vestigial wings, and for the first time, he cried out in pain.

Clay was at him as well, but the Nimble Man knocked the shapeshifter away and then, as if she were no more than a bothersome mosquito, reached up and snatched Eve from her perch upon his back and shoulders. He held her out in front of him by her arms, gazing at her as though she were some child's plaything. Eve struggled but to no avail.

"Keep growing, asshole. You're just a bigger target. You don't know who the hell you're dealing with he—"

The Nimble Man snapped both of her arms, the echo of cracking bone ricocheting around the room. Eve's words were cut off by her own scream. Then the damned creature held her by her head as she hung limply in his grasp, and reached up to run one long claw across her throat. Blood spilled from the gash like a scarlet curtain down her chest. The Nimble Man threw her across the room.

Eve collided with the splintered chrysalis, its magick cascading now throughout the room and across the floor. The collision cracked it open further, so that in several places it had fallen apart completely. Sweetblood's legs jutted out from the base of the thing. Eve lay in a tumble of broken limbs like some forgotten marionette.

"No!" Danny Ferrick screamed, as he raced at the gigantic Nimble Man.

Clay had recovered. Retaining his gleaming angelic form, he darted at the Nimble Man, arriving before Danny.

Clay placed one long-fingered, angelic hand over the Nimble Man's face, and divine light seared his golden flesh. Conan Doyle could have helped them, but only if he had been willing to sacrifice the world. Instead—with the sounds of the combat between Morrigan and Ceridwen behind him—he rushed toward the shattered chrysalis and turned to face the Nimble Man, and the dimensional doorway that had been slit through the fabric of the universe. He could feel Sweetblood's power coalescing around him. It caressed him as though it were a breeze that blew only for him.

The Nimble Man clutched Clay by the throat and tore one of his angel wings off, flesh and bone and cartilage ripping. Clay roared in agony, and even as he did, he began to change again, now a white tiger with black stripe slashing its fur. The Nimble Man crushed his jaws in one massive hand, and then slammed Clay into the floor with enough force to crack the woodwork. The shapeshifter returned to his arid, earthen form and did not move again.

In the strobing light from the magick erupting from the cracks on the chrysalis, Conan Doyle watched Danny Ferrick attack. When he saw the demon boy, the Nimble Man paused, a troubled expression on his face.

"You are horrors," he said, in a voice wet with the moisture of the things writhing in his mouth. Though he was growing, and beginning to recover from his transition to this world, he staggered slightly, unsteady on his feet. *"Why would you fight my coming?"*

"Why?" Danny shouted, snarling the word. " 'Cause this is our world! It's got its problems, but it's home. And you don't belong here!"

Danny leaped up at the Nimble Man, driving his small demon horns into the damned creature's abdomen. Once more the Nimble Man cried out. He glared down at the boy, opened his black-fanged jaws, and the mass of squirming serpent things that filled his mouth spiked out, stretching to impossible length, and punctured Danny's chest, punching out through the demon boy's back.

"Danny!" Conan Doyle roared, and for the first time he nearly lost his composure, nearly surrendered the calm that his next move required. The boy's mother had entrusted her son to him, and Conan Doyle was afraid for him. If Danny was dead, he did not think he could face Julia Ferrick.

He bared his teeth, grinding them together. The magickal energy that trailed from his fingertips and spilled from his eyes seemed to dance with the power leaking from Sweetblood's chrysalis. Conan Doyle felt the two embrace. The fissures in the amber encasement widened. With a loud crack, more pieces of the chrysalis began to fall away. Within that shell, Conan Doyle could see Sweetblood's hand, twitching, fingers stretching.

"The boy was right," Conan Doyle said, starting toward the Nimble Man. "You don't belong here. You don't belong anywhere save that gray limbo. And if you wanted to leave it behind, you should never have left the door open."

Then, unable to resist a dramatic flourish, Conan Doyle passed one hand across his face, disrupting the glamour that had hidden his true countenance.

A spell struck Ceridwen on her left side, her face taking the brunt of the magick. Instantly her flesh began to soften, to melt. She felt her cheek droop, strings of skin dangling from her jawbone like tree sap. Morrigan had the advantage, and now her eyes blazed with malice. All of her fanaticism pulsed just beneath her features, but for the moment it had been usurped by her disdain for her family, for her people, for her land. The Fey witch rose off the ground, floating several inches from the wood floor, and she threw her arms wide. Streaks of oily black energy darted back and forth in front of her, dancing from finger to finger, from hand to hand, as though she were knitting some web of darkness.

"Stupid little girl," Morrigan sneered.

The sensation of her flesh sliding from her skull was the most dreadful thing Ceridwen had ever experienced. She wanted to scream, but could not control the muscles in her jaw. Panic set in, her gaze locked on Morrigan, and she watched as her aunt raised her hands and prepared to hurl that web of black magick at her, to entangle her, to destroy her.

Morrigan attacked. With the crack of a bullwhip, the black net whistled toward Ceridwen. She had expended the power she had borrowed from Sweetblood and knew that if Morrigan meant to kill her now, she would not be able to defend herself.

With a grunt, Ceridwen clacked the base of her elemental staff against the floor. A mystical breeze gusted around her, a traveling wind that lifted her in half an eyeblink from the path of Morrigan's attack and set her down again just behind her mad aunt.

Fear gave way to rage. Ceridwen pressed the ice sphere at the top of her elemental staff against her face and felt the warmth of its energies spread through her. This was her magick, a simple object to channel her own innate power and to help her focus her rapport with the elements. Morrigan was Fey. She was family. Ceridwen easily countered the spell her aunt had cast, restoring her flesh, healing her face.

"You think you can run away from me?" Morrigan asked. Still floating, she spun in the air, glaring down at her niece. "From *me*?"

And for the first time, Ceridwen really saw the familial

resemblance between herself and her aunt. The nose, the eyes, the lips . . . it made her feel sick.

"I have never run from you," Ceridwen replied.

With a flutter of her eyelids and a tugging deep inside her, an ache in her loins, she reached into the wood floor and drew it to life again. Vines burst from the floor and twined around Morrigan's legs, reaching up to encircle her arms, trapping them against her body. Thorns pushed out from the vines, slicing her flesh. It would not hold her for long.

Ceridwen heard Conan Doyle scream Danny's name. She turned her gaze for just a moment from her conflict with Morrigan. In horror, she watched the demon boy impaled and then cast aside. She saw Arthur, grimly determined, bathe himself in the magicks spilling from Sweetblood's chrysalis. As Morrigan struggled to be free of her bonds, Ceridwen saw Conan Doyle pass a hand across his face.

His features shimmered, a glamour dissipating, and Ceridwen felt a stab of despair in her heart as she saw what he had done. Gore streaked the left side of Conan Doyle's face, dried and crusted there. Where his left eye had been there was now a small silver orb that crackled with magick.

The Eye of Eogain.

Conan Doyle had torn out his left eye and replaced it with a magickal construct, with the weapon he would need. Had he brought it into the house in his pocket, or in Eogain's yellowed skull, Morrigan might have gotten hold of it. But now it was his, rooted into his mind, into his brain.

He threw his arms out, let the power of Sweetblood wash over him, and the light around that magickal eye began to pulse, to churn.

"Noooo!" Morrigan screamed.

Ceridwen turned in time to see the Fey witch tear herself loose from those mystical vines, their thorns cutting her flesh to the bone. Morrigan seemed not to notice the pain of those wounds, nor even to remember that she had been fighting Ceridwen moments before.

Conan Doyle had said something about the door still being open. Ceridwen understood. He meant to send the Nimble Man back to his limbo world, and the possibility drove Morrigan to utter madness. She shrieked like the ancient sidhe and thrust herself across the room, staggering into the air, buoyed by a rush of magick so powerful it seemed to give her flight.

Ceridwen would not allow it. Conan Doyle had left her to deal with family business, and so she would.

As she raised her elemental staff, the sphere at its apex lengthened and thinned, wooden fingers closed on its new shape, and now it was a blade, sharp as diamond. Ceridwen screamed as she lunged at her aunt and drove the spear into her side, burying it deep. She thought about how many of her people had died because of Morrigan, about the grief that hung so heavily upon her uncle, her king. She thought about her mother's death in the Twilight Wars and all of the heartache that Morrigan had ever brought to Faerie.

Her aunt screamed and fell to the floor, writhing, struck to her core with the purity of elemental magick. Her black heart was poisoned by it. Ceridwen pulled the spear out of her and thrust it into her again, stabbing her chest and belly again and again. There was no honor in it, but there was so much pain.

Dr. Graves appeared beside her. In her peripheral vision, Ceridwen saw him, took in the look of concern and dismay upon his spectral features, and raised the spear to impale Morrigan again. Graves reached out and his ghostly fingers encircled her wrist.

He was a phantom, nothing more. He could not have forced her to stop. Yet somehow the next blow did not fall. Ceridwen looked down at her aunt, Fey blood bleeding out across the ravaged floor, tiny animal mewling noises coming from Morrigan's mouth, and she felt nothing. Yet she wished that Dr. Graves was more than a wandering soul, that in that moment he could have had flesh so that she could have touched his arm, leaned on him, just to feel something warm.

"Conan Doyle," Graves began.

Ceridwen spun to go to Arthur's aid, but even as she did, the remnants of Sweetblood's chrysalis exploded in a blast of magickal light that blinded her and knocked her back. It passed through her and she had to catch her breath, her every sense excited beyond reason by the touch of this power. She blinked, tried to see through the brilliance, but could not make out even the silhouette of the Nimble Man and the man she had once loved.

THE pain in Conan Doyle's head was sheer agony, like nothing he had ever felt before. It was as though someone were hammering a railroad spike through his skull, a shattering bit of trepanning. He screamed even as the chrysalis burst, and he clapped his hands to the side of his head. In the orbit where his left eye had been, he felt the Eye of Eogain move and pulse of its own accord. It seemed to swell, pressing against the bones of his skull, expanding. At any moment he knew his head would crack wide open.

"Good God, no!" Conan Doyle cried, and he fell to his knees.

Another wave of power from the disintegrated chrysalis passed through him. The pulse of it nearly killed him. The Eye of Eogain gathered up all of Sweetblood's magick, and siphoned all of Conan Doyle's own magick as well.

"You are nothing!" the Nimble Man roared above the blaze of light and sound. *"You are only a man."*

Conan Doyle forced himself to look up at the damned one. The Nimble Man had grown so large that his head and shoulders had crashed through the ceiling above, debris raining down around him. His mane of raven black hair was swept back by some unearthly wind, and several black feathers swirled and eddied on the floor. His ruined wings were still dying.

What will he be like when he has regained his full power?

Behind him, Conan Doyle could see the slit in reality, the door into that limbo world where he had been an eternal prisoner until now. Morrigan had cast the spells, performed the ritual, spilled the blood and the power to open it, but she had not had a chance to close it. And now Ceridwen was dealing with her.

Gray mist still clung to the Nimble Man, residue of that limbo, detritus from nowhere. And Conan Doyle saw that the wind that ruffled the damned one's ravaged wings and jet-black hair did not originate in this room, or even from this world. It was a vacuum, the void of limbo, tugging at the Nimble Man, trying to draw him back to where he belonged, back to the place where the Creator and all the devils in Hell had abandoned him.

"Only a man?" Conan Doyle screamed into the maelstrom that now began to whip around the room, Sweetblood's power and the pull of that doorway merging, twisting together. "There is no such thing as *only* a man! And you, pitiful thing, will never be free until the Lord Himself wills it!"

All of the magick churning in the ballroom began to stream into Conan Doyle's body and he absorbed it, twitching, wracked with pain. He thrust it outward in a burst of magick that required no spell, only thought. His own magick enhanced with Sweetblood's power, Conan Doyle reached toward the Nimble Man, not with his own hands, but with fingers of glistening energy the hue of a forest's heart. Those tendrils of power lashed out, snatching at the Nimble Man.

But that was merely a distraction. For Conan Doyle's magick touched more than the damned one. Shimmering emerald energy whipped at the gray web of strands coming from that limbo realm. The Nimble Man had, all along, been in the process of extricating himself from its hold, as though dragging himself up from quicksand. Its grasp was still upon him, but it was weakening.

"Can you feel it, abomination? Can you feel your prison calling you back?" Conan Doyle snarled between gritted teeth.

He used his magick to strengthen limbo's grasp on the Nimble Man. The emerald energy that he wielded wrapped itself more tightly around the damned one, and Conan Doyle tried to force the Nimble Man back into the dimensional doorway.

The Nimble Man began to laugh. He glared at Conan Doyle with savage eyes and bared his hooked, ebony fangs.

"Arrogant speck. You will exhaust your power soon enough. Mine only grows. When the one outweighs the other, we will have a reckoning, you and I."

Even with Conan Doyle's assistance, the gray clutch of limbo was not enough to draw the Nimble Man back through the portal. It seemed he would need a bit of a push.

"I think not," Conan Doyle whispered.

Surrendering to the pain that threatened to crack his skull, he sank to his knees. Swathed in the power of the greatest mage in the history of the world, with that mystic strength surging through him, he threw back his head and muttered a string of words in Gaelic. The Eye of Eogain burned in his face, as though his skull was on fire, and he released all the churning magicks within him in a torrent of warring colors, a stream of boiling energy that struck the Nimble Man in the center of his chest.

The damned one screamed in rage and pain and staggered backward. He glanced down at the magick that pounded into him over and over. Gray wisps of limbo encircled him, constricted him, binding his arms and wings. Conan Doyle screamed as the magick scraped the inside of his skull, scouring his eye socket. It pulsed as it jetted from the Eye of Eogain, pummeling the Nimble Man, knocking him back further. Closer to the doorway, to that slit in the fabric of reality.

The Nimble Man was smaller now. Shrinking.

It seemed to happen almost in an instant, then. Gray matter erupted from the doorway, sliding over the Nimble Man like a shroud, or a birth caul. One of his arms broke free and those long, terrible claws grasped at the air, found purchase in the wood floor, and then scored long gashes in the wood as limbo swallowed whole this creature who had been cursed and damned by Heaven and by Hell.

There was a sound like paper tearing, and then the Nimble Man was gone, lost inside that limbo realm, gray clouds gathering at the doorway, obscuring any view within.

Some of his pain had subsided, but not all. The magick erupting from the Eye of Eogain ceased, but Conan Doyle could not rise from his knees. He barely managed to lift his hands and whisper. *"Goddef yr brath iachu,"* he said in Welsh, exhausted. And then, as he crumbled to the floor, he added a Gaelic curse. *"Go n-ithe an cat thú is go n-ithe an diabhal an cat."*

The doorway closed.

EPILOGUE

THE roiling energies in that room began to subside. Brilliant colors faded to nothing, and the room was enveloped in darkness. Conan Doyle blinked several times, and then through his one good eye, he found he could see light.

Moonlight, coming in through the windows.

Beyond the glass the crimson fog had departed.

Wincing with every movement, he glanced around. Morrigan was dead. The ghost of Dr. Graves hovered above her corpse, and Ceridwen knelt there, beside the remains of her aunt. When Conan Doyle looked at her, she smiled.

Clay sat against the splintered mirror glass of the far wall, recovering. He held in his hands the wing the Nimble Man had torn off, but even as Conan Doyle watched, it merged into his malleable flesh and he was whole again.

Eve lay on the floor, blood in a pool around her. Conan Doyle had seen her take terrible punishment before, and it always left him heartsick. Her arms were broken and her throat had been torn out. But even as he watched her, she twitched. An hour or so and she would be mostly whole. A handful of hours, and she would be herself again.

The one that concerned Conan Doyle was Danny. A demon he might be, but there was no telling what the Nimble Man's attack had done to him, what might have been damaged within him. He lay crumpled against a wall, and though the moonlight was dim, Conan Doyle thought the boy's chest rose and fell with new breath. He would need their attention, and quickly, but he was a demon. Conan Doyle did not think Danny could be killed that easily.

One hand fluttered up to his bloody eye socket, where that silver ball rested now. None of them had emerged from this conflict unscathed. But they had survived.

"You ridiculous, stupid little man," a voice whispered in the gloom behind him.

Weakly, Conan Doyle turned.

Lorenzo Sanguedolce stood above him, newly emerged from the shattered remnants of the amber chrysalis that had hidden him away from the world for more than half a century. Sweetblood had not aged a day in that time. His swarthy features were made sinister by the thin beard he wore, a style gone out of fashion long ago. His eyes were heavy with disdain.

"Hello, Lorenzo," Conan Doyle whispered.

No one else said a word. With a quick glance around, Conan Doyle saw that the rest of the room had been frozen, as though Sweetblood had pulled the two of them out of time, or trapped them in a stolen moment.

His former mentor crouched in front of him. Sweetblood reached out to grasp his head and Conan Doyle was too weak to resist. The archmage bent to whisper in his ear.

"You little fool. You could never surrender yourself to mystery, Arthur," he said, in a hiss accented with centuries of European influence. "You could never leave well enough alone. This is why I severed our relationship, why

I refused to continue to be your teacher. It may be that I would have been found without your interference. But neither of us will ever know the truth of that.

"So let me tell you what you and the Fey bitch Morrigan have been a part of, both of you unwittingly."

Conan Doyle shivered, the dread in his former master's words too much for him to bear. Sanguedolce was afraid, and that was something Conan Doyle did not think possible.

"I first felt it in the year 1627," the mage went on, whispering, sharing these secrets only with Conan Doyle, as he had done when they were teacher and student. "It was more powerful than anything I had ever encountered. Have you heard of the Demogorgon?"

Conan Doyle nodded, dazed, heart thundering, throat dry. The Demogorgon was a demon of legend, one of the oldest such references in ancient texts, but even so, references to it were scarce. Lactantius in the fourth century. Milton. Dryden. Several others.

"Every myth has a source, Arthur. As you've come to know so well. The Demogorgon is a god eater, a thing of power even beyond my imagining. Your Nimble Man would be a mote in its eye; that is the extent of its power. It dwells in the terrible abyss, or so the stories say. But they do not define this place.

"Well, I have found it. Or, rather, it has found me. For more than three centuries, I searched for answers. When I discovered them . . . The Demogorgon had been here before. That is the source of the myth. But it left this place long, long ago. When I touched it, when I sensed it, out there in that terrible abyss, in a place at the farthest reaches of the universe . . . *it felt me.* Just as I sensed its power, so it sensed mine. God eater, yes. And magick eater as well.

"From the moment its mind first touched my own, on that long-ago, seventeeth-century night, it has been coming this way, making its slow but certain progress across eternity. It is coming here, Arthur. And if it reaches the Earth, no force in all of Creation will stop it. The world will not be overrun with monsters, it will not be cast into darkness, or its civilizations crushed. It will be over, you understand? Over.

"For my own protection, and for the sake of this entire damnable world, I hid myself away, shielded my magick and my presence, so that the Demogorgon could not sense me anymore. It had lost interest once before. I hoped I could make it lose interest again.

"But now . . . well, you've made a mess of it, haven't you? You and your friends and your enemies alike. Not only have you woken me, but you have done so with such flagrant use of my power that it can be nothing but a beacon, a homing flare that will draw the attention of the Demogorgon and bring it here. It has pinpointed us now."

And with this, Lorenzo Sanguedolce at last hesitated. His eyelids fluttered and a look of pain and sorrow became etched upon his face. He shook his head. "I can feel it even now. It may take years, decades, perhaps a century or more. I do not know. But the Demogorgon is on its way.

"I will try to fight it. Just as I know you will. But I fear that the end is inevitable. The clock is ticking toward the fate of the world."

Sweetblood turned Conan Doyle's head in his hands, gazed intently at him. "And I'm afraid that I'll be needing this more than you will," he said, and then he plunged slender fingers into Conan Doyle's face and plucked the Eye of Eogain from his skull.

Conan Doyle screamed, and darkness swallowed him.

• • •

HE blinked. But only one eye moved. The other was so swollen and crusted with gore that it only ached. There was nothing there. Not his own eye, nor the Eye of Eogain.

He lay on his back on the floor. In the moonlight he could see Ceridwen above him, her exquisite face drawn with concern. The ghost of Dr. Graves hovered beyond her, standing sentinel over him.

"Arthur?" she ventured.

At the sound of her voice, other figures moved into the circle around him. Conan Doyle could see the silhouette of Eve, though the dark was merciful in not revealing her wounds. Clay was beside her, stoic and strong. The shadowy form of Danny Ferrick shuffled nearer, the outline of his horns almost elegant in the moonlight.

"My love?" Ceridwen whispered.

"I'm alive, dear lady," he rasped. "I'm alive."

They all were. It was nothing short of a miracle. But Sweetblood's words had kindled a terrible dread in Conan Doyle's heart. He knew that his allies, his agents . . . his friends . . . all had lives of their own. Even the restless spirit of Dr. Graves had business to accomplish before he would go peacefully into the soulstream, past the gate that separated this world from the hereafter. They would want to return to those lives, to those plans, now that the threat had been averted.

And, for a while, perhaps, he would let them.

But eventually . . . probably quite soon . . . he would reveal to them the words that Lorenzo Sanguedolce had whispered to him. And then they would realize that they must stay together. Even if the Demogorgon was years away, they would have to prepare, to gather others like them, to combat the darkness so that when the time came, they would be ready.

The clock is ticking toward the fate of the world, Sweetblood had said. Yet Conan Doyle did not believe that fate had already been written. Destiny, he knew, could be decided by those who were willing to grasp it in their hands and build their own fates from it.

The great darkness was coming. But he and his Menagerie would be there to greet it.

Until then . . .

"Arthur," Ceridwen said, bending low over him, blotting out his view of the others, of his friends gathered round him. He caught her scent, of spice and vanilla, saw her alabaster skin glisten in the moonlight. She kissed him gently, their lips barely grazing one another.

"Rest now."

Yes, he thought. He would rest.

But not for long.